S Sho
Sho

Dark Storm Rising

T.R. Chowdhury &
T.M. Crim

TRIMOON
ECLIPSE

Winter Wolf
PUBLICATIONS

| Cincinnati, Ohio

Copyright © 2016, T.R. Chowdhury & T.M. Crim
First edition: 2011 Loconeal Publishing
First Winter Wolf edition: 2016
Cover Art © 2016, by Carol Phillips
Interior Image Art © 2016, by Carol Phillips
Edited by Jennifer Midkiff
Interior Design by T.R. Chowdhury

Published by TriMoon Eclipse,
An imprint of Winter Wolf Publications, LLC

ISBN: 978-1-945-039-03-4 (paperback)

Shadow over Shandahar:
Dark Storm Rising
Echoes of Time
Whispers of Prophecy
Breaking Destiny
Embers at Dawn
Heroes' Fate

Dark Storm Rising:
Blood of Dragons
Shade of the Fallen
Forging the Bond

The Troubadour's Inn:
(Collections of short stories, poems and artwork)
Tales from the Hapless Cenloryan

Other work by T.R. Chowdhury:
(aka Tracy Renée Ross)

Chronicles of Rithalion:
Elvish Jewel
Dragon Vessel
Fire Heart

Cat Tales:
The Dream Thief
The Time Swiper

DEDICATION

This book is dedicated to those who had such a profound influence on its creation: Dustin Moore (Armond), Rick Meiser (Zorg), Chris Coon (Tianna), Roger Hinton (Dartanyen), Leslie Crim (Amethyst), and Steve Dixon (Bussi). The adventure was loads of fun, and Ted and I couldn't have done it without you!

Table of Contents

Part I

Part II

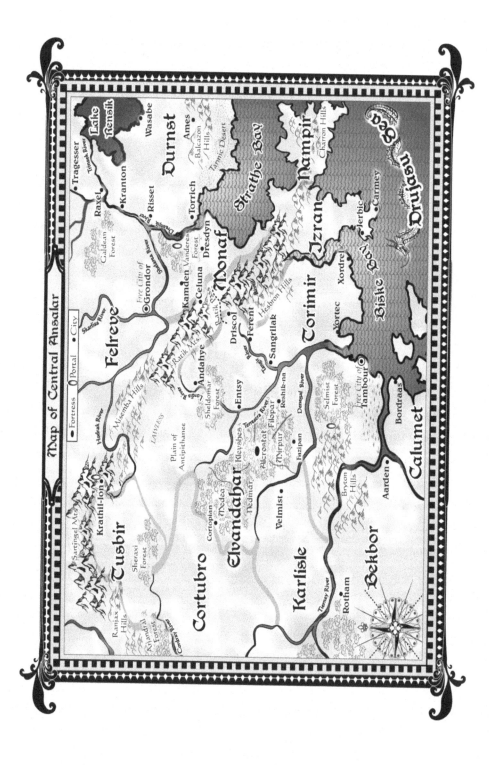

Map of Central Ansalar

Fear the dark storm rising
Over a world covered in shadows
Where dragon and daemon clash
And the air breathes death.
A tipping Balance Cycle after Cycle,
A curse that is unstoppable
By the immortal powers that be.
Enter a whisper of prophecy
Herald to the gathering of the fourteen
Who may break the destiny of the world.

* Excerpt from the Chardelis Prophecies

PART ONE

PROLOGUE

The Historian slowly walked towards the small house. It was dark, and candlelight shone through the windows of every room, but he instinctively knew to which window he needed to go. Peering within, he took in the scene and prepared to document the events about to unfold. Everything, both seen, and unseen were placed upon his mental scroll, down to the things people felt in their innermost minds.

On the bed situated on the left side of the chamber lay a woman. Her hair was like moon-spun silver where it lay in a halo about her head. She writhed as though in great pain, her distended abdomen rippling with muscle spasms associated with imminent birth. Sweat beaded her brow, and the woman seated beside the bed placed a cloth there. As though inside the room, the Historian heard labored breathing, agonized moans, and whispered words of comfort.

At the far side of the room opposite the window, a door opened, and the midwife entered the chamber. Worry creased her brow, along with fatigue. In her arms was a stack of clean cloths. She deposited them near the washstand before making her way to the bed. She positioned herself at the foot, then leaned between the laboring woman's legs. The woman cried out in agony as she was examined.

The midwife shook her head, an expression of deepened concern on her face. "The child has not made progress. I fear the worst."

The woman sitting beside the bed regarded the midwife for a moment, her expression intent. "I fear for my sister more than the child. I don't know how much longer Gemma can endure this. Please, is there nothing you can do?"

Sadly, the midwife shook her head. "Sharra, I have tried everything, but the child will not come. If I reach in to pull the child out, I am afraid I will harm the mother."

Sharra looked back at Gemma as she moaned again. Her sister was weak and becoming even more so by the moment. The contractions leached every bit of energy from her, and she still bled from the birth of the first child. The poor infant lay, untended, in a basket on the far side of the room. Sharra felt the instinctive urge to go to the baby and hold her in her arms, but she dared not disturb the sleeping infant right now when she was needed so much. A tear fell down her cheek and onto the pale hand held within hers. Gemma had been so happy when she first realized her babies were coming. But so many hours had passed since then, and only one had been born.

There was an abrupt knock on the door. The midwife walked over and opened it. At the entrance stood Thane. Behind him was a young boy no older than seven or eight summers. "How is she? How is my wife?"

Sharra regarded the man from her place beside the bed. His face was pale, and dark shadows rested beneath his eyes. His expression was haunted with his fear. Even though nothing had been spoken, Thane knew something was wrong. His son's birth had been an easy one compared to this, and he saw the lines of strain on the face of the distraught midwife.

From behind Thane approached another woman, Mairi. She glanced inside the chamber only a moment before turning to the boy. "Come Gareth, I have prepared your favorite meal." She took the boy's hand, leading him away from the doorway, and the possibility of hearing his mother's desperate cries.

"My Lord, your wife still labors to bring forth the second child. It is proving to be rather difficult, but these things take time," replied the midwife soothingly.

Thane simply nodded and turned from the doorway. At that moment, a tiny cry emanated from the infant lying in the basket across the room. He turned back around, pain written upon his usually stoic countenance. He swallowed convulsively, struggling to keep his emotions in check, and pitched his voice down the hall behind him, "Mairi, could you please come to care for this baby? Sh... she needs you." His voice cracked as he turned from the doorway. Within moments Mairi was there and she passed him to enter the room. The midwife shut the door and his footfalls could be heard as he moved away.

Time crept by. It wasn't until Shandahar's third moon had risen before Gemma's second daughter finally made her way into the world. With all the strength Gemma had left in her weakened body, she pushed the child out in a gush of blood. The midwife quickly scooped the baby up from the sodden bedlinens, cut the umbilical cord, and rubbed the tiny body with a rough towel. The child was blue and hung limp in her hands. The midwife slapped the infant's feet: once, twice, and then a third time. Suddenly there was a cry, the tiniest cry the Historian had ever heard.

Smiling, the midwife turned to Sharra. "She lives! The child lives!"

Sharra looked down at her sister and grinned. "Sister, your daughters are beautiful."

Gemma slowly opened her eyes and looked at Sharra. "I knew they would be. Please, let me hold my youngest daughter. Bring the eldest as well so that I may name them."

The midwife laid the baby within her mother's arms before tending her patient. Blood continued to flow heavily and unchecked, staining the linens and towels. Gemma held the baby close, murmuring soft and tender words while the midwife and Mairi desperately worked to stop the bleeding. Sharra brought the first baby and sat at the bedside. She held the baby beside her sister so that Gemma could see both at the same time. A shock of dark brown hair was like a fuzzy crown on her head.

Gemma placed a trembling hand on the first baby's chest and whispered, "You were born in the light of day, Sheridana D'arya, but you will bring darkness to those who are most deserving of it." She closed her eyes and a few brief moments passed, her face becoming pale as the afterbirth was delivered. She placed her hand on the chest of the second baby, and this time her voice was harder to hear. "You were born in the darkness of night, Adrianna Serine, but you will bring light where once there was none."

Gemma's hand slipped off the baby and onto the bed. Sharra hurriedly took both babies away and moved aside as the midwife took her place at Gemma's side and pressed hard on her abdomen in an effort to stop the bleeding.

When that didn't work, the midwife gave her a pointed look.

Sharra rushed to the door, opened it, and called for Thane. Within moments he was at Gemma's side, holding her small hand within his much larger ones. He brought his face close to hers, his tears falling onto her pale cheeks. "Please, Gemma. Don't leave me. I need you so much..."

She slowly put her hand on his head and her voice was the barest whisper. "I will love you forever, Thane Darnesse." She took her last breaths and the room was silent.

Thane laid his head on Gemma's chest, and his shoulders shook with the force of his sobs. Sharra stood against the far wall beside the two baskets holding the tiny babies. The anguish that permeated the room was suffocating, and her chest tightened so that she could barely breathe. She looked down at the babies and she was overwhelmed with grief. These children would never know their mother. They would never feel her gentle kiss, hear her soft voice, or feel her strong embrace. They would never know how wonderful she had been, and that she loved them so very much. Suddenly she caught movement at the doorway. It was her young nefreyo, Gareth. With wide eyes he looked into the room, saw his mother on the bed, the blood-soaked linens all around her legs. "Father?"

The small voice was hesitant, fearful. Thane didn't move from his place beside Gemma. Mairi went to the boy, wrapping him within a maternal embrace. "Come Gareth. Your father needs to spend some time with your mother for a while..." Mairi's voice trailed away as she led him from the doorway and down the hall.

The Historian despondently stepped away from the window. He was saddened by what he had seen, but many times it was like that when he had to document an event. He enjoyed the happier events the most, those where he got the chance to document some type of victory, the birth of an important person, or the coronation of a great king. Despite this being a birth, it was also the death of someone who had been greatly loved.

The Historian shook his head. Sometimes, he didn't entirely understand the meaning of an assignment, didn't realize the true import of an event until several years later. Something about this particular event was important and would change the destiny of the world. This was the Fifth Cycle. The Historian had seen many events, many of them in duplicate or triplicate. He remembered seeing this one every time, but never figured out why.

Bathed in darkness, the Historian walked away from the house. Soon he would be teleported to his next assignment. He hoped that it would be happier than this one. Equally as much, he hoped it was one he hadn't seen before. Suddenly, there was a small flash of light. When it disappeared, the Historian was gone.

HOMECOMING

*A*drianna walked the dark corridors of the temple. It was eerily quiet, so quiet she heard herself breathe. Her light footsteps echoed on the stone floor and her ornamental belt tinkled softly around her hips. Priests dedicated to Corellian passed her, each one clad in nondescript light brown robes. Each one paused to give her hollow stares from dark pits in their faces. She hastened her pace, somehow knowing the route to her destination even though she'd never been there before.

She abruptly found herself in a round chamber. Fastened to the stone walls were simply made silver sconces within which flames resided. They were small and lackluster, as though they were dampened by the dreariness of the place. Her gaze was drawn to the center of the room to a raised table upon which lay a shrouded figure. The breath caught in her chest. She wondered who lay beneath the white drape even though somewhere within her she already knew the answer.

Adrianna thrust aside her growing trepidation and slowly approached the table. The distance seemed to grow before her even though the chamber was no larger. Her heart thundered against her ribs when, after a moment, she imagined she saw the drape move. She wanted to stop, but her legs continued to carry her forward of their own accord. No, certainly it hasn't moved, at least not by itself. It must have been a stray draft of air.

She moved closer. She saw the movement again but felt no stray wafts of air. Fear took hold of her guts and slowly began to squeeze. The sides of the chamber darkened and began to close around her. Once again, she wanted to stop, but she had to know, beyond any shadow of doubt, the identity of the person beneath the burial shroud.

Finally, she stood before the table. She hesitated briefly before reaching for the drape. She pulled it down to reveal the body of a man. Despite the severe burns, she could tell it was her beloved master. Tears sprang to her eyes and her chest filled with a terrible ache. It was hard to believe he was truly gone, for she had seen him hale and whole just the evening before. She moved to pull the cover back, when a scorched hand reached out and seized her wrist.

Adrianna screamed, but no sound emerged. Flesh peeled back from the grasping hand to reveal bone, and Master Tallek's head turned towards her. One side of his face was recognizable, but the other side had melted away from the skull. A blue eye stared at her from one socket, the other just a blackened hole. Part of the lips were gone, so when he spoke, only the remains moved.

"The Dark Lord is coming for you! Run, run as fast as you can until you find the Warrior of Destiny! Then keep running until you find the one who is sworn to protect her." The hand tightened painfully on her wrist. "Go! Go now!"

Adrianna sat bolt upright, a shout at the tip of her tongue. She gulped in the chilly air, her nightshift plastered against her sweat-soaked body. She pulled her legs up to her chest and rocked back and forth, her face on her knees. She had forgotten how vivid her dreams could be, borne upon manes of darkness and hooves of flame...

Nightmares. Nyxlarian.

Silent tears gathered in her eyes. Tallek had been her savior in so many ways, and sometimes she still couldn't believe he was really gone. Her master's body had been found early in the morning by the city patrol. Due to the strange circumstances surrounding his death, there was a pending investigation for murder. Just like in the nightmare, she'd gone to the Temple of Corellian to identify him and claim whatever possessions of value the kind-hearted priests had removed from his person.

Adrianna glanced around the caravan encampment and slowly lay back down on her bedroll. Fortunately, she hadn't awakened anyone with her cries, and if she'd been noticed, it was only by the nightwatch. She turned on her side and stared at the flames of the nearest fire. As Tallek's apprentice, she'd inherited his tower and everything inside it. She'd also been responsible for the difficult task of informing his journeymen, and any other family or friends that lived outside of Andahye, of his demise.

Journeyman Tannin had been the only one she was loath to contact. Even now she disliked thinking about him. He was Tallek's apprentice before the Master brought her under his wing, and he'd been nasty right from the start. Over time she'd finally figured out why– he was jealous. He hated that she had taken his place as the Master's favored student. She never quite understood how she had earned that status, and obviously Tannin didn't understand it either. She'd been forced to endure the man's hate-filled stares the entirety of Tallek's funeral rites, and when he'd pulled her aside afterward, she suffered his tongue-lashing.

"You don't deserve that tower, and you know it," he spat. "A decent person would give it to its rightful owner." His frown deepened when she made no reply. "Greedy bitch! Fine, we will see about this. Be expecting some correspondence from the High Courts of Andahye."

He'd roughly pushed her to the side and left her standing there, subject to the stares of the people who had been close enough to hear his words. At the time she had been afraid of his threat, but now she didn't much care. *Let Tannin take the tower. Master Tallek is gone, so there is nothing there to bind me to the place and I'm not going to be living there.*

Adrianna breathed deeply and closed her eyes. *Am I a complete fool? Why am I returning to Sangrilak? What does that place hold for me? Most of my memories are filled with heartsickness. The only real reason I'm going back is for Sheri, and she left before I did several years ago.*

Sheri... Sheridana, her twin sister.

When they were children, her beautiful, blue-eyed companion had been her only ray of sunshine. Despite the extenuating circumstances with their father, they had been everything to one another, forging a bond that could never be broken, even after so many years apart. Even though her sister wasn't there anymore, Sangrilak was home– and Adrianna's first step to finding her again.

15 Jicaren CY593

It was almost evening as Sirion sauntered slowly through the city of Sangrilak. Travel-weary and tired, he made his way towards the Inn of the Hapless Cenloryan, his corubis companion bumping against his side as he walked. Irritably, Sirion brushed a lock of copper-brown hair out of his eyes and then buried his fingers into the thick ruff about Dramati's neck. His sister, Anya, would catch up in a few moments, and the rest of the group followed about an hour or two behind her. Sirion had gone ahead to procure their rooms for the night, for he knew the proprietor personally.

An errant breeze blew, and he caught a whisper of what smelled like a bad combination of stale body odor and rotten carcass. Sirion crinkled his nose. He rarely bathed while on the run. His grooming habits were nothing to be desired, for he rarely felt the necessity, or the yearning, to make himself presentable. Yet, upon reentering the world of civilization, he realized how he must seem to the people he passed– a dirty bum from the wilds.

But he couldn't be entirely to blame; his travels had been difficult. He and his companions, otherwise known as the Wildrunners, had been accused of committing a crime they didn't perpetrate. In order to clear themselves of any wrongdoing, they had gone after the foul people who had committed it in their names. They wound up getting ambushed by the enemy and now all they could do was seek shelter and tend to their injuries. Everyone was downtrodden and dispirited, but their rivals hadn't escaped unscathed. As Sirion recalled it, their "twins" were just as wounded.

Indeed, the people who made up the enemy group looked almost exactly like the Wildrunners. There was a mirror image replicate for everyone except for Dinim, the young sorcerer who had joined the group after their doubles had been created. Sirion gave a heavy sigh. *Damn Gaknar! We should never have stepped through that suspicious dark mirror in the temple in Nampoor. The Mehta of the Daemundai couldn't have conceived a better weapon against us. Those heinous men and women not only look like us, but they possess all of our skills and attributes, both physical and mental. When we stepped out of that mirror, we were recreated into the antithesis of ourselves.*

Sirion shook his head. This ambush was the second skirmish the Wildrunners had fought since their doubles' creation. He knew, when next they met, that only one group or the other would prevail.

Sirion walked up the steps of the veranda surrounding the Inn of the Hapless Cenloryan. It would be good to take a much-needed rest in a place where he knew they would be safe. In his native tongue, he uttered a command to Dramati, and pointed behind the establishment. Without complaint, the large canine went to his place at the back of the inn where Volstagg would be sure to give him remains from the evening stewpots.

Sirion opened one of the heavy oak doors that led into the building and stepped inside. He waved to Volstagg as he passed through, and the cenloryan's eyes lit up the moment he saw him. Sirion liked to visit every so often, but this time it had been quite a while. He went to the rear of the establishment where his personal bedchamber was located, wanting to stop there to set down his travel pack and weapons belt. He couldn't resist lying on the bed for a few moments but stirred himself so that he could get quarters for the rest of the group and to get something for them to eat.

Sirion headed back out to the common room but stopped when he reached the entry and just watched for a few moments. Sangrilak was a hub city, considered one of the most diverse in Central Ansalar. It was home to humans, faelin, and halfen alike. It wasn't unusual to see half-breeds, people of both human and faelin descent, and even more unusual, those of human and oroc descent. Even people like Volstagg could find a good place to live in Sangrilak, rare people who were far outside the norm. There were some people in the world who would live their entire lives and never come across anything like Volstagg. Ever.

Sirion was about to move away from the entry when he saw someone enter the establishment, someone he hadn't seen in many years. The young woman approached the bar and sat down, patiently waiting for one of the serving girls to take notice. Her hair was the color of moonlight, bound in a thick plait that lay over one shoulder. Her complexion was a bit more golden then he remembered, most likely sun-kissed from her travels. She was small, even for someone who was of full faelin descent, so the fact that she was partly human made her even more unusual.

It was then Volstagg emerged from the kitchens. He was an interesting individual, one of the only cenloryan Sirion had ever seen. He had the head, torso and arms of a faelin man, and the rest of him was the form of a lloryk. He carried a large pitcher of ale in one hand and a platter of steaming stew in the other. He handed the food and drink off to a serving wench and then began to head in the woman's direction, his massive cloven hooves thudding against the stone floors as he moved.

It was then he saw her.

Volstagg stopped. He stared for a moment, and it was obvious he wondered if his eyes were seeing right. She smiled, and with a wide grin he rushed towards her. She stood up from her seat, and then, much to Sirion's surprise, she climbed over the counter-top to the other side like a child might do. The cenloryan was instantly upon her. Volstagg picked her up, the thick muscles in his forearms flexing as he held her above his head. He gave a hearty laugh and then pulled her close in the type of massive embrace that only Volstagg could give. She wrapped her arms about his neck and hugged him back, the expression on her face showing how good she felt to be there.

In spite of the distance, Volstagg's robust voice was easily heard over the crowd of patrons. "My dear Adrianna! How have you been all of these years?" He set her down. "It is so good to set these eyes on a good friend after so long! By the look of you, it seems you have been traveling for quite a long while. Rest here and I will bring you good food and drink."

Without waiting for a reply, Volstagg lifted her back over the bar. He started towards the kitchens but turned back and looked at her as if to make sure she was really there before moving on. After watching him trot through the swinging oak doors, Sirion heard him roar to his staff to hurry the preparation of a plate of fresh vegetables, grains, and fruits for a special guest. A few moments later the cenloryan emerged with a tall glass of honeyed mead. He set it before Adrianna and leaned his elbows atop the counter with an assessing gaze.

With a raised eyebrow and a slight curve to her mouth, Adrianna asked him something. Sirion looked on as the two began to talk. He just continued to stand there in disbelief. Hells, he hadn't seen Adrianna Darnesse about the city in nearly a decade. He'd always been attracted to her, so when he had finally asked Volstagg about her, knowing that the two were close friends, he had tried to be as nonchalant as possible. Volstagg somehow knew better but answered his questions about Adrianna with a small smile. He always knew better, knew Sirion better than he knew himself sometimes.

A serving girl carrying a plate of food rushed up to Volstagg and spoke in a harried voice. He very quickly excused himself as he set the plate down in front of Adrianna, telling her he would return shortly. She watched him go back into the kitchens to mend whatever mishap had occurred in his absence, and then seemed to go deep into thought.

Sirion couldn't help but just stand there and take her in. For years, even before she left Sangrilak, he wondered about the beautiful girl-child he'd often seen running through the streets. He had never really met her, only noticed her a few times. She grew older, and in spite of the relationship he shared with another woman, he began to notice Adrianna a bit more. He saw how much other people around the city seemed to enjoy her company, and how much Volstagg had come to love her. He was unable to keep himself from being fascinated by her ethereal beauty, her quiet strength, and the way she made the people around her happy.

Sirion pulled away from the entry and walked towards the bar, ignoring the little voice in his mind telling him to stop. *What are you doing old man? She's not for you. She's too young and now a sorceress. What the Hells are you doing?*

He walked across the common room. Is was bigger than most, for Volstagg's inn was one of the more popular places to go when visiting Sangrilak. The tables were strategically placed to maximize maneuverability for the serving wenches, but even so, the place was still crowded and moving was slow.

Before he'd even made it halfway across the room, Volstagg had returned to the bar. Sirion heard him moan about the trials and tribulations of innkeeping. He chuckled to himself, knowing very well how much the cenloryan enjoyed his profession; he just liked to give a show. It was then Volstagg noticed Sirion making his way over. He gave a wide grin and, noticing his shift of attention, Adrianna turned in his direction.

Dark brown eyes calmly assessed him as he took a seat on the stool beside her. She made no indication of it, but he could tell she was taking in his unkempt appearance. He stiffened slightly, now realizing why his subconscious warned him about approaching the bar. The thick, tangled mass of his hair was tied back with a piece of leather, and his clothes were grimy and stained with blood. That nasty stench clung to him, yet she refrained from making any attempt to move away.

Suffused with embarrassment, he chose to ignore her and addressed Volstagg in Hinterlic, "I need rooms for the rest of the group– one for Anya, Laura and Breesa, and another for Sorn, Arn, and Naemmious. They will be here any moment."

Volstagg nodded. "It's already been done, and the baths ordered for later tonight after the evening meal has been taken. I took the liberty of having the food prepared. It will soon be ready."

Sirion nodded his thanks and Volstagg raised an inquisitive eyebrow before turning to another patron who approached the bar. Self-consciousness rose as the focus of his attention once more settled on the young woman beside him. Always before she'd never seemed to notice him, but now she'd certainly seen, and smelled, more of him than he liked. Irritation flared. *How dare she judge me! She doesn't know what I've been through the past few days.*

His nostrils flared. Regardless of his ire, Sirion couldn't help noticing that Adrianna was more beautiful than she had been almost a decade ago.

He also saw that she was watching him.

Ever the perfect host, Volstagg trotted away to get him a tankard of ale along with the one he would get for the other patron. Sirion slowly exhaled and turned towards Adrianna. He caught her gaze and held it, her eyes so dark they could engulf a man's soul. He raised an eyebrow as he speculated about what she saw when she looked at him. He was more than just a few years her senior. Perhaps she saw a filthy old man who stank of the road, himself, and the dried blood of his double.

Incensed, Sirion allowed his gaze to rove over the rest of her. The fact that she was a half-breed didn't bother him. There were many who would berate him for his indiscriminate tastes, but so be it. He had never been one to conform. A maroon winter cloak spilled behind her back, and her tunic, vest, and trousers were finely made, the stitching at the shoulders, sleeves and hem all of excellent quality. The clothes were not form-fitting, but he could see the shape of her beneath them. Her breasts and hips were small, much like that of most faelin women. However, because of her human ancestry, her curves were the slightest bit more rounded, her face not so angular, and her ears not as long and pointed at the upper tips.

Sirion suddenly noticed a tension emanating from her and his gaze swung back up to her face. She struggled to keep her eyes averted, but her skin was flushed, and she shifted uneasily in her seat. Anger rose within him, anger towards himself. He treated her badly by regarding her so wantonly. She was undeserving of his censure when it was he who chose not to make himself more presentable. He abruptly turned away and looked in the opposite direction until Volstagg returned. He accepted the tankard and handed his friend a fat pouch before rising from his seat and leaving to find a table on the other side of the common room. It had been a bad idea to approach the bar; the further he could get away from Adrianna the better.

From lowered lids, Adrianna watched the faelin man walk away. His gaze had raked over her and she'd felt small, like she was... nobody. Volstagg placed the sack beneath the bar and she heard the unmistakable tinkle of coins moving against one another. He was wiping down the countertop beside her when she turned to him. "Volstagg, who is that man? How do you know him so well?"

He smiled. "My dear, that is quite a story and not easily told within a mere sentence or two. But he is Sirion Timberlyn, a member of the Wildrunners. You have heard of them, yes? I met him many years ago, back when he was a boy trying to make a path in the world. And what a name he made for himself!" Volstagg's eyes were bright and he spoke with pride in his voice. "There was once a time when I wanted the two of you to meet, but that was when you had begun to study with old Nahum. You didn't come by as often, and Sirion worked a lot. At the time, he was a hired tracker." Volstagg looked up from his countertop and grinned. She smiled back, remembering the time she spent with her old mentor.

A big woman with and even bigger voice called from the kitchens and Volstagg stepped away once more. Alone, Adrianna pondered his words. *Nahum, my dear friend, I miss you so much. What I would give to have you here again.* She shook her head and continued to eat, relishing the freshly baked bread and the seasoned vegetables. It had been quite a while since she'd had either that tasted so good.

Another man approached the bar and seated himself next to her. She instantly noticed that he was uncharacteristically tall for a faelin, standing almost six foot-lengths high. Black, shoulder-length hair was a startling contrast to his pale complexion, and he wore a simple dark green tunic and brown leather trousers. Two longswords hung from the wide belt around his waist, one at each hip.

Spying a nearby serving girl, he whistled and gestured her over. His speech was slightly accented, "I'm searching for work. You know of anyone looking for a sword to hire around here?" He gave her a debonair grin and followed it with a wink.

The girl blushed and returned the smile. "When he comes back out of the kitchens, I will ask the proprietor. He knows better than I about these things."

The girl left to collect orders for ale and mead, but true to her word, she approached Volstagg when he emerged from the kitchens. Moments later, the cenloryan approached. "I hear you want work. You should meet Sirion Timberlyn. He's sitting over there in the back of the tavern." Volstagg pointed to the man who had behaved like a lloryk's ass not long before. A woman had joined Sirion, one who seemed to share some familial relationship because her hair color and skin coloration seemed to match his beneath the layers of grime he carried.

He nodded. "Thank you for the tip, mister."

The man rose from his seat as Volstagg abruptly turned to Adrianna. "You know, you should go and talk with Sirion too. Maybe he can help you find Sheridana. He might have seen her at some point in his travels."

Remembering the way the ranger had looked at her, Adrianna raised an eyebrow and was about to reply, when she suddenly felt something hit her hard across the backside. She quickly turned on her stool and met the gaze of the tall faelin.

"I'm sorry. They sometimes have a mind of their own." His green eyes sparkled as she glared up at him. He indicated the swords at his hips and gave her a wink.

Adrianna heard Volstagg chuckle under his breath as he turned away and headed back to the kitchens. Irritated, she rolled her eyes and watched as the faelin man made his way to the rear of the tavern. Hesitantly, she rose from her seat. She supposed it wouldn't kill her to take Volstagg's advice in spite of the discomfort Sirion caused.

Halfway across the room, the tall faelin stopped when someone called out. Within moments a human man stepped up to him. This man also stood very tall, even for a human. His sandy brown hair was cropped short, and his bare arms bulged with muscle. The reason hung strapped across his back, a broadsword that appeared longer than she stood tall.

Together, the two men continued, and Adrianna followed towards the table that Sirion shared with the woman and two additional men who seated themselves just before the tall faelin and his human companion arrived. The first to catch her attention was the shortest one, a halfen man standing about four and a half foot-lengths tall. He would have been quite ordinary but for the way he wore his hair, a motley pattern of brown spikes that stood up from the top of his head. Beside him was seated another faelin. From this distance she couldn't see him well, except that he had brown hair and wore a longbow across his back.

Adrianna slowed as she neared the table. The three faelin and the halfen courteously made room as the tall faelin and his human companion approached. Her belly clenched with apprehension. *What the Hells am I doing? I don't know these people.* Then she remembered and quelled her desire to turn around and leave. *Oh yes, maybe they have seen Sheridana. All I have to do is just stay long enough to ask.*

It was then she realized everyone was looking at her. Sirion had an expression of surprise but he quickly schooled it into one of nonchalance. Everyone else just waited patiently. Glancing down, she saw that a seat was open, and she graciously took it and sat down. For a moment silence reigned. She ignored the hooded glances, quite accustomed to them. She didn't understand why people stared so much at her but had come to accept it. There was something about her that people found fascinating, but as of yet, she hadn't discovered exactly what it was.

The woman was the first to speak. She was beautiful, her hair colored a deep red and her complexion a light bronze. She was the epitome of what a Hinterlean should look like, the faelin race that made their homes in the forests of Central Ansalar. This was the archer she had heard about, one of the three women who belonged with the Wildrunners. "Good evening gentlemen," she nodded briefly at Adrianna and continued, "and lady. Thank you for coming over to join us. My name is Anya and beside me is Sirion. We understand that you are interested in some work."

The tall faelin was the first to speak. "My name is Armond. I'm from the mountains of northern Tusbir. My passion is the blade and I am well trained in its use."

23

The large human man beside him nodded. "I'm Zorgandar, but my friends call me Zorg. I'm from eastern Tusbir near the Hodrak River. I am also a sword for hire, and my past employers speak well of me."

The halfen spoke next. "I'm Bussimot, or Bussi if yer a friend. I hail from the Hesbron Hills of eastern Torimir. I'm a bit of a wanderer, I guess. My brother passed away las' year, and without 'im, I had nothin' left ta tie me there. I go where the work takes me."

The man with the longbow nodded. "My name is Dartanyen. I'm originally from the Vanderess Forest in eastern Monaf. I am also a bit of a wanderer, and I have known Bussimot for several moon cycles now. We have become good friends and we work well together."

It was silent around the table for a few moments and it was then Adrianna noticed everyone watching her expectantly. She flushed when she realized they were waiting for her. "I am Adrianna. I was born here in the city of Sangrilak, but I left for several years in order to pursue my profession. Only today have I returned, and Volstagg suggested I come over to answer a personal question I have. I wasn't aware you were here gathering men for a mission, otherwise I would have approached you at another time. But now that I am here, I wouldn't mind listening. Maybe there is something I can do to help."

Out of the corner of her eye, she caught Sirion raising a cynical brow. His sister, on the other hand, gave a nod. "Thank you. The thought is much appreciated."

Sirion's voice sounded a little rough, "As you all probably know already, the advisor to Ristran, heir to the realm of Torimir, has been murdered. Another thing you may possibly know is that my companions and I, the Wildrunners, have been blamed for the crime. We are currently trying to absolve ourselves of any wrong doing. We know the identity of the perpetrators, and it is just a matter of time before we catch up to them."

Sirion paused and turned to look at his sister. The two passed a significant glance before Sirion turned back to them. "We may be able to use your help in this matter. Our enemy isn't so much the persons who committed the crime, but the individual for whom they committed it." Sirion lowered his voice and proceeded in a hushed tone. "The real enemy is a man known as Gaknar."

Adrianna regarded Sirion pensively, familiar with the name of the man about whom he spoke. Gaknar was one of the most powerful magic-users the world had ever known. In her sphere of knowledge, Gaknar was a man of magnificent and awesome power whose influence was surpassed by only a few. Unfortunately, he explored the darker arts, and rumor had it that he was the head of a cult whose goal was to bring daemon-kind into Shandahar. In recent years there was little knowledge of his whereabouts, so now, hearing Sirion speak his name, was a surprise.

Sirion continued. "My companions and I have been doing a little bit of research. When Gaknar became the leader of a private sect decades ago, he created a series of underground temples in order to remain hidden. It is thought that one of them may be near this city. We would ask that you continue our research and discover this possibility for us. Maybe you could even find it. We can't guarantee payment for this service, but if there is, indeed, a temple dedicated by Gaknar near this city, the kingdom might consider giving compensation for your efforts towards bringing about its downfall." Sirion raised a hand. "Just to be clear, we don't expect you to do anything more than contact us when you have sound evidence as to the location of the temple."

Armond drummed his fingers on the table. "Do you have an idea where we should get started?"

"We will be in contact," replied Anya. "Maybe give us a couple of days."

"And exactly how would we contact you?" asked Dartanyen.

Sirion gestured towards the owner of the establishment. "Leave a message with Volstagg. He knows where to locate us."

Sirion and Anya rose from the table, and the others followed suit. Dartanyen presented his arm, and Sirion gripped it in the universal gesture of greeting and friendship. "I will see what I can do," he said. Adrianna watched as he did the same for Anya. The other men at the table followed suit, and then moved away to find their own tables for the remainder of the evening.

Finally, it was only she who stood there. Adrianna swallowed nervously as their eyes met. Without thinking, she mimicked the actions of the others, placing her arm alongside that of the man standing before her. She felt his warm hand close around her forearm, and she suddenly felt a tingling sensation sweep through her. The breath caught in her throat and she thought she saw a flash of surprise in Sirion's amber colored eyes before he swiftly took his arm away from hers. Somehow, with whatever presence of mind remained to her, she turned to Anya and repeated the gesture.

Adrianna then stepped away from the table. Taking deep steady breaths, she slowly made her way to the bar to pick up her travel pack. Once having it in hand, she made her way towards the front of the establishment, hoping that a bit of fresh air would help calm her frazzled nerves. Unfortunately, she still knew nothing of her sister's whereabouts, and Sirion's involvement with Gaknar only made her apprehensive. The Wildrunners had chosen one of the worst individuals with whom to be in conflict.

A commotion at the doors of the inn drew her attention. Both were open, and through it she saw that the men had gathered out on the veranda. However, what really caught her eye was the handsome corubis. The animal was large, at least six foot-lengths high at the shoulder. His fur was tawny and dappled with dark brown spots, a thick tail arced over his back. It was obvious the beast looked to Sirion; he listened intently as the ranger spoke in Hinterlic, ears rotating at the sound of the man's voice. The other faelin were familiar with animals such as these and weren't alarmed, but Bussimot and Zorgandar kept their distance.

Adrianna hesitantly stepped out onto the veranda. She had only been so close to a corubis once before, and that was a very long time ago. She couldn't help feeling a bit uneasy. The huge canine immediately padded over and snuffled her with his nose. Nervous tension swiftly shifted to delight when she sensed his acceptance of her right away. She looked around and saw Sirion standing nearby, leaning with his back against one of the veranda support columns. He regarded her intently, his face impassive, but he gave a slight inclination of his head, letting her know the corubis would allow her to touch him. Adrianna gave into temptation and gently ran her fingers through the soft fur. The creature leaned into her touch and he snuffled her again, this time around her face and hair. She couldn't help giggling like a little girl.

"His name is Dramati. He doesn't take to people very often, but he likes you."

Startled, Adrianna looked up to find Sirion suddenly standing beside her. The corners of his mouth had turned up into a smile and she couldn't help returning the gesture. It was such a drastic change from the offish man she had encountered not so long before, and he seemed like he might be quite handsome beneath the layer of dirt smudging his face. Their eyes met and locked. Delving into two pools of molten amber, she felt a tingle race up her spine and her heartbeat accelerated.

What the Hells is happening to me?

Nonplussed, Adrianna turned away from Sirion and back to Dramati, who was rubbing his large head against her torso, hoping she would take the hint and scratch behind his ears. She happily obliged, keeping her eyes busy and away from Sirion by looking around the porch. Dartanyen was speaking to Anya at the top of the stairs, Armond and Zorg were seated on a couple of chairs, and Bussi was lighting a pipe. Shandahar's largest moon, Steralion, had finished her ascent. The light she cast muted the darkness, giving them just a bit more to see by as night enveloped them.

Adrianna's attention snapped back when she felt Sirion's hand brush hers. He was busy rubbing the corubis' neck and back, most likely not even realizing the momentary contact. Dramati leaned more of his weight against her and she felt lean muscle ripple beneath her palms. The animal made a groan deep in his throat, telling them that he was pleased with their ministrations.

Then Dramati leaned just a tiny bit more...

...and Adrianna unceremoniously toppled backwards.

She tried to catch herself, but nothing was there, and she was falling... falling until she was suddenly caught about the waist. Sirion grinned as she reflexively gripped his arms and pulled closer to right herself. She instantly noticed the warmth of his hands at her waist before he took them away.

"Sometimes he doesn't realize his own weight."

She sensed something pass between them, and by the expression on his face, she could tell he sensed it too. "Quite truthfully, I might not have fallen if I wasn't so tired," she said.

"Why don't we rest then?" With a guiding hand, Sirion helped her down onto the wooden flooring of the veranda. Once settled, she gestured for Dramati to join her, and the corubis was more than willing to lie at her side, his large head in her lap.

Settling beside her, Sirion watched as Adrianna gently caressed Dramati's head and face. He was more than a little awed. *I wouldn't believe it if I wasn't seeing it for myself. I've never seen Dramati like this with anyone but me. This small slip of a girl has never been near an animal like him before, but she allowed him to approach. With one sniff he has chosen her as a worthy companion and, even more, this woman likes Dramati just as much as he likes her. She is even going out of her way to make him happy. She is a rare one indeed.*

Sirion turned to look out into the approaching night, very aware of her side pressed against his. Somehow, it felt natural to have her there. Besides Joselyn, he had never felt so comfortable in the presence of a woman, but he was so tired from his travels, he only briefly considered the import of it. After a while he felt Adrianna's body relax where it rested against his, and she softly crooned to Dramati in Hinterlic. In another time and place, he may have allowed his mind to run free to consider the possibility of this new-found camaraderie. But right now, faced with the possibility of imprisonment, he simply couldn't manage anything but the possibility of that frightening reality.

It was then Sirion realized the language in which she spoke, and he turned back to regard her intently. *Who is she? She is definitely a half-breed, and the faelin part of her is Savanlean by the color of her hair and the cut of her jaw. Where was it then that she learned Hinterlic? Who taught her that language and why?* She had very swiftly become a mystery to him, more so than ever before.

Dramati raised his head from Adrianna's lap and looked out into the darkness. Moments later, the Wildrunners could be seen walking by the light of the lanterns positioned along the street. They were tired, shoulders slumped and feet dragging. Triath, Sorn, Naemmious, Arn, Laura, and Breesa nodded at Sirion and Anya as they stepped up to the veranda and filed inside. It was getting late and Bussi, Dartanyen, Zorg, and Armond followed. Taking the cue, Adrianna stood from her seat on the floor and Sirion followed suit, stretching his weary muscles. He told Dramati to return to his place, gesturing to the side of the inn. With one last look at his new friend, the corubis silently acquiesced and loped away into the darkness.

Sirion opened the door and followed Adrianna into the building. Volstagg was busy at the bar, handing out keys to the Wildrunners. Meanwhile, Armond, Zorg, Dartanyen, and Bussi were already making their way up the stairs to their own rooms for the night. Feeling a light touch at his arm, he turned to find Adrianna standing close beside him. She gave him a tired smile. "Good evening to you, my lord. I hope your sleep is restful." Without awaiting a reply, she moved away to seat herself at the bar, patiently waiting for Volstagg to finish his business.

Sirion remained until everyone had their rooms, and once all was settled, he nodded to each of his comrades as they slowly walked to the stairs that would take them to their chambers. The Wildrunners would share rooms with one another, all except him. He would stay in the personal bedchamber Volstagg always reserved for him on the main floor behind the kitchens. He briefly considered going back to see how the others had fared during the last part of their journey, but then thought better of it. He would find out soon enough after dawn.

Sirion waited until everyone had left before signaling to Volstagg that he was done for the night. The cenloryan gave him a tired wave before turning to Adrianna and speaking to her in a subdued tone. Sirion walked slowly, mentally reviewing what he must do on the morrow. He stepped up to the door to his room just as Adrianna came down the hall towards him. She smiled as she stopped at the entrance to the room next to his. Sirion was surprised. In all the years he'd known Volstagg, he never knew that this young woman had her own room at the inn.

Sirion offered a solemn nod and spoke the traditional words for wishing someone a good night, "May your sleep be restful and your dreams full of peace."

"May you have a good night as well," she replied. Adrianna then opened the door and stepped into her room. He waited for the door to close behind her before opening his own. He was so tired; all he could think to do was shuck all his clothing before lying down on the bed-pallet. He sighed deeply as he settled himself.

His last thoughts were of the young woman who lay just beyond the wall that separated them.

THE LIBRARY

Adrianna entered the common room and looked around. It was empty but for Dartanyen, Bussimot, Armond, and Zorgandar sitting at one of the tables. It appeared she wasn't the only late-riser this morning, for they had just finished breaking their fast. Dartanyen saw her standing there and gestured for her to join them. Pleased that he wished to include her, Adria walked over. Armond made room at the table and pulled over a nearby chair. Meanwhile, a serving girl came to see if she wanted anything to eat or drink. Adrianna asked for a cup of tea and a biscuit with sweet butter and rainberries. The others were silent for a few moments as Adrianna awaited her meal.

"So, are we willing to do this? I mean, are we going to take the Wildrunners up on their offer?" Armond looked about the table as he spoke.

"I think we should. There is the risk that we won't get any-thing out of it, but at least we will have tried to help ourselves get into a position where we could make a little bit of money. And who knows? Perhaps, if we do a good job, we will begin to get a reputation, and it will make it easier for any one of us to find employment later," said Dartanyen.

A deeper voice interjected. "I'm in for gettin' a good reputation and all, but not quite so sure about the possibility of not gettin' paid for what we're 'bout to do. I mean, I don't want people thinkin' that they can get somethin' without payin' for it," groused Zorg.

"I don't think that will be the case," replied Dartanyen. "Most people won't even know we aren't getting paid. Not only that, but we will be getting in good with the Wildrunners by doing them this favor. Maybe they will spread the word about us to others. They do have more than a little influence in these parts."

The serving girl returned with Adrianna's food and drink. The table was silent as she ate. She was just about finished when Sirion walked into the inn. He had awakened early to bathe, and he wore fresh tunic and trousers. He raised his hand in greeting, and Dartanyen gestured for him to join them. The ranger began to make his way over to their table when a man burst through the front door, his chest heaving. He spoke in a broken voice and held his sides. It was obvious he had been running without stop.

"Something has happened!"

Sirion rushed over and grasped the man's elbow. "What is it? What's happened?" Concern shadowed his voice.

"At the library... people killed..." the man gasped.

Sirion looked towards them. Adrianna and her newfound companions had already risen and were quickly grabbing whatever equipment they had brought and moving towards the door. The group ran through the city streets towards the library. Sangrilak sported a rather large one, built just before she had left to study in Andahye. Adrianna looked to find Sirion and Armond running on either side of her, Dramati in the lead ahead of them. She was out of breath when they finally reached their destination.

The library was huge, bigger than she envisioned in her mind. It was constructed of pale grey stone that looked almost white. She had heard that it was also a place of learning and that the older children who lived in and about the city would meet there for classes. It was a far cry from the place she recalled meeting when she went to school.

The city guard had already arrived on the scene and were questioning a few people, probably those who had discovered what was inside the library. Sirion walked up the steps, and when one of the guards approached, the ranger simply gave his name and the man stepped aside. Sirion gestured for the rest of them to follow. Once entering the building, Adrianna paused. The place reeked of death. Slowly, she followed the group into the atrium, and what met her eyes when she entered was a vision she hoped never to see again. She swallowed down the bile that rose in her throat upon seeing the mutilated remains of three men. Blood covered the walls and floor, and entrails hung like garlands from tables, chairs, and shelves. Adrianna vaguely heard someone heaving outside the main entry. Her stomach stirred momentarily, but she wouldn't allow herself to be sick. For once, she was glad she had a hardy constitution.

Slowly taking in the scene, Adrianna saw that the back door of the library was broken and leaned crazily on its hinges. Dramati immediately went over and sniffed around. Within a few moments he gave a loud bark. Stepping away from the corpses he was about to investigate, Sirion went to the corubis while Dartanyen took his place.

Adrianna walked around the area, a hand over her nose in an effort to obstruct the smell. *I never would have thought that three people could have so much blood.* So engrossed in her thoughts, she didn't realize Dartanyen had found anything until he read the contents of a message discovered on one of the bodies. It only registered in her mind when she heard a familiar name. THANE.

"What? What was that again?" She spun around to look at Dartanyen, her eyes wide. He began to read the letter again, but Adrianna was already at his side. She stopped him by reaching a hand toward the parchment. With a concerned frown, Dartanyen handed the crumpled message over to her. She read it with some trepidation, having already heard the name at the end of the message.

Kyrin,

Since I am unable to come to collect him myself, you must bring the sorcerer Dinim Coabra to me. Make haste in this matter for the Master wishes for him to be ready when the time comes. Remember, I am watching you. Do not fail me again.

Lord Thane

Adrianna read the name at the bottom of the page and she trembled. Her palms were sweaty, and she was suddenly cold. She only knew one man with the name at the end of the message. *What does my father have to do with these men laying dead before me, their guts ripped out and their throats gone? Who is this other man, Dinim, whom he had bidden these men to collect for him?*

Adrianna shook her head. *No, it couldn't be my father who wrote this message! Volstagg would have told me if he'd returned to Sangrilak.* She clutched the paper in a white fist. *But the handwriting is so familiar; it is certainly his.* "Sheridana," she whispered. "Where are you?"

Adrianna abruptly realized that Dartanyen was speaking to her. "What in the Hells is going on? Do you know anything about this message?"

She focused her gaze on him and made a stiff reply. "No, it's nothing."

The faelin pursed his lips in consternation. He was undeterred. "I can tell that you know something. Tell me what it is."

Adrianna narrowed her eyes and growled, "I don't know anything! Just leave me alone!"

She stalked away from Dartanyen's immediate vicinity, making her way to a part of the room where the remnants of the massacre had not intruded. Seeking to calm herself, she walked among the tall bookcases. *I shouldn't have spoken to Dartanyen like that. It's wrong of me to keep information to myself, but by the gods, Thane is my father! I need to find the man spoken about in the message... the one called Dinim. Maybe he has answers.*

Adrianna finally made her way back to rejoin the others just as the Wildrunners arrived on the scene. There were seven of them. First entered the lady-archer Anya, followed by a hulk of a man that could only be a half-oroc. Next was a handsome human man with a patch over one eye and another man who appeared to be a cross-race faelin. Then there was a half-breed woman like herself, dressed in traditional clerical robes, and another, larger, human man with a two-handed sword strapped to his back that reminded her of the one Zorg wore. The last was a young human girl with light brown hair and wearing ordinary tunic and trousers fit for travel.

With a smile of greeting, Sirion gestured to the cross-race faelin man. "Sorn, come take a look at this." The man was a bit taller, much like Armond, with pale skin, straight, dark brown hair, and canted violet eyes. Adrianna watched the two as they went over to the decimated door. Meanwhile, the human man with the eye-patch joined them, and the three conferred for several moments.

As the group waited, Adrianna cast a sidelong glance at the half-oroc. He was large, bigger than any other man in the room, standing at least eight foot-lengths tall. His flesh had a grayish pallor, and his hair was so dark it was almost black. His lower jaw jutted out, his bottom canines so long they emerged from his mouth to rest on top of his upper lip. Yet, in spite of his monstrous appearance, there was a human-like side to him as well. His canines were a bit shorter than that of full-blooded orocs, his flesh paler, and his pointed ears smaller. Then there were his eyes. They didn't have the customary reddish cast typical of orocs but were colored a deep medium brown.

Adrianna returned her attention to Sirion and his handsome companion. She was thoughtful for another moment or two, but then she figured out what was so enigmatic about the other man; part of him was Cimmerean. Known also as 'dark' faelin, the Cimmereans inhabited vast labyrinths beneath the surface of eastern Ansalar and the other faelin races considered them outcasts. The Cimmerean soul was known to be as dark as their hair, and the mages practiced the arcane arts to match. Rumor had it that her mother's sister, Sharra, had taken a Cimmerean to her bed. Adrianna had never quite believed the stories, yet now, looking at Sorn, she imagined that it just may have been true.

Sirion turned away from his companion, his gaze perusing the scattered group. He knew something about what had happened here, and she itched to know what it was. With a gesture to Dramati, the corubis emitted a shrill bark. Everyone's attention was suddenly diverted to the animal, and then to Sirion. It was obvious the Wildrunners knew what the bark meant, for they all moved closer. Adrianna followed suit, as did Dartanyen and the other three men.

"I have assessed some of the damages here and I believe a shirwemic played some part in the terror that occurred last night," said Sirion. "Sorn and I have decided that we need to go after him while the trail is still fresh."

Adrianna frowned. Shirwemic were lycanthropes, men who could change into large wemic whenever they chose. She didn't know much about them, only that their affliction was considered a curse and that they enjoyed killing for sport. Anya nodded her assent while the man with the eye-patch continued to stand by with his arms crossed over his chest, a frown pulling at the corners of his mouth. It was obvious he wasn't in agreement, but he said nothing, likely saving his words for a time when he was alone with Sirion and Sorn.

Despite the foul glance sent in his direction, Sirion continued, his gaze coming to rest first on Dartanyen and then herself, Zorg, Armond, and Bussi. "We would appreciate if you all would remain here to further assess the situation, find out what else happened here. We will return as soon as possible and meet you back at Volstagg's inn."

Dartanyen gave a nod of agreement as Sorn turned away and moved towards the library entrance. The rest of the Wildrunners followed behind, each of them offering their forearms in a gesture of camaraderie as they left. Sirion was the last to depart, Dramati at his side. Lifting a hand in farewell, he then followed his comrades. Watching him go, a feeling of foreboding suddenly washed over Adrianna. She had the urge to call out to him yet refrained. He didn't need the added pressure of her fears on top of what he already had to deal with.

Regaining her composure, Adrianna once more considered her situation. Her father had written a disturbing letter to a man who now lay mangled on the floor. He wished to have someone by the name of Dinim Coabra within his possession. The last time she had seen her father, he had been in the company of her sister and uncle when they left Sangrilak many years ago. To her knowledge, they had never returned. *Maybe we can find out if this Dinim Coabra has been here.*

Tentatively, Adrianna turned to the others. "I've been thinking, maybe we should search the other rooms and see what these men had in their possession. Perhaps we will find something to tell us what happened here."

Dartanyen nodded, regarding her cagily. "That's a good idea. Perhaps we will discover some new information that might help us."

They first searched through the bedchamber of Cordellan, the head librarian. They found nothing there but some furniture and his personal effects. Adrianna's flagging spirits lifted when they entered the second bedroom. It was obviously the dwelling of one who dealt in magic. Atop the desk were several scrolls, parchments, and vials filled with unknown substances. Within a locked drawer, which Bussi conveniently smashed open with his battle-axe, Adrianna discovered a spellbook and an obsidian stone hanging from a silver chain. Dartanyen took the chain into his possession while Adrianna pocketed the spellbook followed by some of the scrolls and a personal diary she found on the worktable. The group then moved on to the third bedroom. Finding nothing of import, they finally went back into the atrium.

Adrianna stood there for a moment, pensively looking about the ravaged room. Taking the diary from her pack, she opened it with the hope she might find something. She was disappointed to see it was written in a language with which she was unfamiliar. With a deep sigh, she returned the book to her pack. Unfortunately, they had neither found anything alluding to the reason behind the attack, nor any substantial information that would help the Wildrunners.

Or maybe they had.

Adrianna stared at the scene without really looking at it. The city guard continued to leave them alone to conduct their own investigation, courtesy of the Wildrunners' influence. She spoke her thoughts aloud for the rest of the group to hear, "It's obvious that three men stay here at the library. However, one of the three dead men is not one of those, for none bear any indication that he is a sorcerer. That means one of the dead men is a visitor. So where is the sorcerer? If he'd left early this morning to run errands, he would have certainly heard of the murders by now and returned. That is, unless he had something to do with it."

"It seems we have more questions now that when we started," said Armond.

Adrianna contained her frustration and closed her eyes. *We are getting nowhere, but maybe if I pay a little more attention, I will see something.* Focusing on her environment, she concentrated on seeing the things that liked to remain hidden from ordinary sight. It was an innate ability, one she believed arose from the part of her that was fae, allowing her to look past the obvious and see what wasn't.

It seemed the other faelin had the same idea because she, Dartanyen, and Armond arrived at the same place at the same time, one of the many bookcases within the library. Bussi was there as well, mayhap having the same ability. They were in the literature section and the names of various well-known writers stared at her from the bindings of varying colors and sizes. Her eyes scoured over the massive bookcase, trying to find anything that would give them a clue how they were to possibly move the thing without laying siege to it.

Finally, she caught sight of a book with elegant binding high on the shelf. Adrianna stepped closer, craning her neck to see it better. It looked different than the other books and bore a title that seemed out of place: The Works of Sir Oscar Wilde, 2nd Edition. Glancing beside her she saw Armond. He gave her a lopsided grin and shrugged. He didn't know what she was looking at. Not many people were versed in literature, and as such, she didn't expect him to realize the title was out of place. Zorg stepped up behind them and seeing how tall he was, she gave him a beaming smile.

"Could you get that burgundy volume with gold lettering for me?" She pointed at the book.

Zorg gave a nod, reached up, and pulled the book from its position. Startled, the group stepped back as the entire bookcase slid backwards and to the left behind the one standing beside it.

For a moment everyone just stood there looking at one another, then at the winding, ancient staircase that had been revealed. Zorg gave Adrianna a smile and a nod before taking two short torches from his backpack and lighting them with a flame in from the nearest wall sconce. With barely any second thoughts, the group filed one after the other down the dusty stairwell, and at the bottom stretched a long corridor.

Adrianna walked alongside Zorg behind Dartanyen and Armond, with the halfen bringing up the rear. She felt vaguely out of place. *What the Hells am I doing here with these people? I never met them before yesterday, and here I am, traipsing down an old forgotten corridor as though I've known them for years.*

Without warning, Armond and Dartanyen stopped. She almost stumbled into the tall faelin but managed to stop with Zorg's big hand pulling back on her shoulder. She peered around Armond to see they had come to a dead end. All that existed was the wall in front of them and an old, dust-laden pipe organ. The frame was made of elderwood and had once been rubbed with oils to make it impervious to rot. The smooth keys were made of something else, appearing to be bone. It was the same for the tall pipes that arose above and around organ, each one yellowed with age. Everyone eyed it askance, not knowing what to make of such a thing sitting in an underground tunnel beneath a library.

Adrianna and Armond went to the tunnel wall. They felt around and were unable to find anything that indicated it would open. Meanwhile, Bussimot investigated around the organ. Lying beneath it, he found a dusty, yellowed parchment. He carefully situated the cracked page on the organ's music rack, the place meant to hold a page or book of music. Everyone came to look. What lay before them was almost illegible, the notes drawn on the page having faded over time.

Dartanyen assiduously began inspecting the organ's numerous keys. Bussi frowned. "What are ye doin'?"

"I'm looking for any clues that might show me which keys I need to press in order to play what was once written on this page."

The halfen eyed him speculatively. "Are ya sure we should touch the thing?"

Dartanyen looked at Bussi and then at the rest of the group. "Well, what else should we do? We are at a dead end and there is a pipe organ just..." he shrugged and gave a confused expression, "...sitting here."

Armond joined Dartanyen and Bussi at the organ. He cleared his throat and spoke with a tone of reluctance, "I... I have a little bit of experience with this type of thing."

Dartanyen and Bussi stepped out of the way as Armond placed himself before the instrument. He just stood there regarding the keys and the parchment for several moments. The other two men looked at each other doubtfully and then back at Armond standing before the organ but remained silent. Finally, he poised his hands above the keys. Narrowing his eyes at the page, he finally played the first note. Adrianna jumped as a loud sound, accompanied by billows of dust, was emitted from two of the pipes. She held her breath, waiting. All was quiet. Armond then played another note. The group heard a sound, this one with a tone of discord, accompanied by more streams of dust.

Suddenly, there was a loud *crrrack* from above. Everyone looked up to see a series of long iron spikes racing towards them from the high ceiling. Adrianna fell to the stone floor, squeezing her eyes shut and pressing herself flat. Zorg, Dartanyen, Armond, and Bussi all did the same. She next heard a resounding *claaang* followed by silence.

Adrianna opened her eyes to find herself looking into the crystal-clear blue gaze of Zorg. Together, they slowly looked above them to see the spikes suspended only a farlo overhead. On the side of the chamber where they had entered, the spikes were longer, like oversized spears, and they had crashed to the floor, barring them from escape.

Quickly, everyone was once again standing around the organ. "I thought you said that you had experience," said Dartanyen with a harried expression.

Armond glared at him for a moment before returning his focus to the task, rubbing his hands together nervously. He positioned his hands above the organ keys, pausing indecisively. He was about to press a series of keys but changed his mind at the last moment and shifted a finger to press a different one. Noise and dust filled the air, but nothing else happened. All they heard was the creaking of the iron spikes hanging above.

Armond pressed another series of keys. The sound was discordant, and he cursed extravagantly between his teeth. A slight rumbling filled the room, and as the sound gradually grew louder, the walls around them began to shake, bits of dirt falling from the vaulted ceiling. The dangling iron spikes creaked and moaned with their desire to be freed from the ceiling.

"Gods, the place is gonna tumble down on us!" whispered Zorg hoarsely.

The group pressed together around the organ keyboard. Armond's eyes darted from the ceiling to the keys, tiny beads of sweat covering his brow.

"Hells, man! The mechanism will give at any moment. *Just do it!*" hissed Dartanyen.

Armond pressed the last set of keys. There was a huge crash that resounded from beneath their feet and the floor was falling. Everyone jumped back just in time to avoid tumbling into the pit yawning before them, all except Armond. Unable to regain his footing, he fell into the hole that encompassed the floor in front of the organ.

The rumbling became louder and the creaking of the iron spikes was a frightening counterpoint. Pieces of falling debris struck the organ and any person not quick enough to dodge out of the way. From within the depths of the dark hole, they vaguely heard Armond shout, "I'm all right!"

A shower of dust and debris rained down and the torches guttered. Just as the flames died, the tunnel behind them collapsed.

"Time to go!" Dartanyen shouted.

Zorg gave Adrianna a gentle push as Dartanyen took her arm. She could hardly see, but she vaguely made out a steep stairwell leading into the pit. In single file, the group hastily descended into the black maw. Just as Zorg's head cleared the floor of the tunnel above, the spikes loosened from their rusty prison and crashed down. Zorg fell the remainder of the way down the stairs in a shower of rock and splintered wood. He landed with a massive *thud,* grunting with the impact. Armond and Dartanyen moved aside the rubble and the big man groaned when they helped pull him up. Meanwhile, Bussi bent to retrieve something from the floor and held it before him. It was one of the torches. An ember deep inside continued to burn but was swiftly receding. Bussi blew gently on it and hissed to himself when it wouldn't ignite. He was about to throw it down when she rushed forward.

"No wait, I can help!" Adrianna reached for the torch.

Bussi frowned and handed it to her. "There's nothin' ya can do. 'Tis gone."

She shook her head. "I can bring it back." She cleared her mind and began to concentrate. She briefly wondered at the wisdom of what she was about to do, for she would be revealing her Talent to a bunch of men she hardly knew. But the light was important; none of them had the ability to see well enough through darkness as deep as this.

Adrianna drew a simple runic symbol in the air and whispered the words of magic. It was an easy spell, one that wouldn't make her tired, and it was immensely useful. Within moments the dying ember swiftly grew, and the torch burst into flame. She then handed it back to the halfen. Bussi said nothing, just gave her an appreciative nod. Dartanyen, Armond and Zorg joined them. The men glanced speculatively at the torch, and then at Adrianna. She made no comment, and neither did they.

It was quickly realized that they weren't yet at ground level but standing on a wide landing. Bussi led the way to another staircase and they descended in silence. Armond was scuffed and bruised, but otherwise appeared to be fine. Zorg was a bit shaken but, he too, seemed to be well enough.

Finally, they reached the bottom of the stairwell and came across the other torch lying at the bottom amid a pile of debris. They lit it and found themselves in a wide corridor that stretched several farlo across. They continued onward into darkness, away from the beacon that Dartanyen lit at the base of the stairwell with a third torch Zorg had found in his pack.

They walked. It felt like they walked for days, although Adrianna was sure it was just a few hours. They finally reached the end of the tunnel where it emptied into a huge cavern. She felt a slight chill ripple up her spine as they moved into it. There was something about the place, something that made her feel nervous and edgy. She heard Bussimot mumbling behind her, something about the substrate upon which they had been walking and that it "jus' wadn't right".

The group didn't have long to walk before they saw something in the darkness ahead. Within moments a necropolis came into view, the pale tombstones ghostly apparitions in the darkness. They slowly walked around the place, a paranoid Bussimot constantly looking over his shoulder. Adrianna shivered. It was cold and creepy in the cemetery, a place where she felt they trespassed. The stones were eerie in the flickering torchlight and the shadows jumped out at them with every step. A large mausoleum arose from the center and the group made their way over to it. The building had a set of double doors, each one bearing the head of a kyrrean with a ring in its mouth. Armond, Dartanyen and Zorg felt around on the doors and discussed opening them while Bussi continued to look into the surrounding darkness.

It was then a prickle crept up Adrianna's arms. She looked at Bussi and her breath caught in her throat when she saw his eyes widen with terror.

"By the gods," he croaked.

She heard a sound that reached within to stop her beating heart, an eerie moan emanating from multiple throats in the nearby distance. A stench of rot permeated the air and the hairs on her arms rose. Bussi gave a brief shout and broke from the group to run towards the sound. Zorg spun around and was about to join him when, within the dim light cast by Bussi's torch, creatures of nightmarish proportions were illuminated in sharp relief, oozing out of the darkness. Zombie-like, they shuffled their feet as they walked. They were stooped, their arms hanging loosely at their sides, and decaying flesh hung from white bones. Many of them wore the remains of dark robes.

Bussi stopped abruptly before the advancing horde, then swiftly turned and ran back towards the group. Fearfully, everyone just stood there, not knowing what to do. The mausoleum was at their backs, and the route from where they had come was flooding with the dead. While deciding whether to stay and make a stand, or to flee and give wide berth about the progressing horde, the undead priests advanced until there was no choice left. Their small escape route was blocked.

It wasn't long before the undead were upon them.

In horror, Adrianna watched the battle unfold. Much to her intense relief and gratitude, the men formed a barrier between her and the advancing menace. Swords drawn, Zorg, Dartanyen, Bussi, and Armond pushed forward to meet an enemy they had no idea how to kill, an enemy that severely outnumbered them. Armond was struck down almost immediately, and it was belatedly realized he'd been more affected by his fall than he had let on.

Adrianna squeezed her eyes shut, blocking out the frightening images. *I need to concentrate if I want to aid my comrades!* Finally, she calmed enough to incant the words to her spell, extract the component she needed from her pouch, and make the motions necessary for its casting. She then held her hands out before her, thumbs touching, fingers spread. A wide arc of crackling fire leaped from her fingertips. It swept between Dartanyen and Bussi and struck one of the shuffling corpses. The thing erupted into flame and made no sound as it burned to a crisp.

The men recoiled when they saw the magic, but quickly recovered. *If they didn't realize what I was before when I brought back the torch flame, they certainly do now.* Adrianna wavered on her feet and she put a hand to her head. Casting sometimes made her feel drained, especially after a more powerful spell. *How can I protect myself if I'm tired already? Damn my weakness; these men need me!*

The horde pressed into the group. Dartanyen managed to pull Armond out of reach before leaping back into the fray. In fascination, Adrianna watched the undead priests hacked to pieces. *No blood.* Then she saw Zorg stumble and fall. Fear gripped her anew. *Now only Bussi and Dartanyen remain. Only two of the men are left to keep these monsters at bay.*

Fearfully, Adrianna once more considered her options. The undead priests crowded nearer as they pressed Dartanyen and Bussi back. The men increased their efforts as desperation overcame them. For a moment she considered running, hiding behind the mausoleum at her back. But then she saw Zorg in the distance, his life's blood staining the ground beneath him. *Oh gods...* Her mind whirled and she steeled herself for what she was about to do.

Adrianna ran from the mausoleum towards Zorg. Out from behind the protection of Dartanyen and Bussi she made a wide berth between herself and the continuing battle, making her way towards the unmoving body on the ground left behind as the undead sought to destroy the two remaining combatants. Once reaching him, she dropped to her knees before Zorg. Looking about to be sure that she remained unnoticed, she unsheathed her dagger and quickly cut strips from his tunic. She bound the wound at his shoulder and then moved to his thigh. Her breath caught in her throat as she desperately placed her hand on top of the gaping wound. This one was much deeper, and she felt the warmth of his blood as it spilled from between her fingers. She swiftly cut another strip of cloth from his tunic, this one much wider, and wrapped it tightly about the gash, followed by two or three more strips until she felt confident it would hold. The entire time she dressed his wounds, Zorg neither moved nor made any sound.

Finally, Adrianna looked up from her work. She frowned; it was her first field dressing and it was sorely lacking. Without anymore delay, she stood and rushed to Armond's side a few farlo away. He had lain there for quite some time without attention, his face deathly pale and the wound in his side sticky with congealing blood. In the distance, Dartanyen and Bussi continued to fight and it was easy to see they were quickly tiring. However, they continued their efforts to try and keep the battle away from her and the injured men to whom she tended.

Adrianna sliced through the length of Armond's tunic, fully exposing his injury. Then, just like she did for Zorg, she cut thick strips from it. As quickly as possible, she wrapped the lengths of fabric about Armond's ribs. The blood flowed anew from the wound as she moved his body to complete her work. She hissed when she saw the damage she had wrought, yet she continued and bound him as tightly as she could manage. During her mini-strations, she sensed the battle creeping closer, but she dared not take the time to glance away from her task.

Her hands shook with the strain of continuing despite her fear, but finally she was finished. Adrianna wiped her bloody hands over her skirt and looked up just in time to brace herself...

One of the undead had made it through Dartanyen and Bussi's resistance.

A clawed hand sliced through the flesh of the arm she threw up in defense. She cried out and fell back, but before the creature could make another move, Dartanyen was there. He slashed at it mercilessly until it fell and then dismembered it.

Adrianna breathed deeply, blood running warm and thick down to her elbow, the frayed edges of her sleeve slowly absorbing it. Dartanyen finished off the corpse and turned towards her, offering a hand to help her up. Suddenly it was there, appearing behind him seemingly out of nowhere. Dartanyen went down, the force of the monster's blow too much for his weary body to take. A shrill battle cry pierced the air. Bussimot charged towards the creature, battle-axe swinging wildly. Adrianna scrambled backward out of the way and looked about. The number of undead priests still standing had decreased significantly, but it wasn't enough. It was one against six, and the halfen was already riddled with battle wounds.

But then something abruptly changed. Bussimot seemed to explode into a frenzy of movement. He hacked and slashed with no apparent direction, at a speed that was phenomenal. He seemed larger than life, wild with rage. It was then Adrianna realized she was in eminent danger, and not just from the undead.

Bussi was a berserker, and as such, would slash at anything whilst in a rage, friend or foe.

Adrianna heard a frantic shout in the distance to her left. She was about to turn, but from out of the shadows before her loomed one of the undead, one she hadn't realized lurked so close. It lurched towards her and she suddenly felt something hard connect with the top of her head.

Oh gods...

The crazed axe-wielder was the last thing she saw as her mind swirled into oblivion.

COMMISSION

T he priestess slowly walked up the stairs to her chamber. The morning devotional had just finished, and she had a small amount of time to herself before the day's work began. Today she would be in the kitchen. Tianna crinkled her nose. Cooking wasn't her favorite pastime. There were many days she didn't really mind it, and even seemed to be pretty good at it, but preparing meals was boring business. She much rather preferred to be in the garden tending to her plants. Herbal lore was quickly becoming her area of expertise, and many brothers and sisters sought her knowledge pertaining to the healing properties of this herb or that one.

Once reaching her quarters, Tianna went over to the window and opened it to allow the fresh air to circulate. The room was simple in its décor, having only a bed, a desk, an armoire, and a washstand. The desk was the nicest piece of furniture, large enough to hold several of her books. Many of the volumes contained scriptures about her goddess, Beory. Others had information about the medicinal properties of the local flora, and even a few about common healing techniques and methods that included the basics of humanoid anatomy and physiology.

Tianna leaned out the window, allowing the wind to sift through her hair. *What a beautiful day, and what a shame to have to spend it indoors.* She was startled when she suddenly heard a knock at the door. Tianna spun from the window with a hand to her chest and was relieved to find that it was only her young brother. The boy smiled impishly when he saw that he had alarmed her. She frowned in mock disapproval. "Razlul, you scamp! I almost jumped out of my skin. What do you want?" She put her hands on her hips and glared at him.

Razlul only continued to smile. "Only to bring you a message from Sirion, dear Sister. But if you are busy, I can always bring it to you some other time."

Looking at him, Tianna could easily see that Razlul would be a handsome man. His hair was blond, and his eyes palest blue. His complexion was so fair that he was easily burned by the sun in the summertime. Currently he sported a slender build, but Tianna could see the changes in his body, the muscle developing in his arms and chest. After he completed his growth in height, he would begin to fill out. He would not stay a slender boy for much longer.

Razlul began to back out of her room and into the hallway.

Tianna's blue eyes widened. "Raz, you are such a rascal! Give the message to me at once lest I come to tackle it from you."

"Are you sure you want it now? It's obvious that I have disturbed you. I offer you many apologies. Allow me to come back later when you are not so occupied."

The boy stood in the doorway, regarding Tianna mischievously. He knew that she had feelings for the handsome ranger, and he used this knowledge to his advantage, daring her to chase him down the hallway like she used to do when she was an acolyte. But that was the hitch. No longer was she an acolyte, but a priestess of Beory, and with that title came responsibility and more than a small degree of standard decorum. And it definitely would not be very decorous to chase her younger brother through the halls of the temple.

Tianna couldn't help the smile from lighting her face. It was difficult to retain any semblance of seriousness when Razlul was about. As children, he had been one of her fondest companions, but now that they were older, things had changed. She was not a child anymore, and within but one more year, Razlul would not be a child anymore either, but a fully functioning member of the priesthood.

"Come now, Raz. You know I don't have much time. Let me have the message so I can read it and make a response before I have to tend to my duties."

He gave in and reentered the room. "Here, Sirion just brought it. He told me to give it directly to you."

Tianna concealed a frown. *Why didn't Sirion just bring it to me himself? It isn't like I've seen him anytime recently, several weeks at least.* She took the message and gave him a strained smile. "Thank you."

Razlul noticed her shift in demeanor but didn't mention it. "I suppose I had better be going. Brother Wayne is probably looking for me."

Tianna nodded and watched him leave, closing the door behind him. Not only was Razlul beautiful to look at on the outside, but he was inside as well. His heart was good and his soul pure. He would make an excellent priest someday and, if allowed by the priesthood, a wonderful husband and father. She had never met anyone as devoted to people, and his kindness was unsurpassed. It was these qualities that had always drawn her to him, the young boy who had approached an orphan girl from Elvandahar.

An orphan himself, Razlul had been raised by the Priesthood of Beory. When Tianna had first arrived with Sirion from Elvandahar, she was downtrodden and bitter. Somehow the boy had raised her up and put spirit back into her withered soul. For three years Tianna knew Razlul as a playmate, but when it came time for her to say her vows and take her place within the priesthood, her childhood had to be placed in the past. It was difficult for Razlul, but with time he came to accept the change. For over two years now Tianna had been a priestess of the fold, and soon Razlul would be joining the ranks. He would become a man and they would be equals once more.

Tianna sat down on the edge of her bed and opened the letter. It was a short message, written in fine print. Right away she could see that it was Sirion's handwriting, his being easy to distinguish from most others.

Sister Tianna,

As you read this message, I am on my way to rejoin the Wildrunners. I am a few days behind them, having stayed behind in Sangrilak to see to the welfare of some friends. Currently they are staying within the Temple of Hermod and are slowly recuperating from a mission the Wildrunners had bid them undertake. To our dismay, they were brutally attacked. They were without a cleric, and someone could have easily died before we were able to bring them to the temple.

By now you have probably figured out what I am going to ask you to do. It would be as a great favor to me if you were to accompany our friends on another excursion into an underground temple we think is connected to Gaknar. Their goal is to investigate the area and determine if it is, indeed, a temple dedicated to his worship. They will need someone who is fluent in the healing arts.

My hope is to see you soon. May the sun shine upon you, and your goddess bless you.

Sirion Timberlyn

Tianna carefully refolded the parchment. *How exciting!* She had always wanted to accompany Sirion and the Wildrunners on one of their excursions. Now she would be having one of her own.

Tianna placed the parchment in her belt-pouch. She would show Brother Rashid the message and he would undoubtedly give his blessing since he was a strong supporter of the Wildrunners. She would speak with him later in the day, after the completion of her duties. Despite her desire to leave right away, she would just have to wait until she presented the message to her elder and he had given his approval. Then she would pack her bags and go across the city to the Temple of Hermod. There she would meet this mysterious group of strangers, and she would begin an adventure.

23 Jicaren CY593

Adrianna slowly awoke. Her body refused to move but she knew she was alive because she felt pain. She opened her eyes and blinked several times, hoping to see more than just a gray expanse. She opened her mouth to speak and her lips cracked from dryness. "Where am I?" she croaked. She managed to turn her head and an image of Zorg focused into view. She couldn't make out any details except that he was lying down. Her voice became more insistent, "Where am I?"

A moment later, a woman's face floated into her field of view. "Shhh, hush my dear. You are safe here. Rest now, go back to sleep..." The woman's soft voice faded away and Adrianna closed her eyes.

When next she awoke, the pain was nearly gone. She sat up on the bed and a middle-aged human woman walked over to her side. "Greetings Adrianna. My name is Elainia. It is good to see you awake." Her hair fell in soft brown ringlets about her shoulders and her smile made her eyes crinkle at the edges.

With gentle hands, Elainia checked her healing wounds. One was a large slash that ran the length of her forearm. The other was more substantial, a stab wound in her belly. Adrianna stared at it, not recalling when she sustained the injury. Regardless, it was now an addition to the thin vertical scar that ran the length of her torso, between her breasts down to her navel. Adrianna cast a quick glance at Elainia, knowing the other woman had seen the older scar, but she had just turned to tend to Zorg, who was lying on the bed pallet right beside hers.

Finally, Elainia moved away and they had a clear view of one another. Adrianna smiled. "It's good to see a familiar face."

He nodded. "I'm ravenous. I wonder if they gave us anything to eat while we were asleep."

She thought about it but then discarded the idea. "I doubt it. We weren't awake to swallow."

"Hmmm, yes you have a point."

"Where do you think we are?"

"I don't know, but it has to be a temple dedicated either to Beory or Hermod. Those are the two here in Sangrilak that offer healing."

"Yes, you're right. I should have thought of that."

Zorg grinned. "Easy now. You can't expect yourself to remember much when you've been through what we have."

She vaguely recalled the necropolis and the undead that had come to greet them there. She shuddered and Zorg reached over and patted her knee. "It's over now, nothin' to be afraid of."

She appreciated his comfort and gave him a small smile. "Yes, it's over now. Hopefully it will stay that way."

They looked up when Elainia approached again. "A meal is awaiting you in the dining hall. The rest of your comrades are there waiting for you."

With the help of the priestess, Adrianna and Zorg donned their freshly laundered clothes. She then led them through the temple to the aforementioned room, and once there, opened the heavy oak doors. Their companions sat around a large table, platters of half-eaten food in the center. It smelled delicious. Dartanyen, Armond, and Bussi greeted them with enthusiasm and Dartanyen pulled additional chairs over to the table so they could have a place to sit. The platters were passed around and, with Armond's help, Adrianna's plate was filled to capacity. His movements were a bit stiff, and she was reminded of the terrible injuries he had sustained down in the necropolis, injuries she feared she may have worsened with her makeshift dressings.

Armond caught her haunted expression and frowned. "No worries Adrianna. I'm healing nicely. Actually, we've all been more worried about you and Zorg. For a day or so we thought we might lose you."

"Now don' go tellin' 'er that!" Bussi grumbled. "Ya gonna make 'er lose 'er appetite. Eat up, little lady. Ya nothin' but skin and bones!"

Adrianna grinned at the halfen and began to eat. There was freshly baked bread, cheese, stewed ptarmigan, fried fish, curried lentils, seasoned tubers, roasted legumes, and salad greens. Somehow Armond had managed to pile a little of everything on her plate. She glanced over the table, the mess attesting to mass gorging. Men had absolutely no table manners. However, Adrianna found herself eating with the same voracious appetite that must have gripped her companions earlier. She supposed she couldn't blame them too much for the mess.

She had never been so hungry but found herself full before finishing her plate. Her stomach complained, growling unpleasantly. It felt like it had somehow shrunk, unable to contain the amounts of food she was accustomed to eating. Much to her dismay, Zorg continued to eat ravenously where he sat beside her as if he had no intention of ever stopping.

Movement at the entrance of the dining hall caught her attention. Elainia had returned and a man stood beside her. Adrianna couldn't help but stare. He was a full-blooded Cimmerean, one of the finest looking men she had ever seen. His skin was pale, and he had black eyebrows over eyes the color of deepest purple. The sides of his head were shaved, and short, black hair stood upright on the top and extended down the back in a thick strip to the nape of his neck. He wore a sleeveless russet tunic and billowy trousers. About his narrow waist he wore a shortsword sheathed in a silver-embossed black scabbard.

Elainia spoke and the men quieted. "I know you are still taking your meal, but I thought it was important that you meet Dinin Coabra, the man who was pivotal in helping to bring you back to the surface after your ordeal in the necropolis."

All other sounds were suddenly obliterated from Adrianna's mind and she stared at the man beside Elainia. Her heart increased its tempo, pounding against her ribcage. She'd heard nothing but his name: *Dinim.*

Adrianna's mind chanted as she stood up from her seat, *I can't believe it; I've found him, I've actually found him!* She didn't realize she'd been holding her breath until it abruptly exploded through her parted lips. "Lord Dinim, I have found you!" Her voice sounded strange to her ears.

Dinim's gaze came to rest on her, his expression one of surprise, and her breath caught in her throat. His eyes showed a hint of amusement, and the corners of his mouth turned up slightly. His reply was suave, his eyes twinkling with suppressed laughter. "Well, you can certainly have me if you want."

Adrianna felt the blood rise to her face, and she was about to respond when an angry voice pierced the air, "Don't you talk like that to her!" It was Armond. His gaze on the Cimmerean was deprecating, and he muttered a few oaths beneath his breath before speaking again. "I really don't believe this! Surely it is a joke." Armond's green eyes flashed with rising fury. "Why would someone like *you* want to salvage a group of amateurs who can give you nothing in return?" His eyes narrowed. "Or can we? What is it you want from us, Cimmerean?" Armond threw his arm wide, encompassing all sitting around the table.

Adrianna could see the answering flash in his eyes, but Dinim's voice was as cool as his expression. "Well, this is a fine way to repay me for my efforts."

"So, I will ask again; what do you want, warlock?" Armond's face was suffused with blood, his fists clenched at his sides. "All of you dark fae want something, evil bastards that you all are."

Adrianna's gaze flickered between the two men. The impetuous Armond was about to destroy any hope that she might find the answers to her dilemma.

"From you I want nothing!" Dinim shouted, his eyes blazing with suppressed rage. "We followed the path you had taken and found you defeated at a mausoleum. We called others in to help and brought you here. But it was Sirion who got the gold to..." Dinim stopped speaking, his lips pressed together into a thin line.

"Sirion was there?" Adrianna whispered out loud, but no one heard her as Armond retaliated.

"Yeah, so now I want to know what was in it for you. I know all about you damned people. All you do is take until there is nothing left." Armond threw his arm out again, encompassing the group as he addressed them. "If you want to believe him, fine. But don't expect me to have anything to do with him."

"Bollocks, I've no problem depositing you right back where we found you," Dinim replied hotly, stepping towards Armond with blatant menace.

"Curse you, daemon. Touch me and you will find my sword up your backside." Armond stepped towards Dinim as well, closing the distance. At that moment, Elainia strode into the hall, followed by her fellow clerics. With them were everyone's belongings. Adrianna hadn't even known the woman had left the dining room.

"You think so poorly of me, but I've done nothing to deserve your censure. Actually, it is you who deserves it. I arrived back at the library to find my room ravaged and important items missing. I can't possibly imagine what thieves would have taken them!" With wide eyes, Adrianna looked up at Dinim and found his gaze riveted on her.

Dartanyen rose from his place at the table and, backpack in hand, reached within and pulled out the neck chain he had taken from Dinim's chamber. He walked over and gave it to Dinim. "I'm sorry. I thought you were one of the two dead men on the floor and that you wouldn't be needing it anymore. But even when I realized you couldn't possibly be one of them, I didn't think to return it. My apologies."

Dinim nodded in graceful acceptance.

Adrianna walked over to Elainia and pulled the diary and spellbook out of her travel sack. She then approached the Cimmerean, flinching beneath his scathing gaze, and proffered the heisted items. He said nothing as he accepted them. "When I took these, a part of me hoped they belonged to the man who now stands before me and that he would come for them." She gave a tremulous smile. "It seems my conscious steered me right, albeit not in the most ethical way."

She waited for a moment, but when he gave no reply, she gave a disappointed sigh and turned away. *Excellent, Armond has alienated the only man who can help me find my father. Now that man hates me. Certainly, the fault–*

Adrianna felt a hand on her shoulder and she slowly turned to see a repentant face. "Thank-you," Dinim said. "I..."

Armond's voice cleaved the air. "Don't you dare put a hand on her! You sully her with your foul touch, vile bastard!"

Tension knotted Dinim's features as he turned to face Armond. Adrianna stepped back as Dinim retaliated and the verbal battle began anew. The two faelin were menacing in their fervor, and Adrianna and the others stood by as it escalated.

"Damnation, I've had enough of this." Dartanyen picked up a chair, raised it over his head, and advanced towards Dinim and Armond.

Fear of repercussions prompted Adrianna to rush after Dartanyen. Meanwhile, priests and group members alike urged Armond and Dinim to back down. Finally, to everyone's infinite relief, Armond quit the room with a dismissive wave, the door closing heavily behind him.

A collective sigh of relief swept throughout the hall. The pervading tension instantly lifted, and everyone relaxed. Dinim's gaze sought out Adrianna, and before he could be distracted again, she quickly walked over and pulled out the letter with Thane's signature at the bottom.

Dinim reached for the letter, but before taking it he regarded her intently. "I apologize for my rude behavior when you returned my diary and spellbook. It was unmannerly and unnecessary. Please forgive me."

Adrianna was surprised. She hadn't expected an apology. He seemed almost tense as he searched her face, perhaps even anxious. His gaze was so sincere that her apprehensive feelings began to abate.

Elainia chose that moment to approach, nodding at Dinim. "The cleric that Sirion sent should be arriving shortly." She then smiled warmly at Adrianna. "My dear, how are you faring? You had us worried for a while, you and your big friend." She glanced over at Zorg, who was once more seated at the table, eating ravenously.

Sirion... he was here. He made it possible for us to escape what surely would have been... She swallowed heavily, unwilling to contemplate it further. It was enough to know he had been there. The thought gave her a feeling of security somehow.

Adrianna's mind returned to the present, and as she listened to Dinim and Elainia converse, she got the feeling that quite some time had passed while she and her companions recuperated, her suspicions growing as the conversation wore on. Adrianna finally cleared her throat and interjected, "Excuse me, but exactly how long have we been here?"

Dinim and Elainia exchanged glances of amusement and Elainia patted her shoulder. "My dear, almost an entire week has passed since your ordeal!"

Adrianna's eyes widened in shock, and her voice was a bit high-pitched when she replied, "Are you serious? I've been asleep that long?"

Dinim's expression became anxious. "Shh, hush! Sirion and Anya found you as the battle was ending. The two of them were only able to do so much for your wounds before swiftly trekking back through the cavern and back to the surface for help. It took all of the Wildrunners and several Hermodian clerics to safely remove you, Dartanyen, Armond, Zorg, and Bussi from the cemetery."

Shame rushed through her and she held out a conciliatory hand. "I'm sorry, I must sound terribly ungrateful. Thank you for the help you have given us. Someday I hope to return the favor." She offered a small grin, hoping he didn't think her such an ungrateful wretch.

Dinim visibly relaxed. "You have already done so. Just seeing your smile is a gift." She flushed with the compliment, but remembering the letter, Adrianna handed him the parchment. He took a moment to read it, shaking his head slowly when he finished. His mouth pulled up into a sardonic smile.

"My, I have been popular recently. Everyone seems to want to see me for one thing or another." He arched an eyebrow, his tone amused and sarcastic at the same time. "So, what do you know of this man?"

Adrianna was surprised. *How does he know I'm familiar with the man who wrote the letter? For all Dinim knows, I only want to show him the parchment because his name is on it.*

Dinim placed a hand at one hip and regarded her intently. "I can only help if you tell me all you know, and I can see that you know something of Thane by the expression on your face."

She hesitated before making a reply. "He is just someone I met once."

Once again, she must have given herself away. "That's all right. We can talk about it some other time when you are ready and there aren't so many people around, maybe when you know me better."

"What do you mean?" Adrianna felt her hands dampen with sweat. *Is this man some kind of mind reader? Or are my expressions so readable that even a stranger can fathom my most intimate thoughts?*

As if sensing her panic, Dinim soothed her. "Don't worry. I'm not going anywhere. We will talk later."

Adrianna was about to reply when she noticed activity at the front of the room. Elainia, a man bearing the stripes of the city guard, and a young human woman dressed in clerical robes entered the dining hall. Elainia immediately brought the woman to Dinim.

"The Lady Tianna has arrived in answer to Sirion's message, and the Captain of the City Guard is also here to speak with you." Elainia gestured to the man who continued to stand at the entryway. Dinim nodded and Elainia stepped away, motioning the Captain towards the table and to the fresh platters of food that had been placed there.

Dinim held out his hand. "Tianna, I'm glad you were able to come. Sirion has told me all about you."

Tianna smiled as she grasped his arm. She was very beautiful and moved with natural grace. Her long hair was colored a light chestnut, and her eyes sparkled blue-gray. She had a small waist, rounded hips, and ample bosom. Standing half a foot-length above Adrianna, she was about Dinim's height and seemed to be the perfect model of the way a woman should look.

Adrianna followed Dinim and Tianna back to the table where the rest of the group sat with the Captain. "I am Tianna Trigovise, servant of Goddess Beory. I have been asked to help in your mission in any way I can. I am most proficient as a healer, having dedicated my life to the arts surrounding medical herbalism." Her voice was as beautiful as her face and it had a soothing, musical quality.

Dartanyen rose from his place at the table. "It is good to have you with us, my lady. We owe Sirion a favor. Thank you for accepting his summons. Your skills will be invaluable."

Tianna smiled and nodded as Dartanyen returned to his seat. Meanwhile, the Captain cleared his throat. He immediately got to the point. "Since introductions are out of the way, I want to get down to some business. I want to hire you. I want you to return to that cemetery and discover what is being guarded there. I have a thousand gold to offer for the service."

The room was silent for a moment before Dinim replied, slightly agitated. "I have heard that thirty of your men have gone down there and not returned. You honestly want us to do this service for only a thousand gold?" Dinim grunted. "You claim to protect this city but expect us to do your dirty work for minimal reimbursement?"

Adrianna looked on in fascination as Dinim continued to harangue the Captain, and in the end, with the aid of Tianna's charm, free room and board was acquired for the group for the duration of their mission, as well as free weaponry and provisions. This was in addition to the thousand gold they would all split equitably.

When the Captain finally left, grumbling and cursing to himself, Dinim turned to the group with a big smile. "How about us all getting a drink somewhere to help us think about this list of provisions we need to make? The tab is on me."

Everyone collected the travel packs and gear that had been left at the entry of the dining hall. They gave their thanks to the benevolent Hermodian priests and proceeded out the front doors of the temple. It was midday, and once making it to the main thoroughfare, they were surrounded by the bustling activity of a burgeoning city. Adrianna hung behind with a hand over the healing injury on her belly. *This aches a bit more than it should, and I'm tired. I don't feel like I've been asleep for an entire week! I can't let myself get too far behind...* She hastened to catch up and ahead saw Dinim and Tianna walking close together. The woman's long, creamy-white clerical robes were a sharp contrast to his darker trousers. She laughed at something Dinim said, her arm bumping against his.

"If you come any closer, I'll have to dance with you," Adrianna heard Dinim say as she finally caught up to them.

"I don't do that when I first meet a man. I have to get to know him better," Tianna replied in a hushed voice.

Adrianna's cheeks burned and she rolled her eyes. Tianna definitely knew how to use her charming smile and alluring body to her advantage. It was obvious the woman liked to flirt. Adrianna had walked up at the tail end of their conversation, but she heard the hidden message in their exchange. Or was she just imagining Dinim's sexual invitation?

Memories surfaced in her mind, memories she wished would fade into the depths of oblivion and never come to haunt her again. *How can Tianna stand there, so inviting and enticing, and come away unscathed, when I, merely walking down a road, dragging my feet tiredly and covered in dust, could not?* Startled by the thought, she swatted it away, not wanting such misfortune to descend on anyone, especially someone who was a healer. *This woman spends her life helping others. What is wrong with me? I'm not normally so selfish. I wish I had never heard them talking!*

Saying nothing, Adrianna urged her body into motion and passed the pair. The ache in her belly grew into a dull pain, but she ignored it to be away from the influx of negative emotions and the feelings of not belonging whenever she was reminded of her painful past. The group turned down the road leading to The Inn of the Hapless Cenloryan, when Armond appeared walking from the opposite direction. He was a bit out of breath, and smears of soot marked his tunic. He stopped when he saw them and looked at Tianna inquiringly before turning at the sound of Dartanyen's voice. "We have been hired by the city to continue our investigation at the mausoleum. We are going to the Inn of the Hapless Cenloryan to sit down and compile a list of needs for our mission. You are welcome to join us. I am sure there are some things you will want to add."

Indecision shone in Armond's eyes and he hesitated. "I have some work to do. Maybe I will join you later."

Seeing his expression, and feeling much the same way herself, Adrianna stepped up beside him and put a light hand on his arm. "You should come with us. The city is paying handsomely for our services."

Armond shook his head. "Well I would, but it's essential that I return as quickly as possible since I left the forge burning. I'm not turning down the work though. I will be joining you when I can."

Adrianna saw the truth reflected in his gaze and nodded. "All right. We will see you later then."

Armond quickly took his leave and continued down the street. The group proceeded onward, and it wasn't much longer before they walked into the inn. Adrianna immediately went to the bar where Volstagg stood drying some mugs. When he saw her, an expression of relief washed over his face. "My dear Adria! I heard about what happened and I've been ridden with worry!"

Without waiting for her to respond, he came around the bar and enveloped her in his massive embrace.

Adrianna closed her eyes, luxuriating in the warmth of his hug. It was just what she needed. Finally, she stepped back. "As you can see, I am hale and whole."

Volstagg's tone was serious. "Sirion came and told me what had become of you. I went to the temple and requested to see you, but the priests said it would be best if I waited. They said you were severely wounded and that you were in a deep sleep."

Adrianna was touched that he cared so much and that he had come to see her. She gave him a smile. "No more worries. I am much better now; we all are." Adrianna paused and looked around the common room. "So where is Sirion? I would like to thank him."

"He waited a few days to be certain of your recovery, but then he left." Volstagg lowered his voice, "Supposedly the Wildrunners have some business in Grondor."

Adrianna nodded. The whereabouts of the Wildrunners was not meant to be common knowledge. The fact that Volstagg told her their location indicated that he trusted her. The Captain had mentioned their excursion back into the necropolis wasn't public knowledge either, that most of his force wasn't aware of the goings on beneath the city. She was sure that, in part, it was because the Wildrunners were involved.

When Adrianna turned back to the group, everyone was seating themselves at a large round table. Food and drink were ordered, and once they were served, everyone began to tell Dinim what should be included on the list of provisions. Adrianna tried to tell Dinim what she needed as well, although she wasn't sure he heard her over the other conversations going on around the table.

Adrianna listened attentively for a while, sometimes making a few comments about this issue or that one, all the while looking about the common room. It was good to rest, and the pain in her belly had subsided. She relaxed in her seat, taking note of the people that came and went. At some point she noticed a human girl of Denedrian descent. She was small and pretty, with black hair and a bronzed complexion. Adrianna imagined she took particular note of the girl because she seemed a bit out of place in an establishment that usually catered to older folk.

The place soon became busy, and there were many people coming in and out for a late midday meal. A Hinterlean man made his way through the crowd towards their table. For the most part, he was quite nondescript, albeit large in stature for one of the forest-dwelling fae. He had dark hair, and his thick eyebrows converged together above his nose. He smiled and greeted everyone in the Common tongue when he reached the table, grabbing the empty chair beside Adrianna and sitting down.

"It isn't my intention to intrude, but the innkeep told me you all know a friend of mine by the name of Sirion Timberlyn. I was wondering if you would give him a message from me. We haven't seen one another in several years, and I am anxious to meet him again after so long. I will be staying in town for a while, and the message tells him where I will be."

He held out the sealed letter, and when no one else took any initiative, Adrianna reached out and accepted the parchment. A chill crept up her spine as he gave a self-satisfied grin "May I ask your name, my Lord?"

His smile widened. "It's Sydonnia. Thank you for your aid. Sirion will be happy to know I am back. Have a good day and may the gods smile upon you." Before she could mention that Sirion was no longer in the city, the fae had risen from the chair and left.

Adrianna looked at the parchment in her hand for a moment before putting it in one of her pouches. Everyone at the table resumed their interrupted conversations and Adrianna watched the man make his way out of the inn. At the entrance, he and Armond almost ran into one another. Each man excused himself politely and Armond continued over to the table and sat down. She looked around at the group. No one inquired about the letter. She thought it more than a little strange, for she was naturally very suspicious about the contents of a message left in her hands by a stranger for a man she hardly knew.

Adrianna dismissed her thoughts and looked about the common room again, her gaze passing over the young human girl she had noticed earlier. She was sitting by herself at a small table beside one that seated two blond-haired, blue eyed faelin. They were Savanlean, those fae that made their homes in the northern mountains of Centeal Ansalar. They were a common sight in Sangrilak, but Savanleans tended not to stray any farther south.

Still feeling tired, Adrianna closed her eyes. Her mind detached from the activity around her and she allowed herself to relax. She vaguely realized when Tianna returned from wherever she'd been and sat back down at the table in same seat that the strange man had commandeered not long before.

A commotion on the other side of the room made Adrianna open her eyes again. During the time she'd dozed, the common room had filled with people. Her gaze was drawn to the two Savanlean men she had noticed before. One was complaining in a loud voice and held the black-haired Denedrian girl by the front of her blouse, shaking her as he emphasized his words, "I know you stole my money pouch! It was with me before you bumped me and gone after you left!"

57

Out of the corner of her eye Adrianna noticed Dinim rise from his seat and she watched him walk over to the scene. "Is there something wrong here?"

"Yeah. This girl stole my money and I would like to have it back." The man shook her again, and her head snapped back on her neck. She said nothing, remaining calm and silent throughout the accusation.

Dinim regarded the girl intently. Adrianna and the rest of the group arrived just as he questioned her. "Do you have this man's money?"

The girl shook her head.

Dinim looked back up at the men. "Please release this girl. She claims not to have it–"

The Savanlean interrupted. "I know she has it. She is a thief and a liar. I have seen her kind before." The faelin's face was red with suppressed anger, and he shook her again.

The girl's face visibly paled. Dinim held up his hands. "Well now, it's your word against hers, my friend. Let her prove that she doesn't have it and search her." Dinim looked at the girl for the answer to an unspoken question and received a nod.

The Savanlean glared at Dinim. "Well I don't see as you have a say in the matter, *friend*. So why don't you just step away and let me finish my business with this little imp," he growled.

Adrianna glanced around at her companions. Armond seemed slightly amused while Dartanyen appeared tense, his gaze intent upon the situation. Bussimot didn't seem to care, and neither did Zorg, who had stayed behind at the table to continue eating. Adrianna sensed a flurry of movement beside her. She turned just in time to see a mug fly from Tianna's hand, striking a bearded man a couple of tables away. The man shouted and stood from his seat, his hand at the back of his head.

Tianna gripped Adrianna's arm and gave her a pointed look. "What in damnation is that?" Her eyes were wide, and she was gesturing towards the front of the room.

Everyone, including the angry fae and his companion, looked towards the front entrance. What they saw was a confused man holding the back of his head, looking around the common room in order to ascertain who had thrown the mug.

The angry Savanlean glanced scathingly at Tianna and then returned his focus to the girl. Meanwhile, the man who had been struck by Tianna's mug was suspiciously looking in their direction and was making his way over. Tianna's hand tightened about Adrianna's arm. The Savanlean angrily shook the girl once more, and Dinim raised his voice. With a frown of irritation, Mug Man approached the table. "Who threw that mug?" he asked gruffly.

He was ignored by everyone except Tianna, who kept herself inconspicuous behind Adrianna.

"What is going on over here?" Volstagg's voice was almost as loud as he was big. "I will have no trouble in my tavern! If you have something to settle, do it outside!"

With a raised brow, Volstagg listened to stories from Dinim, the Savanlean, and Mug Man. The cenloryan then quickly remedied the situation. With the flick of a wrist and an upraised forefinger, Volstagg's burly cook came over to the table and the outraged Savanlean and his companion were escorted out of the establishment. Volstagg turned to Mug Man. "I'm sorry you got caught up in this. How about I make your next ale on the house?"

Mug Man smiled. "Thank-you Volstagg, that would be much appreciated."

After the man left, Volstagg turned back towards the group. "I don't know exactly what's going on here, and I don't care. What I *do* know is that I don't want any trouble. I think it's time for you all to leave as well."

Adrianna just shook her head as the group took their possessions and walked out the front door. For a while, everyone just stood quietly about at the entrance to the inn. The Denedrian girl stood among them, her dark head bowed. Evening was approaching and soon they would need to find lodging for the night. Adrianna didn't worry about herself; she knew she was welcome anytime. It was the others...

Adrianna abandoned her thoughts when the girl finally spoke. "Why did you do that?" She looked up, her brown eyes searching Dinim's face.

"What?" asked Dinim.

"Why did you help me?"

Dinim shrugged. "You looked in need of helping, so I obliged."

"But I stole the money. You know I stole it, so why did you help me?" The girl's voice was both imploring and accusing, her expression one of confused suspicion.

"You have skills that may be valuable to us."

The girl's eyes narrowed when she realized he had helped only to place her within his debt.

Her retort was ardent, "I owe you nothing!"

Dinim's gaze became cold. "Oh, I believe you do."

Adrianna watched the interplay with mixed emotions. Fear flashed in the girl's eyes and her gaze wavered. *She is afraid he will call the city guard if she doesn't cede to his demand. What the Hells are we doing? We have to force people to help us out?* She felt Dartanyen shift beside her. *He doesn't seem quite comfortable with this turn of events either. Mayhap this all could have been done differently. We could have given the girl a choice...*

The girl continued to stand there for a moment, but then she shrugged nonchalantly and seated herself on the top step of the veranda.

Adrianna was thoughtful about the girl's sudden change of heart as Dinim began to discuss the few remaining items that were needed for their mission. A few moments later he turned back to the girl. "What types of things do you need in order to do your job well? Keep in mind, everything is paid for."

"I need a new set of lock picks."

He nodded. "And you shall get a new set of daggers as well."

She gave a small smile and her body lost some of its tension.

"By the way, what should we call you?" he inquired.

She pondered the question for a moment. "Amethyst."

Dinim grinned. "Welcome to the group, Amethyst."

Astride Dramati, Sirion moved through the small wood. His body was attuned to his surroundings and every sense was alert to any change in the environment. As a ranger of Elvandahar, it was his business to know everything there was to know about his terrain of preference: the wooded regions of central Ansalar. He knew every plant and animal by sight alone and had studied them all so he knew many of their other attributes: the different voices of the songbirds, preferred vegetation of the various hoofed beasts, which plants had medicinal properties, and which bushes had the tastiest berries. But even if he wasn't in a wooded area, he would continue to see, hear, taste, smell, and feel the world around him.

Because that was simply who he was.

Sirion and Dramati scouted ahead of the group. He was glad for the solitary nature of his work, for it suited his personality perfectly. It allowed him to think without the interference that being social brought. But this day, his thoughts were not only on his work, but the memory of what he had witnessed just over a week before.

Sirion and Anya rushed through the wide corridor, the light from their torches casting eerie shadows on the walls. The sounds of battle up ahead kept Sirion from faltering and he hoped they weren't too late. The tunnel emptied into a huge cavern where the darkness tried to swallow the light from their torches, making it difficult to see what was happening until they got closer to the cemetery. The sight that met their eyes was frightening and almost made his heart stop in his chest. In shock, Sirion watched as an undead abomination shuffled towards a young woman kneeling on the bloody ground at the side of her fallen comrade. Beside her was another one of her companions; the man was reaching down to help her up.

Sirion would recognize her anywhere. The woman was Adrianna.

Terror swept through him. He tried to shout, but the words somehow got stuck in his throat. By the time he could speak, the wraith had struck the man down.

A shrill battle-cry pierced the air. The only warrior left fighting was the halfen axe wielder. Bussimot savagely destroyed the wraith that took down the other man before careening away to find the next opponent. Sirion swept past his sister as Adrianna scrambled away from the battle crazed halfen. She seemed to recognize the danger she faced, that it wasn't just from the undead.

It was then he saw it, another wraith approaching from out of the shadows.

"Lady, 'ware behind you!"

Adrianna turned just as she was struck. Fear gripped him as the monster stooped over her prone form. It slashed downward and its dagger dripped red with her blood as it straightened again.

Sirion careened past the wraith, lopping its head off as he swept by with his quarterstaff. Out of the corner of his eye, he saw the halfen fell another one. Bussimot was covered with splatters of blood, some from his comrades, but most from himself. The man was working only on energy reserves and would need just as much medical attention as his fallen comrades when his rage ended.

Anya entered the fray, methodically dispatching the undead with swift efficiency while Sirion knelt before Adrianna. He cursed eloquently in Hinterlic as he placed his hand over the deep cut below her ribs, dark blood flowing freely from the gaping wound. She moaned and slipped more deeply into unconsciousness. Adrianna was lucky, for the wound could have been much deeper, the wraith's dagger waylaid by the lower-most rib. He tore open her vest, and once feeling around the area, he discovered the rib was broken. He removed the blue sash from about his waist and wrapped it around her ribs and over the hole, hoping to stop the blood-flow and keep the rib from doing further damage when she was removed from this place.

It was then Sirion stopped to consider what he and Anya would have to do in order to save Adrianna and her comrades. Oh gods...

The halfen fell as the last undead priest toppled to the ground. Anya disdainfully kicked at the bodies of the hideous creatures as she made her way over to Sirion. Her hand gripped his shoulder tightly. "Come, we must find aid as soon as possible."

Sirion shook his head. "I can't leave her."

Anya turned away. "Fine, I will go alone."

Alarmed, he moved to catch her arm before she could step away. "No!"

Anya frowned. "We have to go now, Sirion! We are wasting time!"

He sighed heavily, knowing his sister was right. He was loath to leave, but he didn't want Anya to travel through the tunnel alone, not with the dangers they now knew to be present. He bound the wound tightly, hoping it would be enough. Then Sirion rose and swiftly ran back through the tunnel, Anya right behind.

Sirion tightened his fist in the thick fur around Dramati's neck. His mind still recoiled at the sight of the ghoulish monster's bloody dagger as it rose from its victim. In slow motion, he remembered swinging his staff and seeing the grotesque head fly through the air to land a few farlo away. He remembered his fear as he knelt beside Adrianna's body, the warmth of her blood pumping against his palm, and the paleness of her face where she lay beside her fallen companion, her head in the crook of his arm. Then he remembered running, running like he never had before, back to the surface to find the only people he knew who would be able to save her and the others.

The Wildrunners had come just in time. If left any longer, Adrianna and her companions would have died from blood loss. The Wildrunners took them to the closest temple, one dedicated to the god Hermod. In return for the services the priests and priestesses provided, Sirion and Volstagg had combined their resources and donated over twenty-five hundred gold.

Despite pressure to be on the road, Sirion had refused to leave Sangrilak until he knew Adrianna would live through her ordeal.

Now, on his way to the city of Grondor to face trial, he wondered about Adrianna and hoped she fared well. He and Dramati had run for three days and nights to catch up with the rest of the Wildrunners. As he travelled, thoughts of her never completely left his mind, and much to his surprise, it didn't bother him; he never tired of thinking about her. It was such a change from what he had always known before, even when he was with Joselyn. Despite the strong feelings he had once borne the druidess, she had never been able to take him away from his work. But now, a mere slip of a girl did more than just that. Sirion smiled to himself. Adrianna consumed more than just his thoughts.

Joselyn. It has been a long time since I last thought of her. Whatever has become of her? What has she accomplished? For quite a while, with the exception of his profession, Joselyn Quemirren had consumed both his mind and his body. He was a tracker, and after each job, he would come to see her where she lived in a small town at the outskirts of Entsy. They would share a few days with one another before he was off to his next assignment. In many ways, he had honestly cared for her, maybe even loved her. However, the feelings never transcended his desire to be a successful ranger, and neither would she give up her own endeavors to be with him.

So, in order to pursue their professions, they had mutually decided to end their steamy acquaintanceship. Looking back on it now, he couldn't refer to their relationship as anything more; it had been a meeting of their bodies and very little else. All he knew of Joselyn's dreams and goals were that she wished to rise in the ranks, to be known as one of the highest in the order. At the time, it had been the same for him, to strive to be the best at his own chosen vocation.

Thus, it had ended. A few times over the years he had thought he might regret it, but in all honesty, he never did. Now, as he thought of the young woman Adrianna, he imagined that he just may have given it all up... just to be with her.

DEEPENING MYSTERY

A drianna wandered out into the common room and found she was the first one to breakfast. Once seated at the bar, she began eating the meal brought to her and thought of the previous evening. With more than a small amount of haggling, their list of provisions was approved by the secretary of the Captain of the City Guard, right down to the lloryk and larian she had jokingly suggested that Dinim place at the very bottom. The group had then come back to the Inn of the Hapless Cenloryan and she had beseeched Volstagg to allow the rest of the group to stay there for the next few days until they went back down to the mausoleum. He'd halfheartedly agreed, and she knew the only reason he did so was because it was she who did the asking.

Quite truthfully, she was more than a little glad she and the others had some time to rest before returning to the necropolis. The thought of going back there was terrifying, and her mind had fabricated the idea that the place was a pit belonging in the Nine Hells. Not only that, but she would have time to visit Mairi. She felt guilty for being in the city so long without seeing the woman who had raised her, even if she had good cause for not doing so.

Tiredly she picked at the remains of her meal. She hadn't slept well; her nightmares having returned full force since leaving Andahye. More than once she'd wondered if Master Tallek had cast a spell to keep them away whilst she lived in his tower. She wouldn't be surprised if he had, for he'd always striven to give her what happiness he could in spite of his rigorous training.

It wasn't long before the rest of the group entered the common room. Everyone broke their fast, and soon they were ready to begin the day. Dinim informed them that he had some personal business to address and would see them later for the evening meal. Without any further explanation he left. Adrianna thought it a little odd but said nothing as she watched him depart.

The first part of the day was spent with the weapon-smith and the armorer, haggling over how soon everything could be made. Finally, it was agreed the items could be ready in four days, albeit for a handsome price. The group agreed to the increased cost, knowing it would be covered by the city. The end of their day was spent on a farm at the outskirts of Sangrilak owned by a man who bred and sold larian and lloryk. He had come highly recommended by several informants, and he was knowledgeable and friendly. His stock was of excellent quality, all of his animals healthy and strong. Everyone picked out a beast they favored. In spite of her small size, Adrianna chose one of the lloryk, a dark steel grey animal with white markings. Everyone else chose a larian, those smaller animals being more appropriately sized for faelin and small humans. Zorg was the exception, whose larger frame was more easily carried by one of the lloryk. He chose a white animal with only the merest hint of coloring in his mane, beard, and tail tuft.

Once their business had been concluded, everyone led their beasts back into the city and housed them in Volstagg's stable. The boys who worked there took over the animals' care upon their arrival. Adrianna and Dartanyen, both knowing a bit about larian and lloryk, remembered all that the breeder had told them about keeping the animals in good condition. They gave the boys strict instructions for the feeding and currying of each of the beasts and then followed the rest of the group into the inn.

Dinim was already there, sitting at a table in the back. The men went to the bar to give their orders for the evening meal and Adrianna studied him as she, Tianna, and Amethyst approached. He appeared upset, his dark brows pulled together into a frown. However, once realizing their presence, his countenance changed. Adrianna watched as he schooled his features into an expression of pleasant welcome that didn't quite reach his eyes. He stood as they arrived at the table and seated themselves.

Dartanyen, Bussi, Armond, and Zorg returned with some mugs and a tankard of ale. It wasn't long before their food was brought. Throughout the meal Dinim remained distant and aloof. Not once did he try to join in the conversation. Adrianna cast surreptitious glances in his direction, noting how different he seemed from the animated and free-spirited person she had met the day before. She had meant to speak with him later this eve about her father, to ask for his help in discovering what had become of the man after he'd left Sangrilak all of those years ago in the company of his brother and daughter. But with his aura of indifference he seemed so remote, and she was reluctant to say much of anything at all.

Once they were finished, the food platters were removed, and the men got another tankard of ale. Tianna joined in the drinking, but Amethyst seemed a bit out of place, her dark eyes cautiously taking in everything all around. After a while she rose from her seat and excused herself from the table.

Dartanyen's authoritative voice stopped her. "Where are you going?"

Irritation passed over Amethyst's features. It was obvious she hadn't answered to anyone before, or at least, not for a while. "Nowhere in particular. I just want to take a walk in the cool night air."

Adrianna smiled to herself, hearing the annoyance in the girl's voice, and it was at that moment she realized who would be leading this group. It was the way he spoke to Dinim about knowing everything on their list of purchases, how he'd insisted that Adrianna tell him what she knew about Thane, and when he always asked everyone's whereabouts, even if someone was just going to the privy. Dartanyen showed his authority just by his self-assured saunter.

Adrianna watched Amethyst make her way past the tables to the front of the inn. Once the girl was at the door, Adrianna turned back toward the table. Her eyes were immediately drawn to Dinim, whose gaze was locked on Amethyst as she left the establishment. His brows were drawn together in a frown above cold, dark eyes. A chill walked up Adrianna's spine. *He looks so menacing...*

Abruptly his gaze shifted, and those eyes were fastened onto her. She suddenly felt trapped. A tingling sensation rose over her flesh, and her breathing slowed, almost as though her body sought to still itself. Then he smiled and his expression was transformed. Once again, he was the handsome, dynamic man she had met the day before.

Released, Adrianna looked away. Suddenly, she too, felt the need to get out. She rose from the table and glanced around at her comrades. "I'm going out for a ride. I will see you in a couple of hours." Zorg offered her a brief wave as she stepped away and Dartanyen gave her an appreciative nod.

Adrianna made haste as she left the inn and walked to the stables. The visit to Mairi was overdue. It had been too long, much too long since she had last seen the woman who had sacrificed so much to be a mother to her and Sheridana after their mother passed. Adrianna went to the stall that housed the lloryk she had chosen earlier that day. The dark shape inside moved as she approached the door. He was a fine animal with a thick arched neck, a sturdy chest, well-muscled legs, and friendly eyes. He was a large creature, larger than what was needed to carry her person. Yet, above all the other lloryk and larian she'd seen, it was this one who had captured her eye.

He had a name, one that didn't suit him, so she gave him a new one– Sethanon.

She unlatched the door and entered the stall, offering a handful of hartbeetles to show that she was his friend. The lloryk ate every last one, including the ones that tried to crawl away up her arm, gently plucking them off her flesh with his soft lips. The sensation was ticklish and caused her to shiver. She patted his silky scaled hide, then quickly and efficiently saddled him.

Once out of the stable, Adrianna vaulted onto his tall back. His muscles rippled beneath her as he expressed his happiness to be away from the stall confines. He pranced about, head held high, nostrils flared. He awaited her commands before beginning a trot. His stride was excellent and his footing sure. She rode to the front of the Hapless Cenloryan and saw the group out on the veranda: Dinim sat between Bussi and Dartanyen on the steps, Tianna was seated in a rocking chair, and Armond leaned against one of the support columns. Everyone seemed to be enjoying some light-hearted banter. She felt a momentary twinge of longing, a part of her wanting to go back to share in the camaraderie. But she thrust that feeling into the back of her mind as she urged Sethanon into a canter, riding past the inn and into the darkness.

Adrianna rode through the city towards the northeastern periphery. The buildings became sparse and shifted solely to residences the farther they moved from the central square. After a while the houses became spaced farther apart, each one claiming several plots of land used for farming.

Once out in the open, Adrianna urged Sethanon faster. The air was cool and crisp, the wind sweeping over her face to make her eyes tear and her hair whip about behind her. She hadn't realized how much she missed riding; Master Tallek used to take her all the time. The raw power of the animal beneath her was phenomenal, his muscles stretching and bunching to carry her so far so fast, and she controlled that power with naught but the simplest of commands. She imagined that it was much the same with magic, and she hoped she could be a really good spellcaster someday.

She was there before she knew it. Out of the darkness appeared the house in which she had spent much of her childhood, and she bid Sethanon slow and finally come to a halt. Adrianna dismounted and patted the lloryk's sweaty shoulder. He probably needed a good cool-down walk, but it was already getting late. She wasn't sure she wanted to be riding about in the middle of the night without someone there with her. If Dartanyen knew she was riding so far, he probably would have requested someone to accompany her.

Hoping for the best, she chose not to loop Sethanon's reins around the pole in front of the house. This way, he could walk about freely by himself, and help himself to the nearby trough of water near the side of the house. He stood still as she gently took his head in her hands and placed her forehead against his soft muzzle, "Please stay close. I need you to take me back into the city. Don't leave me, my friend."

With that she patted him again and turned away to look at the house. It was the same as it had been several years ago except maybe a bit more run-down. Most likely, Hafgan didn't have the funds to hire someone to help him anymore. She walked up the porch steps, the very ones she had run up and down as a young girl, and it felt like forever had passed. She knocked on the door and she had only to wait but a moment before a familiar figure appeared.

Mairi opened the door and gasped when she saw Adrianna, her brown eyes lighting up with joy. "My dear, sweet Adria, I have waited so long to see you!"

"Oh Mairi, I have missed you so much!" Adrianna held the woman close, guilty for not writing more often. But then she was enveloped within the warm embrace of the woman she had called 'mother' as a child, and found it was the same she had always remembered. Mairi hadn't allowed Adrianna's lack of communication to influence the love she felt.

The two women held one another for several long moments, and when they finally parted, Mairi had tears in her eyes. She bade Adrianna enter the house and led her into the sitting room where she offered biscuits and tea. Once all had been prepared and set before them, Mairi gave a deep sigh. "It is so good to have you here, Adria. There has been so much I have wanted to share with you, and when you stayed away so long, I wished we had spoken more before you left."

Adrianna rose and went to the older woman, kneeling on the floor at her feet. She then laid her head in Mairi's lap. "I am here now." Adrianna swallowed heavily and closed her eyes, feeling the tears seeking to be freed. She sniffed and straightened, knowing she needed to ask the question although she wished not to. "How is Hafgan?"

"Ah, my husband sleeps. He is old and tired." Mairi smiled her sad smile, the one Adrianna remembered the most. "Such is the price I pay..."

Mairi's voice trailed off, but to Adrianna, the older woman need not say more. A half-faelin had married a human, and for that, Mairi would spend many long years without her mate. Adrianna shivered momentarily, struggled to take her mind away from Hafgan, the old memories resurfacing. She had resolved to forget the abuse she had suffered at his hand, refused to allow it to affect her life. She wouldn't allow his past treatment of her to ruin her reunion with Mairi, who had never known the full extent of her husband's cruelty.

The two women spoke for a while, not about the shared past like many would have done, but of Adrianna's training in Andahye, what had recently befallen her in the necropolis, and dreams of what the future could hold for her. Adrianna balked when it came time that she should leave. There was a part of her that wanted to stay, but it was getting late, and Mairi should be in bed beside Hafgan. He would be irritable if he awoke to find her not there.

Adrianna rose. "I should go. I am weary, and I have much ahead of me on the morrow."

Mairi stood and placed a hand on her arm. "Adria, wait. There is something I want to tell you."

Adrianna noted the solemn tone in Mairi's voice and regarded her questioningly. "What is it?"

"We should have spoken more about her years ago when you were yet still a girl, but I couldn't bring myself to do so knowing how much it could hurt you to hear about her, especially the way your father treated you. But now, looking back with wiser eyes, I feel that it could have helped you to hear more about her, to have known how wonderful she was, and especially how much she loved you."

Adrianna responded in a monotone. "My mother."

"Oh, yes. I so much wish that you had known her. She was a special kind of person, so genuine, and so caring. It is frightening to know just how fragile life is, and that it can be taken away in just the space of a heartbeat."

Adrianna's voice cracked. "Mairi, please..."

"A long time ago, before you were born, I knew your mother. We were the best of friends." Mairi smiled with the memory, a sad smile that seemed to touch Adrianna's soul. "Your father was gone much of the time, so we got to know one another quite well. Gemma was so vibrant and full of life. After she became pregnant with you and your sister, she couldn't wait to show you the world.

"But it wasn't meant to be. The labor went on for far too long, and she became weak from blood-loss. She knew she was dying. After you were finally born, she held you close. She spoke so softly that I could hardly hear. She said, 'You will be the child of my heart. You have a part of me that will always be with you. You will have knowledge of those things that have passed and of those that will come to be. Listen to your innermost soul, and you will be free.' She named you just before she died."

Mairi's eyes shimmered with tears, and one escaped to trail down one cheek. "Your mother seemed to know things– things that would happen in the future. Moon cycles before your birth, when you and your sister were naught but seeds within her womb, she knew something of the circumstances under which you would be born, and she gave something to me. She told me that it should be given not to the child born in the light, but the one who would be born in darkness. Even then she knew that there wasn't just one child inside, but *two*.

"When the time finally came, your dark-haired sister was born during the light of the day, and the sun shone upon her as she emerged from your mother's body. Much later, you were born in the darkness of the night. Not even the light of the moon touched you. Despite your lighter coloring, I knew it was to you that your mother meant for her gift to be given."

Mairi sighed. "You have grown into such a lovely woman Adrianna. Your mother was right. You definitely are the child of her heart. You look just like her." Mairi shook her head. "I hid the gift that your mother left for you, knowing how special it is and how important it was to her that you have it because I was afraid that Thane would take it and keep it away from you. Now I will find it, and when next you come to see me, I will give it to you."

Adrianna took Mairi within her arms and held her close. "Thank you so much for everything. You are the only mother I have ever known. I love you."

"And I love you, my dear. I have always loved you, just as I would have loved a daughter born of my own womb."

Several moments passed before Adrianna released Mairi. "I will come back as soon as I can. Take care until then."

With Adrianna's hand held within hers, Mairi led her to the door. Adrianna stepped out into the cool night to see Sethanon waiting patiently. With a vault onto his tall back, she mounted the lloryk and waved as they trotted away into the darkness.

After a few moments, Adrianna turned her head to look back at the house. In the distance she could still see Mairi framed by the light in the doorway.

Adrianana stepped away from the bath. Her thick hair hung past her shoulders and down her back. The ends were already beginning to curl a bit, and this was the straightest she would see it for a while, the water making it heavy and holding the strands down. She slowly dried it with a towel as she settled down before the desk. She appreciated the bath Volstagg had brought, and she would thank him for the luxury tomorrow morning when she went to breakfast.

Adrianna opened her book, the one she'd just begun studying when she left Andahye. It was taking much too long for her to get through it, and despite other obligations that had taken her away from her studies, she felt guilty. For several moments she focused on the text, combing her hair and braiding it as she read. She had to get up to find something to tie it off with and suddenly remembered the message she had taken for Sirion the day before. She grabbed her belt-pouch and fumbled around inside it for the folded parchment.

Adrianna pulled out the message. It had been folded in such a way that it was open only at the corners, and those were sealed with colorless wax. The opening was also sealed. She frowned, never having seen anything quite like it before.

Thunder rumbled outside. The window was ajar, and she could smell the scent of impending rainfall. She suddenly realized how dark it had gotten and her gaze darted around the room.

A loud knock sounded at the door. She put a hand to her chest when her heart leapt. "Who is it?"

"It's me, Volstagg."

Adrianna rose from the bed and opened the door. She motioned him inside and shut it behind him. "So how was your visit with Mairi? She is well, I hope?"

"She is well enough I suppose." Adrianna walked back to the desk and sat down. "She missed me. I wish I'd written her more."

He chose his words carefully. "You probably could have." He was quiet for a moment. "But you recognize your fault. It is what you do now to make reparations that's important."

Adrianna smiled. "I like that. Once I'm back from our mission, I shall make more efforts to reach out."

Volstagg grinned. "Is there anything you need before I had off to bed?"

More thunder rumbled outside, and Adrianna tapped the folded message on the desk. "Well... no I suppose not."

He noticed the hesitancy in her voice and raised an eyebrow.

She sighed. "I have this message for Sirion. It was given to me by a strange faelin I'd never met before, and no one else in the group had met him either." Adrianna indicated the folded parchment in her hand.

Volstagg waited for a moment and then got a puzzled expression on his face. "What is the problem?"

"Don't you think it's strange? Why would this man place his message into the hands of a person he doesn't know?" She forbore mentioning the mixed feelings she had concerning the large Hinterlean man.

Volstagg squinted his eyes and looked at her closely. "Adria, people do it all the time. Hells, they even rely on birds to send messages to others who live far away."

Adrianna nodded. *Oh yes, I hadn't thought of that.*

"Did he say anything when he gave it to you, anything about what it might say?"

She shook her head. "Not really, just that he hadn't seen Sirion in a long time, that he would be in the city for a few days, and that the message has the location of where he is staying."

"Did you tell him Sirion is no longer in the city?"

"I never got the chance because he was so quick to leave."

"You get the man's name?"

She wracked her mind. "I can't recall it."

Volstagg turned to leave. "I could take it if you really want, but the message was entrusted to you."

She shook her head. "No, that's alright. I'll give it to Sirion when I see him next."

"Help herself to anything in the kitchen if you need it, day or night. You are not a guest, but my family. You understand?"

She nodded and somehow spoke around the lump that suddenly formed in her throat. "I do. Thank you for everything."

"You are very welcome." He gave her a wink and then de-parted, closing the door softly behind him.

Adrianna turned back to the open book lying on the desk. The room was quiet except for the rain that had begun to fall outside. She got up and settled herself back onto the edge of her bed, looking at the folded parchment. *There is just something about it, something not right.*

The moment she chose to open the message, the rain began to fall harder. With a bit of trepidation, she broke the wax seal and unfolded the letter. Lightning flashed outside her window and a troubling scent filled her nostrils as she read the words on the page. Thunder crashed and a gust of wind blew into her room. One of the candles blew out.

Sirion,

I have you in my sights. It will not be long before I catch up to you. I will crush you and then drink the blood from your shuddering heart. You are a dead man walking.

Sydonnia

Adrianna trembled. She could smell that the words had been written in blood. She read it a few more times, and then with shaking hands, refolded the disturbing message and placed it back into her pouch.

She whispered, "Sirion, who is this man who desires the taking of your life?" She rose once more from the bed and went to the open window. Her hair blew in the wind before she shut it. Then she stood there, still shaking. She was afraid, afraid for a man she hardly knew. She thought of telling Volstagg about it, but quickly discarded that notion. First of all, he would know she had opened a confidential message, and second, there would be nothing he could do, and it might make him worry.

Adrianna took the book from the desk and lay down on the bed. She tried to study, but her concentration was long gone. The storm had been short lived and had quieted down, the thunder now rumbling unobtrusively somewhere in the distance. She didn't know how long she lay there, only that she had calmed enough to feel tired.

Another knock rapped at her door, this one softer than the last.

"Who is it?"

"It's Tianna." She paused and then spoke again before Adrianna could break free of her surprise long enough to form a reply. "You know, the healer Sirion sent for?"

Adriana was already at the door. *Why is this woman coming to my room, especially at this late hour?* She opened it and courteously motioned for the other woman to enter. As she moved back towards the bed, she gestured for

Tianna to sit in the chair at the desk. The young woman obliged and for a moment there was silence.

Finally, she spoke. "Listen, I don't really know anyone in the group, and I was hoping to get to know you first. You know, as one woman to another."

Adrianna raised an eyebrow. *This is unexpected.* "All right," she replied, wondering what this "woman to woman" thing entailed.

Tianna smiled, a pretty smile that not only turned up the corners of her mouth but shone in her misty blue-gray eyes. She then pulled the chair closer to the bed, turned it around, and sat on it backwards. She regarded Adrianna a moment before talking again. "Well, I was wondering," she paused and licked her lips nervously, looking down at her hands folded neatly in her lap, "what exactly happened down there in the cemetery?" Her voice shook a little. "And why were you all down there in the first place?" Tianna's eyes rose to meet hers. She had a haunted look, as though dreading what Adrianna would say.

Adrianna looked at the young woman perched on the chair before her. She could tell that Tianna was going through some type of emotional struggle. That fact alone made her uncomfortable, not to mention that she was talking with someone she hardly knew about one of the darkest days in her life. She breathed outward in a gust before responding. "We searched the library as a favor to the Wildrunners. They hadn't the time to do it themselves. Although I wish they had, for then all of this would never have taken place."

Adrianna then proceeded to impart most of what she knew about the situation, as well as what she knew about the other members of the group, which was not much. She forbore mentioning the message that Dartanyen had found on one of the mutilated corpses, not willing to speak about her father.

As Adrianna neared the end of her rendition, Tianna seemed to become restless, shifting about on the chair, and picking at the sleeve of her blouse. "And that was when they came–"

Adrianna's words were cut off as Tianna covered her face with her hands, her body shuddering convulsively. She instantly stopped, watched as Tianna struggled to compose herself. The other woman's face was pale, and her hands shook as she placed them back in her lap. The haunted look in her eyes had returned. Adrianna knew fear when she saw it, and in a flare of sympathy, quickly started speaking about waking up in the temple where Tianna had met them. After Adrianna was finished, the room was quiet.

"I don't like to hear about the undead." Tianna breathed in deeply, her eyes shifting about the room until they finally rested once more on Adrianna. "But I had to hear your story." She paused again. "Something similar once raided my childhood home... something frightful... something *dead...*" Tianna's voice trailed away, and her eyes got a sad, faraway look. After a moment she shook herself out of the memory.

Tianna smiled wanly, and then rose from the chair. "Thank you for having me. I hope I wasn't too much of an inconvenience."

Adrianna shook her head, "No, it was fine."

Tianna swiftly walked to the door and opened it. "I suppose I shall see you in the morning. Good night."

Adrianna stared at the closed door for a moment before returning to the bed. She lay down and looked up at the ceiling. Her thoughts returned to Sirion and the eerie message she had read prior to Tianna's arrival. *What in the Hells is going on? What should I do?*

Then it hit her. *I must try and warn him. Somehow, I have to get a message to Sirion and warn him of Sydonnia's intentions.* Adrianna jumped out of the bed and went over to the desk. She opened the drawer and pulled out a small sheet of parchment. She then opened the ink jar and picked out a quill. The first words that came to her mind found themselves on the parchment.

Sirion,

I write to offer thanks for your aid in helping us out of the temple. It seems we had walked into a situation that seeped over our heads without our knowing it. At the request of the city guard, we will once more walk in the Underdark. This time we hope to gain access to the temple proper.

However, there is something more I need to share with you. I have told no one else about it, not really knowing who to tell. But it is here, sealed to the bottom of this page. The message worries me, and although I don't really know you, I am concerned for your welfare. Watch your back, for I fear that this man may be lurking about one of the turns.

Take care and give Dramati a pat for me. May you transcend all obstacles and may the sun shine upon you.

Yours truly,
Adrianna Serine Darnesse

Adrianna stared at the message she had written, then rolled it up, placed his name on the outside, and sealed it with wax. She would figure out how to get it to him in the morning. For the last time, she went over to her bed and

75

lay down, extinguishing the lantern on the way. Despite her feelings of foreboding, she finally fell into a restless sleep, her dreams troubled.

Adrianna awoke early, making it to the common room before Volstagg became too busy. She sat down at the bar and put the rolled message on the counter. "This is for Sirion, but I'm not sure how to get it to him. I remember you saying he went to Grondor, but do you know *where* in Grondor?"

Volstagg nodded. "He and the rest of the Wildrunners are going to the courthouse to be tried for the murder of the advisor to the Prince of Torimir. The courthouse has an aerie, so it won't be a problem to get your message to the right place." He picked up the message. "If you would like, I can take it to the Sangrilak aerie-keeper later today. He and I are good friends, and I can get it sent for minimal cost."

Adrianna raised an eyebrow. "Sangrilak has an aerie?"

Volstagg nodded. "Yes, for the past five years."

She smiled and leaned across the counter to give him a hug. "You are too good to me Volstagg. Thank you."

He just gave her a smile and pocketed the message. "Like I said last night, you are my family. As it turns out, Sirion is too. For family I will do anything." He gave her a wink. "I'll be right back with something to break your fast."

Noticing Dartanyen had entered the common room, she gestured in the archer's direction. "I'll be sitting with the group."

Volstagg nodded and disappeared into the kitchens. Adrianna then joined Dartanyen at the table situated in the farthest corner of the room. It wasn't long before Dinim, Armond, Zorg, Tianna, and Bussi arrived. A while later, Amethyst was the last to approach. Either she had spent half of her night awake, or she simply wasn't a morning person. The sour expression on her pretty face told all at the table that she was not in a sociable mood.

When everyone was finished with the morning meal, Dartanyen suggested they go to the bazaar to purchase any things they would need to make life easier while on the road. "For all we know, this may not be the last of our assignment. I mean, let's think about this. Sirion sent for Tianna to come to us, knowing that she is a healer of some renown." Dartanyen, turned pointedly to the lady of discussion. "Am I correct in saying this?"

Tianna smiled. "Perhaps. I am a healer. That much is true. But the well-known part..."

Dartanyen chuckled. "Hmm. A modest healer of some renown." Dartanyen turned to the rest of the group. "But don't you see what I am saying? Sirion sent for her knowing we would need her skills. Would he have done so if he thought everything would be resolved with just one excursion into a temple?"

Armond nodded. "You do have a point."

Bussi frowned. "Eh, methinks ur puttin' too much inta this."

Dartanyen waved dismissively at Bussi and turned to Dinim. "You know the man better than any of us. What do you think?"

Dinim seemed to consider it for a moment. Regarding him furtively, Adrianna thought she saw a glimmer of irritation in his eyes before they became hooded. "I think you are probably right. I would dare to guess that the Wildrunners, after this assignment, are considering asking you to help them further."

Adrianna considered it as well. She wasn't quite so sure. She believed that Sirion would have asked for Tianna to help with just this mission, especially if he felt it important enough. However, it was possible that what Dartanyen said could be true. Though, Adrianna wasn't so sure that she liked that idea. She had her own worries. She needed to find her sister and her uncle, find out how the dead man in the library knew her father, and why Thane was looking for Dinim.

Adrianna remained silent throughout the rest of the exchange. It was decided they would take Dartanyen's suggestion and go to the marketplace. She had no money of her own, having given much of it to the priests who had taken care of Master Tallek's body. The remainder she had spent on her journey to Sangrilak in the form of food, lodging, and protection.

It was a beautiful spring day, mild and seasonally warm, a good day for a walk through the bazaar. The merchants had opened their doors at the crack of dawn. It was a day of rest, so the street vendors had set up their booths early as well, laying out their wares for the coming day. Adrianna and her companions wandered in and among the shops and booths, the merchants smiling at them warmly in the hopes that one of them would stop long enough for him or her to come over and begin preaching upon the virtues of this length of fabric, that pair of boots, or another string of beads.

Finally, they stopped, Bussi fascinated first by a carved wooden pipe, and then by the varieties of dried herbs and leaves offered by the same merchant. The big man lumbered over to the halfen and Bussi began to bombard the merchant with questions. The rotund man answered them all with good-natured patience and was sincerely pleased that someone else was as interested in the varieties as he.

The group stood by for a few moments as Bussi and the pipe merchant conversed, but eventually dispersed to nearby booths. Adrianna found herself wandering over to the beautiful stall of a fabric merchant. Many colored and textured lengths of cloth waved in the mid-morning breeze. She walked among the billowing waves of color, silently choosing those shades she liked best even though she hadn't the money to purchase any.

"This one would look best on you, I think."

Startled, Adrianna turned to find a woman holding out a silken length. It was indeed beautiful, a soft shade of brown. When it was held this way and that, the hue shifted from light to dark. Adrianna shook her head. "Oh no. I can't. I was just looking. You have so many beautiful pieces."

Adrianna turned away from the woman and began to continue her perusal when suddenly she found Dinim standing in front of her. "She's right, you know. With just the right touch, it would be most becoming on you." Dinim held out a strip of textured red cloth.

Adrianna felt her cheeks flush. Slightly embarrassed, she glanced first at Dinim, and then at the stall owner, who continued to hold the brown silk. "Really, I can't. It must cost a small fortune." *What the Hells is he doing?*

She silently wished that Dinim had never come upon her, wished that she had never decided to have a look in the fabric booth in the first place. It was true she needed a new cloak; the one she wore would soon be too thick and heavy for her to carry in the summer heat. She didn't know how it would be possible to acquire one unless she borrowed money from Volstagg. It was something she really didn't want to do, not because he wouldn't give her the money, but because he would give her more than she needed.

And then he would never allow her to pay him back.

Adrianna frowned inwardly. *Why didn't I include it on the list of provisions to be purchased by the city? Sometimes I can be so daft.*

Dinim raised a dark eyebrow. "Don't you like it?"

His question caught her off-guard. She looked up to find him regarding her solemnly. Adrianna shrugged. "Sure, I like it. But that's not the point."

"You're right. That is not the point... precisely. More like, you need the fabric, and you may as well like the thing that you need to have."

Adrianna sighed heavily and put her hands on her hips. "Dinim, what in the Nine Hells are you talking about?"

He smiled broadly, and his eyes glinted with mischief. "Just what I said. You need the fabric. You may as well like it, and it may as well look good on you."

Adrianna rolled her eyes. "Dinim, you don't understand." She pointed to the fabric. "That length of fabric will cost a fortune! I am not in any position to be purchasing clothing of any such kind, especially one so costly."

"No, my dear. It is *you* who doesn't understand. *I* am in a position to purchase such an item, and I will. Knowing that you like it makes it that much easier."

Adrianna felt her eyes widen. "You will do no such thing! I haven't the means to repay you!"

"I didn't ask you for repayment, nor would I ever expect it of you. You are supposed to consider it a gift and accept it as such." With that, Dinim took the strip of red fabric to the merchant, who wore a satisfied smile on her face. Dinim didn't even bother haggling with the woman over the price, for she already knew he would buy it. The woman gently placed the brown swath of fabric in a cloth sack, followed by the red piece, and gave it to Dinim, who then gave it to Adrianna.

Numbly, Adrianna took the sack. Smirking to himself, Dinim took her by the elbow and led her from the booth. The rest of the group continued to wander around in the near vicinity. Zorg was found in a leather shop being sized for a new pair of boots. Tianna was found in yet another fabric shop, haggling with the merchant over the cost of a shock of deep green fabric. Dartanyen and Bussi lounged against the wall of another nearby stall.

Amethyst was nowhere to be seen.

ATTACK

With an open book in her lap, Adrianna sat in the rocking chair on the veranda of the Inn of the Hapless Cenloryan. Sighing, she leaned back, and moving back and forth, she closed her eyes and remembered the last time she had spent out on the veranda. Sirion had been there, and Dramati. She looked back on that memory fondly, for it was one of the only good memories she had experienced since coming home. That and seeing Volstagg again, visiting Mairi, and meeting Dinim.

Dinim. She found that she liked him very much, her wariness having given way to an easy camaraderie. It was thoughtful of him to purchase the cloth, and afterward he'd gone with her to see a tailor who would shape the fabric into a fine summer cloak trimmed with the red satin he had chosen. Afterward she had returned to the inn to spend the rest of her day with her books.

Adrianna had let her studies slide since her master's death and she felt she shamed his memory. She knew what he would have said had he been alive to say it. In her mind's eye she could see him sitting at the lesson table in the laboratory...

"A mind unused is a vessel for mischief. A mind without intellect is a waste, a repository for the useless garbage that it takes in on a common day. A mind without something to learn will go stagnant, rot like the thousands of other minds in this world of monotony. It is up to you to use the Talent bestowed upon you, to extend your mind to reach the farthest of horizons. And it is my job merely to guide you on your way."

He would try to keep a frown, but within moments he would break out into a smile, his clear blue eyes crinkling at the corners. Rightly chastised, Adrianna would meekly return to her lesson, ashamed that she hadn't met his expectations... all because she hadn't kept up her studies.

Adrianna sighed again. She thought she would have heard something about the investigation on Tallek's death. There was no reason she shouldn't be informed, for she'd made it very clear where she would be going after leaving Andahye. Now, looking back, she realized maybe she shouldn't have left so hastily. Her decision to leave had been based solely on emotion, and there were things she could have made sure were done properly, especially in regard to the tower. Journeyman Tannin's threats to take it from her, however, were all made of hot air. The legal counsel she'd sought had easily recognized her firm hold on all of Tallek's assets, including the tower

After a couple more hours of study, Adrianna went to the common room where she discovered that Amethyst had finally returned. The young girl had been away all day without a word to anyone. Adrianna remembered Dartanyen's silence as the group returned to the inn after visiting the tailor. By the set of his lower jaw and the sparkle in his blue eyes, she could tell he was angry. Now Adrianna was just in time to see the verbal battle that was to ensue.

"It's about time you decided to walk in here." Dartanyen's tone was icy from where he sat in his chair.

Amethyst shrugged noncommittally, her expression impassive. "I was just out and about."

"Just 'out and about', hunh? Well, next time why don't you consider telling someone you are going to be 'out and about' before you just go traipsing off to only gods know where."

Amethyst sneered disdainfully. "I'll do whatever I damn well please. I don't recall anyone naming you my keeper. So just bother off, will ya?"

Dartanyen rose from his chair. His next words were loud, louder than Adrianna thought they would be. He was furious, his eyes flashing dangerously. "For your information, little miss, I named myself your warden, and as such, you will come to me when you plan on going anywhere. That includes 'out and about', inside out, and sideways. Do you understand?"

Amethyst's brown eyes narrowed angrily. "Piss off," she hissed.

She turned on her heel and began to walk away, but quick as lightning, before she could go two paces, Dartanyen was upon her. Brown eyes widened as he grabbed her arm and spun her around to face him. They stood face to face, she being almost as tall as he. However, that didn't diminish him, anger fueling his body to make him appear larger than she by far. His voice was menacingly soft, "Never turn your back to me in an argument. You may one day come to regret it."

Amethyst's tone held none of its previous hauteur, "Don't threaten me."

"Oh, it's no threat." Dartanyen leaned in closer. "It's a promise."

Amethyst was silent for a moment as she regarded him, her eyes taking in his face and judging his sincerity. Then she stiffened. "Let me go," she said as she began to struggle.

Dartanyen abruptly released her and she stumbled back. Amethyst blinked with surprise but said nothing as she rubbed her arm.

"You will agree to tell one of us when you are going next time. It's not my job to be your nanny. You made me, and everyone else here, worry needlessly over your absence. Another hour or so and we would have begun to search for you." Dartanyen paused and then continued. "I know that you are not accustomed to this, but I can't have the integrity of this group threatened by the impetuous nature of a child. It's about time you start to grow up and take responsibility for your actions. Dinim won't always be there to save your silly hide."

Amethyst's gaze went to where the mage was seated. He hadn't stirred from his place, lazily taking in the scene before him. Her eyes then swept over the rest of the group, who silently watched the scene playing out before them. She momentarily turned back to Dartanyen, whose temper had begun to cool. But then, saying nothing, she turned away and slowly walked up the stairs to her room.

Adrianna stared after the girl for a moment before going to the bar and asking for some of Volstagg's special mash of cooked grains and a cup of tea. In a way, she felt sorry for Amethyst. However, at the same time, she disliked the lack of respect the girl had shown Dartanyen, and for that matter, the rest of the group when she left without a word. It seemed that Dartanyen had taken care of that type of behavior, commanding her respect with a show of aggression. As she awaited her food, Adrianna wondered why he hadn't shown such anger in the library when she had refused to tell him what she knew about Thane's letter. She had spouted off by raising her voice and turning her back on him the same way Amethyst had just done. Mayhap the difference lay in the disbelief he saw mirrored in her eyes, the helplessness. Perhaps he had been able to see that it was anger and fear that spoke, rather than arrogance and lack of respect. Dartanyen just might be more perceptive than she gave him credit for.

Armond had been at the forge since early in the morning, helping to complete the weaponry the group needed for their mission back into the Underdark. He had some training in the craft and was able to take some of the burden off the weary smith, who had kept hours long into the night to complete their requests. From the veranda railing, Adrianna watched as he walked slowly towards the inn. It was obvious Armond had been working hard. His face and clothing were covered in the dark grime that came with working at the forges. His hands were black, and she was sure there were numerous cuts and abrasions beneath the layer of ash. When he reached the top stair, Adrianna went to the door and opened it. Armond smiled and gave her a grateful nod as he entered. Stepping in behind, she heard him call for a bath on his way up the stairs to the room he shared with Zorg.

On her way down, Tianna crinkled her nose and gave him a sideways glance. Once reaching the bottom, she stepped up to Adrianna. "So, how do you feel about a midday walk?"

Adrianna shrugged. "Sure. I suppose my body could handle a little physical stimulation." Inwardly she cringed at her offhand comment. It was such an understatement. While apprenticed under Master Tallek, she had been accustomed to so much more. Within the first week of her apprenticeship, he had taken her to Lady Wilhelmina, who had taught her the art of controlling the movements of her body through the art of dance. Much to her disbelief, Adrianna had excelled at the exercises, but it wasn't just the body control, or the physical stimulation. It was the release... that little piece of something that her mind and body could devour without the need for intellectual challenge.

Adrianna and Tianna stepped out onto the busy street. An umberhulk cart loaded with lumber rumbled by, followed by a group of boys chasing a mangy worg. Adrianna glanced after the boys as they passed. She had been much like them once. She had never chased animals through the streets, but she had definitely spent much of her time wandering around from one place to another, getting into whatever minor mischief she could until she had been forced to attend school.

Adrianna was jolted out of her thoughts as her companion suddenly clutched at her arm. "Effin calotebas," muttered Tianna, glancing back at the offending passerby, a tall man with a dark cloak who had brusquely bumped into her without bothering to stop. She then turned back to Adrianna. "Sorry, living in the temple and spending most of my time there, I had forgotten how rude most people can be."

Adrianna smiled. "That's all right, I can probably remember enough for the both of us."

The two women continued to walk, enjoying the day. It felt good to have female companionship, something she hadn't experienced since her sister left Sangrilak, and she appreciated Tianna reaching out to her. She unexpectedly recalled Sirion's disturbing message hidden in her belt pouch. *Maybe I should tell Tianna about it. She seems to be a kind person, someone who would be a good friend, and maybe even someone I can trust. Not only that, but Tianna knows Sirion personally and she might have some insight about the man who gave it to me.*

The women turned down another street towards the central square. Today was not a bazaar day, packed with the make-shift stalls and street vendors they had experienced a couple days ago, but the place would still be bustling with people. The aroma of freshly baked honey buns wafted through the air and Tianna turned to her with a mischievous grin. "On our way back to the inn we need to get some of those!"

Adrianna chuckled. Tianna looked like a little girl doing something naughty. *I'm going to tell her about the message. It will be good to have someone else who knows about it.*

Suddenly a commotion could be heard in the distance. The women glanced at one other before rushing in the direction of the sounds of fighting. It wasn't long before they made it to the scene. Between themselves and the combatants was a quickly growing mass of spectators. They squeezed between a couple of burly men and a group of gaping women to make their way closer. They abruptly stopped when they recognized one of the fighters.

It was Dinim.

The Cimmerean's pale face was contorted with rage as he leaped at his dark-robed, human opponent, a glowing shortsword in his right hand. The other man parried Dinim's blow with a longsword. Both of the men sported wounds: Dinim with a slice to his arm and shoulder, and the other a nasty gash at his side. He clutched the wound a couple of times, almost as though to be sure to keep his insides from coming out.

Amid the noise from the growing crowd, Adrianna heard the two men shouting at one another, but was unable to make out their words. She could see Dinim was getting angrier and that he wanted to use his magic; any sorcerer would. But, in the presence of so many onlookers, it would be sheer stupidity.

The Talent to harness magic was a rare one. Master Tallek had taught her that only the most gifted of the Talented could learn to use their innate faculties to harness and tame the energies that flowed between and among all living things. The ability to use magic was an awesome thing, but to the common masses it was nothing less than frightening. Those who knew how to do it were a mysterious lot and much under the scrutiny of those who didn't posses the capacity. If Dinim were to use magic here, he would receive much fear and prejudice, more than what he was getting already as a result of his race. Granted, he used a magical sword, but most of those gathered wouldn't notice it as such, seeing it only as an item of quality and beauty.

The men lunged at one another again, the magic of his sword offering Dinim more power and finesse than he might have had he not wielded it. But the other man was a more practiced swordsman and, despite the arcane nature of Dinim's blade, turned the tables of the fight into his favor. With a quick twist of a wrist, the man sent Dinim's weapon flying from his hand.

The crowd gasped and Tianna put her hand to her mouth. Adrianna caught a glimpse of a big man making his way through the press of people on the other side of the combatants. After another moment she recognized Zorg. Dinim cursed at his opponent as the other man spun past, but Dinim didn't turn to follow. Instead he kept his back to the other man. The human saw his opportunity and took it. He leaped, but at the last moment before impact, Dinim spun around. He sheathed his dagger deep into the man's belly, using the force of the man's momentum to aid his thrust. Dinim then staggered backwards, the weight of the dying man falling on top of him.

Adrianna heard herself and all of those around her exhale. She watched as Zorg succeeded in pushing past the front line of the crowd on the other side. He rushed towards the fallen men and pulled the enemy off Dinim. Worried, she watched for any signs of movement. Finally, he stirred. The big warrior was instantly at his side, and after a few words were exchanged, the mage was picked up by Zorg and carried from the scene.

Adrianna and Tianna were pushed from behind as the crowd surged forward to get a closer look at the dead man. The companions quickly got out of the way and followed Zorg. From the left, a regiment of the City Guard rushed down the street towards the square. Needless to say, they were much too late. Dartanyen and Bussi moved behind Zorg and they ducked down a side street to the right. "They will be going back to the inn," said Tianna. "Let's go."

The women ended up arriving right behind the three men and their burden. Bussi swung open the inn door and Zorg hurriedly carried Dinim inside. Luckily there were no customers. "Volstagg, come quick. Dinim has been injured," shouted Dartanyen.

The cenloryan came bursting out of the kitchens and was up and over the bar within a single moment. His massive hooves made indentations in the wood planking as he landed on the floor, the sound of it like thunder in the common room.

Dartanyen ran to the nearest table and swept the bowls, mugs, and anything else atop it onto the floor. Zorg lay the semi-conscious Cimmerean down while Bussi stood at the door. In one hand he carried Dinim's blade. Meanwhile, Amethyst had also entered the common room and stood near Bussi to watch what was going on.

By the time Tianna reached the table, Dinim's clothing had already been stripped away from the wound sites. "Bring another table and move it up against this one," she ordered. "Then someone bring my medicine bag down from the bedchamber."

While Amythyst rushed back up the stairs, Zorg and Dartanyen were quick to move the table. Feeling that Tianna might need an extra pair of hands, Adrianna stood silently on the other side. Armond arrived through the front door, nodding at Bussimot, who stood guard. With a look of concern, he walked up to Dartanyen and Zorg, who filled him in on what had happened.

Tianna climbed onto the table, giving herself better access to Dinim while she worked. She then leaned over her patient, her left hand grasping the amulet around her neck. Within her mind she prayed. She closed her eyes and clutched the symbol of her goddess, Beory, tightly in her grip. For several moments she remained that way, then, opening her eyes again, Tianna placed her hands near Dinim's wounds. He stirred for a moment beneath her touch and then subsided.

She frowned. There was something amiss, something not quite right about this man. She sensed something from his bodily vibrations that she had never encountered before.

Tianna continued her ministrations. With the gifts bestowed by her goddess and her skills as a healer, she analyzed the wounds. They were not severe and would be easily mended. She picked up the wet cloth Volstagg had the presence of mind to set beside her. He had even known enough to boil it so that it wouldn't be the cause of any infection that might enter the wounds. The water was hot, very hot, but she stayed focused on her task.

Tianna squeezed out the excess water and laid the cloth over the wounds on Dinim's upper arm and shoulder. He stirred again as she thoroughly cleansed the areas. She wouldn't know for sure if there would be any infection for a day or two, but in her professional opinion there would be none. When she was ready, she asked Adrianna to hand her a small pot of salve from the bag Amethyst had brought, the one with the green lid. Tianna had prepared the ointment herself: gathered the dark brown bark from a khaobab tree, pulverized it, and steeped it in water over a flame. She had then added leonine to it, not only to make it soothing as it was applied, but to make it thick and oily. It had a strong medicinal smell, and a person could reek of plants for several days. But it was worth the inconvenience to avoid the massive infections that so often took the limbs and lives of many a good warrior.

Finally, Tianna was finished. She lay her hand on Dinim's brow and was pleased to feel no fever. However, she couldn't keep a frown from creasing her forehead. It was the same sensation she had experienced earlier, the feeling that there was something unnatural about this man, something not right. But unable to put her finger on it, Tianna was eventually forced to dismiss it.

That evening, the group sat around the dinner table. Zorg and Armond indulged and ordered large tankards of ale for everyone to share. It was the second to the last night before their excursion back into the Underdark, and they felt they deserved it. Adrianna enjoyed the taste of the ale, it being one of Volstagg's best. However, she decided not to drink too much, disliking the sensation that imbibing larger quantities of such beverages brought. Dinim was unusually quiet; it was expected considering the events earlier in the day. But inevitably, the conversation shifted in his direction, Dartanyen being the first to bring it up. Adrianna had been wondering when he would.

"So Dinim, what happened this afternoon? That was quite a fight." Dartanyen stopped and waited.

Dinim shrugged nonchalantly. Adrianna noticed a slight frown of irritation before he quickly covered it up. "I really don't know. The man bumped into me as we were passing in the street. He stopped and gave me an attitude. Of course, I said words back to him. The man became angry and unsheathed his sword. In order to protect myself, I was forced to do the same." He cast a glance around the table. Adrianna followed his gaze and it stopped at Amethyst. She regarded Dinim with a strange expression on her face, then looked down into her lap.

Zorg whistled. "That was it? You was fightin' because you bumped each other in the street? Gads, it sounds like somethin' I would do." Zorg guffawed loudly, the drink beginning to take hold of him. Armond and Bussi snickered as well.

The men threw around some jokes before Bussi took control of the conversation, telling them a tale about his earlier days. Not much later, Amethyst rose from the table. The girl nodded to the group and left. Not even Dartanyen stirred from his seat, for it had become common knowledge that Amethyst took a walk every night before retiring to bed.

It wasn't long before Dinim also rose from the table. Everyone glanced up as he spoke. "I think I am going to get some rest. I am more tired than I thought I was."

Tianna stood as well. "Are you feeling all right? Is there anything I can get for you?"

Dinim grinned and raised his hands. "No, no. I'm fine. I just need some sleep is all. You have done more than enough to help me. I'll just see you all in the morning." Dinim then stepped away from the table and walked up the stairs to his room.

Well into the night the men talked. Adrianna and Tianna just sat and listened, entertained by the stories the men told about their lives and the lives of those they knew. Finally, with bellies full of drink, the men stumbled up the stairs with the help of the two women. They giggled as they tucked the men tightly in their beds. Adrianna remembered that she wanted to tell Tianna about the letter, but she was so tired, she decided to do it in the morning.

She slept a restless sleep.

The group gathered in the common room. Everyone had eaten breakfast and was ready for the day. They had agreed they would go together to procure their weapons from the smithy. Each item would be checked for proper balance and handling. Armond was certain of their caliber and guaranteed the quality himself. Dartanyen gave another gusty sigh of impatience. They were waiting on one person.

Amethyst still had not emerged from her room.

Adrianna grumbled to herself. No one showed any inclination of going upstairs to get her. She rose from the table at the same time as Tianna and they nodded to one another and left the rest of the group sitting there talking about the restless relationship between the realms of Elvandahar and Karlisle.

Once making it up the stairs to Amethyst's room, Adrianna knocked. When there was no response, she put her face close to the door and spoke loudly enough that someone would be able to hear through it. "Amethyst? Amethyst, everyone is waiting for you downstairs."

There was no reply. Adrianna frowned. She put her hand on the doorknob and turned, expecting it to be locked. To her surprise, the door opened. She glanced at Tianna. The other woman nodded, and they entered the room. They looked around in consternation when they saw it was empty. The only evidence that someone was staying there was a back-sack sitting on the nicely prepared bed.

Tianna shook her head. "It looks like she didn't come back last night."

An uneasy feeling swept through Adrianna. "I wonder if something happened."

"You mean, you wonder if she got caught?" Tianna cast her an apathetic glance.

Adrianna rolled her eyes. "Of course."

"But don't you think she would have found a way to get a message to us?"

"From prison... no."

Tianna huffed. "It probably serves her right. This was bound to happen. I mean, look at the circumstances that brought her to us in the first place."

"I know, I know. But before we speculate any further, let us first find out if she is, indeed, imprisoned for a crime. Let's go tell the others."

The two women went downstairs and approached the group. "She's not in her room," said Adrianna.

Dartanyen looked up, his brows drawing together into a scowl. "What do you mean?"

"Exactly what I said. Amethyst is not in her room. In fact, it appears she never came back last night."

Dartanyen's lips drew into a thin line. "All right." He stood from his seat. "We go without her then."

Adrianna continued. "Well, Tianna and I feel that she may have gotten herself into trouble. We were thinking of looking around for her a little. You know, check out the local jail to see if she's there."

"Forget it." Adrianna turned in the direction of Dinim's voice. He wore a frown of irritation across his face. "Let her deal with the consequences of her actions. We can't always be here to get her out of trouble."

Adrianna frowned. "You see, that's just it. We were never here before. Think of all the years she has been living on the streets. She obviously has always been able to elude trouble before we came along."

"Yeah, maybe with the help of the local thieves' guild," quipped Armond.

"But how do we know that?" replied Tianna. "We have to give her the benefit of the doubt. I mean, she is a member of this group, right?"

"At least let's check out the jail, just to be sure she's there. We have to know for certain," said Adrianna.

Dartanyen sighed. "All right. We'll go."

The group filed out of the inn. Adrianna noticed Dinim shaking his head. Zorg, Armond, and Bussi just shrugged and followed behind. In silence they walked to the jailhouse located on the north side of the city. Once there, everyone waited while Adrianna and Dartanyen went inside. The rotund man sitting behind the desk nodded as they entered.

"Who ya here for?"

"We are looking for a girl, human, maybe having seen fifteen or sixteen summers," said Dartanyen. "She appears to be of Denedrian decent, with black hair and brown eyes. If she's here she would have been brought in last night or early this morning."

The guard smoothed his moustache thoughtfully, then shook his head. "No, no one's come in with that description, not that young." He frowned. "Come to think of it, we don't have any women in here right now except for old Mattalyn. She was drunk again last night, schmoozing with all the men in the Tilted Tankard and propositioning them." He waggled a bushy brow, but his countenance remained solemn. "I fear that one night a few men will finally take her up on it and rape her. Poor thing." The guard shook his head sadly.

"Well, I appreciate your time, but if you do happen to see her, my name is Dartanyen and I'm staying at the Inn of the Hapless Cenloryan. Please send me a message and I'll be right over."

The guard nodded. "Will do."

"Thank you."

Dartanyen took Adrianna's elbow and they walked back out. She shook her head, and everyone gave a collective sigh. For a few moments they just stood outside the jailhouse. Finally, Dartanyen spoke. "All right, so she's not here. Maybe she has no intention of coming back. I mean, she acts like she doesn't want to be a part of our mission anyway."

Adrianna shook her head. "No. I don't think that's the case. Tianna and I saw her slingbag still in her room when we went to check on her this morning. We feel that she has every intention of coming back."

"Where the Hells is she then?" asked Armond.

"Listen, I don't have time for this," said Dinim petulantly. "I have a lot to do before we go back down to the cemetery tomorrow."

Dartanyen planted his fists at his hips and growled under his breath. "I know. We all have a lot to do before then. Let's just go and complete our business for the day. Maybe she will have shown up back at the inn by the time we get back."

"But what if something has happened to her and she needs our help? Maybe we should search for her," said Tianna.

Adrianna had just been thinking the same thing. A feeling of foreboding crept up her spine. "It seems that she didn't return from her nightly walk. Perhaps we should just search around some of the main streets. Maybe someone has seen her."

Dinim threw his hands into the air. "Well, you all can spend the rest of the day standing here talking about it. I have a lot of business to take care of. I'll see you later."

Adrianna looked after him as he walked away. *He acts like he doesn't care if something happened to Amethyst.* Her eyebrows furrowed in thought. *He doesn't even want to bother with conducting a search for her.*

"All right, why don't we do this? Armond, Zorg, Bussi and I will go to the smithy and the armory. That is important business we simply can't ignore. In the meantime, Adrianna, you and Tianna begin searching. After the rest of us have finished our business, we will join you. We should meet back at the inn a quarter past midday."

"Agreed," piped Tianna. "Let's go, Adria."

Adrianna was surprised as Tianna looped her arm around hers and led them down the street. Her new friend had used the name that Sheri called her when they were children. Strangely, it made her feel good. She grinned to herself for a moment. Perhaps she could make a place for herself back here in Sangrilak after all.

For two hours Adrianna and Tianna searched for Amethyst to no avail. No one had seen her; they had searched all the main streets, and even some of the side streets. "Tianna, we should return the inn. Who knows, maybe Dartanyen and the others were able to find her. Or maybe Dartanyen was right and she went back to the inn on her own."

Tianna cast her a withering glance. "And you really believe that?"

Adrianna frowned. "Well, no. But we still need to get back. I don't want to find out later they sent out a search party for us too. Besides, I think we are in over our heads and we need to ask for some professional assistance."

"You mean you think we should ask the City Guard to help us? Don't you think we have made ourselves high profile with them enough already?"

"Yeah, but one more thing won't hurt us any more than we have already."

Tianna nodded. "True. All right then, let's go back. But you know, I think that if we just look a little longer–"

Adrianna shook her head. "No, no, no. We must go. Maybe the others have found out something."

When the women returned to the inn, they found Dartanyen, Bussi, Zorg and Armond waiting for them. Dartanyen stepped towards them. "So, did you find her?"

Adrianna frowned. She had been nursing the secret hope that, despite her feelings that something was terribly amiss, Amethyst either would have returned to the inn, or that the others would have found her. "No. We searched everywhere. What should we do?"

Dartanyen shook his head. "We'll have to go to the City Guard. They have professionals who do this type of thing all the time. Every city usually has at least one on duty. They are called Streetsliders. They are the ones that discover those who are missing and probably murdered."

"How are we going to get one of those people to search for us?" asked Tianna. "Amethyst hasn't even been missing for an entire day. Not only that, the possibility still remains that she decided not to return, slingbag or no."

"My dear," began Dartanyen, "it is always possible to get others to do the work one wishes of them. One needs only to use a bit of style."

"You mean lie," replied Tianna, her eyes narrowing.

Dartanyen spread his arms, his expression the epitome of seriousness. "It is merely a matter of viewpoint. I see it differently."

"Come on," said Armond. "Let's go and get this over with. I'm not beyond a bit of manipulation myself."

"I knew someone would see it my way." Dartanyen grinned mischievously.

"Yeah, well I just want to get a full night's rest tonight. I don't relish the idea of being awake all night long searching for children who should be at home in their beds," grouched Armond.

"Hear, hear," mumbled Zorg as he followed Dartanyen and Armond out the door.

"Whatever gets the job done," whispered Adrianna to herself.

Not much later, they stood before the Captain of the City Guard. He eyed them speculatively. "How long did you say that she has been missing?"

"Almost three days," said Dartanyen.

"And she was one of the ones hired to contribute to our efforts in the temple?"

Dartanyen spread his arms. "Of course."

"And you have reason to believe that something may have happened to her?"

"Yes. Just being in contact with us could cause anyone to be endangered. For all we know, Gaknar has infiltrated this city with his spies. They could have caught her unawares."

The Captain leaned back in his chair. "You know, you people are turninging out to be a pain in my backside. Do you know what kind of money you have cost me already?"

"And I am sure it is worth every copper of it to keep the citizens of this province safe from the machinations of one such as Gaknar," said Dartanyen.

The Captain glared at him. "Fine. I will call in Harris. Maybe he can find your friend. Just bring me the proof I need that it is Gaknar's temple when you come back." The Captain then waved them out of his office.

It seemed like hours that they waited. Just when Dartanyen was about ready to go back inside to ask if they had been forgotten, a man called to them as he emerged from the side of the building. Behind him followed two other men. They were armed with crossbows and each had a longsword that hung from his hip.

The men approached the group. "Good evening. M'name's Harris. This is Darric," he indicated to his right, "and Burke". We will be working on your case. The Captain gave us a description of your companion. We had best hurry before we lose our light. Where can we reach you?"

"The Inn of the Hapless Cenloryan," replied Dartanyen.

"All right. See you there when we're done." Harris turned on his heel and the two others followed him down the street.

Dartanyen turned back to the group. "Now we wait."

In silence they walked. Once back at the inn, the group found Dinim waiting. Dartanyen filled him in on the events of the day, ending with hiring the Streetsliders to find Amethyst.

"I tell you that it's all a waste of time. She's gone. You should have let it be." The Cimmerean shook his head, slouching down in his chair and crossing his arms at his chest.

"Perhaps, but Tianna and Adrianna seem to feel otherwise. At least now, no one can say that we didn't try," said Dartanyen.

Dinim made no reply, a dark brooding expression on his face. Adrianna regarded him out of the corner of her eye. He seemed so uncaring and abrasive, very unlike the way he had been before his skirmish in the city streets. She felt Tianna step up beside her. Adrianna glanced at the other woman and noticed her watching Dinim strangely. Perhaps she also sensed the duality of Dinim's nature.

Hours passed and the last of Volstagg's patrons began to leave for the night. But no one, including Dinim, was willing to climb the stairs to his or her bedchamber. All waited expectantly for the arrival of the urban rangers. Finally, they came. The front doors swung open, causing Adrianna to lurch up from her seat. The three men strode into the room, Harris carrying a limp body in his arms. "Hurry, she needs a cleric as soon as possible!"

Tianna jumped up from her chair and ran towards the stairs. "Bring her up to my room. All of my supplies are there."

Harris followed Tianna up the stairs, the rest of the group following behind. Once in her room, Harris laid the body down on the bed. He pulled aside the tangled mass of dark hair to reveal a battered face. It was Amethyst. She had been beaten so badly she was hardly recognizable.

Adrianna had already collected the washbasin and cloth and brought both to Tianna. The healer already had her eyes closed, her talisman gripped firmly in her hand. Adrianna dipped the cloth in the water and began to wipe the blood from Amethyst's face. The girl didn't move, and her breaths seemed shallow. Her clothes were torn and covered with blood. Her flesh was pale, almost like she was a ghost, and she was cold, like the warmth of life had already left her.

Tianna lay her hands on Amethyst's face. Adrianna caught the whispers of her prayers but couldn't entirely make out the words. Tianna released the remaining fasteners on the blouse and pulled it open. Adrianna heard the sharp intakes of breath from around the room. In horror, Adrianna looked upon the bruised and beaten body. Unbidden, tears sprung to her eyes. *That was me, once.* Then she shook her head, willing the memories away. Her gaze went to Amethyst's trousers and found them still intact. *At least the perpetrator hadn't raped her.*

Tianna looked up and glanced around the room. "Please leave us." She then went back to work, removing the rest of the girl's clothing. Dartanyen nodded and went out the door, the others following suit.

"I hope we found her in time milady," said Harris as he and his men left the room behind the other men. Adrianna placed the cloth in the reddening water in the washbasin and rose to leave with the others.

"No, Adrianna wait." Tianna put her hand out. "Please stay. I could use your help. It's just that I didn't feel comfortable having the men here. Besides, they weren't doing any good just standing there anyway. I want to afford the poor girl as much privacy as I can. It's the least I can do."

Adrianna smiled warmly. "I would be happy to help. Here, let me get a fresh basin of water." Adrianna went downstairs and retrieved some of the water that Volstagg had boiled, as well as some fresh cloths. When she returned, she found Tianna praying over Amethyst again, her delicate hands resting over the bruises on her ribs and belly. Adrianna sat beside the bed and once more began to cleanse the girl's face and head. She was careful not to wash away the blood that had clotted at some of the cuts and abrasions. She then began to wash the dirty matted hair, knowing it could ultimately carry infection to the wounds.

Quite a while later, Tianna looked up from her work. Her shoulders sagged and she had hollows beneath her eyes. "Her wounds are severe. Her right wrist is broken, several of her ribs are cracked, and she is bleeding inside. I have done all I can to help her. She needs more than I have the strength to give. Obviously, she will not be going to the cemetery tomorrow. I think we should take her to the Temple of Hermod to heal and rest until our return."

Adrianna regarded Tianna with open concern. The woman looked haggard, like she hadn't slept in days. Her hands shook as she took them through her reddish-brown hair. It was obvious to Adrianna that she had spent every last vestige of energy on the girl lying between them. Such was the price that Tianna paid for the prayers to her goddess, much like the price that magic exacted from Adrianna when she opted for its use.

"Come then," she said. "Let us take her there now. We need to get as much rest as possible before tomorrow morning."

Tianna nodded. Adrianna went downstairs and told the others about their decision. Zorg followed her back to the room. Gently, the big man picked Amethyst up from the bed and carried her back down the stairs. Only Dartanyen accompanied them to the temple, for Armond, Dinim, and Bussi had already gone to their beds. The priests at the Temple of Hermod had no problem keeping the girl with them until the group returned from their mission, happy to help anyone who aided the Wildrunners.

Then the three companions left, hoping Amethyst would be well when they returned.

He walked in darkness, seemingly one with it. His tattered dark robes swished about his ankles and from within the crevices of the walls he could hear the skittering of tiny feet. Scrats. Although he was accustomed to them, had lived his entire childhood near them, he hated scrats. They were vermin, scavengers, not even worth eating.

Dinim stopped. The dark tunnel seemed to continue, but for him it ended. Half a farlo away was a barrier, an invisible wall. Slowly he made his way forward. Before the ward he stopped, knowing exactly where it lay. He put his hand out, felt the hum of the magic behind the barrier, and withdrew. He had touched it several times, trying in vain to escape, and he'd been pulsed with electrical energy.

Dinim had quickly learned the confines of his prison. He rotted within the confines of Gaknar's wretched temple, an angry spirit that roamed the corridors. Not many entered this section, the dumb guards thinking it to be haunted. Several he had maimed, and a few he had killed. In the beginning they didn't know any better, but now hardly anyone came.

Deep within, anger stirred. Dinim turned and moved away from the ward. He thought of the creature who had stolen his identity and now lived his life in the above world. Shapeshifter daemon... doppelganger. Ixitchitl had used the magic of Aasarak to capture him, defeat him, and then assume his form. With sickening clarity, he remembered the invasion of his mind, how the creature had scoured his memories, learned his strengths and his weaknesses, acquired his skills, incorporated them unto itself. And then the creature had left him, picked clean of everything he had ever been.

But, unfortunately for Ixitchitl, Dinim knew how to reclaim all that.

With a cruel grin turning up the corners of his mouth, Dinim made his way to the next ward. He checked them all every day, hoping, always hoping, he would find a weakness and discover a way out. Deep in his mind, he knew that the daemon Ixitchitl would return. The Deathmaster would eventually come to claim his prize, and the creature would be with him.

Dinim would be ready.

THE TEMPLE

Everyone was awake and in the common room before dawn's early rays pierced the thick, low-lying clouds resting over the city. The men claimed they were up prematurely because they wanted to get an early start. Adrianna and Tianna knew it was because they couldn't sleep. It didn't take the group long to prepare, for they were eager to go. Armond, Bussi, Dartanyen and Zorg donned their armor, the only thing that had been left behind on their first excursion. They then made sure their weapons were properly strapped in place. Tianna, Dinim, and Adrianna did the same, also making sure all their belt pouches were accounted for.

They walked through the foggy streets to the library. The lack of customary noise was eerie, and shivers ran up Adrianna's arms. They approached the new front doors, Dartanyen opening them with the key placed in his care. Once inside, it was good to see that the mess they had seen the last time was gone. The group silently went over to what had once been a hidden passageway. The bookcase was propped open and the corridor well lit with a multitude of torches set in sconces along the walls, a courtesy provided by the City Guard.

The group continued to move in silence. Bussi and Dartanyen led them while Adrianna, Dinim, and Tianna comprised the center. Zorg and Armond brought up the rear. When they reached the area that had collapsed, they saw that the tunnel had been cleared of large debris. They had only to step over bits of the walls and ceiling to get to the staircase they recalled was located at the very end of the corridor. When they reached it, remnants of the old organ were littered about among the rocky debris. Much to their delight, more torches continued to line the walls. One by one they progressed down the steep winding staircase, not stopping until it ended.

When they finally reached ground level, the group arrayed themselves in a diamond formation. Once again, Adrianna and Dinim were in the center while Bussi stayed in the front. Zorg and Armond took the sides and Dartanyen moved to the rear, his bow cocked and ready. The group walked for several moments before Armond spoke. "There must be another way to get down here. I mean, it's quite obvious that no one has come this way for a long time. This passage has only been disturbed by us, the Wildrunners, and whatever forces the City Guard sent."

"Yeah. I was thinking about that myself," said Dartanyen. "We must have found the one Gaknar's priests and clerics would use if, for some reason, they were unable to access the main entrance. But I am sure that one is just as hidden." Dartanyen chuckled. "It seems this one will have to do."

The group continued, and a couple of hours later, they reached the entry into the cavern that housed the cemetery. Slowly they walked inside. Adrianna shuddered as she remembered what happened when last they had been there. The place was eerie in its silence, the dead waiting for something to happen. She looked at Tianna and saw the other woman's face was white with fear.

Together the group moved towards the massive double doors of the mausoleum, the warriors flanking them strategically. Once there, they were confronted with the kyrrean heads they had seen last time, each one with a ring in its mouth.

"What do you think we should do?" inquired Armond.

Dartanyen grimaced. "I don't know, but we may have triggered the attack when we touched the doors the last time."

Suddenly they heard a deep voice. "Entrance can be gained, you will see. Answer correctly and the locks will be freed."

Startled, Adrianna jumped.

Zorg pointed to the left head. "That thing just spoke to us."

The kyrrean on the right continued. It was so strange, for the jaws of the bronze object moved when it spoke. "Round they are, yet flat as boards, the altars of the lupine lords. Jewels of black velvet, pearls of the sea, unchanged, yet changing eternally."

For a moment the group was silent. Adrianna spoke the answer to the riddle at the same time as Dartanyen. "The moons." They both glanced at one another when there was a faint click. The sound of the doors opening was like thunder in the stillness of the cemetery, and everyone looked furtively about to see if anything had been drawn to the noise.

Nothing emerged from out of the dark stillness.

The group slowly filed into the mausoleum. Zorg lit two torches and handed one to Armond. The bones of humanoid skeletons littered the floor. She couldn't be certain, but Adrianna thought most of them appeared human. Everyone tried not to step on them as they walked through, almost as though afraid they would inadvertently disturb the spirits of men long gone. For a moment, the group walked through, unchecked. But their luck was too good to be true for long. While they made their way through the remains, the dead began to rise.

A ripple raced up Adrianna's spine just as Bussi shouted a warning. He drew his battle-axe, wasting no time as he rushed towards the nearest skeletal form rising from the floor, his face florid with excitement. The first skeleton burst apart as he swept through it, the bones splintering with the impact and colliding against the stone walls. Zorg and Armond dropped their torches and joined the fray. The threesome hacked and slashed at their adversaries before many of them even had time to even stand upright. These skeletons were quicker than the zombie-like undead priests they had encountered during their last visit, but they were no match against Bussi, Zorg, Armond, and Dartanyen, especially now that they were endowed with their battle armor.

Adrianna considered holding back her spell when she saw how well the men were doing against their opponents, but then thought better of it. She wanted to help in what way she could, even if the men could handle it themselves. She incanted the spell, her delicate fingers weaving intricate runic patterns in the air. She threw a hand outward in the direction of her target and a missile of magical energy flew from it, scorching the skeletal monster closest to her. Tianna easily finished it with a swing of her scimitar.

The battle was shortly over. Tianna treated the minor injuries the men had sustained while Zorg, Armond, and Bussi animatedly discussed the improvement in their ability to fight with their new weapons. It wasn't long before they were walking deeper into the mausoleum. The musty, dark passageway forked, and after walking for a short while it forked again. It branched twice more before Dartanyen stopped. "I think we need to start drawing a map," he said.

"Yes, I'm pretty sure we've been this way," said Armond.

Dartanyen frowned. "How do you know?"

Armond pointed to the wall. "I remember seeing this broken sconce before."

"I will draw the map," volunteered Dinim.

Dartanyen nodded and they continued, the passageways twisting and turning, getting so narrow in some places to where they had to move single file, Zorg barely able to move comfortably through. Adrianna began to wonder if they were making any progress when she heard Armond hiss an expletive behind her.

"Everyone hold up. We've been down this way before. We are going in circles," said Dartanyen.

"Effin Hells, this place is like a maze! Dinim, I thought you were drawing the map," said Armond.

The Cimmerean regarded him with a scowl. "I am, but I must have gotten turned around. Like you said, this place is a damned maze!"

Armond held out a conciliatory hand. "All right, why don't I mark the passages? That way we will more easily know where we have been. It will also help you with the map." He rummaged around in his pack and took out a lump of charcoal. He drew a large X on the wall beside him. "All right, let's go."

After getting turned around a few more times, the group found the appropriate passages. After a while they were walking through the halls of an ancient pagoda. The stonework was very different, much older than the rough stone passageways they had recently left behind. Slowly and quietly, they walked through deserted chambers, their torchlight casting strange shadows on the walls and ceiling. What once had once been a place teeming with activity was now nothing more than a hollow shell. In their wanderings they saw no one, and Adrianna thought it more than a little strange. It seemed that Dartanyen felt the same, his tension mounting with each step they took deeper into the temple. Adrianna looked around at the rest of the group and noticed similar signs of strain, except, possibly, for Dinim. He seemed just fine.

Finally, they stopped. They placed their packs against the wall opposite the entranceway and settled down beside them. With the exception of a few large empty chests, the room was empty. Adrianna sat and leaned against an adjacent wall. She opened her pack and removed the bread and cheese she had packed that morning. She was so hungry– gods only knew how long they had been going, for it was difficult to tell the passage of time in the Underdark. Tianna settled down beside her. She took two cannis fruits out of her pack and held one out to Adrianna. Smiling appreciatively, she took the firm yellow sphere. She then tore a piece from her bread loaf and offered it to Tianna, who accepted it graciously. Everyone else had decided to take a meal as well. The men passed their food around, all having packed something a little different.

"We should rest here," announced Dartanyen. We don't know when we will have another opportunity. Who wants to take the first watch?"

Zorg raised his hand. "I will."

Armond raised a hand. "I don't mind taking the second one."

"I will take the third one," piped Dinim.

Adrianna looked up, instantly on edge. She didn't want him taking any of the watches. A part of her liked Dinim, for he'd been very friendly and generous with her, but his disinterest in finding Amethyst, even going to far as to show his irritation, gave her pause. He was unpredictable; one moment he was a kind gentleman, the next an uncaring bastard. She didn't trust him, and for that reason alone she didn't want him watching over while she slept.

Dartanyen was about to nod his acceptance when she hurriedly spoke up. "Dinim, I know you want to help, but maybe you should let one of the others take the watch. We should be getting as much rest as we can, and maybe do a bit of studying tonight to be ready for any fighting that might take place tomorrow."

Dinim narrowed his eyes. "No, I'm perfectly capable to take the watch. I don't mind taking the opportunity to let the other men rest; I got plenty of sleep last night."

Adrianna took a deep breath and held it. Really there was nothing more she could do to keep him from taking the shift unless she made a scene.

Dartanyen nodded. "Adrianna has a good point. You should rest, Dinim, for we will need your skills tomorrow to help us out of any trouble we might find. I will take the last watch."

Adrianna exhaled in relief. Dartanyen looked at her and gave an almost imperceptible nod before talking with Bussi. She blinked in surprise– he had noted her unease and chose to back her up on it. She glanced over at Dinim to find him glaring her intensely for a moment before turning away. A chill rippled through her, the brief flare of undisguised malice only making her wariness towards him increase.

Everyone unpacked any bedrolls or blankets they might be carrying. Adrianna hadn't brought anything, unwilling to bog herself down with bedding material when she didn't know how long they would be in the temple. She watched the others for a moment and then took out her spellbook and began to read. Master Tallek had always taught her to be as prepared as possible, over prepared if need be.

Adrianna startled when she suddenly felt a touch on her arm. She looked up to find Tianna standing above her with a woolen blanket. "You know, you should at least pack one of these. It will keep people from feeling so sorry for you."

"But I..." Adrianna halted when she saw the twinkle in Tianna's eye. "Don't worry. I have another."

Adrianna accepted the blanket. "Thank you. This means a lot to me."

Tianna gave her a wink. "You are welcome."

The other woman went back to her bedroll and sat with legs crossed beneath her, palms resting on her knees, and eyes closed. Adrianna imagined it was in preparation for prayer. Dartanyen, Armond, and Bussi already lay on their bedrolls, wrapped in light blankets. It was cold in the Underdark, so they wore all their clothing, the edges of the blankets tucked securely around them. Zorg settled against the wall adjacent to the one she and Tianna occupied. He had taken out his dagger and appeared to be examining it for any blemishes. Looking up to notice her watching, Zorg gave her a friendly grin. She just smiled back and went back to her reading.

The rest seemed much briefer than it probably was, but Adrianna wasn't as tired as she could have been as the group moved cautiously through a part of the temple they had not yet explored. As they walked, the corridors became much less dusty and lanterns hung along the walls. Strangely, none of them were lit, and they didn't come across anyone. However, they came across a well, and once determined the water was safe, everyone had the opportunity to drink their fill and top off their flasks.

Once moving again, the group passed through a series of rooms, each one as empty as the last, and when they reached the bedchambers, they were met with chaos. Clothing, bed linens, books, parchments, and other possessions lay scattered over the floors, and the furniture had been overturned as though someone had been looking for something. They proceeded onward, and still came across no one.

Eventually they came upon a laboratory. It, too, was left in shambles. The group quickly made their way through it, picking up things here and there and keeping a few things they thought they might possibly be able to use. Adrianna broke away from the others and moved to the back of the room where it looked a bit more interesting. Vials, flasks, and beakers lined the shelves. Many were empty, but some had questionable contents. She picked up one that appeared to have little eyeballs floating around in it and she shuddered.

She smelled it before she saw it, and her senses immediately heightened. Death. Proceeding cautiously, she stepped behind a large table to find the body of a priest lying on the stone floor. She covered her nose and mouth and looked back towards the rest of the group circulating the large laboratory. Dartanyen noticed her and made his way over, Bussi right behind him. Adrianna moved aside to allow them access.

Dartanyen knelt beside the body. "It's been a while." He then plucked at the black fabric of the man's vest. "He died of a chest wound. Sword."

"What in da Hells is going on 'ere? Everthins' been deserted 'til now," grouched Bussi.

Dartanyen shook his head. "I don't know, but it makes me nervous. Whoever killed this man could still be around."

"Not too much of a loss if you ask me." Adrianna turned at the sound of Tianna's voice at her side. Behind her stood Armond and Dinim.

"An' why da Hells not?" asked Bussi, raising a bushy eyebrow.

Tianna shrugged. "He's on the dark side. I can tell just by the color of his robes. No imam priest of the light arts would wear such dark robes and vest."

Dartanyen searched the priest and found only a talisman attached to a thick silver chain about his neck. He pulled it out from beneath the robes and held it in the palm of his hand. Tianna moved to kneel next to Dartanyen. "That is Gaknar's insignia," she said.

Dartanyen frowned. "I don't understand. This is supposed to be a temple dedicated to Gaknar. Why would one of his followers have been killed like this?"

"Maybe he did something he shouldn't have," replied Armond testily. "Come on. Let's get out of here. We are kyrrean-bait standing around like this. Just because we haven't seen anyone doesn't mean we haven't been noticed."

"You are right. Let's go." Dartanyen took the talisman and rose.

"Do ya think t'would be enough ta prove this place is bein' used by Gaknar?" said Bussi.

Armond raised a brow. "I don't see why not."

Dartanyen's expression was skeptical. "I'm not sure. I was under the impression they wanted something more concrete."

"What could be more concrete than this? You can hold it in your hand," argued Zorg.

"What I mean is, I think they want something more than just us finding a talisman on a dead man."

They left the laboratory the same way they had entered it and continued deeper into the pagoda. No one was unduly surprised when they came across more bodies of dead priests, all bearing the symbol of Gaknar. The men collected a few more talismans, handing them to Dartanyen to store in his bag, but stopped at the sixth one. When Zorg removed the chain from around the dead man's neck, the talisman began to crumble.

"Whad'ya do to it?" said Bussi.

Zorg shrugged. "Nothin', jus' picked it up." He let the pieces fall from his hands, and once hitting the floor, one would never have known they were once the pieces of Gaknar's insignia.

"It doesn't matter. We have the other five to take back with us." Armond turned to Dartanyen. "If we head back now, we can possibly make it back to the surface before our food runs out."

Dartanyen nodded. "I agree. Five talismans should be proof enough for them."

Tianna knelt beside the remains of the talisman. All that was left was the chain from which it had hung. She shook her head. "This doesn't seem right."

"What doesn't seem right?" asked Armond.

"Things like this don't generally fall apart quite so easily, especially those dedicated to someone as powerful as Gaknar."

Dartanyen knelt beside her. "What are you trying to say?"

She held out a hand. "Give me one of the talismans from your bag."

He did as she asked, pulling the bag off his shoulder and feeling around the inside. Frowning, he dug a bit deeper when one of the talismans didn't immediately come to hand. Finally, he took hold of something, his eyes widening as he pulled it out. He opened his hand and the crumbled remains of something poured between his fingers.

"Effin Hells," whispered Zorg.

Tianna nodded. "I have seen it before with other objects dedicated to a particular god or goddess, priest or mage. The one to whom it is dedicated will enchant it and bind it to the follower for whom it is meant, usually during a ceremony that involves bloodletting. So, if ever the object is taken too far away from the wearer, or if the wearer dies, the object will disintegrate."

Bussi shook his head. "But why?"

"Simple; so no one else can use the properties held within it."

Dartanyen gave a gusty sigh. "Well, it looks like we are stuck staying a bit longer. Let's head out."

Tianna looked around at everyone and her shoulders slumped. "I'm sorry."

Dartanyen patted her back. "It's not your fault."

The group continued onward, no one in any mood to say anything. Everyone hated the Underdark, and to have the possibility of leaving pulled out from beneath their feet so cruelly was hard to overcome. Tension escalated as they quietly proceeded, for still they came across no one living, and questions remained unasked and unanswered.

The group finally found themselves going up a flight of stairs, past another series of disheveled rooms, and through a hallway that finally ended at a large audience chamber. The area was dimly lit by large, round floor braziers containing small fires. Weapons drawn, they cautiously entered after taking a few moments to scrutinize the place, walking slowly towards the double doors on the other side. They had almost reached the doors when Bussi called out a warning. The group turned in unison toward the halfen, just to see a dark figure slowly walking toward them from across the room. They held their ground until the figure was distinguishable. It was a Cimmerean faelin. He was hooded, but his eerie eyes shone crimson red in the firelight. He wore dark trousers, tunic, and a long cloak that swept the floor as he moved. He carried a gnarled black staff in his left hand.

The Cimmerean continued towards them, his glittering eyes regarding them menacingly. As he neared, Adrianna noticed he was concentrating on something, his lips moving silently. It took her less than a moment to realize he was in the middle of casting a spell. Just as she was about to say something, Dartanyen raised his longbow, arrow already knocked, and let loose the projectile. In fascination and horror, the group watched as the faelin caught the speeding arrow just as it penetrated his chest. He then proceeded to pull the half-embedded arrow from his flesh and throw it aside. His lips pressed into a thin line, the only indication of his increasing anger.

Bussi's battle cry echoed throughout the room as he, Armond, and Zorg sprinted towards the dark faelin. They didn't get far when the Cimmerean uttered a few words and swept the gnarled staff in an arc before him, blanketing the room in blackness. Muttered curses floated towards her as the men shuffled about in the dark. Tianna's soft voice reached her ears, and a moment later the room once again had light as she countered the *Darkness* spell. The Cimmerean had moved, and a swift look around found him near a large support pillar on the other side of the room. The men hurled more oaths when they realized they were further away than they were when they first rushed the mage.

Adrianna tensed when she felt a shift in energy to her right. She turned to see Dinim cast his spell. The set of his shoulders was rigid, and she could tell by the downward turn of his mouth and the gleam in his eyes that he was angry. Fire burst from his fingertips and raced towards the dark cloaked faelin. In shock, she watched the fire diminish as it neared the enemy Cimmerean, and it sputtered away completely before touching him.

Oh gods, I can't believe his spell just failed...

Adrianna's gaze swept back to Dinim, but he was turned away from her, his hands balled in fists at his sides. The dark faelin had either cast a protective shell around himself, or he was naturally immune to the magic that was cast. The possibility that he had immunity told Adrianna that he was an experienced magic user and the staff he carried made him more powerful. She thought better of casting her own spell, not wanting to waste her energy needlessly. *By the gods, I've never been in a situation like this before. This isn't just some test given by a few crazy mages in Andahye. This is for real.*

Feeling utterly defenseless, with uncertainty and fear battering her mind, Adrianna unconsciously backed away from the threat. The room was silent, the enemy's gaze riveted upon Dinim. With lightning-quick speed, she watched as Dartanyen nocked another arrow in his bow and let it fly. This time it caught the Cimmerean unawares, hitting him full-force in the chest. The shaft went in deep and the Cimmerean stumbled backwards, his hand above the place where the arrow protruded. He fell onto the floor, and for a few moments his body thrashed about, his throat gurgling as he tried to take a breath.

Finally, he was still.

It took a few moments for Adrianna to begin to breathe normally. She looked around and found her backside pressed firmly into the door. Realizing the threat was gone, she unclenched her bloodless hands and relaxed her muscles enough to step gingerly away. She followed as the group went over to the body of the fallen mage. Dinim reached him first, and when the rest of the group arrived, they found him searching through the folds of the fallen man's robes and cloak. The dark hood had fallen away to reveal long ebony hair that shone in the dim light. He was young, younger than Adrianna would have thought him to be, and very easy on the eyes. Adrianna was coming to realize that, despite the darkness of their nature, the Cimmereans were a physically handsome race.

Finally, with the dead man's staff in hand, Dinim rose. "There is nothing else on him. Any other valuables he might have are probably located somewhere in this temple." Dinim indicated the staff. "I would like to keep this, if no one objects."

Dartanyen nodded. "Keep it. 'Tis a wizards' thing and fit for you to have. That is, if the lady doesn't mind." He turned to indicate Adrianna.

For a moment, she was surprised. It was the first time anyone in the group had made mention of her profession. She had wondered what they thought of her, knowing where her skill lay. She found herself relieved that they seemed to think nothing much of it at all, at least not anymore. Any reservations they may have had when they first discovered her Talent had been set aside.

"No, of course I don't mind." Adrianna said the words even though she wasn't quite so sure that she meant them. That staff would give a man she didn't trust even more power. Yet, she didn't know quite what else to say, not wanting to openly repudiate him.

The group followed Dartanyen through the doors that led out of the room and, for a while, the group uneventfully passed through many more corridors. After a while they stopped to eat and rest, but then they were up again despite their fatigue. No one really knew what time of day it was, nor *which* day it was, for that matter. Such things just didn't mean much in the Underdark.

Adrianna's thoughts kept returning to their fight with the enemy Cimmerean. She was pleased with the outcome, at the ease and rapidity with which the group was able to dispatch him. However, she was very unhappy about the fact that she had not borne a contribution to that outcome. She hadn't even tried. *I should have cast the spell. Just because Dinim's spell failed didn't mean mine would too. Have I not learned a single thing from Master Tallek? Maybe, just maybe, my spell could have broken through the enemy's resistance. I didn't even give it a chance.*

Shamefully, she remembered the role she *had* played during the fight. Even now she could feel the press of the doors against her backside, the erratic beating of her heart, the sweat gathering beneath the pits of her arms. For a moment the group had faltered. There had been a pause, that brief moment in time when she could have made a difference, albeit a small one.

But that wasn't all. It was more than the fact she hadn't acted when needed. It was her fear. It had consumed her, eaten up all rational thought. While the rest of the group disposed of the threat, all she could think about was escape.

Much to her relief, in the hours since the fight, no one had mentioned that she had failed to contribute to their victory.

The group stopped to rest again. Tianna sat beside her, acting like nothing was amiss. They ate what remained of the food they had brought and then settled down for a brief rest. Tianna spread the blankets over the two them and then paused to regard her intently. "Are you all right?"

Adrianna nodded. "Yes, just tired."

Tianna nodded. "You just lean against me then. Maybe something softer than the hard wall will help you sleep better."

Her throat suddenly threatened to close up, so she just nodded and rested against her new friend. She looked around at the men. They looked just as bad as she felt, with pale faces and hollows under their eyes. Armond and Zorg had agreed to keep watch and she heard their whispers from where they sat close by.

"This isn't just a temple," said Zorg. "'Tis a damned sprawling city."

Armond nodded. "I imagine it was once a Cimmerean stronghold."

"Thank the gods for the wells we've come across, but we're outta food. We are spendin' all our energy trekking about down 'ere burdened wi' dis armor and our travel packs. After dis rest we'll no longer be at our optimal."

Armond clasped his hands together. "We will need to decide if we should turn around and head back or continue forward."

Adrianna shifted her attention to Dinim, his spell book open on his lap. He hadn't said anything to her, but she had caught him watching her a couple of times as they had walked, his gaze calculating. He undoubtedly considered her a weak Talent, one not worthy of her master's praise, one that would be a hindrance to the group.

But Dinim had more than proven his worth with the spell he'd cast. *Flamesphere* was a deadly weapon. In the most powerful of hands, it could incinerate entire villages. Now he studied, perhaps to recall the incantation to other spells like the *Flamesphere*. He showed his dedication to the welfare of the group in a way that she had not. Adrianna was about to turn away but stopped. As unobtrusively as possible, she regarded Dinim more keenly. His attention appeared to be focused on something else besides the book, perhaps a dirty fingernail. She watched him for a while as he dabbled about, looking at this, that, or the other... all the while giving the impression he studied his text. Finally, after the rest of the group had settled beneath their blankets, he closed the book and lay down himself.

Adrianna continued to watch Dinim for several moments, wondering. *Perhaps he doesn't need to study. After all, he cast only one spell today. But why the subterfuge? Am I just being overly critical, looking for faults in others so that I can make less of my own?*

She didn't know, and so she turned away, disgusted with the fact she didn't recognize herself anymore.

Dinim pressed himself against the cold stone wall, blending with the dark shadows. The priests hurried past him, intent upon their destination, heedless of the warnings provided by their peers– that a creature resided within the walls in this part of the temple city, a monster who would maim and kill. Silently, Dinim slipped behind the priests, considering how he could slay them. The fact that they belonged to Aasarak instead of Gaknar didn't change his desire to feel their blood on his hands. To him they were all the same, although he was a bit concerned about what the newcomers had in store for him.

Keeping himself hidden in the shadows, Dinim eagerly followed. Aasarak's priests and clerics had taken over the temple and the surrounding city after mercilessly slaughtering Gaknar's followers. He didn't know much about the situation, only what Aasarak's assassins had said to one another as they bragged about their exploits.

Somehow, Gaknar had angered the Master of the Dead, and his priests had paid the price.

Dinim didn't really care about the reason behind the attack. However, he *did* find himself caring about the current subject of the conversation between the two priests he now followed. They were human and spoke in Common. The syntax of their speech was a little strange, but easy enough to follow.

The taller priest spoke in hushed tones to his shorter companion. "They are here, have been for at least a couple of days. They have made it through the older temple and are traveling through the northern quadrant in this direction. Minos was sent to cut them down and they killed him."

The short priest sniffed. "Humph. How come I haven't heard about this before now?"

"You don't pay enough attention. You wouldn't know it if a tornado swept through here."

He didn't bother with a retort. "So how did they kill him?"

"It was an arrow through the heart," replied the tall one. "Now that I think about it, I believe he offered to go alone."

"Humph. Minos always was a fool."

"Luckily, one of us travels with them."

"Then why did Minos meet such an unfortunate demise? Did our man not try to stop it?"

"Who knows?" The tall one paused for a moment before he continued. "They say that Lord Thane will be here soon."

"That man gives me the shivers. He is chaos incarnate. I wonder how the Master keeps him?"

"Are you sure that he does?"

The shorter man almost stopped in the passageway. "I am sure you jest. The Master has powers we can't even begin to imagine."

The tall one chuckled. "Believe what you will, but I feel that Lord Thane is seriously underestimated, has become something more than what the Master planned."

There was another pause. "So, what are they doing about the intruders now?"

"We have blocked the route they used to enter. It's the only way they know. When they meet our forces, they will seek an escape only to find themselves trapped."

"Why toy with them? Why not just kill them and be done with it?" asked the short one.

The tall one chuckled again. "Where's the fun in that? They will be an interesting diversion from the monotony of our lives down in this stinking pit."

Dinim stopped in the passageway. The two priests continued on, unknowing they had been followed and overheard. *Someone is here, more precisely, a group of someones, and they have created unease among Aasarak's priests. Perhaps they are someone to be reckoned with. Not only that, but Lord Thane is coming. I wonder, what does that mean for the creature who stole my identity? I would sincerely like to see Ixitchitl again.*

He turned and began to make his way back down the passageway. He would go towards the northern quadrant. Perhaps these people would stumble into his prison. Maybe he could use them to his benefit.

Volstagg swept the last of the refuse into a dustpan, then took it to the nearest trash bin. He emptied it and gave a heavy sigh. It had been a long day and he was glad to hear nothing but quiet. He had let the inn wardens go just a few moments before, and the only ones that remained were Nolan and Mia. His cook and serving girl were cleaning up the last few things in the kitchens before calling it a night. They both resided there at his inn, so they were the perfect ones to help out at the end of every night. For their help he always gave them a bit extra in the way of food or coin. To his knowledge, neither had any complaints.

Suddenly the cenloryan felt a chill. He paused for a moment, then frowned and shook his head. *It's nothing. I've diverted my fair share of small catastrophes this day and I'm just being paranoid.* He continued with his work, hoping to be resting soon. A good night of sleep would see him ready for a new set of catastrophes on the morrow.

Volstagg heard a noise outside and was instantly on alert. He swiftly moved behind the bar and took up his massive battle-axe. His arms began to prickle, and the hairs rose. Something was wrong...

The front doors burst open. With mist swirling around his feet, a tall, dark figure strode into the common room. His platemail was black as pitch, as was the cloak that trailed behind him. A horned helmet concealed his face, and he wore a longsword at his right hip. Reeking of death and decay, the dark warrior glanced about appraisingly.

"We are closed for the evening," said Volstagg, his grip on the axe tightening reflexively.

The mailed warrior turned towards him, and the cenloryan tried valiantly not to cringe. For a few moments the warrior didn't move. Finally bringing his hand to his left hip, the man took a flanged mace from his belt. Volstagg stiffened and prepared himself for a fight. He noticed the arrival of two more dark robed figures but didn't take his eyes off the one standing before him. Just as he remembered that he had staff in the back, he heard the doors leading from the kitchens swing open.

Mia and Nolan burst into the dining room. Each held an old sword in his and her grip, the ones Volstagg kept for situations such as these. But, unfortunately, this was an extremely bad situation. There was something very amiss with these men, and Volstagg knew the pair should have remained out of sight.

Before Volstagg knew what was happening, the two men standing at the entrance had cocked their crossbows and let fly. Volstagg heard the bolts strike their targets. He closed his eyes tightly shut for a moment as he heard one body hit the floor. When he didn't hear the second one, he turned back to see Mia standing there, her dark eyes wide with fear and shock. The bolt protruded from her belly, her small hands grasping the blood-stained shaft.

"Master Volstagg... Nolan..."

A small part of him died inside when saw the tears in her eyes. The girl knew what was about to happen. Her body rocked back as another bolt struck her in the chest. She fell, her hands still clutching the shaft in her belly, her eyes echoing her fear, even in death.

Volstagg turned back to the dark warrior. The man had not moved to strike him even though he very easily could have. Despite his fear, Volstagg spoke with grief and barely suppressed rage. "Get out of my inn. Now."

In response, the warrior cocked his head to the side. He then raised his mace and rushed forward. Volstagg raised his own weapon just as the mace came crashing down. The cenloryan staggered with the force of the blow, stunned. Volstagg was a large creature, and having some physical power of his own, he was surprised at the strength behind the dark warrior's strike. The warrior then took advantage of the cenloryan's weakness and hit again. This time there was no axe to parry the attack, and the mace struck Volstagg in the right shoulder. The cenloryan cried out and clutched at the wound, the pain overpowering.

It took a moment for Volstagg to collect himself. He then regarded the warrior through slitted eyes. "Who are you?"

The reply was almost otherworldly in quality, the voice low and deep. "I suppose I shouldn't expect you to remember me. It has been quite some time since we last saw one another."

Volstagg sensed that the warrior smiled behind the helmet and he couldn't suppress feelings of dread. He would surely have remembered had he met one such as the warrior standing before him now. "What do you want?"

The warrior chuckled, the sound causing a chill to race up Volstagg's spine. He then raised gloved hands to his helm and lifted it from his head. The reek of decay intensified and Volstagg felt his heart stop in his chest. The one who stood before him was no longer a man. Lank, dark hair fell around a semi-skeletal face that was pale as death. The eyes were sunken with irises consumed by blackness, and bloodless lips pulled back to reveal two rows of white teeth. The creature standing before him was familiar, a man he had once known as Thane Darnesse.

"Ah, so you *do* remember me. Then you will also know my daughters, Sheridana and Adrianna."

Words tumbled out of Volstagg's mouth before he could control them. "So strange, this is the first time I have heard you refer to Adrianna as your daughter. Death has changed you, Thane."

The warrior's eyes narrowed. Before Volstagg could react, he swung his mace once more. Volstagg staggered as it struck his side and he felt his ribs crack. Thane then kicked him in the abdomen— once, twice, and then three times in quick succession before his gauntleted fist struck Volstagg on the side of the head. He fell to his knees, one hand covering the wound at his temple. Blood flowed between his fingers and it dripped onto the ale-stained, wooden planks of the floor.

Thane looked down at him from cold, emotionless eyes. "Let's start again, shall we? Oh yes, my offspring. We were talking about my wonderful daughters. Where is the one named Adrianna? I know you are her good friend."

Volstagg's body shuddered with fear. Beyond any shadow of doubt, he knew that if this man knew Adrianna's whereabouts, he would kill her. "I... I don't know what you mean. I haven't seen her in years."

Thane's eyes narrowed once more. He kicked Volstagg in the gut once again. "Lie. You lie!" he shrieked. "I haven't the patience for your stupid, insignificant desire to protect her from me. My sources tell me that she was seen here not so long ago!" Thane pointed his finger downward, indicating the inn.

"I swear, I really don't know where she is. She left days ago!"

"And if you did know her whereabouts?" Thane leaned over Volstagg, his black eyes piercing deeply into his soul.

With effort, Volstagg returned his gaze. Despite his fear, he refused to back down, refused to play the coward. He would keep his pride, at least some measure of it, as well as his honor. Adrianna's life would depend on it, even if his own life was forfeit. "I still would not tell you."

Thane paused for a moment and then laughed. It was like nothing Volstagg had ever heard before. It groped about within his chest and tried to wither his soul. The sound of it was fearsome with undertones of evil in its purest form.

"Still protecting my weak little Adrianna, hoping that I shall never find her. Such an endearing quality! I am touched... really. You are indeed her good friend, aren't you?" Thane paused for a moment, regarding Volstagg intently. "My other daughter is on her way here to Sangrilak. Most likely she will stay at your inn, remembering it to be the one Adrianna preferred. You will tell me when she arrives here."

Volstagg clenched his jaw. "What makes you think I would do that?"

Thane smiled. "You have seen how effortlessly I killed your cook and serving wench. I will kill your precious Adrianna the same way if you do not accede to my wishes."

"Why are you looking for your daughter?"

Volstagg watched as Thane studied him, the warrior realizing it wouldn't matter if he knew the information or not. It wouldn't save Adrianna or her sister. "Her bastard child must die, and I will be the one to kill it," the warrior replied.

So Sheridana has a child... Volstagg swallowed heavily. "How will I contact you?"

"With this." From within the folds of his black cloak, Thane pulled out a small horn. "You need blow on it for a moment and I will know that Sheridana is here. It will make no audible sound to your ears, but I will hear it, no matter where in Shandahar I may be."

Volstagg took the horn. Thane placed the helmet back over his head and motioned to the other robed figures standing at the entrance to the inn. Volstagg had forgotten they were even there. "Remember my promise, innkeeper. I don't make idle threats. I will kill Adrianna if you don't deliver." The warrior then turned on his heel and strode from the inn, the others following behind.

Volstagg listened to the sound of receding hoof-beats until all was silent. He looked around his inn, saw the fallen bodies of Mia and Nolan. Tears streamed down his face. Somehow, he knew theirs were the first of many, and that it would not the last he saw of bloodshed.

ESCAPE

A drianna stumbled and cursed inwardly as she caught herself against the wall. She would be happy when this was over, and she could once more see the sky above her head. The stone walls of the temple made her feel so trapped. All her life, she had much preferred the open sky to the confines of wood, stone, or brick walls. In more recent years, she hadn't much choice in the matter, and had settled for the stone walls of her master's tower. Despite the distance between the interior of Andahye and the forest to the south of the city, the wild had still called to her. But now, so far beneath the surface of the world, she felt no such call. It made her want to be out of the Underdark that much more...

...but not as much as she wanted to discover the truth about her father.

Adrianna looked up to find Dinim watching her again. He averted his gaze, making it seem as though he had only been glancing in her direction, but she'd seen his derisive expression. It made her nervous, this watching and sneaking around. She had caught him several times already and had the distinct impression that his thoughts were not of the savory variety. *But what am I to do? Mayhap go to Dartanyen and say, "Excuse me, but can you make Dinim stop watching me? He is scary when he does that."*

Adrianna rubbed wearily at the ache in her temples. It was just as well no one spoke as they walked, the group sullen and withdrawn. The silence wasn't companionable; the situation was much too uneasy for that. She was sure that everyone had thought the same thing at least once– *what the Hells am I doing here?*

Adrianna looked behind her once again, past the taller forms of Armond and Zorg at the rear of their small procession. She saw nothing lurking in the shadows through which they had just passed, yet she couldn't escape the creepy sensation that they were being followed. The hallways they tread showed signs of recent use and they knew they now walked among the enemy. They couldn't go on much longer; they had to be nearing their destination, whatever that was. The others sensed the same thing and it made them tense and expectant.

The sound of someone approaching in the corridor ahead bid them pause. Dartanyen and Bussi glanced at one another in alarm before rushing forward, the rest of the group quickly following. Someone was speaking and the voices became louder as they sidestepped into an unlit adjacent hallway. Keeping to the shadows, they pressed against the walls on both sides. Meanwhile, the voices passed and continued on down the corridor they had abandoned. The sound of multiple footfalls revealed that there were several persons in the company.

After a few moments they detached themselves from the walls and gathered together. A sheen of sweat beaded Dartanyen's brow. Without saying a word, he beckoned them back out into the main corridor. Quietly they continued on, and at the end of the corridor they found a downward-leading staircase. They took it and emerged into another corridor. At its end was a door. Beyond it was the sound of someone speaking.

Slowly the group approached the door. When they stood about a farlo away they stopped. Dinim moved to the front of the group and held up a staying hand. He then motioned his intent to open the door and look beyond.

The door made no sound as Dinim slowly cracked it. He hesitated, and as everyone stepped closer, they saw that no light came from the opening because of a curtain hanging a few feet beyond the door. Dinim disappeared into the narrow space and everyone waited in tense anticipation for him to make some kind of signal that all was well for them to follow.

"Who are you and what are you doing here?" Almost in unison, they turned to the sound of the gruff voice behind them. A limp Tianna was held in the arms of a Cimmerean, a wickedly curved dagger pressed against her throat. Two others flanked him. "Keep your arms to your sides and step back into the worship hall."

The group hesitated, glancing at one another.

"Back up into the worship hall... *now*," repeated the Cimmerean. He pressed the dagger into the flesh of Tianna's neck and a thin trickle of blood flowed from the cut.

Swords drawn, the other two Cimmereans stepped forward until the group moved back into the curtained chamber beyond the door. Adrianna was manipulated into the center of the press of bodies, Zorg, Armond, and Dartanyen surrounding her. Behind them there was an exclamation of surprise from Dinim.

The group pressed back and into the curtain. As it shrouded them, Dartanyen leaned close to her and whispered, "Be ready." But she had already begun to incant the words to her spell. She moved slowly to give herself extra time, and the warriors did the same, maintaining their circle around her.

The dark faelin pressed forward. "Move it," one of them growled.

Slowly they emerged from the curtain. Her spell completed, she whirled around and let it fly. Dartanyen stepped aside just in time. A vivid fan of rainbow color sprang from her hands and struck the six priests closest to them in the foremost pew of a grand worship hall. All but one of them dropped to the floor. The other placed his hands to his eyes and yelled out, "Agh, I can't see!"

As pandemonium ensued, Adrianna glanced around. They stood atop a raised dais. To her right was an elaborately robed high priest standing before a pulpit, and to his right stood an altar. Adrianna sidled to her left, hoping to remove herself from the thick of the fight, and noticed the old priest did the same.

Adrianna turned her attention to the hall below. The room was split down the middle by a wide aisle with rows of pews on either side. The priests were shouting and jumping over the pews. Five men lay on the floor between the first and second rows on the left side and she wondered how long they would remain unconscious. The one who was blinded by her spell had fallen over one of his unconscious companions. He crawled about on the floor, cursing and moaning to himself. One priest tried to get past him. Beside her, Dartanyen nocked an arrow and let it fly, swiftly followed by another, and another. They all hit the same target in the chest, one after the other, and the priest crumpled over the blinded one, who shrieked when he felt the weight descend upon him.

Adrianna's eyes widened as the clerical priests from the right side of the hall stepped up onto the dais, angry shouts and curses preceding them. She retreated as Dartanyen dropped the bow and unsheathed his sword. He and Bussi met them and a melee ensued. A few others remained where they were, concentrating on their spells. They were the imam priests, specializing in magic while the clerical ones specialized in weapons.

She felt a little drained from the last one, but Adrianna had the energy to cast another spell, one she would use on one of the imam priests. They would be the most dangerous to her comrades, for many of their spells had the ability to exact control over others, either by causing them to feel fear, to render them stationary, or to command their actions.

Just as Adrianna was about to begin her incantation, a heavy hand settled onto her shoulder. A strange sensation swiftly overcame her, and as she turned to face her adversary, she began to feel the pain of several wounds being inflicted over her body. They simply appeared of their own accord, no weapon being used to put them there. The imam priest gave her a grim smile before slipping away.

Oh gods... Involuntarily, Adrianna sank to the floor. Fatique washed over her and she was tired, so tired she could barely stand anymore. *I will rest, just for the briefest moment.* As she lay there, she watched Zorg and Armond engage in a fight near Tianna, who lay motionless on the floor beyond them. She also saw Dartanyen and Bussi where she left them not long before. She frowned, knowing there was someone whom she hadn't accounted for. Oh yes, it was Dinim. She couldn't see him anywhere. *Curse that man. Where is he?*

From behind the curtain, Dinim watched the battle unfold. The infiltrators were a weary lot, tired from maneuvering the maze of Gaknar's temple-city. But just as he'd hoped, they wandered into the confines of his prison. They were an interesting mix— two humans, a halfen, two faelin, and a half-breed. Ixitchitl he did not count. The daemon would be dead within the hour. Everyone seemed common enough, all but one. The half-breed woman, Adrianna, had a presence about her, one that intrigued him immensely. Her beauty was extraordinary, almost godlike in quality. She seemed more faelin than human, for she was small and delicate, with slightly canted, dark brown eyes and long flaxen hair that she kept in a thick plait that ran the length of her back. Dinim watched her carefully, and he noted that she seemed to distrust the daemon imposter who had taken his form. He liked her already.

All morning Dinim had trailed the group. He'd kept his distance, not wanting the doppelganger to sense his presence. However, the creature definitely had him on its mind, its furtive backward glances making Dinim smile smugly to himself.

Dinim took in the battle scene. The Hinterlean/Terralean faelin crossbreed they called Dartanyen fought opposite a clerical priest wielding a *Flameblade*. The priest made an unexpected move, causing Dartanyen to stumble. The fiery sword sliced into his side and he screamed, his flesh cauterizing where it had just been cut. Meanwhile, the big human man, Zorg, was beset by two opponents. He handled his broadsword with swift efficiency, but Dinim knew the man would soon tire.

As the stench of burning flesh filled the hall, he noticed something from the corner of his eye and his gaze shifted to Adrianna. In dismay Dinim watched the young woman sink to the floor. One of the dark imam priests had touched her and open wounds appeared over her body. Some of them bled and she tried to staunch the flow with the hem of her tunic. Something within urged him to go to her, but he restrained himself. He didn't wish to give himself away, not yet.

With narrowed eyes, Dinim turned back to the place where Ixitchitl had placed itself. The coward had found a place out of harm's way, hiding behind the same curtain as Dinim, only at the other end closest to the high priest. The creature would wait until the battle was almost over before it emerged once more, offering one excuse or another for its inability to help the group.

The high priest abruptly caught his attention. The man raised his staff and aimed it at Zorg. A spurt of flame emerged from the top and struck the big warrior in the back. Zorg's thick, studded leather vest ignited and began to burn. He bellowed a series of curses, then dropped and desperately rolled around on the floor. His adversaries maximized on the distraction, and lunged, trying to pierce him with their scimitars.

Suddenly, a bolt of magical energy raced towards the high priest. He made as if to ward it off, but it slammed into his chest. The man stumbled backward and out of sight. Dinim looked towards the source of the spell and saw Adrianna sitting up a few foot-lengths away from Armond and Bussi. The halfen swung his battle-axe, severing the leg of his opponent. With a cry the cleric dropped to the floor, and another took his place. Adrianna's eyes widened as the fight got dangerously close. She slid herself out of harm's way before encountering Armond on her other side, fighting another cleric.

Dinim watched Armond for a moment, crinkling his brow in thought. There was something about him that he couldn't quite figure out. The man was skilled, his movements fluid and graceful. He had an intense look of concentration as he fought, an intensity he only saw...

Dinim blinked. Armond's swords glowed for a moment and then his movements started to accelerate. His swords moved faster and faster, and for the briefest moment they were almost a blur. The head rolled off the priest's shoulders and hit the ground at Armond's feet, the body crumpling after it.

Dinim chuckled to himself. This man was a blade-singer, a Talent who used his arcane ability to enhance his skill with swords. Armond could learn to become very powerful, indeed. He saw Adrianna shake her head and he knew she'd seen the same thing, but she had something else on her mind. She crawled away from her place near the curtain and made her way towards Dartanyen. Somehow the man had found the strength to vanquish his enemy before succumbing to his injuries. He lay slumped on top of the fallen priest and Dinim hoped the fiery blade hadn't touched one of Dartanyen's vital organs.

Tianna opened her eyes to the harsh sounds of battle all around. Groggily lifting her head from the floor, she saw a massive pair of boots standing right in front of her face. The boots stepped closer, and just as she was about to get trampled, she rolled out of the way. As best she could, she hastened to her feet. The owner of the boots was burned, and he sported numerous other injuries. Rivulets of sweat poured down Zorg's forehead and into his eyes. He shook his head and she felt a spray across her face.

Backing away from Zorg and his opponent, Tianna saw Adrianna kneeling beside a fallen Dartanyen. Just behind her was Bussi, wildly swinging his battle-axe. Beyond the halfen there was a drop and a small group of three imam priests nestled among the pews. They had cast their spells, the effects wreaking havoc among the group. Bussi was bellowing with rage, and Tianna could see the heat emanating from his chainmail. Dartanyen suffered the same, his semi-conscious mind registering the pain the metal studs embedded within his leather vest caused.

Praying to her goddess, Tianna touched the ground and brought forth her spell. The *Darkness* enveloped the three imam priests and the area around them. They wouldn't be casting their spells now, at least, not until the *Darkness* was dispelled by a counter spell, or it lifted at the end of its duration. Tianna hurried to Adrianna and Dartanyen. She heard Bussi howl again and knew that he was close to the end of his endurance. Tianna knelt beside her friend and saw her body covered with wounds, her face so pale it was white.

Hells, they have gotten her too. I so want to help her, but I know I need to focus on Dartanyen. She bent to examine him, and realizing the extent of his injuries, she worriedly shook her head. She placed one hand around her amulet and the other over the jagged, cauterized wound across his belly. She then closed her eyes and whispered a simple prayer.

Dear Goddess Beory, I pray to you
Please help me accomplish my task
Please give me strength
Please give me power
Please help mend this man
Dear Goddess Beory, I pray to you

She repeated the prayer twice more and felt the healing power of her goddess sweep upward through her body and out through the hand on Dartanyen's wound. It was painful, more painful than usual. She had learned to tolerate it over the past couple of years since being inducted into the priesthood, but it never ceased to take her breath away. She ground her teeth, refusing to cry out like she used to do when she was an untried novice, and finally it subsided. This prayer wouldn't heal Dartanyen completely– far from it. But it was a beginning, and mayhap the thing that would save his life if left untended.

After a few moments, Tianna opened her eyes again. She quickly surveyed the scene and saw Bussi fall. She quickly glanced down at Dartanyen to be sure that she'd managed to help him, and when she saw that the cauterized wound had lost a substantial amount of the redness, she felt relief and pride. She was getting stronger, just like Father Erszan had said she would.

An agonized scream abruptly pierced the air and her heart lurched. *Dear Goddess, please no, not Adria!* She lunged to her feet and looked over to where she had last seen her friend. Adrianna knelt beside Bussi, moving back and forth with her hands against her chest. *She's been hit, please help me save her.*

Tianna rushed over to Adrianna, and once there, fell to her knees. "Tell me where you were hit. I can help you."

Adrianna looked up, her eyes filled with tears of pain. "I wasn't hit. I touched his armor and it burned my hands."

Alarmed, Tianna glanced at Bussi. Just by looking at him, she never would have known his armor was so hot. He was un-conscious, and a deep gash marred the area over his left shoulder and chest. Bright red blood trickled from the torn chainmail and was pooling on the floor beneath him.

Careful not to touch his armor, Tianna dragged Bussi over to where Dartanyen lay. In spite of his shorter stature, he halfen was heavy, and if it had been any further, she wasn't sure she could have managed it. Adrianna slowly followed but collapsed back onto her knees when she reached them. She moaned pitifully and Tianna knew the pain was near excruciating. She'd heard that burns ranked as one of the most painful injuries a person could sustain. When Adrianna turned and vomited on the floor beside her, she no longer doubted it.

Dinim knew when the time had come. Taking Tianna's lead, he cast a *Darkness* spell of his own within the area in which he knew Ixitchitl was hiding. Then he left the sanctuary of the curtain. The group had been greatly outnumbered by the priests, and they were suffering for it. Two of them had fallen, and the others were barely standing. He wanted to give them a hand, show them some measure of thanks for bringing Ixitchitl to him, albeit unintentionally. But he had something to do first.

Sword drawn, Dinim slunk between the rows of pews on the left side of the hall. No one noticed him scurry across to the other side. Dinim passed silently towards the imam priests who were ensconced within the *Darkness* cast by Tianna. He waited. After only a moment, the spell was diffused and there was light in the area once more. Dinim stealthily slipped into the row of pews behind the priests. He waited patiently as they assessed the situation– the battle was in their favor since the enemy had been so greatly reduced. They then began to concentrate on another volley of spells they hoped would take the infiltrators out for good.

Dinim took his chance. He placed his dagger to the throat of one of the priests while embedding his shortsword into the belly of the second. Blood sprayed onto his face as he slit the first priest's throat, but he paid it no heed as he stared the third one in the eyes. Dinim saw the priest's fear as he scrambled about desperately for his weapon. He pulled his sword free from the second priest and swiftly impaled this one, feeling the blade catch on the man's ribs as it passed through. Dinim then pulled the weapon back and watched him fall beside his companions.

Dinim looked back up onto the dais and saw the large human and the tall faelin dispatch the last of their opponents. One of the priests was missing; he had fled the scene with the intention of bringing others to the fight. In the meantime, Ixitchitl had diffused Dinim's *Darkness* spell and finally emerged from its hiding place. He watched the creature interact with the rest of the group, as always making excuses for itself.

At first no one noticed Dinim standing there among the pews, but then he sensed her. The half-faelin's dark eyes were on him, watching. She said nothing, just merely stared. The other woman they called Tianna was too busy to note her friend's preoccupation. But one other did notice, the one that mattered the most, and that was when Dinim began to move.

Dinim strode towards Ixitchitl, the damnable creature who had stolen his life away. For several weeks he had dreamed of this moment, and nothing could take it from him. He could see the fear mirrored in the doppelganger's eyes...

Suddenly the daemon bolted. It darted past the rows of pews to the rear of the worship hall. Dinim swiftly turned and began to follow. *I mustn't let the creature step outside the bounds of the prison!* Dinim heard shouts from the group, heard them beginning to follow. *No, they can't interfere! This is my only chance to escape the prison of Gaknar's temple before Thane arrives.*

He slowed to cast a *Force Projection* spell. When it was complete, Dinim stopped and swung around with his hand raised. A wavering disturbance in the air sprang from his palm and struck the ceiling between he and the group. The stone crumbled down with a thunderous crash. He turned and ran as debris rained down around him, just barely making it out of the worship hall.

Continuing to run, a wicked smile curved his lips. He knew these corridors better than anyone; it would be easy to determine where the creature was going and take a shortcut to that location. He would then have the daemon all to himself.

Oh gods, where is everyone? Keeping her breath shallow, Adrianna slowly picked herself up from the floor, her eyes tearing up as she tried to see through the thick layer of dust pervading the air. She kept her hands cradled against her chest, more afraid than ever that dirt would get into the extensive wounds covering the palms. Coughing and shifting debris gave her a feeling of relief; the others were nearby and hopefully they were all well.

Adrianna finally chanced a deeper breath and was awarded with a fit of coughing. *Damn Dinim... or whoever the Hells he is! Which one is the real man? Does it matter? Either way we are trapped here.* Nearby there was a thump followed by a curse and she turned to look. The air had cleared enough for her to see Zorg righting himself after stumbling over Armond.

The big man's gaze took her in, followed by Tianna, Dartanyen, and Bussi. "Is everyone all right?"

Armond grunted. "I *was*."

Zorg shot him a quelling look.

"Dartanyen and Bussi seem to be all right for now, but they need help. There is only so much I can do for them down here," said Tianna.

By the tone of her voice, Adrianna could tell that she was tired and probably had injuries of her own. She put the back of her hand on Tianna's arm comfortingly. "We will do the best we can for them."

Armond limped over and sat beside Tianna while Zorg sat on the other side next to Adrianna. "Adrianna is right; just try to do what you can for now." Armond glanced around as he continued, "Who knows when the priests will return, and with *whom*." His tone became ominous.

Zorg stared at the felled ceiling. "That wreckage is a barricade keepin' us from escapin' beyond this worship hall. It'll be easy for tha priests ta pick us off now, 'specially in our condition. Mebbe we should try'n make a way through the debris."

"Yes, I was just thinking the same thing," nodded Armond.

The two men rose to make their way to the massive pile of stone, wood, and glass. The dust was clearing more every moment, making it easier for Adrianna to see them as they methodically began shifting around the rubble. Tianna busied herself making Dartanyen and Bussimot comfortable and tending them as best she could with limited supplies. After a while, Zorg and Armond stumbled past with a large stone, climbing atop the dais and behind the curtain. Adrianna realized they were placing it at the doorway with the hope of keeping the priests out as long as possible. The two men placed several more such stones there before returning to the more arduous task of clearing a path.

Nudging Adrianna in the side, Tianna gently took one of her hands and looked at it, hissing beneath her breath when she saw the extent of the damage. A swath of flesh had torn away when Adrianna pulled her hands off Bussi's chainmail. Unfortunately, there was very little water to wash the exposed burns, which were now coated with a layer of filth despite her efforts to keep them covered. By the look in her eyes, she could tell Tianna feared they would become infected along with the other wounds covering her body, wounds that were caked with dirty, dried blood. But Tianna said nothing, merely pulled a pouch of water from her pack and tried to rinse the hands as best she could without using all of it. She then extracted a jar of salve from the pack and applied it to the raw flesh. Adrianna mewled piteously, fat tears making streaks down her dusty face. Afterward, Tianna wrapped the hands in clean cloths and wiped the tears with the hem of her robe.

Exhausted, Adrianna lay on the floor beside Dartanyen. She felt drained, and the throbbing of her hands made her stomach queasy. Tianna went back to tending Dartanyen and Bussi, praying first over the latter and then for a second time over the former. Dartanyen moaned in his sleep and Adrianna rested a bandaged hand on his arm, the one free of burns. The sound of

Tianna's soothing voice, combined with the *thump-thumping* of moving rock as Armond and Zorg worked to clear the debris in the distance, lulled her.

She slept.

"Adrianna... Adrianna. You have to wake up now."

Groggily, she awoke to Tianna shaking her. It felt like no time had passed as she looked around the darkened room. Most of the torches had expired, and those that remained were in the vicinity of Zorg and Armond. From this distance, she could see they had cleared a large portion of the rubble away, although it would take them a bit more time before they reached the doorway.

But, unfortunately, time had run out.

Muffled sounds emanated from behind the curtain; the temple inhabitants had finally decided to come and finish what they'd started.

Tianna hurriedly packed away her ointments and salves. She had taken the armor and other accouterments off Dartanyen and Bussi, leaving them only in their trousers, and had treated their wounds the best she could. Much of Bussi's chest was covered in wet cloths. Adrianna could smell the medicinal odor emanating from them and wrinkled her nose. The cloths covered the flesh that had been in contact with the searing armor. The chainmail lay in a heap beside him, much of it scorched and darkened. The integrity of the armor had been compromised and would probably never be useful again. The studs on Dartanyen's vest were similarly blackened, and the leather surrounding them was crispy. It also would never be used again.

"Will he live?" Adrianna asked

Tianna paused and regarded her for a moment. "With the proper help, yes. Nothing critical was hit by the *Flameblade*. He is very lucky." Tianna went back to packing her bags.

Adrianna slowly stood. She felt slightly woozy and rocked back on her heels. The pain had diminished, probably because of Tianna's salve. She looked toward the men, hard at work moving as much of the debris as they could, their bare chests shining with sweat. Zorg was an example of brute strength. The muscles in his chest and arms were well-defined and they rippled as he moved. In contrast, Armond's build was slender. His belly was almost concave and rows of abdominal muscles on either side of his midline were clearly visible. The men worked diligently on their task, unwavering despite the various cuts, burns, and bruises covering their bodies.

Crack! Adrianna startled and jumped. "Zorg! Armond! They are coming," Tianna called out, a note of desperation to her usually calm voice.

The men stopped their labor and jogged over. Zorg went to his knees before Dartanyen and looped the man's arm about his broad shoulders. Dartanyen moaned and his eyes fluttered open as Zorg stood. Adrianna heard Bussi curse as Armond did the same. The men then helped their comrades toward the mound of rubble. Tianna hastily shoved some packs towards

Adrianna. She hissed as she caught them, her palms burning with the impact. Tianna glanced over in sympathy before picking up her own load of bags.

Zorg and Armond went to an empty area to the right of the pile of debris. It was a relatively secluded spot that was more defensible than any other. They settled their companions on the floor, then donned their grimy tunics and armor.

Tianna stood over Bussimot and Dartanyen, clutching her amulet. The sounds of destruction from behind the curtain became louder, the enemy working to break the door down. Once through, they would eventually overcome the obstacles Zorg and Armond had placed there and infiltrate their resting place. Fear coursed through Adrianna like a river, her heart beating a staccato rhythm in her chest. The men readied their weapons and walked a few farlo and stood in front of them.

It would be their last stand.

HIDING

U nder cover of darkness, they shuffled down the main road through Sangrilak towards the Inn of the Hapless Cenloryan. No one else was about, no one to witness the weary troupe of half beaten men and women walking down the main thoroughfare covered in dust and blood. When they finally stumbled up the steps leading onto the familiar veranda, they slumped into chairs and against the side of the building.

One of the men stood apart out on the street, his dark robes blending with the night beyond the wan light of the lantern Volstagg had promised he would have lit for them every night until they returned. Dinim. He had returned to the worship hall to lead them out the temple. They had trusted him because they had no other choice. But now that it was over...

Everyone just sat there for a moment, each regarding the other. "It wasn't me, you know, but a doppelganger." Dinim's quiet voice reached their ears. "The man who had settled within your midst was no man at all, but a daemon who had stolen my form. I don't know if you believe me, nor do I care. But I wanted to say the words so that you may hear them and know the truth." Dinim paused for a moment, then turned to walk away.

Armond called out, "Thank you for your help."

Dinim paused for a moment and nodded without looking back. Adrianna stared after him as he continued down the street. It was strange; she felt that she knew him, but that wasn't possible. She shook her head, remembering how she had warred with herself whenever the doppelganger was in her mind. *It was as though a part of me had known something was very amiss...*

"My lord, Dinim, wait!" Adrianna descended the steps and followed him out into the street. He stopped to wait for her, and once standing before him, she suddenly forgot what it was she was supposed to say. *Oh gods, not again!*

He waited patiently as she collected herself. "Will we be seeing you again?"

Much of his face was thrust in shadow, but what she could see showed her a man who was just as surprised about the question as she was. One side of his mouth curved up. "No worries. When my business is complete, I will come looking for you here at Volstagg's inn."

Relief flooded her and she returned his half-smile with a nod. "Until then, my lord."

He inclined his head and walked away. She watched until he was swallowed by the darkness.

Dinim had returned for them. Blasting away the remaining ceiling debris, he completed the pathway Zorg and Armond had worked so hard to clear just as the priests burst through the fortified door on the other side of the curtain. He had led them out of the worship hall, and they scurried through the passageways like scrats, skulking about in the shadows and behind the corners as best they could. Their fallen comrades dragged at them and their pursuers dogged their footsteps. Yet, they had finally emerged from the bowels of the Underdark by climbing a rock wall, and once reaching the top, Zorg and Armond pulled Bussi and Dartanyen to the surface with ropes Zorg had in his pack. The danger over, they had found themselves at what looked like a deserted well, another hidden entrance into the temple. They rested there a short while before heading to the inn.

Once Adrianna returned to the veranda, Zorg knocked heavily and pulled the rope that hung alongside the doors. It would ring a bell that was suspended within Volstagg's chambers, one alerting him to visitors that came in the wee hours of the morning. After only a few moments, the cenloryan threw open the doors. Saying nothing, he stood quickly aside as the group filed inside. He took in their battered condition and relieved Adrianna and Tianna of Dartanyen's weight. He led them to the rear of the establishment and into an empty room. He lay the faelin on a bed while Zorg and Armond did the same with Bussi.

As Tianna went to find clean water, Adrianna found herself being swept into Volstagg's embrace. He whispered in her ear, "Dearest Adria, thank the gods you are safe!" He then held her out at arms' length, his dark brown eyes scrutinizing her from head to toe, making sure she was hale and whole.

"Aye, but what happened to you?" Adrianna regarded him in return, her brows pulling together into a frown. One side of his face was red and swollen, his left eye half-closed. His ribs were bound, and he moved with the stiffness of someone who suffered broken bones.

Her voice was distressed. "Who did this? Who..."

Volstagg tightened his hands on her upper arms, led her out of the room away from the rest of the group. His tone was deep with suppressed anger and his eyes shone with fear. "Adria, listen, someone was here. A man. He was looking for you. He overpowered me..."

Adrianna's world spun and her heart hammered against her ribs. She must have wavered on her feet because Volstagg reached out to steady her. "Wh... who was it?"

"It was Thane. He was here looking for you and your sister."

She stepped away from Volstagg, but her legs were still unsteady. Just as she was about to fall, she reached out and braced herself against the nearby wall. She made herself breathe deeply in and out through clenched teeth. *My father was here seeking me. What could he possibly want after so many years of doing everything he could to believe I didn't exist?*

"Adrianna," Volstagg lay a comforting hand on her shoulder, "all will be well. I am here, and no harm will come to you while I yet live."

She looked at him and into his eyes. She searched their depths and found what she already knew. This man wasn't her father, her brother, or her son. He wasn't an uncle, a cousin, or even a nefreyo. But he would die for her.

His hand tightened with emphasis. "Come, you must hide. He searches for you still, and I would not have him find you."

Adrianna paused. She had put her friend in danger, albeit unintentionally. As long as the rest of the group was with her, they would also be in danger. Adrianna looked back inside the adjoining room. Armond stood in the center, hands on his hips. He regarded her intently, his solemn face framed by long, dark hair. By his side stood Zorg. The two looked like they had overheard portions of the conversation. Tianna sat on the bed next to Dartanyen, worry and confusion written upon her features as she looked back and forth from Adrianna and Volstagg to Zorg and Armond.

Silence reigned. Everyone was waiting, knowing there was a decision she needed to make, and that she was the only one who could make it. They also knew she had to make it now. Adrianna looked back to Volstagg and nodded.

Tallachienan Chroalthone slouched in his favorite cushioned oak chair. He clasped his hands before him, knuckles touching his chin, one leg crossed over the other, staring broodily into the surrounding darkness. He'd known this time was coming but hadn't realized so many years had come and gone. For him, having lived so long already, Time had a way of doing that, and the years blurred into one another.

Tallachienan thought about the message he'd received earlier that day. His student, Dinim Coabra, had contacted him via the travel notebook, a method Tallachienan had devised to keep communication open between himself and his journeymen whilst they were away from the citadel. The young man wrote about a young Talent he had found, one that had potential, great potential. Dinim had then described her as "the most beautiful mortal woman he had ever seen".

Tallachienan pursed his lips. For the third time he would have to face Adrianna Darnesse, take her as his apprentice and train her to be the best she could be. It bothered him that Dinim had found her, not behind the walls of his citadel like the two Cycles before, but out in the open world where anyone could go anywhere and experience anything. Tallachienan had ceased believing in Destiny centuries ago, but it was things like this that made him wonder...

He shook his head and slumped deeper into the chair. *No, who cares about the past when I have the future to worry about?* Deep in his chest he felt a familiar ache and he placed a fist over his heart. *I still have some time. I will prepare myself a bit more and then bring her here.*

Tallachienan took a deep breath and closed his eyes. Memories of the long ago past came to the fore. In his mind's eye, she regarded him from dark eyes that could look beyond what lay in his heart, all the way to very depths of his soul. A cool breeze swept through the room, brushed his shoulder, and whispered hauntingly in his ears.

"I do swear, that I'll always be there.
To give you anything, and everything,
And I will always care.
Through weakness and strength, happiness and sorrow,
Through all space and all time I will love you,
With every beat of my heart."

Tallachienan came back to himself. Remembering her words, spoken so long ago, he grimaced in pain undiminished over the centuries. He put his head in his hands and his heart cried out in agony, echoing throughout the world, all of its dimensions, and the very fabric of Time...

Adrianna suddenly jolted awake. She didn't know exactly what had awakened her, but it was full of pain and loneliness. She looked about her room in the citadel, seeking it within the shadows, but found nothing. She reached out to pat the bed beside her even though she knew Tallachienan wouldn't be there. He'd told her he had a lot of work to do in his laboratory before he could even think about sleeping.

However, Tallachienan had bid Adrianna to sleep, and to sleep well, because she would need all of her strength and wit for the upcoming battle with Aasarak. Unfortunately, she wouldn't be able to go back to sleep now. Whatever had awakened her had been only feelings and emotions, but they had seemed so real. To think someone, somewhere in the world, was feeling that miserable...

She got out of bed and sought out Tallachienan, drawn to do so although she knew not why. She found him in his library, pouring over a thick tome. She stepped up behind him and put her hands on his shoulders, gently kneading the taut flesh beneath his velvet tunic. Her unbound hair fell in golden waves, a stark contrast against the dark fabric. Tallachienan brought his head back and looked up at her, a smile curving the fullness of his lips. She came around the large oak chair to face him, and he moved it back so she could settle onto his lap. Adrianna then wrapped her arms around his neck and put her head on his shoulder.

For several moments he simply held her there, but then began to softly caress her skin through the thin nightgown. She slowly brought her head up and looked deep into his lavender eyes. They smoldered with desire. But this time she saw something more, something she had noticed before but been unable to place. It was love...

Adrianna cupped his face in her hands and gently kissed his lips. His arms wrapped around her, and she was enfolded within his warm, strong embrace. She held on to him in return, never wanting to let him go. "I do swear..."

Dinim opened one of the doors to the inn, slipped inside, and then closed it behind him. His gaze quickly surveyed the room, took in the nicely swept floors, the freshly wiped tables, and the thoroughly stocked bar. The place was empty, save for himself and the cenloryan coming through the doors leading into the kitchens. Volstagg saw him and stopped. A multitude of emotions passed over the man's face before he spoke. "Dinim, I wondered why you didn't return with the others."

Dinim blinked, then he remembered. *Ah yes, the creature Ixitchitl had been with Adrianna and her group for a while. Volstagg would have encountered the daemon and thought it was me just like everyone else did.*

Dinim shook his head. "Volstagg, I don't have time to explain. There is someone following me."

The cenloryan was instantly on alert. "Who is it?"

"I'm not sure, but it may be the one who had me imprisoned for the last few moon cycles." Volstagg frowned. He opened his mouth, a question poised there, but Dinim raised a forestalling hand. "Please, I will answer all of your questions, but tell me... is the Lady Adrianna here?"

Volstagg stiffened, his eyebrows coming together into a frown. "Why? Don't you know?"

Dinim sighed heavily. This was proving to be rather difficult. "Please Volstagg, just tell me. Is she still here?"

He inhaled, his chest puffing out. "Yes."

"All right, good." Dinim hesitated. "I need a place to hide for a day or two. How about it?"

The cenloryan frowned once more. Dinim could tell what he was thinking: *Where has this man been? What does he mean by 'imprisoned'? I just saw him several days ago when the group left to go down into the temple. Now he acts as though he doesn't know the whereabouts of the group and asks to be hidden.*

However, Dinim had the advantage. Volstagg would be hard pressed to deny him a place to stay. Dinim was a member of the Wildrunners, and he had sworn to support and aid them in any way possible.

Volstagg eyed him warily, lips pressed into a thin line. "I suppose."

Dinim followed Volstagg into the back of the establishment. He knew the cenloryan was confused, and he applauded Volstagg for his patience, but he would have to wait and explain it all a bit later when Lord Thane was no longer in the vicinity. Dinim had taken great pains to avoid being followed, but he couldn't be certain he had succeeded or that Thane's spies didn't already know where the Lady Adrianna was located. Everyone with whom she had come into contact was in grave danger, including Volstagg, but Dinim didn't know what to do about it. They were up against something powerful, something he'd never encountered before now...

Azmathous.

Finally, they stopped. It was only then Dinim realized he'd followed Volstagg into the cellar. The cenloryan pulled away the massive rug in the center of the floor to reveal a heavy wooden door. "This is it."

Dinim nodded. "Volstagg, where is the Lady? I have reason to believe she is in danger. She needs to be in hiding as well."

Volstagg regarded Dinim intensely, then nodded towards the door. "You had better get yourself inside. You will find your companion within."

Dinim nodded. Her welfare was of paramount importance, not only to himself, but to his master. Tallachienan had taken a rather undisguised interest in the potential that lay within this young woman, and he'd made it his personal mission to make sure she was kept safe.

"Thank you, Volstagg. I am in your debt."

"You have already been in my debt," replied the cenloryan solemnly. Volstagg lifted the heavy door. It moaned on its hinges as it opened.

"Nevertheless, I thank you."

"You are welcome."

Dinim climbed down into the darkness and the door was cast down behind him. "Praise the gods for those such as Volstagg," he whispered to himself.

With a massive sigh, Adrianna closed the book. *I simply can't study this stuff anymore. All these theories and algorithms are making me wither away with boredom.* She flung herself back onto the bed and stared up at the ceiling. *All I really want to do is just get out of here. Volstagg has a great place, but all these walls are killing me.*

Volstagg's fortified sanctuary was a series of rooms, each with its own bed, desk, storage chest, and vanity table. There was also a common area with sofas and tables. It was safe; she had felt the magic of the wards when she passed them by on her way down the curving staircase under the hidden door.

Everyone was still recovering from the wounds they had suffered in the temple. Dartanyen and Bussi were still bed-ridden, but Tianna was certain they would be up and about in another day or two. Because of the curative properties of Tianna's salve, Adrianna's hands were healing nicely. The pain was almost gone, and new flesh covered the areas that had been scorched by the burning metal. Just this morning, Tianna had removed the bandages and told her that, at this stage in the process, the wounds needed the air to touch them in order to heal completely.

Adrianna stretched and then paused, sensing someone watching. She looked toward the entrance to her room and, there in the doorway, stood Dinim. She sat swiftly upright on the bed but the Cimmerean continued to silently watch her. Likewise, she regarded him solemnly. He looked different; his hair was grown out, the hair on top longer than that on the sides. He wore new tunic and trousers, the dark colors accenting his pale complexion, dark hair, and lavender eyes. Now that he sported more hair, Adrianna could see a streak of silver that sprang from the peak at his forehead and fell over the left side.

Adrianna stood from the bed. She walked across the room to the doorway, then stopped about three foot-lengths away from him. There was something magnetic about the man, something she found hard to resist. He was handsome, his face finely chiseled, the planes delicate yet pronounced. The one who mimicked him had been the same, yet there was something different about this man, something...

Dinim gave a half-bow. "Milady, 'tis good to see you again."

Adrianna smiled to herself. He was so formal; it was almost endearing. She nodded to him. "Likewise, my Lord."

Dinim shook his head. "No, please call me Dinim."

"Certainly, but only if you call me Adrianna."

Dinim paused and then smiled. "As you wish."

"I do." Adrianna smiled in return. "Please, come in."

Dinim entered and looked around. "Cozy."

Adria grinned and raised an eyebrow. "I thought the same thing."

Dinim smiled for a moment, but then his countenance became serious. "Adrianna, I think that someone is hunting you."

She lost her smile. "I know that someone is hunting me."

Dinim regarded her solemnly. "Do you know who it is?"

She swallowed heavily and then cast her eyes to the floor. She couldn't look him in the face. "Yes."

133

Dinim waited, clearly wanting her to elaborate. Adrianna was suddenly afraid. She had never spoken the words aloud before– that her father wanted to kill her. *What man wanted to kill his own daughter?* "His name is Thane."

He frowned. "Why does Lord Thane want you? Besides being a Talent, what are you to him?"

"He..." she almost choked on the words. "...he is my father."

Silence. Adrianna slowly looked up. She saw Dinim watching her with an expression of grim understanding. His tone was quiet. "Does the rest of your group know about this?"

She shook her head. "Maybe. I think Dartanyen is suspicious. He knows that Thane means something to me, but not exactly what." She sighed. "This is all new to me. I had no idea my father was looking for me until we arrived back at the inn. Needless to say, I was more than a little shocked to find his name on a message belonging to a dead man we found at the library. And then to discover he had been here whilst we were at the temple–"

Dinim's expression suddenly shifted to one of alarm and he interrupted her. "What? Thane was here?"

Adrianna frowned. "Didn't Volstagg tell you?"

He shook his head, cursing eloquently in Cimmerean beneath his breath. He paced the room, his fists clenched at his sides. Her eyes widened, his anger making her nervous.

Dinim swung back to face her, but once seeing the expression on her face, his anger immediately died away. He shook his head apologetically. "I'm sorry. I didn't intend to frighten you. I forget how intimidating I can be." He hesitated. "It's just that I had rather hoped he hadn't followed you this far. It means we aren't as safe as I thought."

"But we are well hidden down here, and the place is warded. How would Thane possibly find us?"

Dinim raised a dark brow and expelled a gush of air. She sensed he knew much more about her father and what was happening than he cared to let on. He regarded her intently, deciding how much he should tell her. A flare of frustration swept through her. *I have every right to know exactly what is happening! I don't need to hear little bits and pieces here and there. It's more than my life at stake now; other people are involved!*

"Tell me what you know." She surprised even herself with the commanding tone of her voice.

Dinim must have recognized something about her demeanor, because after another pensive moment he nodded. He was the epitome of solemnity as he gestured to the bed. "You had best sit. There is much to share with you, none of it pleasant."

Adrianna did as he suggested and seated herself on the bed. Dinim did the same but kept enough distance between them so as not to cause any potential discomfort. It took him some time to gather his thoughts, and as the moments passed, her anxiety grew.

"I just want to start by saying that some of what I am about to tell you is speculation. Granted, it is speculation based upon fact, but speculation, nevertheless. I also want to say that I don't have all the details. Unfortunately, those are left for us to discover someday in the future."

She nodded understanding. Dinim looked directly into her eyes as he spoke again. "Adrianna, your father is no longer the man from your youth. Somewhere, somehow, sometime within the past few years he became something else... something no longer truly mortal. At some point, he became Azmathous. Thane Darnesse sold his soul to the Deathmaster."

Adrianna took the prompt. "What? Who is this Deathmaster?"

"Another name for him is Aasarak. Within his possession he has an awesome artifact known as the Azmathion. Academicians say it is a geometric work of art, and that whoever can master the puzzles contained within it will have access to its secrets. Of course, it is an arcane thing, its use driven by the power of the sorcerer who possesses it.

"The Azmathion is what gives Aasarak much of his power. It is through this object that he has created the Azmathous, an elite group that has been reborn through the power of the Azmathion. These beings possess the skills and abilities they had in life, as well as whatever added benefits they acquire through the process of rebirth."

During his recitation, Adrianna slowly began to frown. She shook her head and blinked rapidly. "Are you sitting here trying to tell me that my father is dead?"

Dinim regarded her intently for a moment. "That is exactly what I am telling you."

Adrianna rose from the bed. She walked as far as the farthest wall, then turned and made her way back again. She couldn't stop shaking her head back and forth, mumbling to herself. "This can't be. No, he is wrong. This just can't be."

It wasn't until after her third circuit that she was reined in. With a gentle hand at her arm, Dinim pulled her around to face him, his expression one of sympathy. "Adrianna, I am sorry. Mayhap I should not have told you—"

"No, you were right to tell me. It's just... I can't believe... why? Why did he do it?"

Dinim shrugged. "That is one of those details to which I have no answer."

Adrianna turned, taking her arm from his loose grip to move a few steps away. Then she stopped. "He wasn't always a bad man," she said. "Mairi, my foster mother, once told me the stories my mother used to share with her about my father. Thane was good once, and he loved my mother more than life itself. Gemma gave him a son, my brother Gareth. And then she gave him my sister and myself."

Adrianna paused for a moment to collect her emotions. "As the second-born twin, it was my difficult birth that caused my mother's death. Thane never forgave me." She then turned back to face Dinim. "And now it seems he wants retribution: my life for hers."

She watched the play of emotions that crossed his face. She could see the part of him that was bewildered by her words. But there was the other part that sympathetically understood, almost as though he had experienced something like it himself.

"If that is the situation, then we must get you out of Sangrilak as soon as possible. It has taken him this long to place a price on your head. Mayhap with distance, Thane may come across another reason to occupy his time and efforts."

Adrianna took a deep breath. "I hope you're right."

Armond's voice was the first one Adrianna heard when she entered the common room. "What I'm trying to say is that I don't think the Wildrunners are even thinking about us right now. They have their own concerns that obviously don't involve us. They weren't even there when we awakened after our recovery. I don't think they were considering us to help them after our excursion into the temple. Actually, they were lucky to have happened across us. They were able to foist the temple off on us while they went to pursue bigger, better, and probably more dangerous things."

"You're probably right," replied Dartanyen. "In his message, Sirion didn't mention us coming to join them. So, I guess we all need to think about where we will go from here."

For a few moments the room was quiet. Tianna motioned Adrianna over to the sofa where she was sitting and patted the space beside her. Adrianna obliged, and then looked from one person to the next. Armond leaned with his shoulder against the wall. In many ways, he seemed to be a voice of reason for the group. He had the ability to state facts in such a way that the truth could be found amongst them. His statement about the Wildrunners was most likely correct. Adrianna had thought the same from the start. But she had been so consumed with her own worries, she hadn't bothered to voice her opinion.

Zorg was slumped in a chair, his feet crossed and propped up on the table before him. He was a quiet man and not very good with words, but he was a good fighter, and he and Armond made a great team. With Armond's speed, and Zorg's brute strength, they could conquer many an enemy. Adrianna turned to Bussi. He also was a good fighter, yet he frightened her.

His maniac display in the cemetery didn't repeat itself in the temple, but she knew that it was there, crouching like a kyrrean waiting to be set free.

And then there was Dartanyen. He was doing well for someone who had been injured so extensively. Adrianna turned her gaze to him to find him watching her. His blue eyes bore into her, but she didn't look away. *He is wondering about me, wishing he understood what I am about. The others must have told him what transpired between Volstagg and I on the night of our return.*

Finally, he spoke again, continuing to look at her. "A part of me feels that something remains unfinished. Sure, we brought proof from the temple that it was dedicated to Gaknar and that it has been taken over by another power that now has control there. Yet, there are so many parts to this puzzle that we still don't understand."

Dartanyen raised an eyebrow before glancing around at the rest of the group. His attentions had not gone unnoticed and Armond and Tianna looked back and forth from him to Adrianna. Discomfort brought a rise of heat to her face. *I hate how he's going about this; he could just as easily have questioned me privately. Sometimes the man has absolutely no decorum.*

Dinim chose that moment to saunter into the chamber. "Good afternoon, everyone."

Adrianna sighed with relief as attention shifted away from her to greet the Cimmerean. The group was more interested in Dinim and what exactly had happened down in the temple after the ceiling collapsed. Beneath lowered lids he shifted his gaze to her and gave a wink she never would have caught if she hadn't been watching. Dinim then turned his attention to the other people around the room. He poured himself a mug of water and tore away a chunk from the bread loaf in the center of the table before sitting down across from Zorg. The other man promptly removed his feet from the tabletop and instead placed them on the closest chair.

The room was quiet as Dinim ate. The group was dying to question him, but just didn't know how to broach the subject. Adrianna thought it more than a bit humorous, especially since Dartanyen was more than willing to thrust the spotlight onto her bare moments before.

"So, who are you really? *What* are you? I mean... what the Hells is going on?" Tianna leaned forward a bit as she spoke.

He shook his head and chuckled. "My name is Dinim Dimitri Coabra, and I assure you I am very much a man. The creature you had thought to be me was a doppelganger, an intermediate daemon called Ixitchitl. By someone's order, it was bade to take my likeness, my skills and abilities, my memories, and most everything else about me that would allow him to live my life.

"You see, in their natural form, doppelgangers are thin humanoids with grayish flesh. They are hairless and don't really have any distinguishing features. In truth, they are templates for what they wish to become. When they choose a victim and touch him or her, their shape shifts into the form of that particular individual. They then enter the mind of their victim, learning all they can about the person: their personality, temperament, skills, and interests. They replicate that person in almost every way. Most people would never be able to tell the doppelganger was an impostor.

"So, I became a prisoner within Gaknar's temple. Why, I still don't know. When the place was taken over by priests dedicated to Aasarak, I discovered that a man by the name of Thane was supposed to come for me. However, it seems that Thane had other matters about which to address in addition to bringing me to his master."

Dinim paused and for a moment everyone was asking questions at once. He cast a glance towards Adrianna. She was taken aback by the intensity reflected in his eyes, a pressure perhaps compounded by the questions lurking there. It was tempered only by the upward curve of his lips that softened his expression.

Armond's voice rose over the others. "So, what happened between you and the doppelganger?"

Dinim grinned. "Ixitchitl was surprised to see me when I emerged from the pews in the worship hall. He must have thought I couldn't extend the walls of my prison so far, but he was wrong. He never realized the extent of my power and determination, and he died for that."

"Wait, wait," Tianna interrupted. "The creature... it seemed so temperamental, so unpredictable. Is... is that who you truly are? I mean, did the doppelganger replicate you in *every* way?"

"In many ways the daemon replicated me in every detail," Dinim began. "But it could only go so far– when the environment and its own natural bent begin to exact their own influences. In some ways, I am quite temperamental and unpredictable, but not to the extent in which you found Ixitchitl to be. Doppelgangers tend to be that way, and the creature's natural inclination was beginning to show through his disguise."

"You know," Armond cast a withering glance at Tianna, "I've been waiting to hear about the details of your battle."

"I was just thinking about that myself," said Dartanyen, leaning forward in his chair.

Tianna put up her hands in mock defense. "Sorry, I just had to ask him my question before I forgot."

Armond rolled his eyes and Dinim chuckled.

THANE

The group stood in the center of the inn common room. Splintered tables and broken chairs lay overturned. Plates, bowls, and cups were scattered about, and shattered glass covered the floor near the bar. Rivers of ale had soaked into the floor and the planks were swollen and distorted. Volstagg had issued a warning when he led them from out from hiding, but the image was so much worse than the words he'd used to describe it.

Adrianna took in the destruction. "Volstagg, I'm so sorry."

The cenloryan frowned. "Now stop that. You have nothing to be sorry for."

"If it weren't for me, Thane would never have come here." Her voice rose. "I can hardly imagine the gold you will need to replace all these things, not to mention the lives of Mia and Nolan lost during his first visit–"

"I say stop!" Volstagg interrupted with a growl. "I say it isn't your fault!"

Dartanyen moved up beside her. "Adrianna, what the Hells is going on? We have a right to know!"

She breathed deeply to control her emotions. *Dartanyen is right. The rest of the group deserves to know about me. Their danger increases with every moment they spend in my company.* She turned around to face him and saw the others arrayed behind, all with expressions of bewilderment.

Tianna walked over to stand beside Dartanyen, her eyes reflecting concern "Adria, what's going on?"

"I know I should have told you before, but I didn't know it would go this far!" She wrung her hands. "The man who wrote the message we found in the library is my father. I know this must sound crazy to you, but he is hunting me. He... he always disliked me as a child, maybe even hated me, but never did he try and kill me!" She took a deep, tremored breath. "I don't know what has changed, but you can see the threat is very real. He is dangerous and you all should not stay here!"

Disbelief was the prevalent emotion written upon the faces of the people she had come to call her friends, and Dinim's expression was one of sorrowful regret. Silence reigned as everyone collected their thoughts; even Dartanyen didn't know what to say.

Adrianna slowly turned back to Volstagg, his expression mirroring Dinim's. "What did my father say?"

Volstagg drew his lips into a thin line. She knew he didn't want to tell her, but she wouldn't accept that. She waited patiently until he realized she expected an answer. "He said he would kill me if he had to return a third time."

Silence. Her voice trembled. "What else?"

Volstagg blinked several times and his eyes became wet. "I asked him why he wanted you so much. He said he would slay the daughter who killed his wife and that he would not rest until he stilled her beating heart."

Adrianna somehow swallowed past the huge lump in her throat as she looked away from Volstagg. Now she knew that Dinim was wrong. Thane would not stop until he had found her.

"I told him nothing, even though his informants told him they had seen you walking towards my inn the night you returned from the temple. His minions demolished the place, but they didn't find the hidden door. Thane was enraged..."

Volstagg's voice trailed off and once again there was silence. "Do you know where he went?" Dartanyen asked.

Volstagg shook his head. "I have no idea. But I fear his informants continue to watch my establishment."

Adrianna numbly stared at the floor for a moment. *By the gods, what should I do? Where should I go? I can think of nowhere I can hide without him eventually finding me.* As her mind mulled over those questions, she had the strange feeling that she was forgetting something.

Volstagg reached into the pouch at his side and pulled out two folded parchments. "Here, these arrived just today." He gave one to Adrianna and the other to Dartanyen. "They are from Sirion."

"Sirion," she breathed his name softly as she held the parchment. Slowly she opened the sealed page, pleased he had chosen to respond to her message personally.

Lady Adrianna,

I received your message. Thank you for taking the time to warn me. It means so much that you consider my welfare as something of import to you. I regret we were unable to stay in Sangrilak to help you and the rest of the group, however, urgent business called us away. I hope you understand.

Please be careful. Sydonnia is a very dangerous man and could ultimately cause you harm. I will have to deal with him myself when I am finished here. Good luck with your endeavors and be sure to take care and keep a good watch. Danger is afoot and I fear that the Powers That Be may have caught wind of you all.

Sincerely,
Sirion Timberlyn

Adrianna read over the letter once more, pondering over words filled with thankful concern. She folded the parchment as Dartanyen told the rest of the group that Sirion had thanked them for their help. She caught Tianna watching her, but the other woman swiftly looked away.

Adrianna seated herself on one of the only chairs that remained intact. Hunching over, she put a hand to her forehead and an elbow on her thigh. *I wish Sirion was here. Certainly, he would know how to help with my situation. I feel so lost.* She felt a hand on her shoulder and looked up into the friendly face of Volstagg. She placed her hand over his and then brought her cheek to rest on it. Silent tears sprang to her eyes. She just couldn't escape her feelings of guilt. She had placed her old friend in danger not once, but two times. She thought of the group, knew that the longer they were in association with her, the more endangered they became as well. And then she thought of someone else...

A wave of fear abruptly crashed over her. It was the one thing she had not thought of, something she should have realized when Volstagg first told her that Lord Thane had come seeking her out. If her father had known to look for her at the inn, he would also have traced her... *home.*

Adrianna choked on the words as they left her mouth. "Volstagg where did Thane go after he left here last night?"

Hearing the acute agony in her voice, his eyes widened, and he stuttered over his words. "I... I don't know."

Adrianna thrust herself from the chair and ran for the front door. Volstagg followed behind, his voice filled with fear. "Adria, wait! Where are you going?"

She stopped and looked back at the group. Everyone stared at her, their eyes wide as they were caught up in the unfolding drama. Her lips trembled and her voice was small when it left her throat. "Mairi."

Realization flooded Volstagg's face, and he swallowed convulsively. "Oh gods..."

Armond strode towards her. "Someone should go with you just in case."

"I will also come with you," said Dinim.

Adrianna just nodded and started back toward the entrance.

"At least use the doors in the back of the kitchens! I don't know about the rear exit, but I know that the front is being watched," said Volstagg hurriedly.

Adrianna paused, and then turned around and ran to the rear of the inn. She rushed through the kitchens and out the back doors, Dinim, Armond, and Dartanyen following closely behind. Racing to the stables, Adrianna went straight to Sethanon's spacious stall. The animal raised his head and whickered a greeting. She slowly approached the lloryk, patted him soothingly and murmured to him in Hinterlic. *Forget the saddle; it will take too long...*

Adrianna took several steps away from the lloryk, but then turned back around and sprang towards him. Sethanon didn't even flinch as she vaulted onto his back and gripped his mane in her hands. She dug her heels against his sides, and he burst from out of the stall. They swept past Dartanyen and Armond who were still leading their larian from the barn. Adrianna heard Dartanyen shout for her, but she kept going.

But then she heard Dinim's voice. "Adrianna, wait!"

She leaned back and Sethanon instantly slowed. With commands given by her legs and feet, the lloryk turned around. Sensing the tension in his rider, he pranced about nervously. Dinim rushed towards her, anxiety written over his face. "I don't have a mount, and I've never ridden..."

Before Dinim could finish his statement, Adrianna extended her arm down to him. He quickened his pace, and once beside the lloryk, he reached up and clasped her arm. He propelled himself upwards as she pulled. Sethanon surged forward and Dinim landed awkwardly on the lloryk behind her. His arms wrapped around her waist and his legs pressed into the lloryk's sides as he righted himself. Sethanon took the unintended cue and took off. They cantered through the streets of Sangrilak, Dartanyen and Armond close behind. It didn't take them long to make it through the city and out into the surrounding farmlands. They rode for almost a zacrol and Adrianna slowed Sethanon as they neared Hafgan's fields. She frowned with unease, for she should have seen the house by now. They rode onward and her worry strengthened. Then she saw it, a scarred place on the landscape, a blackened heap of rubble in the distance.

Panic swept through her. "No... no. This can't be..."

Adrianna tightened her legs and Sethanon broke out into a run. Adrianna lowered herself over the lloryk's back and his speed increased. She felt Dinim clutch her more tightly, leaning forward with her. The lloryk's mane whipped at her face and her heart thudded erratically in her chest. Within moments Adrianna sat back up as they reached the area. Sethanon slowed, but even before the animal could come to a halt, Adrianna was off his back.

The foundation was all that remained of the house. Flame blackened stones lay crumbled about where once walls had been. The charred remains of wood planks lay scattered about the interior along with some broken cookware, serving plates, and bowls. There was a twisted lantern, some shards from Mairi's favorite lamp, and something that looked like it may have once been part of a bed.

Adrianna stumbled forlornly about the wreckage. A few shreds of burnt cloth blew about in the breeze and glass crunched beneath her boots. With devastation such as this, it was hard to believe that simple flames destroyed the house. Anyone who worked with magic would recognize it, even a novice such as herself– wizards' fire.

Thane had a sorcerer with him.

It was then she saw them. Adrianna ran over and fell to her knees, shards of fractured glass stones biting into her flesh. She sobbed hysterically, taking great gulps of air that made the world tilt crazily and dump her sideways. She expected an impact, but instead her fall was cushioned by someone who wrapped his arms tightly around her. It was Dinim. He knelt there among the debris and held her close as she cried. Overwhelmed by pain and loss, Adrianna beat her fists into his chest. She screamed, not in the Common tongue, but in Savanlic, the language of her mother's people. Dinim only tightened his arms around her and murmured in a soothing tone, rocking her slightly back and forth.

She didn't know how much time passed, but finally she regained control and pulled away. She let her gaze travel over the blackened, skeletal bodies of Mairi and Hafgan. They were close in death even if they may not have always been so in life. Mairi's existence with her husband had not been an easy one, yet she'd loved him very much. Despite the increasing winds, Adrianna lingered. *If only I could hold you just one last time. I was so wrong to stay away so long without coming back to you. I love you more than you will ever know.*

It was then she saw it, something hidden beneath the remains of her foster mother.

Adrianna reached down and gently moved aside the skeletal arm. Beneath it, almost completely hidden within the ashes, was a small box. She slowly pulled it free, the debris falling away from it to reveal an object of great beauty. Unharmed by the inferno that had destroyed the house, the box was made of the finest wood, probably from one of the silver oak trees of Elvandahar. The engravings were exquisite, made by the most brilliant of artisans. The delicate flowers seemed to dance across the surface, and tiny inlaid gems made them sparkle. Adrianna ran her hands over the silky-smooth wood. She sensed the magic of the box, knew that it was the reason why the fire had been unable to harm it. She also knew that this was the gift her mother had left for her, the gift that Mairi had spoken about the last time they were together.

Adrianna looked up from the box. Dusk was falling and the winds were increasing even more. It was going to rain; she could smell it in the air. Dinim watched her intently but kept his distance. Behind him, not far away, were Armond and Dartanyen. They stood next to their larian, unobtrusively watching.

Adrianna looked back down at the box. On the front of it there was a small metal hook that fit into a loop. She pulled the hook free, surprised that it opened so easily. Surely the magic of the box should have kept it locked, but then she remembered the box was meant for her. Adrianna slowly opened the lid. Inside, sitting on a bed of scarlet satin, was a tightly coiled golden serpent. The creature was beautiful to behold, its scales glistening in what was left of the sunlight. The object was artfully designed, perfect in every detail. Its eyes were tiny rubies, looking at her from a delicately sculpted head. Amazed, Adrianna put her forefinger on the small serpent.

Suddenly, the thing moved. Adrianna jerked her finger back, but the serpent was quicker. Like lightening it shot up her hand and slithered around her arm until it reached the spot it wanted. There it settled, wrapping its small body just above the crook of her arm. In shock, she and Dinim stared at the creature, who glared balefully back at them from ruby eyes. Adrianna touched the serpent once more, but it didn't move from its place about her arm. She exerted pressure on it, thinking perhaps to remove it. Adrianna only felt the metal coil more tightly about her arm.

Adrianna stopped and looked up again at Dinim. It began to drizzle, and thunder sounded in the distance. He frowned at the serpent wonderingly. The thing didn't seem to be harmful, and mayhap felt that it had found its place. Dinim reached out and touched it, but the serpent didn't move. The creature had flattened and molded itself to fit Adrianna's arm perfectly.

He reached down to take her hand as the rain began to fall more heavily. "Come, there's nothing more we can do here."

Adrianna balked. She didn't want to leave Mairi, but the woman was dead, and there was nothing she could do change it. Slowly she rose, the box cradled under one arm. Tears fell once more, mixing with the rainwater streaming down her face and neck. "Goodbye dearest Mairi," she whispered. "I will always love you."

Adrianna then went with Dinim, followed him away from her past toward a strange and unknown future.

It was late. Deep in thought, Dinim tapped his fingers on the desk, deciding what he should do next. He thought about the young woman who slept downstairs, one who's father wanted to kill her. Already four people had died in Thane's quest to have her, and it was such an evil twist of fate that made her suffer so much all at once.

Homicide was almost unknown within most faelin cultures. In general, faelin had the utmost respect for life, and didn't believe in the act of killing. The exception lay with Cimmereans, most of whom lived their lives by progressing up the social ladder by stepping upon the bones of those who got in their way. Many Cimmerean mothers committed infanticide, not wanting to bother with the male children they bore. Dinim had been lucky; his mother hadn't killed him at birth, but he remembered times during his life when he'd wished she had.

Dinim shook the memories away, refocusing his thoughts on Adrianna. He leaned back in the chair, stretching his legs beneath the desk. Almost instinctively he had reacted. Once seeing her pain, he had run to her, knowing she needed someone. He imagined that person could be him. He could still feel her arms around his neck, and he'd crooned nonsense phrases to her in Cimmerean, phrases that he'd devised on the spur of the moment...

Because very few phrases of sympathy, friendship, or love existed in his native tongue.

Despite his efforts, Dinim's thoughts once again spiraled back into the past to a life spent in the Underdark. A matriarchal society ruled by priestesses of the Queen of Darkness, the goddess Tholana, life was a game of survival for most boys born within the dark recesses below the surface of the world. Very quickly he'd learned how to tread quietly, to hide within the shadows, and to use a dagger with frightening skill. There was always someone out to use another as a stepping-stone to their own advancement. The death of the unfortunate individual who had been thusly used was of no consequence, for it was just one less Cimmerean to impede future advancement. Most of the time, not even one's family could be trusted; the treatment he had received from his own mother had been appalling to say the least, and his brother had used treachery of the worst kind against him...

The memories slowly ebbed away as he recalled what happened next. There had been a light at the end of his tunnel– a man by the name of Tallachienan Chroalthone had decided to save his wretched life. The man had taken him to his citadel in the distant north and trained him in the ways of a sorcerer. And now, many years later, Dinim sat within the comfort of a well-kept inn, with thoughts of a lovely lady.

Damn, I wish I had more time, but I need to get to the Wildrunners. They have a big fight ahead of them and they will need me more than ever. But I really want to stay with Adrianna and the others. I want to help uncover more of the mystery surrounding her father. There is so much more to Thane than meets the eye. The man has power, and I want to know more about how he obtained it.

Dinim breathed a deep sigh. That would all have to wait. Not only did he need to join up with the Wildrunners, but Master Tallachienan had given him the task of discovering why Talents around central Ansalar were being hunted. Dinim himself had been one of those captured but had never figured out why. Many of them where being killed, and Lord Thane may have something to do with it. In this case, Dinim was working for the same cause as Adrianna, albeit for a different reason. However, Master Tallachienan had cause to believe that a secret cult was behind the murders. Dinim felt that it was the one headed by Aasarak, for Thane was one of his minions. Unfortunately, he still couldn't be sure. It was possible that Dinim hadn't been singled out by Aasarak at all, but by Gaknar for his skills as a Dimensionalist. His capture mayhap had nothing to do with the deaths of the other Talents at all.

Dinim finally stood from the desk and blew out the candles. He was tired, and he needed as much rest as he could get before his journey to catch up with the Wildrunners. In spite of his desire to stay with Adrianna, he had a duty to his comrades.

Early the next morning found him making travel preparations. His pack lay open on the bed, the contents strewn all around it so that he could see what he still needed to acquire before his journey. He wrapped a navy sash around his lean waist and secured pouches of his most useful spell components on it, arranging them near his right hip. At his left side hung the shortsword he had the good fortune of recovering from the mangled body of the doppelganger. It was his most valued weapon, the one he had bespelled with extraordinary *Sharpness*.

Dinim looked up when there was a soft knock at the door. "Enter."

Volstagg walked into the room. The cenloryan had to bend only slightly to fit through the doorway. When he'd had the inn constructed, Volstagg had everything designed to allow his larger frame easy passage. It meant that the doorways were taller and wider. Dinim found he rather liked it, for it was a change from the dull norm.

Once closing the door, Volstagg turned to regard him intently. Dinim gave him a brief nod and a smile. He wondered what this was about, for he had already apprised the cenloryan of the details of his capture and stolen identity. He continued to prepare for the day while he waited for Volstagg to speak, having learned early on that Volstagg was one of those people who preferred to act in his own time and that patience was a virtue.

Volstagg cleared his throat. "I just came to find out when you were leaving. I need to know when to have your meal pouch ready."

Dinim was surprised by the kind gesture. He didn't get much of that from other people, his race setting him apart. For good reason Cimmereans had a negative reputation and it acted to his detriment. However, the people of Sangrilak were accustomed to seeing him about and knew he was a friendly sort. In any other city he was given scant courtesy, if that.

"My plan is to leave tomorrow morning. I need to get a few supplies, and I would like to have one more night of good rest before I depart."

Volstagg nodded. "That's good. I received a message from Sirion. Even though he doesn't say it, I can tell the Wildrunners need you. They have left Grondor but provided the name of the town where they will be waiting for you."

Dinim simply nodded. Duty called, and he couldn't put it off any longer, no matter how much he wanted to.

Volstagg gave a sigh of sympathy. "I know how torn you must feel right now, and I feel the same. I am going to try and convince Adrianna to return to Andahye. At least there she has a better chance of finding protection."

Dinim felt a surge of frustration. *Who the Hells is going to get her all the way to Andahye? Damnation, I'm probably the only one who can get her there alive!* He had tried contacting Master Tallachienan last night via the travel notebook, but he'd received no reply. "Hmph, good luck."

Volstagg prickled. "What do you mean by that?"

"I mean that you will have a difficult time with that venture. I have the feeling she won't be willing to go back there."

"And why is that?" asked Volstagg, frowning. Dinim raised a brow. "Don't you know?"

"Stop being so cryptic, Dinim. It gets on my nerves, not to mention, I don't have the time or inclination for guessing games."

Dinim sighed explosively and frowned. "Oh, and your warm personality has always been one of your better qualities, Volstagg."

Volstagg pursed his lips. "So, tell me, why won't Adria want to go back to Andahye?"

"Because of the reason why she left in the first place. The master under whom she was apprenticed was murdered. She has nothing there now, no one to turn to."

Volstagg's eyes widened with incredulity. "Why didn't she say anything to me?"

"Why would she? She hardly got a chance to realize that she had finally come home when everything started happening so fast. She didn't even have the chance to see her foster mother but that one time."

Volstagg nodded slowly. "You're right. She wouldn't have had the chance. But how do *you* know all of this?"

"We got a chance to talk while we were in hiding. You can learn a lot from a person if you just take the time."

Volstagg had the decency to look chagrined. He shook his head and looked down at the floor. "You are right. I was so focused on her safety that I wasn't a very good friend to her. I didn't even come down to ask her how she was doing..."

Dinim stepped forward and put a hand on the cenloryan's arm. "Listen Volstagg, you are a great friend; it wasn't my intention to make you feel otherwise. And you are a good man. Few others would have done what you have for Adrianna. She is lucky to have a champion like you."

Volstagg raised his head. "Thank you. That means a lot to me."

Dinim nodded and turned to walk over to the desk. "So, the message says where the Wildrunners will be waiting?"

"Yes, a town by the name of Elsador located south of Grondor."

"Then that's where I'll be heading." Dinim picked up his journal, ink, and stylus and carried them to the bed where his travel pack lay.

"There is something else I want to discuss with you. It has to do with Thane."

Dinim turned back to Volstagg and quietly waited for him to elaborate.

"From speaking with Adrianna, you probably know she has a sister."

Dinim nodded. "Yes, I do seem to remember her mentioning that."

"When Thane came here looking for Adria, he also told me to keep a watch out for Sheridana."

Dinim frowned. "Why?"

"Sheridana has a child. He wants to destroy it."

Dinim shook his head and said nothing. The plot surrounding Adrianna was thickening, and he was forced to leave her to fend for herself.

Volstagg continued. "Adrianna doesn't know about this child."

Dinim was thoughtful. He remembered Adrianna telling him that she hadn't seen or heard from her sister since before she left for Andahye. "Are you going to tell her?"

Volstagg shrugged. "I'm not sure if I should. It might make things that much more difficult for her. Right now, she needs to think of herself. She could end up getting herself killed trotting all over Ansalar trying to look for the woman."

By the tone of Volstagg's voice, Dinim could tell that the cenloryan didn't think very highly of Sheridana. "She could end up getting herself killed no matter what," he replied flatly.

Volstagg frowned. "Well, I don't see you offering any alternatives."

Dinim slumped his shoulders. "I know. I'm sorry Volstagg. I'm just not very good company right now."

Volstagg nodded. "Then I shall leave you to your preparations."

When Volstagg left, Dinim sat down on the bed. *I just need to stop thinking about Adrianna and her problems for now and focus on getting to the Wildrunners as quickly as possible.* He shook his head and put it in his hands. That was going to be hard to do.

It was a quarter past midday when Dinim finally walked into the common room. Save for Dartanyen, Armond, Bussi, Zorg, and Tianna the place was empty. Volstagg had closed the establishment to any other patrons, the damage to the place too extensive to have other persons occupying the premises. He walked over to their table, one of the only ones that had remained unscathed during the destruction that Thane's minions wrought. They greeted him as he pulled over a chair and sat.

"I want you all to know I will be leaving on the morrow. I have important business that has yet to be tended since my absence from the Wildrunners. I am assuming you all must have some idea of what you are going to do next?" He posed the last as a question, wanting to find out where everyone would be going in the hopes that Adrianna might have someone to stand by her despite the risk involved.

"Well, employment is paramount on everyone's minds right now. We will be paid handsomely for our services here, but that coin won't last very long," said Dartanyen.

"I have been entertaining thoughts of going to Karlisle," mentioned Armond. "The nobles there are always looking for a sword to hire."

"Before I answered Sirion's summons to help you, I had heard that Elvandahar has been suffering a lycanthrope infiltration," said Tianna. "My family lives in the southern tip of the domain of Filopar, so I was going to go and assess the severity of the situation. I thought about asking if you all might consider accompanying me there. I don't know how dangerous the situation is and I am loath to go alone."

Dartanyen nodded. "Sure, I'll go with you. I know that Hinterleans don't take well to strangers, but maybe I can get a position as one of the fortress guards. I'm good with the bow, and perhaps they won't turn me away once they see my skill."

"Armond, maybe you'll want a companion with ya to Karlisle," said Zorg.

"Certainly, I would appreciate the company," Armond replied.

Dinim just looked from one person to the next. He had hoped the conversation would take a slightly different turn, but he couldn't really blame them for thinking of themselves. For a moment he considered taking Adrianna with him, but then discarded the notion. He would be taking her into a very dangerous situation. He knew that she was in the middle of one already, but he didn't know if he was willing to take responsibility for her life if something were to happen to her when he and the rest of the Wildrunners finally met up with Gaknar.

"Well, I'm going to see about some of my preparations. I will see you later this afternoon," said Dinim, rising from the table.

"Yes, we will have dinner this evening and see you off in the morning," replied Dartanyen.

Dinim nodded and made his way to the front door. He opened it and stepped out onto the veranda. He was surprised to see Adrianna sitting on the top step, easily visible to anyone who might be looking for her. He hid a frown of disapproval as she turned to glance up at him. The sad smile she offered made his chest deflate. She looked so forlorn, almost as though she was giving up. "I didn't know you had such immediate plans to leave."

Any question he may have had if she'd heard his conversation with the group was answered.

"Yes. The Wildrunners are expecting me to join them as soon as possible. Volstagg and I sent the message just this morning."

Adrianna looked down at the ground, hoping to hide her expression of disappointment. "I see."

Dinim regarded her intently and his heart went out. Once more he had the urge to take her with him, but he knew that the Wildrunners, and Triath in particular, would be upset by that decision. It was too dangerous for her, but Dinim wondered if it was any more dangerous than what she faced already. "Listen, I will return to you as soon as I can."

Adrianna looked up at him once more. "You promise?"

"You have my word." Dinim noticed a smile tugging at the corner of her mouth and he immediately began to relax.

Eyes colored like the darkest mead danced, striking against her pale complexion and curling silver-gold hair. "You know what they say about Cimmereans though."

Dinim grinned in return. "No, what would that be?"

"Only a fool would trust one."

"Well, what do *you* say?"

"That I must be a fool."

Dinim's smile widened, pleased she would even consider trusting him, especially after what had happened with the doppelganger.

"Come. I will accompany you while you collect the supplies for your journey." Adrianna reached out a hand and he pulled her up. He then offered her his arm and they walked down the steps and into the street. Suddenly she stopped, her eyes wide as she turned to look at him. "That is, if you want some company."

Dinim grinned. "Always. I would be honored to have you at my side whilst I shop for supplies."

Relief suffused her features. "Oh, good! I'd hoped so."

Dinim's stride was light as they began to walk again. He had the impression she preferred his companionship, and it was it was difficult to comprehend this shift of fortune. Only several days ago he was trapped within an underground temple waiting to meet a destiny that likely would have ended with his death, but now he walked down the streets of Sangrlik with one of the most beautiful women he'd ever met.

Dinim bathed in Adrianna's attention for a while, taking his time to reach the apothecary. He had some to spare, for he wouldn't leave until the morrow. They had just passed his favorite clothier when he heard a voice behind them. "Sir! Excuse me, sir! Could you please wait up a moment?"

Dinim and Adrianna turned and looked back in the direction of the clothier. Travel-stained and dusty, a weary man hastened towards them. He was a faelin of medium build, with unkempt brown hair. His ears weren't as elongate and arched as the Savanleans and Hinterleans, easily showing that he must be of Terralean decent.

The man stopped when he reached them, his voice breathy. "Please, could you show me the way to the closest smithy?"

"Of course. You will go up this street. When you pass the apothecary, you will turn left down another street. The smithy is located at the end of it," said Dinim, pointing the way out to the man.

"Thank you. I appreciate you stopping." Then the man paused and regarded Dinim intently. "Do I know you?"

"I don't think so."

The man nodded. "Yes, I am sure of it. We have met before. My name is Sabian Makonnen. I apprenticed under Master Tregorn."

Dinim's eyes widened. "Yes, I remember you now. Whatever happened to the old man? It just seemed that one day he'd suddenly disappeared. Master Tallachienan always wondered where he had gone."

Sabian smiled. "Master Tregorn is doing well. Whenever he begins talking about Master Tallachicnan, you can't get him to stop."

Dinim smiled in return. "So, what brings you to Sangrilak?"

Sabian's expression became serious. "No good reason actually, except for the fact that I'm being followed. Someone means to do me harm, and I honestly don't know why. I was hoping on finding refuge here for a night or two before heading north. I hear that Grondor is a good place to get lost if you don't want to be found."

"I've heard the same," said Dinim. "Perhaps you would like to travel together? I will be leaving tomorrow morning. Is this too soon for you?"

151

"Not at all. The sooner the better, and I must say, a companion would be good to have on the journey. But are you sure that you want to hitch yourself with me? You may be putting yourself at risk."

"No, it won't be a problem. I am also being followed. It may even be the same people who have been pursuing you. Perhaps I will be able to discover more about them if we travel together."

Sabian nodded and then glanced at Adrianna. Dinim noticed and put his palm to his head. "Oh, excuse me. I'm sorry I didn't introduce you. Adrianna, this is Sabian. I met him in Andahye a few years ago while I was still an apprentice. Master Albus Tregorn, Sabian's mentor, is a good friend of Master Tallachienan's. The masters knew one another in their younger days, and even had a few adventures together."

"Yes, Master Tregorn told me about some of those. I must say, they were some reckless days." Sabian laughed and Dinim joined him. "Well, I had best get myself to the smithy. Where are you staying? Perhaps I can join you there later."

"I am staying at the Inn of the Hapless Cenloryan. The innkeep isn't allowing any additional patrons right now, but maybe if you give him my name, he will consider allowing you to stay for just one night."

Sabian nodded and walked away in the direction that Dinim had indicated before. Dinim stared after him for a moment before turning back to Adrianna. "It is good to see an old face. Master Tallachienan will be happy to know that Master Tregorn is well. Come, let's collect those supplies. Perhaps there is something you need as well?"

"Yes," she replied. "I can repay you as soon as I get my share of the monies Dartanyen and the others will be collecting from the city today."

"Aha. So, you were able to escape that onerous task. You are a smart one."

Adrianna gave him a winning smile. "I like to think so."

From across the table, Dartanyen leaned forward in his seat with an intent expression. "What do you remember from the night you were attacked?"

Amethyst looked around at everyone through wide eyes, obviously unaccustomed to having so much attention. Tianna caught her gaze and nodded encouragingly. "Well, I guess I could start with what I noticed earlier that day."

Dartanyen nodded. "Yes, what happened? Tell us everything you remember."

"Well, I was walking through the streets, minding my own business, when I saw Dinim. He was talking with another man. They were in an alleyway.

Most people wouldn't have noticed them, but it's my job to be aware of everything going on around me, even when it's in the periphery."

Dartanyen nodded understanding, his expression neutral.

"I got closer, keeping sure they didn't see me. I got close enough to hear snippets of their conversation. Dinim got angry about something and he and the man argued. Dinim mentioned disposing of something when he got to the temple." Amethyst paused, furrowing her brow. "I remember someone bumping into me. The person got angry and cursed. Dinim turned, and before I could get out of his line of sight, he had seen me.

"I was afraid. The expression on his face was terrifying. Dinim kept staring at me while the other man was trying to get his attention. He started to yell at Dinim and pushed him. Dinim pushed him back and before long they were brawling and everyone on the street was getting out of their way. They drew their swords and the rest you remember."

"We brought him back to the inn and Tianna used her prayers to help him," said Dartanyen.

From her place beside Amethyst, Tianna nodded. "Yes, I remember sensing something strange as I called upon my goddess to help me heal him. Something wasn't quite right."

"So, what happened when you left the inn that night while the rest of us were drinking?" asked Dartanyen.

Amethyst took a deep breath. "Well, I remember walking through the streets as I usually do, keeping to the shadows, and watching for anything out of the ordinary. I walked for quite some time before realizing that I was being followed. I stopped and tried to determine who it was and where they were coming from, but he was good. He came at me, seemingly from out of nowhere. He threw me to the ground, and before I could utter a cry, a cloth was stuffed into my mouth. When I saw Dinim's face hovering above me, I was scared. By his expression I knew that he wanted to kill me and that it was because I'd heard what he said–"

Amethyst abruptly stopped speaking, her eyes cast away from the group, trembling hands clutching the edge of the table. Tianna's heart went out to the girl and she put a gentle hand on her shoulder. Amethyst instinctively cringed away, but within moments, self-loathing replaced the fear in her eyes. Tianna knew the reason why– Amethyst hated her weakness and felt stupid for letting it show.

"Amethyst, I want you to know that you're safe now. The man who did that to you is gone. He was an imposter, someone who made himself look like Dinim. The *real* Dinim is a good man and he helped us escape the temple. Please don't be alarmed when you see him." Tianna smiled reassuringly.

Amethyst frowned. "An imposter? I don't understand. How can that be?"

153

"It was a daemon who took over his likeness, but now he's dead. The real Dinim killed him."

Amethyst just sat there for a moment, then nodded and stood from the table. Tianna watched her walk over to the bar, where she asked for a mug of mead, knowing she just needed a moment to contemplate what she'd heard. By the time she returned, Dartanyen had just begun to speak again.

"Listen, I know everyone has begun to make plans for where they will go when they leave here. I was tempted to do the same." Dartanyen paused and looked at Tianna before he continued. "But when I thought more about it, I realized I couldn't just leave."

Zorg grunted. "An' why not? You're just as free to do as you please as the rest of us."

"I wish that were so. But that's just not the case, not for any of us." Dartanyen looked around the table. Armond wore a ponderous expression and Bussi and Zorg looked mutinous. Tianna frowned.

"Now see here, Dartanyen. What are ya tryin' ta say?" said Bussi angrily.

"I thought you were planning on coming with me to Elvandahar," interjected Tianna.

Dartanyen shook his head. "I think we all need to stay together for now. By association, we are currently in a dangerous situation."

"What in the Hells are you talking about?" asked Tianna.

Dartanyen opened his mouth to reply, only to be cut off by Armond.

"Because we have been in Adrianna's company, Lord Thane won't think twice to hunt us all down and slaughter us. Our association with her has put every single one of us at great risk. You saw how Thane came for Volstagg. If he was a weaker man, he may not have survived Thane's visit."

The room was silent. "So, what are we going to do?" asked Amethyst hesitantly.

Dartanyen gave a deep sigh. "That has yet to be decided."

Just then the front door opened. Adrianna and Dinim walked into the inn. "Good afternoon everyone," said the Cimmerean affably as he made his way across the common room.

Adrianna followed slowly behind Dinim. Tension hung around the place like cobwebs and she wondered what it was from. She noticed the girl, Amethyst, had rejoined them. She looked well, and no worse for the beating she had suffered at least a fortnight ago.

Dinim pulled over another table and opened the packages they carried. While the rest of the group talked, she helped him sort through the things they had purchased. They discussed each item and then placed a portion of each into their personal stash.

Everyone heard Volstagg before they could see him, shouting at the new boy he'd hired to help replace Mia and Nolan. He walked through the kitchen doors and smiled a greeting. "It's good to see everyone is here and doing so well. How about a meal? I have some leftovers heating over the fire."

Adrianna instantly spoke up, her belly grumbling with hunger. "Food would be wonderful, Volstagg!"

The cenloryan walked over to her table. "It should be ready soon, my dear." He stood there for a few moments before clearing his throat uncomfortably. Adrianna finally noticed Volstagg's looming presence and glanced up at him questioningly.

His expression was the epitome of solemnity. "Adrianna, I've been thinking. Perhaps you should return to Andahye."

She frowned. "What? Why?"

"You will be safer there than anywhere else. Even though Thane may think to look for you there, Andahye claims the most powerful seat of arcane influence in all of western Ansalar. Surely there are many who would offer you some measure of protection. Besides, you have a home..."

Adrianna's frown deepened. "I may have a tower there, but I do not have a home. Home is where one's family lives. I have no family in Andahye," she interjected.

"But Adria, surely you must have friends. They will have the capacity to offer you protection that no one else will be able to match."

"No. I have no one." Adrianna's tone was clipped. "There is no reason for me to return to Andahye." Adrianna's firm tone brooked no argument. "I have decided I shall search for my sister. It is about time I found her."

Volstagg pressed his lips into a thin line. "So, there is nothing I can say that will change your mind?"

Adrianna regarded him intently. "No, nothing."

"Fine. Be stubborn then," Volstagg grumbled. "Supper will be ready shortly." He disappeared back into the kitchens.

Silence reigned. "So, you plan to look for your sister?"

Adrianna swung her gaze over to Dartanyen. "Yes. It has been a long time. She is the only family I have left; we need each other."

Dartanyen nodded. "Do you know where to begin looking for her?"

"Not really. I will think more about it tomorrow. I want to see you all off on your respectable paths and then sit down and decide what to do."

He shook his head. "Wherever she is, I'm sure it will be a harsh road to travel alone."

She gave a sigh. "Yes, I suppose. But I don't really have a choice."

"Do you really think you can do it?"

"Do what?"

"Travel that road alone with no one at your back?"

"Dartanyen, I don't know," said Adrianna irritably. "Why are you asking me all this?"

He shrugged nonchalantly. "I was just thinking you should hire someone to accompany you, someone who can protect you while you are on the road, someone you can trust."

She narrowed her eyes. "Oh, and I suppose you know someone? I hope he comes cheap because it's not as though I'm swimming in gold or anything!" Adrianna suddenly felt like a fool. *Why did I ever think I could find Sheridana? I have no idea where she is, and Ansalar is a large continent. She could be anywhere!*

Dartanyen raised a placating hand. "Actually, I do know someone, and he will work for free, for a little while, anyway."

Adrianna abandoned her thoughts and raised an eyebrow. "Really? Who is this gentleman?"

Dartanyen stepped forward, walked to her table, placed his arm at his waist, and bowed. "Dartanyen Hildranis at your service, my Lady. I will aid you as long as I can. My sword and bow will protect you as you set forth upon this endeavor."

Adrianna just sat there, stunned. Then, with a tremulous smile, she placed a hand on his arm. "Dartanyen, you will never know what this means to me."

Adrianna's attention was drawn away when she noticed movement behind Dartanyen. Armond and Zorg approached, and they, too, bowed at the waist. Armond gave her a half smile. "We also would like to extend our services to you."

She blinked in surprise, and before she realized it, the whole group was there standing alongside the two men. "Yes Adrianna, we will all come to help you find your sister," said Tianna.

Adrianna looked at all the faces before her. Tears sprang to her eyes and she hurriedly wiped them away with the back of her hand. *What could I have possibly done to deserve their allegiance?* "Dear gods. You are all so good to me. I don't know what to say..."

"Jus' say you will have us with you," said Zorg.

She nodded. "Yes, yes! I would be honored to have you!" Adrianna stretched out her arms and walked towards them. Dartanyen reached out first and hugged her close. She cried onto his chest for a moment before moving on to Armond, Zorg, Bussi, Tianna, and Amethyst. Then she realized Volstagg was there and she hugged him too. Finally, he pulled away. "I'm glad you all have decided to stay together. I was so concerned for you, Adria, but now I needn't worry so much." He gestured towards the table. "Here, I have brought food for you all to eat, with ale and mead to wash it down."

Adrianna felt a hand on her shoulder. She turned to find Dinim standing behind her. She smiled happily up at him, still in disbelief over her good fortune. "Come," he said. "Let us sort out the rest of these things. Then we can focus on food and drink."

Adrianna nodded and they set to work. Meanwhile, the rest of the group helped themselves to the food and everyone was in high spirits. It only took a short while longer for them to complete their task, and then Dinim and Adrianna joined their comrades. The stew was delicious, and the mead flowed easily. Talk of travel plans was abandoned for storytelling. Adrianna rose to get herself another serving when she noticed someone enter the establishment. It was the Terralean man she and Dinim had met in the street that morning. Adrianna tapped Dinim's shoulder and gestured toward the entry.

Dinim looked in the direction she indicated and stood from his seat. He went over to Sabian and they spoke for several moments. Finally, he led the other man back to the tables. "Everyone, I have someone I would like to introduce."

The rest of the group looked up towards Dinim and the new arrival.

"This is Sabian Makonnen. He is someone I met a few years ago while I was still an apprentice. Adrianna and I came across him this morning and I invited him to join us all here. He will be leaving with me in the morning."

There were nods all around and an invitation to join them for their meal. Sabian graciously accepted and helped himself to a bowl of stew and a mug of ale. The banter went on well into the evening, but after a couple of hours Dinim declared that he would have to turn in for the night. "I have a very long road ahead of me on the morrow," he said as he rose from his table.

Sabian rose as well. "Thank you for the meal and the camaraderie. It was a pleasure getting to know you all."

Adrianna watched as the two men left to return to their chamber for the night. Dinim was right; he had a long road ahead of him, and she did as well. Adrianna rose from her own seat and bid everyone goodnight. She then slowly made her way to her personal bedchamber. Tomorrow morning, she would have to see Dinim off. That would be difficult for she had hoped he would remain with her.

Adrianna donned her nightshift and settled into the bed. Despite Dinim's absence, she was happy to have Dartanyen and the others. They were placing themselves in danger by staying with her. Despite their association with her, their chances of leaving the threat of Thane behind were much stronger if they were to all go their separate paths. Yet, they had chosen to pledge themselves to her cause. Together they would help find her sister, and together they would stand against Thane if it came to that.

Now all Adrianna could do was have a little bit of faith, not just in herself, but in the people who chose to follow her.

PART II

PROLOGUE

5 Tiseren CY590

T hane wiped a shaking hand over his face. Just like the rest of him, it was damp with sweat in spite of the cool evening air. The forest floor crackled as he turned in place once more, his breaths shallow and ragged. Even feeling as sick as he did, he sensed that something followed, something dark and sinister. It was the faelin part of him that noticed it, for he believed no typical human had the ability or intellect to perceive such things.

It was so unfortunate that weak human blood made up the rest of him. Perhaps it was the human half of him that made Thane feel as though he was going mad.

What started out as a soft chuckle ended up being a hearty laugh. *Yes, mayhap it is insanity causing me to see shadows at the periphery of my vision, to hear whisperings just barely within my auditory capacity, and to sometimes catch the brief scent of rot.* It was a good excuse for why, even after all these years, he couldn't let his beloved Gemma go.

Thane resolutely turned back to his path. Darkness was falling and he needed to make it back to the encampment before everyone started to wonder about him. He remembered the expression of concern on his half-brother's face when he left and knew Ian awaited his return. Sudden anger coursed through him and he clenched his hands into fists. *Ian must think me a fool. I've seen the glances he casts my daughter when he thinks no one is watching, seen the lust in his eyes. I should never have fostered such a close relationship between he and Sheri and taken the entirely of her training upon myself.* His fingernails dug into his palms and he hastened his pace. *Ian has noticed I am unwell and claims he is concerned about me. I know better. He feigns care for me in hopes I won't realize what he wants to do with my daughter, a girl nineteen years his junior.*

Thane continued for several moments. He stumbled a few times, but managed to regain his balance. The shadows lengthened more swiftly than he thought they should, and once again he stopped. He brought his hands to his temples and squeezed his eyes shut. By the gods, the images that arose in his mind... terrible images of blood, torment, and death. He shook his head to free it of the ugliness. He hated that he was so drawn to the visualizations, and that he was pleased by their grisly outcomes. To say that they were macabre was an understatement, and for a moment he wondered if perhaps Ian was right to feign concern.

He heard something and Thane jerked his head up, blood-shot eyes raking across low lying scrub and towering hardwood trunks. The stark trees loomed over him, many of them just barely showing signs of new growth after the harsh winter. He heard it again, a whispering just beyond his hearing, emanating from some smaller, gnarled trees to his right. He thrust his fingers through greasy brown hair, most of which had escaped the loosely made plait that rested over one leather-clad shoulder. The other hand he rested on the hilt of his broadsword.

By the gods, what is wrong with me?

Shaking his head, Thane continued onward through the lengthening shadows, the sparse canopy overhead rustling in a breeze that carried the scent of death. He began to wonder why he hadn't yet seen landmarks showing he was getting closer to his encampment and he frowned. He changed his direction to the south, allowing intuition to lead him onward. *It's possible I shifted course, especially thinking about my damned brother and silly daughter. Effin Hells! Curse them both!*

He muttered a string of epithets, this time focusing on Sheridana. He liked to believe she was a smart one, but her behavior as of late made him rethink that. She preened under Ian's attention, and seemed to pay a bit more heed to her appearance. She definitely spent more time in his immediate company. She was turning out to be a damn fool just like any other woman. Any other woman, that is, except her mother.

Gemma, his beloved wife, gone almost two decades.

It had been about this time of day when Gemma went into labor. Even now he could hear her agonized cries through the sturdy oak door of the bedchamber. Right from the start he had sensed something wrong, terribly wrong. Gemma had brought their first child into the world, but the second resisted. His wife had continued to labor, her body weakening as the hours passed. Finally, she birthed the second child, but at a terrible cost. The midwife was unable to stop the bleeding that persisted after the difficult labor, and the woman he loved more than life itself died in his arms.

Thane seethed to himself. Over the years he had come to despise his youngest daughter. In truth, he hated to claim her as his own– the child who fought so hard that she refused to be born soon enough for the midwife to save her mother. If Thane had it his way, he would have abandoned the second twin to the elements after her birth. Instead he had been forced to endure the sight of her, making him relive the night of Gemma's death over and over and...

Thane stopped again, wiping a hand across his face. He hissed when the fingernails raked across his cheek, not noticing the stiff curve of his fingers until it was too late. He shook his head at the absurdity, when he saw something at the periphery of his vision. He instantly felt a tingling along his shoulders and back; danger was afoot.

He turned as a dark robed figure glided out from the shadows of the trees a few farlo ahead. His eyes widened and his heart raced in his chest. The familiar odor of decay he'd sensed every now and again during the past few days intensified. His every instinct told him to run, but his mind had already rationalized it would do him no good. It seemed Death had found him, and everyone knew there was no escape from Death.

Thane stood there as the cloaked form approached. It seemed to float over the ground, for it had no discernible stride and made no sound as it passed. The tattered black robes fluttered eerily about it, the edges having a strange ethereal glow that shifted and wavered. As it got close enough, the face within the recesses of the hood slowly became more visible.

The image within was something from his most hideous nightmares.

Thane's heart skipped a beat and breath caught in his throat. The flesh was shrunken around the skull, giving sharp definition to the cheekbones and making the lips almost nonexistent. The nose was almost gone, represented by a dark hole, and the ears were missing. The most disturbing feature was the eyes, glowing like hot coals from a banked fire. The apparition stopped before him, those eyes burning right into the very depths of his soul.

The voice was like the whisper he had been hearing, only magnified. It was creepy, chilling him to the core of his being. "I have heard your cries, Thane Darnesse. I have felt your sorrow, tasted your bitterness, and smelled your despair."

Thane swallowed heavily and stammered. "Wh... who are you? W... why have you come to me?"

The figure cocked his hooded head to the side and regarded him intently from smoldering eyes. "I am called Aasarak, and I am here to offer you a bargain."

Thane took a moment to compose himself. "Wh... what kind of bargain?"

The hideous face grinned widely, showing a row of perfect teeth. "I have seen your innermost soul. You want strength to persevere over your opponents, skill to be the best at your profession, and power to influence those who surround you. I can give you all of these things, ten-fold!" Aasarak's eyes burned brighter. "But even more than these things, you yearn for vengeance. The power I can grant you will give you the means to achieve your desire."

Thane gave a swift inhalation. *By the gods, how does this being know so much about me? How can he possibly know my innermost secrets? Even more, why is Death be striking bargains with his victims?*

Thane shook his head slowly. "What is your price for these things?"

The smile disappeared from Aasarak's face. "Only your soul."

Thane became still. "What?"

Aasarak regarded him intently. "Your soul is all I require to transfer these gifts to you. Then, just to make it permanent, I need your sworn allegiance to me."

A few moments passed and Thane eyed Aasarak speculatively. "You promise to give me all of these things?"

"All that and mooooore." Aasarak breathed the words and held out a skeletal hand. "Come to me, and you shall have what your soul most desires."

Thane hesitated. He noticed the word Aasarak used– soul. The sorcerer would give what his soul desired, but not his heart. He supposed no one could do that, give true life to someone who had already known Death, no matter how powerful he might be.

But at least he could have his revenge.

"So how do I know you will keep your end of our bargain?"

Aasarak cocked his head to the side once more. "You don't."

Thane frowned, not liking that response, but moving on to his next question. "How do I give you my soul? Is it by some kind of magic?"

Aasarak reached within his voluminous robes and brought forth an intricately carved object that appeared to be made of bone. The runic designs danced over the eight faces, each one melding into the next. It was a geometric work of art, and Thane wondered at the significance of it.

"My Azmathion shall help you," said Aasarak.

Thane paused. If he swore his allegiance to Aasarak, he would be leaving Ian and Sheridana behind. He supposed he didn't really care all that much, for he already felt that his brother deceived him. And Sheri, well, mayhap her loss was worth the gain. "How do we start?"

Aasarak regarded him intently. "Do you agree to the terms, then?" Thane nodded his agreement.

"You must speak the woooords aloud," breathed Aasarak.

His voice shook. "I agree to the terms of your agreement."

The thing sitting in the palm of Aasarak's skeletal hand flared with a red luminescence for a moment before subsiding to a paler glow. Aasarak gave a small smile. "Now we can begin."

Thane swept a hand across his damp forehead and repeated the question he had asked earlier. "What do I need to do?"

Aasarak grinned more widely, and a shiver of trepidation raced up Thane's spine. As the sorcerer reached his other hand towards him, Thane felt a sudden tension surround him. He tried to move his arms and legs but found they had been bound by some invisible force. "There is only one way a man can surrender his soul," said Aasarak. "He needs to die."

Thane's eyes widened in alarm just as a wave of pain swept over him. The Azmathion's glow shifted to a dark blue and his body contorted with agony. He felt a pulling sensation from deep within, felt his insides being sucked away. He wrapped his arms around his belly and sank to his knees. *By the gods, I never imagined I would die this way. What will Ian and Sheri think happened to me?*

What have I done?

Sweat dribbled down the sides of his face and down his neck. He barely recovered before the second wave struck. He fell onto his back and lay there on the ground, unable to move through the agony gripping his every muscle. Aasarak moved to stand over him, the purplish glowing Azmathion illuminating a ghastly grin stretched across the skeletal face.

Thane was only able to gasp a few more breaths before the third wave washed through him. This time he screamed, the pain ripping through him like a scythe. Now he knew what Gemma had endured when she birthed his children. Now he knew what she endured when the child Adrianna refused to be born. He barely had a moment to breathe before the fourth wave came...

The torment was unbearable. All he could do was stare at the dark form hovering above him, at the burning eyes that cruelly watched his suffering. The fifth wave came and he fought for breath. He heard his heart stutter within his chest, felt it struggle to continue beating. Adrianna, Adrianna... the wretched child who was his ultimate downfall. Without her, Gemma would have lived. Without her, he would have kept his sanity, human blood or no.

The sixth wave crested over Thane. His heart slowly shuddered to a halt. Time seemed to become still as he lay there, his tortured body sprawled on the ground. Blood trickled from his nostrils, and urine wet the front of his trousers. Then there was a moment when Time had no meaning...

...and as Thane's consciousness shifted to darkness, he only saw Aasarak's burning eyes.

THE PATH

It was early and dawn had not yet begun to paint the horizon. Adrianna, Dartanyen, Armond, Zorg, Bussi and Tianna sat around the largest of the rebuilt tables. Tianna had tried to rouse Amethyst to no avail. The young girl simply refused to awaken, and Tianna's efforts had been rewarded only by muffled curses and threats to her wellbeing.

It wasn't long before Dinim and his companion walked into the common room. Both men were garbed for travel and wore tunics and trousers with reinforced stitching. Thick vests were worn over the tunics and sashes around their waists sported a myriad of easily accessible pouches used to store spell components. Leather boots were worn up to their knees; Dinim's were the ones she'd chosen for him the day before when Adrianna accompanied him around the city to conduct his business. Each man's pack was loaded with all of their belongings and included several days of food packs that Volstagg and his cook had assiduously prepared the previous night.

Everyone arose from their seats as the two men stopped by the table. Dartanyen put out a hand. "Thank you for all that you have done. I don't think we could have escaped the temple without you. I hope you have a safe journey."

Dinim grasped Dartanyen's forearm and nodded. "The best of luck to you all. I hope that you can help Adrianna find what she is looking for." Dinim glanced over at her. "However, I have spoken to my companion and he has agreed to accompany you."

Sabian stepped up beside Dinim. "I hope you will accept me into your ranks. I have much I can offer your group. My Talent is strong and I've had many years to hone my skills. I know the areas in and around the central kingdoms and the free cities rather well, so I can help there as well."

"My friend, this is not necessary. I assure you that Adrianna will be safe with us," said Dartanyen. His serious gaze swung to Dinim. "You have nothing to worry about."

"Please, for my own peace of mind, take Sabian with you. It can't hurt to have another spellcaster in your midst."

Dartanyen stared fixedly at Dinim for a moment. Adrianna looked from one man to the next. Finally, Dartanyen took in a deep breath. "All right. I suppose he can accompany us."

Dinim smiled. "Good. It is settled then." Dinim clapped Sabian on the shoulder and the other man returned the gesture. "Thank you, Sabian. This means a lot to me."

Sabian nodded. "Take care on your journey."

"I will." Dinim turned to Adrianna. "Would you walk with me to the gate?"

Everyone walked out onto the veranda. It was still dark, but the first rays of sunlight were beginning to light sky. Dinim waved as he and Adrianna stepped down onto the street. She was quiet as they walked, her eyes downcast. After a few moments Dinim broke the silence. "Adrianna, don't stay here much longer. Thane has surely caught wind of you by now." She nodded and looked up at him. He regarded her thoughtfully, his lavender eyes intent. Suddenly he stopped. He turned and took her shoulders in his hands. "Adrianna, believe me when I say we will meet again."

She gave a small smile. "I believe you."

Dinim smiled back and then pulled her forward into his embrace. It felt good to have him hold her, and she reached up to wrap her arms around his neck. Finally, they stepped apart and walked the rest of the way to the city gate in silence. Once there, they regarded one another for one last moment before Dinim raised his hand in farewell. Adrianna returned the gesture. She watched as he walked out of the city towards the people who awaited him. *Sirion, he is going to Sirion. I wish I could go with him, but I have my own responsibilities that don't include the Wildrunners and their troubles.*

Adrianna finally turned and made her way back to the inn. Dinim was right, her time in Sangrilak was running out. She had the day to find out anything she could about Sheridana and her possible whereabouts. After that, she would go from city to city and town to town, everywhere and anywhere that she could think of where anyone could know anything about her sister.

The caravan had pulled out of the city of Tragesser a few days ago. Her wagon was one of several that comprised the large procession of merchants and wanderers. It was a dangerous land through which they traveled, and there was safety in numbers. One wagon with bright blue tassels carried a few bards, each playing his or her instrument of choice throughout the day as they traveled. The one with the harp annoyed Sheridana to no end. He didn't want to take 'no' for an answer, and constantly found new reasons to be near her. He had requested the 'pleasure of her company' several times, and her negative response was always the same. Unfortunately, his wagon happened to be just ahead.

Sheridana quickly rode past the bards' wagon, escaping before the one with the harp could even think about speaking with her. He would have found something new to discuss, something quirky, trivial, or terribly mundane. *What was his name again?* She could scarcely remember, although she thought it was Kling, or maybe Klon. Sheridana waved as she passed the other caravan drivers, most of whom were friendly and unobtrusive, and nodded to the other riders on patrol. They would circle the caravan perimeter several times during their shift and then pass the responsibility on to the ones who rode after. This was Sheridana's last pass before she returned to her own wagon.

She smiled to herself. Fitanni was probably still awake, waiting for her to return before settling down for a late morning rest. The baby always awakened early, appearing to enjoy the discomfort she caused her mother and nanny. She cooed with delight when Sheridana picked her up from the furs in the morning, and would stare at her as she nursed, wide blue eyes exploring every contour of her mother's face. The baby would tap Sheridana with her tiny hands and try to grab the errant strands of dark hair that liked to come loose from her long braid.

Fitanni had brought joy to Sheridana's life that had never existed before, yet something was missing. Sheridana regretted many things in her life, and the one thing she lamented most was leaving her sister behind. While she, Ian, and their father sought fortune on the open road, Adrianna was left alone in Sangrilak. Sure, her sister had Mairi and her friend Volstagg there, but it wasn't the same. Sheridana would never forget the expression on Adrianna's face when she and the others rode away that fateful day.

Sheridana shook herself free of the memories. Several years had passed since she'd last seen Adrianna and she wondered about her. *Has she stayed in Sangrilak or did she leave to study magic? What does she look like? Does she forgive me? Do I expect her to?* Sheridana had written several times when she first left, determined to keep contact, but she'd never received a reply. Finally, she stopped sending the letters and for a while she was angry, telling herself that Adrianna was selfish and mean-spirited. But then, after a while, she couldn't hold up the façade. It was she who had been the selfish one— Sheri had been the one to leave, not Adrianna.

Sheridana rode until she passed the wagons nearest the one she used for herself and her family. Carli enjoyed preparing their meals and she would have breakfast ready when Sheridana got there. It was a good thing, because she returned every morning with a rumbling stomach. Sheridana counted her blessings. Carli was a wonderful friend to her and an excellent care-giver for Fitanni. With the girl's help, Sheridana needn't have motherhood interfere with her other duties, allowing her to earn a bit of coin by serving as one of the caravan guards as they traveled.

At the age of twenty-one summers, Sheridana had become pregnant. For a woman with faelin blood, this was very uncommon because she'd still been in adolescence. For eleven moon cycles she carried the child. Any human woman would have carried for approximately nine, and a full-blooded faelin woman almost fourteen. Because of her youth, Sheri had difficulty during labor, and when the child was finally born, she became very ill. She had lost a lot of blood during the birth, and her depression over Ian's loss impeded her ability to recover.

Carli's family had generously taken her into their home and cared for her until she was well again. Carli herself had taken most of the responsibility of caring for the baby and Fitanni developed an attachment to her. When Sheridana had sufficiently recovered and began preparation for her journey back to Sangrilak, Carli made the decision to accompany her. Carli's parents were distressed, for they were loath to lose their eldest daughter. But when Sheridana explained how Carli had become like family to her, and that they would always be together, Carli's parents gave their blessing.

Now, several weeks later, they were slowly but surely making their way towards Sangrilak. Riding with caravans made it an even slower process, but she would not place Carli and Fitanni at risk by traveling alone. There was safety in numbers, and although there was still a chance that they could be ambushed by thieves, the risk was smaller with herself and the other caravan guards taking turns at the patrols. It would take some time, but eventually she would make it home. Finally, she would see Adrianna again, and she couldn't wait for her sister to meet Fitanni.

And they would be a family again after so long being apart.

Clad in a hooded cloak to keep prying eyes from possibly recognizing her, Adrianna slowly walked up the steps to the veranda of the Inn of the Hapless Cenloryan. She had been all over the city. Most of the people to whom she spoke were merchants, as they were often privy to information that came in from the outside. They were the ones most likely to hear about anything happening in another city or town, even one located in another kingdom. She also spoke to some caravan drivers and a couple of wandering bards. Unfortunately, none of them had information about her sister or the two men with whom she'd been traveling.

The front door to the building opened and Dartanyen and Armond stepped out onto the veranda. By the expressions on their faces Adrianna knew they'd had no success. She slumped despondently into one of the rocking chairs, dismally contemplating the route she and the others would take on the morrow. It would be best if they left under the darkness of night. She knew the others wouldn't complain much, for they wanted to get out of the city just as much as she. Besides, most of the group had been resting throughout the day with the exception of herself and these two.

Adrianna looked out toward the street in the direction of the city gate where she had left Dinim early that morning. He was traveling north, and within two or three days he would reach the town of Ferent. He would then cross the Tangir River, a tributary of the mighty Terrestra, and travel to the city of Driscol, the last city he would see before he had to cross the Ratik Mountains. He would take the Ratik Pass through the mountains and then go to the city of Celuna. There, he would prepare for his several days journey to Grondor.

She rubbed her chin thoughtfully. *I wonder, should we go in the same direction in our search for Sheri? Or, perhaps instead travel west? Within the day we should be able to make it to the Terrestra River. We would take a ferry across and then be on the southern outskirts of Elvandahar. We would then skirt the timberline until we reached the Denegal River. Once crossing into the realm of Karlisle, we would make our way north to the city of Velmist. I wouldn't be surprised if Sheri went there because it is a place rich with opportunity.*

As Adrianna ruminated over her choices, she noticed a small group of men and women walking up the street. She didn't pay them much heed until she realized they were making their way towards the inn. They were obviously very weary, packs weighing heavily upon stooped shoulders, and boots worn from many zacrol of travel. They had just reached the steps when Armond called out, "The inn is closed. You will need to find other accommodations for the night."

The travelers eyed them skeptically. "I see. I suppose you are just hanging around here for the view then," one of the men replied sarcastically.

"We are friends of the proprietor," said Dartanyen. "He has allowed us to stay, but we will be leaving on the morrow. Many repairs must be made to this place before it will be ready to accommodate travelers again."

The man nodded and his shoulders slumped. "I hope you can direct us to the next closest inn."

Dartanyen pointed down the street. "Macey's Tavern and Inn is just down the road. You can't miss it."

The man raised a hand in farewell and the group turned to leave. Adrianna felt sorry for them, hated for them to have to walk even further, just so they could take a rest. She noticed that their clothes were not only dusty from the road, but bloodstained as well, as though they had seen some trouble. One of the women seemed weaker than the rest, and she leaned against one of her companions.

"Wait," Adrianna called out. "Do you happen to know anyone by the name of Sheridana Darnesse?"

The man stopped and turned toward her. His expression was ponderous as he regarded her for a moment. "Darnesse. That name sounds familiar to me."

Excitedly, Adrianna stood from her chair and approached the man. "Please, try to remember. How long ago have you heard that name?"

"Several moon cycles ago." The man paused. "Wait. I remember now. It was a man who bore that name. He traveled with a group called Thritean's Pride. The last time I saw them was out near Kranton, a city in the northern province of Durnst."

"Do you remember what he looked like?"

The man shook his head. "Can't say as I do, but I think I heard his lady companion call him Ian. It is an uncommon enough name that I remembered it."

"Do you remember what *she* looked like?"

"Yes, as a matter of fact I do. Her hair was dark, almost black, and her eyes were blue. Her features were out of the ordinary, but she was a beautiful woman. She looked like her bloodlines were crossed– you know, a half-faelin." The man looked closely at her. "Perhaps like you, milady."

Adrianna smiled, brimming with excitement. This was her first lead, her first step towards Sheri!

"Well, we had best be off. We have some beds somewhere calling out to us." The man gave a tired grin and turned away once more. He stepped down from the veranda and the group began to make their way down the street.

"Wait." Adrianna heard herself calling out to them again. She wanted to do something for them, a favor in return for the one they had done her. Adrianna hurried down the steps and approached the group. The man turned to her once more. "I am sure Volstagg could keep you for this one night. He owes me a favor. Please, come inside and share a meal with us."

The man regarded her speculatively for a moment before turning to the rest of his group. The others nodded. He turned back and held out his hand. "My name is Vornec. Thank you for the offer. This means a lot to us. As you can probably tell, we have had a rough journey."

Adrianna grasped his arm in welcome. "I am Adrianna. Please come inside and make yourselves comfortable..."

The three companions walked down the main street of Sangrilak, enjoying the early evening air. It was unseasonably chilly and the women wore their hooded cloaks. Shandahar's first moon, Steralion, had made her ascent, and soon the second moon, Hestim, would follow. They spoke of the route they would be traveling, how long it would take, and the last of the supplies they would need. No attention was paid about the hour, not realizing it was getting late. The activity of the day had died down, and the shadows that usually existed only in the alleyways began to encroach onto the street.

This was Dartanyen's first chance to talk with Adrianna. He felt that it would be a good idea to get to know her a little better before their journey. Through the course of the conversation he shared with her as they walked, he found her to be as much of a mystery as ever. Honestly, he couldn't entirely figure her out. She was obviously quite intelligent and knowledgeable, and her charisma was unsurpassed. Hells, there was little he wouldn't do for her if she asked.

Yet, in spite of those things, she lacked confidence. He wondered briefly about the reason, but it suited Dartanyen rather well for he was rather accustomed to being in a leadership position. Ultimately Adrianna was the leader of the group, and he merely a hired hand. However, he got the impression that she was going to leave much of the decision-making up to him. Although, he did note that Adrianna was a woman who knew what she wanted. She didn't hesitate to tell him the route she wished to take in search of her sister.

Dartanyen, Adrianna, and Tianna walked for some time, discussing their options, forging plans, and making light conversation. He hadn't the chance to get to know the women very well whilst he drank and joked with the menfolk in the evenings after supper, but he found the company was good. He now had a better idea of their background, some potential strengths and weaknesses, and some of their motivations.

Before long, Dartanyen realized that they had come to a poorer section of the city. Most of the buildings had crumbling brick along the edges, and many had broken windows. Some of those were covered with bed sheets to keep the elements out. Metal railings along crumbling staircases were rusted, and wooden doors were moldy from lack of upkeep. There was a filthy smell to the place, and the mess of the streets was testament as to why.

The fading light cast wickedly eerie shadows from the side streets and alleyways and it was then Dartanyen took in the state of his person. He wasn't wearing his customary leather trousers and vest and all he had was a dagger for protection. He put a hand on Adrianna's shoulder and was about to tell her they should head back to the inn, when they heard a scuffling sound accompanied by a strange noise in the alleyway up ahead.

Instantly they stopped. The noise continued for a moment and then receded. It was an odd gargling sound, like someone was struggling to breathe through water. They heard the scuffling again, this time accompanied by groaning. Adrianna and Tianna instinctively pressed together. Dartanyen remembered the hardship they had recently endured. His heartbeat increased in tempo and he realized he was afraid, an emotion he didn't feel very often. *Oh gods, it's too soon. I just finished healing from the wounds I acquired in the temple...*

Dartanyen quickly assessed their surroundings. They were currently in the middle of a deserted street. However, there was a smaller side street they had just passed. He figured they could reach it in a few strides if they ran, however, he was unwilling to make the mistake of their footfalls being heard by whoever was up ahead. Suddenly they heard a peel of laughter followed by some voices. All of them sounded masculine, and they came from the same place as the gargling sounds from moments before.

"He held out longer than I thought he would," said one voice. "Over two days."

"Grimwell's business in this city is over," said another voice. "Let his master come here to conduct it his damn self."

"He'd better not," growled a third. "This is MY city. I'll not have..."

"Just stay quiet," whispered Dartanyen, taking advantage of his chance to speak while the men continued back and forth. "Parley might be our only option. If it comes to it, let me do the talking."

The women nodded mutely. He pressed them back slowly, hoping to make it to the side street they had passed before the unknown men possibly made it around the corner. Dartanyen had a bad feeling the men were trouble, their mocking laughter telling him that they had overcome some poor, unfortunate soul who happened to be in their way somehow.

They were lucky, making it to the side street and slipping into it just as three men emerged onto the main road. They were muscular, wearing thick leather vests with fur at the collars. The leader radiated a strong aura of unbridled power that made Dartanyen even more apprehensive. He looked vaguely familiar, with thick brown hair that touched the tops of his broad shoulders. Dartanyen was jostled from behind and Adrianna's whispering reached his ears, "We should leave! This man is dangerous!"

He tried ignoring it and focused on the men. Indeed, it did look like they were dangerous, making it imperative for the women to keep their mouths shut.

"Sirion warned me about this man. We have to leave. Please..."

Dartanyen frowned and motioned for Adrianna to remain quiet, keeping his eyes fixed on the men. One of them carried a mean crossbow and the leader had a massive broadsword strapped over his right shoulder.

Tianna's voice– "Adrianna, you have got to be quiet." There was a pause. "What's wrong?"

"That man, Sydonnia. He wants to kill Sirion."

"Wh... what are you talking about? Why..."

Dartanyen couldn't help paying attention to the unfolding conversation behind him even though silence was of the essence.

"I don't know. He gave me this message and–"

Tianna's voice rose. "What message? Why didn't *I* know about this?"

Dartanyen cringed. Her loud whispers had attracted the men in the street and they were heading in their direction. He reached back and tried to grab Tianna's arm, but she pulled away from their hiding place and defiantly strode towards the burly men. Dartanyen whispered a curse and pulled himself and Adrianna further back into the lane. They could hear the guffaws of the men as Tianna neared.

Tianna stalked towards the men. *Oh yes, I remember him now. The one in charge is Sydonnia, Sirion's deranged uncle. I never understood why Sirion was always so concerned about the man; he doesn't look very imposing to me.* Her frown deepened when she saw the leers on the men's faces. *I'll take care of that really quick!*

The man with the crossbow chuckled and nudged his companion. "Hey Sy, it looks like we have a wench to play with."

Tianna stopped in front of Sydonnia. She'd met him only once before, but she remembered her initial impression. He was the shady type and it was hard to believe he was actually a blood relative to Sirion. Her friend had told her to always steer clear of the man, but she refused to lie low this time. Sydonnia had issued a threat to Sirion's well-being and now he would regret it.

"I have your wench right here, you bastard!" Tianna slammed her fist into Sydonnia's smirking face, his head turning with the blow. The painful impact traveled through her hand and up her arm. She was so tempted to groan and hold it close, but she resisted.

For a moment, the street was silent. The men looked at one another and abruptly began to laugh.

Irritation flared and she narrowed her eyes. "You think this is funny? Well maybe I should give you another–"

Tianna's words were cut short as Sydonnia caught her flying fist. His other hand grabbed her just beneath the jaw and brought her face close. "Now listen here, bitch. I don't take kindly to wenches offering me this kind of treatment unless it's in my bed."

The other men laughed raucously and fear coursed through her like a wild river. Tianna had to struggle to keep herself from trembling. She felt the power in Sydonnia's grip and saw the darkness in his eyes. Shaggy brown hair fell to the furred collar of his vest, some of it concealing one side of his face. His arms were thick with muscle and covered with curling dark hair uncharacteristic of someone of faelin descent. If she didn't know better, she would have thought he bore some human heritage.

His voice was gruff. "You had best answer me quickly. Why are you here and what is the meaning of this?" Sydonnia's grip on her jaw tightened and the pain was enough to make her want to cry out. He had suddenly become

173

very imposing after all, and he expected an answer. She dreaded his wrath if she didn't cooperate.

Tianna was loath to mention Sirion's name. "I... I heard you are looking for a friend of mine." Tianna could barely get the words out through her fear, and the pain of Sydonnia's grip intensified the more she hesitated.

"Well now, I'm looking for a lot of people. Who might *this* person be?" Sydonnia's eyes narrowed into slits.

Suddenly there was a familiar voice. "Hey now, how about letting the woman go? She has had way too much to drink and she doesn't know what she's talking about."

Sydonnia shifted his gaze to look at Dartanyen. Next, he glanced at Adrianna, merely taking note of her presence, then looked back at Tianna and frowned. "You know, if there is one thing in this world I hate the most, it's a terrible liar. I don't mind a good liar, or even a halfway decent one. And a man can always tell something about his enemy by the way he lies. My dear, your friend is definitely a bad liar, is he not? I don't smell the least bit of brew on your breath, and let me tell you, I would definitely be able to tell if you had *anything* to drink today." Sydonnia gave her a smile that didn't quite make it to his eyes.

Just then, a fourth man stumbled out from the alley from which the men had come. Covered in blood, his clothes appeared as though they had been shredded by a gigantic claw and he sported several deep lacerations to his face, arms, and chest. He held one arm across his abdomen and used the other to hold himself up against the nearest building. Sydonnia looked to see what had caught their attention and then turned to his companion with the crossbow. He gave a nod, and within the blink of an eye, three bolts struck the beaten man in the chest. He slid down the side of the wall until he lay in a crumpled heap on the ground.

Sydonnia returned his attention back to Tianna, releasing her jaw. "So, my dear, what were you saying? Oh yes, you were about to tell me about this person whom I am looking for."

The moment he released her, Tianna took an involuntary step back. She couldn't believe what she had just witnessed: the murder of a man in cold blood out in the open for anyone to see. Sydonnia was arrogant, and it was obvious he felt he could do whatever he wished, to whomever he wanted to do it.

Tianna was silent, not knowing how to answer. She didn't want to say Sirion's name, afraid of what Sydonnia's response would be. Dartanyen and Adrianna stood a few foot-lengths behind her, but this fact offered her little comfort. She had the terrible feeling this man could do whatever he wanted with them in the blink of an eye. Sydonnia watched her like a predator inspecting its prey. He knew she was afraid– she could see it in his eyes. And something else lurked there waiting.

The corner of Sydonnia's mouth curved up in mild amusement. "Tsk, tsk. So closed-mouthed we have become. Well, at least tell me where he is from." Sydonnia put his hands on his hips, waiting for her to respond.

Tianna swallowed, her mouth and throat dry. "El... Elvandahar. He is from Elvandahar."

Sydonnia's gaze suddenly intensified. He glanced at Adrianna once more and a wave of realization passed over his face. He hadn't recognized her because of the hood that disguised her unusual features, most notably her hair. "Ah, my wayward nefreyo. You are right, my dear. I *have* been looking for Sirion. Now I remember why you look so familiar to me. We met once, a few years ago while I was passing through your village. You are the human girl that likes to tag along on Sirion's bootheels– much like a lovesick corubis cub."

Tianna prickled at the mocking tone in Sydonnia's voice. He was goading her, urging her to react. Her hands clenched into fists at her sides and she obliged. "You bastard," she hissed. "I knew you were a pile of umberhulk dung when I first laid eyes on you. You are nothing more than a wretched snake who only feels like a real man when he's intimidating others."

Dartanyen was suddenly at her side. He grabbed her arm and roughly pulled her back and held her there against his chest. "Shut up, Tianna. What the Hells is wrong with you?" he hissed.

Sydonnia's eyes were slitted once more. "Yes, you are indeed a rude little wench. You would do well to watch where you waggle your tongue, my dear, lest you find it down your throat," he growled.

Tianna allowed herself to be pulled backward in spite of the pain that made her eyes water. "Just excuse us," said Dartanyen. "It is late and we have comrades who are undoubtedly awaiting our return. I wish you a good evening." Dartanyen continued to haul her back and she pressed her lips together to keep from crying out. She glanced to the left to see Adrianna being pulled alongside her. Once far enough away, he abruptly turned Tianna around and pushed them both down the street.

As the three made good their escape, they heard the tauntingly wicked sound of laughter. Tianna palpably sensed the evil they left behind. She heard Dartanyen whispering words of thankfulness beneath his breath. It was only then she realized exactly how afraid he'd been. *I feel like such a fool. I placed all of us at great risk. There is something about that man, something predatory. Sydonnia would have derived much pleasure from killing us and I can't help wondering why he didn't.*

175

The sun was beginning to set. It was his favorite time of the day, a time in which his powers, many of which were dormant during the daylight hours, began to strengthen. There was just something about it– the lowering of the sun and the surge of power rushing through his veins. It was excruciating and invigorating at the same time that make him feel like a croxian addict taking his first hit after several hours of having had none.

Thane stood out on the plain between Sangrilak and Andahye, the sky wide and open before him. The setting sun bathed it in hues of blue and lavender. The first moon, Steralion, would soon become visible, followed by her sisters, Hestim and Meriliam. It was at that time, when all three of the moons could be seen in the midnight sky, that his powers were greatest. And when Thane was strong, his followers were strong.

Thane looked back towards his band. After leaving Sangrilak, they had begun to travel towards the next place he thought his daughter would go, the place where she had lived the majority of the past several years. It was as good a guess as any, for certainly she had allies in the mystical city of Andahye. Within the small copse of trees they waited for darkness to descend. He frowned, for he so much hated waiting, but it was nearly over. Then, in the distance he caught sight of a small speck. As it got closer, the speck turned into a blob, and eventually into the form of a larian and rider. As the twosome thundered into camp, Thane frowned once more. The man had been riding hard. His animal was lathered in a sheen of sweat, and the breathing was labored. The rider himself was in a state of weariness, obviously having ridden without stopping. He slid from the back of the larian, and immediately went to Thane, bending in obeisance.

Thane tapped his servant on the shoulder and the man straightened. "So, what news do you bring me? I assume it is of some importance." Thane paused and regarded the poor larian, whose head hung close to the ground. "Especially since you have nearly killed your beast to bring it to me."

The man looked at Thane. "My Lord, we have located the group for which you have been searching. They are in Sangrilak; have been there the entire time. I came as quickly as I cou..."

Thane swiftly reached out and wrapped his hand around the man's throat. The man gasped and brought his fingers up to his neck, clawing at the hand as it began to tighten. "Fool! Why did you not contact me through Grimwell? I would have known immediately they were there, and I would have been in Sangrilak by now!"

The man continued to gasp and opened his mouth as though he wanted to say something. Thane suddenly released his grip and the man fell back, holding his neck with his hands. His voice was hoarse. "My Lord, I tried to find him, but was unable to do so. I don't know where he is."

Thane clenched his hands into fists. *Why? Why am I surrounded by idiots? Poor fools who haven't a brain amongst them all?* The group had gotten away once already in the temple when his Master's priests were supposed to have been able to keep them there until he arrived. When he reached the temple, he had found the worship hall in shambles. The doppelganger, Ixitchitl, was dead, as were several of the Master's priests. The wizard, Dinim, had escaped, as had Adrianna and the small posse of people with whom she had aligned herself.

Thane had gone into a fit of rage. He'd murdered several more priests before finally controlling himself. He didn't care about the loss of Dinim, hadn't really cared to capture the young Dimensionalist in the first place. He had only done it because the Master wished to seek revenge on his nemesis. But really, who gave a damn about Gaknar anyway? That man was down a bad path. Consorting with daemons was a risky business at best.

However, the loss of his daughter was something that Thane *did* care about. He wanted her dead, wanted her to be gone from this world, gone the way Gemma was gone. He hated her with a passion he didn't understand, didn't care to understand. And then there was her twin, the daughter who had betrayed him by sleeping with his brother and conceiving his whelp. The whore. He thought about killing her, but then realized it would be sweeter if she had to see her brat die first. He would kill the little bastard with his own two hands.

Thane grabbed the man again, hoisting him to his feet. Somewhere in his mind he knew his servant was not at fault, but he didn't care. Thane needed an outlet, and the man was right there– so pathetic, so vulnerable. Thane took the man's head between his hands and gave a savage twist. He felt a pop as the skull separated from the spine and the body went limp. He then let the dead man crumple to the ground.

Thane spun away and strode towards the trees. He felt only marginally better, but better nevertheless. He walked among the foliage and came to where his band waited with their shadowy steeds. He took the ropes of his lloryk from one of his knights and swung effortlessly up into the saddle.

He gave a shout, "We ride to Sangrilak!" He raised a fist into the air and ground his heels into the lloryk's sides. The animal trumpeted and sprang forward, the others following behind.

DEPARTURE

Tallachienan strode purposefully through the northwestern tower of the citadel, his mind full of the preparations he needed to make for his students' arrival. A couple of them had come already, two young men whom he'd been tracking for quite some time. Their Talent had been difficult to determine, but that probably had much to do with the circumstances surrounding each one's upbringing. They had potential– all of his students had potential, and that was why he chose them. Out of all of the Talents of Shandahar, Tallachienan always chose those with the brightest aura. Only they would have enough of the gift to succeed in the rigorous training required to become a Dimensionalist.

Tallachienan opened the door to the area dedicated to his research. He made his way to the rear of the study and walked into the next room. There, sitting upon a wide pedestal, was a large orb. When he approached it, the orb glowed softly green. He splayed his hands over the surface, bringing to the forefront of his mind the person he wished to see. The dense mist within the orb eddied about, the colors varying from blue and green to pale yellow. Then, within the center, appeared the face of a young man.

He was Cimmerean, with black hair, lavender eyes, and pale skin. He appeared to be riding in a wagon, his image moving rhythmically about in a swaying motion. The man appeared strained, but Tallachienan couldn't tell if it was because of the fact he was forced to endure a wagon ride, or if he was overly tired. Tallachienan shook his head. It was obvious Dinim had yet to reach the Ratik Pass. He'd hoped his journeyman was well into the mountains by now, but he had a tendency to forget that most people had to use mundane modes of travel. It had been decades since Tallachienan even considered riding in a wagon to reach a desired destination. As it was, Dinim wouldn't reach the Wildrunners until it was too late. *Damn Aasarak! If that crazy mage hadn't put his nose into business that wasn't his own, Dinim would be with the rest of his companions by now.*

Tallachienan turned from the orb. Without Dinim, the Wildrunners would be hard-pressed to achieve victory over the Daemundai. Their leader, Gaknar, needed to be destroyed. With the knowledge he possessed, Gaknar had become more than just one of the greatest sorcerers who had ever lived– he had become a great threat to Shandahar. With power and wisdom he'd gained over the centuries, Gaknar was quickly learning how to bring Bra'hatra, or greater daemons into the world without the use of the rifts. The rifts were guarded, and as such, the Pact of Bakharas had the potential to still be upheld. Without the Pact...

The Wildrunners needed to find the sorcerer before he could make his next attempt, and if Gaknar happened to succeed, the Wildrunners would need all the help they could get.

Tallachienan expelled a heavy sigh. The Wildrunners and their upcoming tribulation wasn't the only thing on his mind. The preparations he'd been making were primarily for one person. Adrianna's training needed to begin soon. A part of him longed to see her, to have her there in the citadel with him once more. The other wanted nothing to do with her. It was one of the reasons why he'd left Dinim's calls for help unanswered. That, and he had vowed to have very little to do with the girl until the last moment when he would be forced to take her for training.

Well, not *forced*. Tallachienan wasn't *forced* to do anything. More that he chose to train her under duress of the consequences.

Tallacheinan left the laboratory. He needed to complete a few things before he went to Dinim. First, he would write a message in the Travel Notebook, telling his journeyman to be expecting a visit. Once there, Tallachienan would ask Dinim a few questions about Adrianna, just to determine how much she had changed since the last Cycle, if at all.

Hellfire! I so much hope things will be different this time. Is it really so much to ask? Do I not deserve to be freed from this eternal torment of want and desire?

With a sudden surge of emotion, Tallachienan raised a hand, and with all of the anger and anguish within him, focused on his spell. A huge roll of fire sprang from alongside him and tore down the corridor. It incinerated everything in its path and then exploded into the wall at the end. The concussive force then swept back down the corridor towards him. He didn't move. It swept over him in a heated wave, making his robes and hair whip wildly about behind him. When it was over, Tallachienan lowered his hand.

For a long time he just stood there in the blackened hallway.

Shrouded by the darkness of the night, the group traveled northeast, leaving the city of Sangrilak behind. It was with a light heart Adrianna left, knowing that when she returned, her sister would be with her. A lloryk pulled the small wagon they had purchased with the gold they received from the city. Everyone loaded most of their travel gear onto it, making the burden for their larian much lighter. Adrianna rode Sethanon, and the only other person to ride a lloryk was Zorg. Everyone else rode a larian, everyone except Amethyst, who didn't know how to ride, and Bussimot, who refused to ride.

"It jus' ain't meant to be... halfen ridin' on these animals. We needs ta be havin' our feet on da ground. Can't know what da land is tellin' ya if yer not walkin' on it."

Throughout the night, they traveled in silence. Dartanyen's mood was serious and contemplative. Adrianna imagined it might have much to do with their encounter with Sydonnia. The experience had left a chill that wouldn't dissipate even in the light of the following day. Tianna had been sullen and withdrawn as they'd prepared for the journey, and now that they were on the road, Adrianna hoped it would soon pass. Armond and Zorg had noticed, but didn't say anything, allowing her the time she needed to recover. Since he refused to ride, Bussi accepted the task of driving the wagon. Adrianna thought it rather interesting, remembering the words he had spoken in regards to riding astride. His feet wouldn't be on the ground while riding on the seat of a wagon either, but of course she would say nothing of this, recognizing it for the excuse that it was.

The group traveled with ease into the morning. The land was flat and easy to traverse, the long prairie grasses sweeping beneath the larian's bellies as they walked alongside the road. Dartanyen acted as their scout, riding up ahead to view the terrain before they rolled over it. Meanwhile, Zorg and Armond rode alongside the wagon, their mounts a stark contrast to one another. Where the lloryk were large, muscular, and pale in coloration, their larian cousins were smaller, slenderer, and more colorful. Most lloryk were colored varying shades of grey, with darker or lighter dapples at the hindquarters. Some few were known to be white, and even fewer that looked so white they could be pale blue. The larian varied from palest blond to deep bronze. They tended to be more docile and were the preferred beast for riding purposes. The group was very lucky to have found a docile lloryk female to pull the wagon, preferable to the alternative, one of the less intelligent umberhulks. Sabian brought up the rear of the procession and managed to perch a book in front of him to read as he rode. Amethyst sat in the wagon, her legs dangling from the back. Her shoulders were slumped and boredom was prevalent in her demeanor. Oftentimes, Adrianna would glance over to see an expression on her face that asked, "What the Hells am I doing here with these strange people?"

After midday, Dartanyen announced they would soon be finding a place where they would rest for the night. "I know it's a little early to be stopping, but considering that we were riding all night, I feel that we need the extra rest."

Everyone concurred and they finally found a place hidden within a small stand of trees several farlo from the road. Everyone laid out their sleeping rolls for the night. No fire was lit, for they didn't care to attract any unwanted attention. They ate pack rations: bread, dried meat, cheese, and figs that

Volstagg provided before they left. For a time there was silence, everyone too busy eating to say much. And then, after the meal was packed away, they were too tired. The watch was set. First Zorg would sit, then Sabian, Tianna, and finally Amethyst. Adrianna, Armond, and Dartanyen were left out because they hadn't found a chance to rest the day before. Adrianna was grateful for the reprieve and fell asleep the moment her head hit the blankets.

Early the next morning she awoke to the sound of shouting. Groggily she opened her eyes and saw the sun had barely begun to rise over the distant horizon. She sat up and looked around the camp, her focus soon riveted on the scene at the far side of the space the group had occupied throughout the night. Amethyst stood there, her hands on her hips, a disgruntled expression on her face.

"What if someone, or some*thing,* had happened upon us while you were dozing? We could be murdered in our sleep. You know it is very possible that we are being followed, yet you allowed yourself to become derelict in your duty. Everyone's lives are in your hands while you are on watch!"

Amethyst rolled her eyes skyward. "Dartanyen, I already told you I was sorry. I didn't mean to fall asleep."

"Well, 'sorry' isn't good enough. Not when it's as important as something like this. Our lives are at stake out here, and we need everyone to be trustworthy. If you can't handle something as simple as the nightly watch, then maybe you should just go back home."

Amethyst narrowed her eyes, hiding the hurt that lurked there. Despite her golden complexion, Adrianna could see the smudge of color that suffused her cheeks. "Fine, I will do just that." The girl stomped over to her bedroll and began stuffing things away into her pack.

Tianna's voice cut through the air like a knife. "Dartanyen! Just who the Hells do you think you are? I didn't know we had voted you master and commander here." She stalked over to him, chestnut hair flying about her shoulders. "Lay off of the girl. She apologized for her mistake. What more do you want?"

Dartanyen's expression turned from anger to surprise.

"What really is the issue here?" she continued. "The fact that Amethyst made a mistake, or that she is young, much younger than you feel she should be in order to participate as a fully functioning member of this group?"

His expression shifted to bewilderment and then to chagrin. He regarded Tianna intently for a moment and then looked back to Amethyst, who continued to prepare her pack for the trip back to Sangrilak. Dartanyen hesitated a moment but then walked over to the girl. "Amethyst, wait. Maybe I was a little too harsh on you. Tianna is right, I *do* feel that you are too young to be traveling with us. But here you are." Dartanyen paused. "I will try to remember that all of this is very new to you if you try a little harder not take some things too lightly."

Amethyst looked up at Dartanyen. Her lips were pressed obstinately into a thin line. For a moment, Adrianna thought she would reject his apology, but then she shrugged. "All right. I can do that."

Dartanyen nodded and then turned to put his own bedroll away. He walked by Tianna on the way over to his belongings, patting her on the shoulder and nodding as he passed. Adrianna saw Tianna's mouth curve into a small smile before she, too, began to pack up. Adrianna watched the silent exchange, realizing that Dartanyen harbored no ill feelings towards Tianna, had even seemed to appreciate her input about the situation. Adrianna's respect for the faelin archer grew. It was a good leader who took the opinions of his group members to heart. And only a man who had the utmost confidence in himself would take the censure of another, and go so far as to amend his behaviors.

The group resumed their journey. Unfortunately for Adrianna, she was sore from the ride the day before, her muscles unaccustomed to being in the saddle for so many hours at a time. Before moving out, Tianna rubbed Adrianna's sore leg muscles with an ointment that suffused the areas with warmth, helping her to better deal with the ride. In spite of their aches, no one wanted to stop, the risk of being followed too high a possibility. The repercussions they would suffer if they were caught were much too hideous to contemplate.

The two women rode together for most of the day. Adrianna was glad Tianna seemed to have recovered from the shock of meeting Sydonnia, and subsequently discovering the message that had been sent to Sirion. Their easygoing friendship seemed to be back to normal. As they traveled, Tianna kept Adrianna's mind busy with natural lore. Tianna would point out a particular tree, bush, or flower, and tell her the name of the plant, its characteristics, and healing properties, if any. Adrianna appreciated the thoughtful gesture.

The group rode until dusk, and then they quickly found another place away from the road to set up camp. Once again, they lit no fire and ate only the pack rations provided.

At the end of the next day, the group would reach the town of Ferent. There, they would replenish their supplies and rest for the night. Then they would journey to the Tangir River. They would take a ferry across and then continue northeast to the city of Driscol. They would re-supply themselves again and rest up for the journey through the Ratik Pass, the safest path through the mountains. They would spend at least four days in the pass before emerging on the other side. Adrianna took it all in good stride, despite her aches. Everything was all so new since she had never journeyed to the mountains before. And each step they took northward brought her closer to her sister.

Dinim cursed eloquently in Cimmerean and slammed the book shut. *This is useless. There's no way I can concentrate with this!* The bumpy terrain rocked him about within the wagon. It was to the point where he needed to constantly catch himself lest he risk falling over even though he was sitting down. Dinim berated the wagon, but actually felt lucky to have found it. He'd met the owner in Ferent, and was happy the man was willing to take a passenger with him to his destination, which happened to be the same place Dinim needed to go. Grondor. The Wildrunners awaited him there.

Dinim didn't look forward to this meeting. His companions were most certainly irate about his behavior in the recent past. Even though it hadn't really been his behavior, but that of the doppelganger, he would have a jolly time trying to tell them that story. Sirion would be the most skeptical. To this day, even after all the moon cycles they had fought beside one another, Dinim had yet to win that man's trust. There was no love lost between them, for Dinim disliked Sirion almost as much as Sirion disliked him. So, it was much to his surprise to discover that it was Sirion who had made the decision to have him stay behind with Adrianna's group after they were rescued from the temple.

Only, it hadn't really been Dinim at all, but a daemon...

The wagon went over another bump and Dinim growled under his breath. Before he was captured, he had made an important discovery that would potentially increase his powers of spell-casting ten-fold. It could be pivotal in their fight against Gaknar. Spell reversal was a common practice among most spell-casters. It was something that could be achieved rather easily, if one knew how. With only a slight modification of the incantation, one could accomplish the opposite effect of what the original spell had intended. One day, while doing some research in the library in Sangrilak, Dinim found an old text. It was a strange book he'd thought mostly to be full of nonsense. However, as he read on, he began to see the power behind what was being stated.

Dinim had secreted the book within his robes and took it back to his chambers. It was there he had read the volume to completion. The most interesting thing he had read was the practice of casting a spell backwards. At first, Dinim thought the words had been erroneously scribed. Surely the writer was talking about spell reversal. But as he continued to read, Dinim realized he was wrong. The author was most definitely talking about casting a spell backwards, speaking the words of an incantation in the reverse order. Dinim was flabbergasted. He had never heard of such a thing.

That evening, Dinim had been captured by Gaknar's priests. He was imprisoned, and his identity stolen by the creature Ixitchitl. During his several weeks of incarceration, Dinim had a lot of time to think. He wondered about what he had learned from the book. As he worked to slowly increase the size of his prison, he was finally able to come across some scrolls and other books. He had practiced reading the passages backwards, and after a few days, was able to read backwards at a rather decent rate.

Finally, when Dinim had been able to defeat Ixitchitl, he took the scroll that imprisoned him and destroyed it. He helped the group to escape from the temple, and then left them to return to the library. He had found the book still resting on the shelf in the room he had inhabited there. He took the book and left the library. In the middle of the night, Dinim walked through the streets towards the Inn of the Hapless Cenloryan, the place where Adrianna said she would be. He kept to the shadows, not wanting to bring any attention to himself. He knew that someone would come in search of him, for Thane would not give him up easily. As he continued to walk, he started to hear whispers in the alley ahead. Very cautiously he crept closer, and when he was close enough to hear what was being said he stopped.

What Dinim heard surprised him. Adrianna... they were looking for Adrianna. Someone wanted her, and Dinim quickly discovered that it was Lord Thane. The young woman was in grave danger to be wanted by someone like Thane, a creature that was the epitome of evil and cruelty, no longer human or faelin, but Azmathous.

In spite of his extensive knowledge of most things arcane, Dinim knew little of the Azmathous. What he had told Adrianna about them during their days in hiding beneath the inn was most of what he had learned since he first heard of them. It seemed that the conditions had to be just right in the making of an Azmathous, and the death was particularly tortured. They were extremely powerful beings. Dinim guessed that their strength was at its highest only during certain times. At other times he suspected they were rather weak. It had to be the reason why Thane and his minions simply didn't remain within Sangrilak themselves instead of relying on others to give them information about Adrianna.

That weakness was the only thing that had saved Adrianna thus far. He could only hope that she and the others could continue to thwart Thane long enough for Dinim to learn more about the Azmathous, perhaps even find the best way to destroy them. Dinim was glad Sabian had agreed to accompany her group instead of accompanying him to Grondor. He felt that the benefit of having a more experienced spellcaster in their midst outweighed the fact that Sabian was being followed by someone. At least he hoped so.

The wagon went over yet another bump. Dinim cursed and rubbed his backside. It was going to be a long trip.

25 ENAREN CY593

On the sixth day out of Sangrilak, the group reached the foothills of the Ratik Mountain Range. In the distance, the taller swells were seen rising from among the hills, large and imposing. Adrianna and Amethyst stared in awe, for they had never been to the mountains before, much less traveled through them. For everyone else it was old hat.

The group veered true north, keeping the foothills to their east. The land was littered with bushes and scrub of all types, offering a break in the monotony of the steppes. Tianna had finally fully regained her former spirit. Much to Adrianna's happiness, the other woman sought her out the most. They rode side-by-side next to the wagon, often near the rear. Adrianna caught Amethyst listening in to their conversations a time or two, but her interaction tended to be minimal. It was the same with Sabian. Adrianna thought him to be a rather strange sort, keeping to himself most of the time. He seemed friendly enough, and participated in basic group functions. However, the man held an air of mystery about him, and Adrianna was left wondering exactly what he was about.

For a day more they traveled, stopping only for the midday meal. Then it began to rain. Cloaks were donned, hoods up for additional cover. The animals walked with heads lowered, their cloven feet tromping through mud puddles that splattered onto their fur, turning their undersides a dirty brown. The riders also had their heads down in misery, the rain seeping through all their layers of clothing. Nothing was dry. Even clothing items that had been tucked away deep within their packs became soaked. That night they slept on wet bedrolls, and no fire could be lit for lack of dry kindling.

The next day the rain ceased and the sun shone. Spirits lifted and clothing dried out. While scouting, Dartanyen noticed something and he raised his hand for Bussi to halt the wagon. He jumped down from his bronze larian and knelt at the ground near the animal's feet. "Trolag sign. They aren't far."

Tianna dismounted as well. "Yes, there is a small group, maybe about seven or eight of them. Most likely it's a family group. The males will be excessively protective. The trail continues down there." She pointed straight and a little to the left down the hill.

They sat there for a moment, deciding what course of action to take. "Let's skirt around the beasts, mayhap about a half zacrol berth to avoid them completely," Armond suggested.

Dartanyen nodded and Zorg grunted his approval. The group moved off their path and into the tall grasses and scrub. For most of the day they moved at a rapid pace, arcing about the main trail so as to avoid the trolags. After several more zacrol, they finally made their way back to the road. It was near nightfall when Dartanyen and Tianna searched the other side for signs of trolag passage. They found none.

The group decided to continue traveling until they reached Driscol. It would be late when they finally arrived, but they would have warm beds with a shelter over their heads. They ate as they rode– fresh bread, cheese, and produce purchased in Ferent. Sometime after sundown the weary group entered the city. They approached the first inn they noticed and were glad to discover rooms available for the night. Dartanyen paid the inn-keep for three: Tianna, Amethyst, and Adrianna would share one while the men split up into pairs to occupy the other two. Once reaching their room, Adrianna was happy to slump down onto one of the two beds. She would share it with Tianna. The two women had already discovered that Amethyst wasn't a good sleeping compan– ion; she was much too restless, and kicked out in the night. Adrianna shucked her outer garments and crawled beneath the blankets. Sleep was quick to come, and she was so tired that she dreamed no dreams.

Early the next morning, the group awoke later than usual, adhering to the strategy devised the evening before– to be well rested for their foray into the Ratik Pass. Quickly and efficiently they purchased the supplies they would need while traveling through the mountains. They were forced to sell the wagon because it would be too difficult to take within such rocky terrain. Instead of pulling the wagon, the extra lloryk would help carry any excess baggage.

A little before midday the group left Driscol, traveling north through the foothills that would lead them to the pass. The mountains rose precipitously before them and Adrianna stared in awe at their majesty. There was something about them, an aura of power and mystery she couldn't help but appreciate.

A few hours later, the pass lay before them, twining ever upwards. The riders dismounted, and they evenly distributed their belongings among the lloryk and larian. The group then started their ascent. The way was slow, the animals taking time to find proper purchase for their cloven hooves. For the rest of that day they moved, and as dusk approached, they camped among trees that rivaled those in the largest of Ansalarian forests. Adrianna felt comforted by them, their beauty and grandeur wonderful to behold. Tianna, Dartanyen, and Armond also seemed to find solace in the presence of the magnificent trees. However, Amethyst, Zorg, Bussi and Sabian just passed as though they hadn't a care in the world. To them, the trees were just like any others, except bigger.

The band awoke early the next day, hoping to use as much sunlight as possible since the going was slower than it had been across the plains. As they traveled, the journey became more laborious, the air thinning as they moved ever upwards. Meanwhile, the climate got cooler, prompting them to don warmer clothing. The terrain became rockier, and the tree cover sparser, giving more brush-like vegetation a chance to proliferate. Along with the trees, grass grew a bit less abundantly as the group climbed in altitude. To compensate for the loss of grazing, the burden beasts were awarded extra handfuls of grain and hartebeetles at midday while they rested. However, water was bountiful and flasks were refilled in the cool mountain streams they passed.

Everyone plodded doggedly onward. Dartanyen and Bussi walked in the front of the group with Tianna and Adrianna close behind. Tianna constantly searched the ground for evidence of anyone passing, yet, in spite of their caution, the monsters happened upon them without warning.

Out from behind the rocky outcroppings they emerged. The trolags were hideous creatures, standing about eight foot-lengths tall, much of their stooped bodies covered by dirty brown hair. Their eyes were purple with white pupils and jagged black teeth were revealed when one of them opened its mouth in a vicious snarl. They were smarter than most animals, but primal in their desire to maim and kill.

The lloryk and larian screamed and reared. Immediately, Bussi swung his battle-axe, Armond and Zorg close behind. Dartanyen sought to get hold of his bow while attempting to keep his larian from fleeing the scene. Astride Sethanon, Adrianna moved into the group's center, mentally reviewing her list of spells. A couple of them she disregarded as soon as they came to mind, fearing the radius of those spells would encompass her comrades. Frustration flared. *By the gods, how can I cast my stronger spells when my companions are in the way?*

Zorg and Armond engaged the enemy while Dartanyen shot one of the monsters with his bow, finally deciding to let his larian go. To Adrianna's dismay, Tianna also entered the fray. Her irritation grew. *How can she possibly help anyone with her healing skills if she is busy playing warrior?*

Adrianna glanced at Sabian as he finally made it to her side, the man assessing the situation with similar disgust. She shook her head and cursed, quieting Sethanon with a pat on his muzzle and focusing on one of the seven trolags. She cast her spell and watched the two missiles of magical energy unerringly strike their target. It startled Bussimot, almost giving his foe the upper hand when he inadvertently fell back. The halfen was quick to regain his feet and struck the massive forearm coming at him with his axe, nearly severing the limb from the body. The trolag howled and lashed out, knocking Bussi away with the other arm. The halfen sailed through the air and landed a few farlo away from his angry adversary. Stunned, he lay there for a moment before sitting up. Then, seeing the massive creature coming for him once again, he leaped back to his feet.

Meanwhile, Zorg made short work of another of the trolags, sheathing his huge, two-handed blade within its belly. The monster gurgled as it fell forward, blood bubbling from between sharp, uneven teeth. Zorg tried to move aside to avoid being squashed, but unable to retrieve his blade from the body quick enough, he was forced down as the creature fell until the pommel was twisted from his grip. The trolag fell heavily on its belly, forcing the blade deeper until it emerged out the other side, the once shiny blade covered with thick, dark blood.

Sabian completed his incantation and the ground rumbled ominously. Adrianna's eyes widened as the rumbling became more insistent. Then, from out of the ground a few farlo in front of them, five thick, black tentacles emerged. Rope-like, they sprang from the substrate, whipping about wildly. In horror, she watched as her companions scattered. Immediately, one of the tentacles grabbed hold of a nearby tree, tearing it from the ground and waving it about. Another of the tentacles found one of the trolags. The hairy creature wailed in terror and soon was gasping for breath. Slowly, the trolag was squeezed to death, and when it finally died, it hung limply from the tentacle, blood dripping from its open maw.

Meanwhile, two of the other tentacles gripped two more of the trolags, and while he was busy trying to extricate his sword from the fallen enemy, the last one found Zorg. As the sinuous form wrapped around the big warrior, Zorg cried out and clawed at the tentacle. Adrianna turned to Sabian. "Stop it! Stop the spell!"

Sabian's eyes grew wide. "I can't! The spell has to wind itself out!"

Adrianna cursed and then incanted the words to her own spell. Once more the glowing missiles found their intended target. They left deep lacerations in the tentacle holding Zorg, but not enough to sever it. Bussi rushed forward, swinging his axe. He chopped at the waving tentacle until it finally fell, releasing its death grip. Armond was instantly there, pulling the big warrior away from the other four tentacles. The mindless things continued to wave about, three of them holding the limp corpses of trolags, and one an upended tree.

Armond stepped aside as Tianna knelt beside Zorg. He struggled to breathe, and when she exposed his torso, it was already colored pale blue with extensive bruising. Adrianna suspected that several of his ribs were broken. Tianna gripped her pendant and placed her other hand on Zorg's belly. She then began to pray to her goddess.

The rest of the group wearily prepared the encampment. Sabian and Armond worked to clear away the dead while Amethyst collected weapons that had been used in the fight: Bussi's axe, Zorg's sword, Dartanyen's arrows, and her dagger. After a time, the tentacles receded back into the ground, leaving only holes as testimony they had ever been there. Meanwhile, it was discovered that Adrianna was the only one who had been able to keep her mount throughout the battle. All of the other lloryk and larian were nowhere to be seen.

The group continued to make camp while Dartanyen and Sabian decided to track down the beasts. Sethanon balked briefly as the two began to lead him away from the encampment, but Adrianna was able to calm him down. It was near sundown when the men returned, leading the missing animals. Adrianna rushed over to help and Dartanyen gave her a broad smile. They were fortunate, for each animal still carried their load.

The three companions led the beasts to the place Adrianna had prepared for them. While she started to unload each one, Dartanyen and Sabian went to rest before the fire. Amethyst came over and Adrianna showed her how to rub the beasts down. Once finished, each one was offered a few handfuls of hartebeetles and grain before the women stepped away to their bedrolls. Too tired to do anything but eat a few bites from her travel rations, Adrianna settled immediately into the furs. She saw the silhouette of Bussi outlined by the light of the moons as she fell into sleep, glad they were all still hale and whole after their encounter.

Stealthily, Sirion crept through the undergrowth. Every sense was on alert, and focused on his quarry. It a small group, extremely conspicuous since they made no effort to conceal their passage. There were eight of them, four men and four women. Three of them were faelin, four were human, and one a half-oroc. There was also a large corubis. Everything about this group was an anathema to him, and one person in particular was his antithesis in every nuance of the word.

Sirion was an Elvandaharian ranger, one who knew the natural world in a way few others could. When he worked, he was one with nature, every aspect of his body attuned to the environment around him. It was not so with his antagonist; the natural world shunned this man. As such, his double was easy to trail, for nature shrank away from him, exposing him like a merchant displays his wares in the market place.

For quite some time Sirion trailed the other group, Dramati at his side. In most ways they were just like the Wildrunners. They wore the same type of clothing, carried the same weaponry, had the same bodily physique, and even had the same faces. It was frustrating to know that many people thought these deranged individuals were the real Wildrunners. And when there was trouble, as there always was when these imitators were around, the Wildrunners were blamed for the crimes. This group was ruining the Wildrunners' good reputation, and they had to be stopped before any more innocent people could be hurt. Walking through that mirror all those moon cycles ago had been one of the worst mistakes the Wildrunners had ever made. The magic had duplicated them with an opposing alignment, creating a group of psychopaths that he was now forced to track down and eliminate.

Sirion stopped to take stock of his location. He frowned, immediately realizing he was moving in the direction from whence he'd come. Buried in his thoughts, he hadn't realized it when he'd made a complete circle. *Damnation! The imitators are heading towards the rest of the Wildrunners!* He vaulted onto Dramati's back and urged the corubis into a run. He had to reach his comrades before the other group.

They sprinted through the shrubs and tall grasses. Mentally he berated himself, knowing that he should have been paying better attention. Mayhap the Wildrunners were not that far behind and he would have a chance to warn them. He made a call, one he used as a distress signal, hoping the Wildrunners would hear it before the other group reached them.

But it was too late. Sirion smelled them before he saw them. Just as he reached the Wildrunners, the other group emerged from out of the surrounding foliage.

Dinim hid among the tall bushes, and watched the scene unfold. He had rejoined the Wildrunners just two days ago; without Master Tallachienan's help, he would have spent at least another two or three weeks on the road. Dinim never got the chance to find out why the Master had decided to break protocol and teleport him there, but the aid had saved everyone some much-needed time. Nothing that he'd been told about this renegade group prepared him for the scene before him. Many of them wore the same clothes, armor, and weapons as their duplicates. Dinim heard Dramati growling deep in his throat, the large corubis eying his twin menacingly. The other animal reciprocated the gesture and the two beasts circled one another.

Suddenly there was a flurry of activity. As the two corubis leaped at one another, the antithesis of Sorn rushed Sirion, slicing his scimitars across the left side of Sirion's back and arm. Sirion spun around, but before he could retaliate, Sorn was there, and he had captured the attention of anti-Sorn. Anti-Arn rushed at Laura, but he was lifted into the air and slammed into the nearest tree trunk. What seemed to be a gigantic, invisible hand was actually Triath's psionic ability– the rare power to manipulate the world with his mind. Anti-Arn rose from where he had fallen and came face-to-face with Arn. The two warriors drew their swords and began to fight. Anya loosed a couple of arrows at anti-Triath, only to have them freeze in mid-air and drop to the ground. Anya was then struck by an arrow herself and she spun around to find that it was her double. She pulled the arrow free from her arm and sprinted towards her look-alike.

It was then Dinim realized the members of each of the groups had located one another and paired off. It seemed that each person bore an inexplicable hatred for their 'twin' that caused him or her to automatically seek out the other. After another several moments passed, Dinim started to become confused. Sirion was fighting anti-Sirion, one of the Sorns had the other backed against a tree, and Naemmious was beating Naemmious into a bloody pulp. One of the Triaths was using his mental energy to attack his nemesis. The unfortunate recipient held his head in his hands, screaming from the mental lashing. Breesa, the only one without a double, seemed to be trying to create some kind of illusion, but she was having a difficult time of it. Arn was at a stalemate with Arn, neither man getting in a successful attack. At the edge of the battle scene, Laura was grappling with Laura, each woman clawing wildly at the other.

Dinim wiped the sweat from his brow. A fog began to roll in, and right away he could tell it was magic-made. *Damn, what do I do? Whatever it is, I have to act quickly!* He no longer knew who was who, and he was afraid that he would do more harm than good. *Perhaps I should break Breesa's concentration...*

By the time Dinim made his decision, the fog was thick. He incanted the words to his spell, and when he was finally about to cast it, the fog abruptly lifted. To his consternation, the people standing before him comprised only one group. He immediately diffused his spell, intuitively knowing it was the Wildrunners. He emerged from behind the shrubbery and approached. All were blood-stained, weary, and confused. The burning question was, where had the other group gone?

He slowly drifted into consciousness. It was a strange sensation, like something kept trying to pull him back into the thick blackness surrounding him. Sluggishly he made an attempt to move his arms and legs. The sound of the moan escaping his lips startled him into further wakefulness, and pain burgeoned in every joint of his body in the form of a relentless ache. As his mind slowly freed itself from slumber, it became more alert. He felt the cool air on his bare flesh, the hard ground beneath his prone body, and the abominable dryness of his parched throat.

The boy slowly opened his eyes. All he could perceive was inky blackness. Once more he tried to move and he realized his arms were bound behind his back. His muscles, sore from the abuse, wailed for freedom. Again he heard himself moan and it echoed within the enclosed space. He smelled the damp and mold, and dirt shifted beneath him as he tried to move. He strained his eyes trying to see something, anything, in the darkness.

By the goddess, where am I? Is this some kind of dream? I should be at home, at the temple, in my bed.

Like a river, fear coursed through him, giving him the impetus to struggle against his bonds. The ropes sawed into his wrists, making him want to struggle all the more, the fear of being unable to escape urging him on. His body protested as he made it onto his knees. Suddenly nauseous, he heaved, but all that emerged was a spattering of foul-smelling fluid. It burned his throat as it passed through, causing him to groan yet again.

How long he knelt there, he didn't know. After a while he stopped working at the ropes. Sticky blood had dribbled down to his palms, and the wounds around his wrists stung. His head hung until his chin touched his chest, and when he swallowed, his dry throat felt raw.

For some reason someone poisoned me, took me from my bed in the night, and brought me to this place. Will they ever return for me? Or will I stay here until I die of thirst?

Suddenly there was a loud noise, a grating sound that made him cringe. There was a click, and then a light so bright he clenched his lids tightly shut. There were footsteps, and they got closer until they paused before him. Silence reigned.

The boy struggled to open his eyes, and when the lids finally parted, a dark robed figure stood there in front of him. The light cast by the lantern had been muted so it was easier for him to see. He had yet to hear the person speak, or to see his face, but he knew the visitor was a man.

The figure stared down at him, a hood pulled over his head to conceal his face. The boy could feel the weight of the stare despite being unable to see the eyes. The visitor slowly placed the lantern at his feet and pulled the hood down from his head. The boy's gaze widened when he saw the misshapen face. But it wasn't so much the face, but bright, red eyes with slits for pupils. The cheekbones were prominent, and the brow-ridge. The nose was long and had a slight downward curve to the tip. The lips were a reddish purple, and were thin on the long face.

"Ssso, you have finally awakened."

The boy startled when he heard the sibilant voice, so accustomed to silence that the sound was loud to his ears. The strange man offered a ceramic bowl filled with what appeared to be water.

"Drink thisss. It will make you ssstronger."

The man put the bowl to his mouth and he drank greedily. The liquid was cool, and slightly sweet. It cascaded down his parched throat, bringing life back to his bruised body. After several swallows, the man withdrew the bowl.

193

"Not too much," he warned. "It could make you sssick if you drink too much all at oncsssse. I shall give you more later."

He watched the man place the half-emptied bowl beside the lantern. Then the man sat on the floor in front of him and removed a dagger from his belt. The boy's breath caught in his throat. The man leaned forward, took the rope that bound his feet, and swiftly cut it before sitting back and placing the weapon back into its sheath.

For a moment the boy just knelt there, regaining his equilibrium. Then he painfully maneuvered himself into a seated position. His mind whirled. He sensed the visitor was a being of great evil, someone who had conducted many acts of terror upon many people. Yet, the man had shown him some measure of kindness. The fear resurfaced. *What does this man want me for? What purpose could he possibly have for a young acolyte?*

His voice was barely a croak. "Wh... why have you brought me here?"

"I have sssome ssspecial planssss for you. You are a very important young man, dessserving of great honor. I would be the one who would bessstow that honor."

"Th... then why am I tied up? Why did you steal me from my home in the middle of the night?"

"You are bound becaussse I was afraid you would try to get away before I could exssssplain thingsss to you. Now that you know, and are a willing recssipient, I can remove them. My people took you in the middle of the night becaussse your Brothersss and Sssistersss would not underssstand. The priessthood hasss ssuch a limited outlook on thingsss. But sssoon you will have knowledge and power you can't begin to imagine."

The boy shook his head slowly with the ache in his neck. "But, why me? How am I so special?"

"It took my people a long time to find you. Of all of the many young men we came acrosss, only you have the traitsss we are looking for."

He gave a deep swallow. "And what would those be?"

"Goodnesss of heart and purity of sssoul." The man paused. "You alssso have a peacssefulness of ssspirit that very few posssesss. You will be the perfect recssipient."

The boy frowned. "What is it that I will be receiving?"

"Now, that is sssomething we will have to dissscusss at a later time. Come, food awaitsss usss outsssside." Once again, the man took his dagger and sliced through the bonds. The ropes fell away from his torn wrists. "Tsssk, tsssk. Look what you have gone and done. Thisss is just not accsseptable. We will have to treat thessse woundsss before we partake of the evening meal."

The boy nodded and slowly rose to his feet. The man was beside him, perhaps there just in case he should fall. He followed the man out of the small, dungeon-like room, his body aching with every step. His stomach rumbled; indeed, he was hungry. His fears had been eased somewhat, but not alleviated. There was something the man wasn't telling him.

"By the way, what isss your name?" The man turned just before they reached the stairs.

"Razlul. My name is Razlul."

THE WILDRUNNERS

Sirion and Dramati entered the small wood. They moved silently... stealthily. He had bid the rest of the Wildrunners to stay just outside the area. It was up to him to find out what they were up against, where Gaknar and his priests were located. The group would be close by if he got into any trouble, yet far enough away that they wouldn't hinder his reconnaissance mission.

It wasn't long before he found the dilapidated temple. For the most part, it was a heap of ancient stone that had been scoured by the elements. There was only a hint of where the entrance once stood, but now there was no need for one, time having taken it away.

Sirion crouched in the shadows. The sun would be setting within the hour. He needed to quickly assess the situation and get back to the group. There was evidence of activity, but no one was about. He frowned. *Where would everyone be at this time of the day, when most people are settling down to partake of the evening meal, winding down after the day's activities?*

Sirion slunk around within the trees surrounding the ruins. Once he reached the other side he stopped again. He saw no one. Dramati suddenly raised his head, the muscles in his body stiffening. The corubis' ears rotated at the hint of a sound Sirion could not yet detect. Sirion slightly turned his head and closed his eyes in concentration. Then he heard it, the sound of chanting emanating from within the ruined structure.

With a deepening frown, Sirion cautiously crept towards the rubble, and once amongst the fallen stones, he saw a staircase leading down beneath the surface. He could more clearly hear the chanting emanating from the bowels of the ruins. Motioning for Dramati to stay, he slowly made his way down. He was placing himself at risk, but he saw no other way. It was best if he found out what was going on now, by himself, instead of getting the rest of the group and taking the chance of being discovered.

Once at the bottom of the stairs, Sirion moved in the direction of the voices. It was dark, the torches few and far apart set in sconces along the dank walls. After a few moments he reached a doorway. The chanting had stopped, but this was where it had been coming from. When Sirion peered through the narrow crack of the doorway, the sight that met his eyes caused a rush of alarm to race through his body.

Oh gods, I have to get the Wildunners right away! The ceremony has begun and I don't know how much time we have left before this daemon is brought into Shandahar.

Once back outside, Sirion vaulted onto Dramati's back and they sped back towards the group. Warning them with one of the many calls he used to communicate while he was scouting, the Wildrunners were on the alert before he reached them. Within moments the group was on the move through the wood, quickly making their way to the fallen temple. Once there, Sirion led them to the staircase and they paused at the entrance. Triath motioned to Dinim and the mage stepped forward. Triath gave a nod and he stepped in behind Sirion as they made their way down. Once at the bottom, the rest of the group arrayed themselves behind.

In pairs they made their way through the corridor. Sorn and Laura walked behind Dinim and Sirion. Triath and Breesa were next, followed up by Anya and Arn. Naemmious brought up the rear. The group moved within the shadows cast by the flickering torchlight. The place was eerily silent, as though the air itself waited for what would happen next.

Dinim walked as a leader before the group. For the first time, he would be playing a key role as a member of the Wildrunners. He felt a charge in the air; magic was being called– used in some twisted plan devised by one of the most powerful sorcerers upon Shandahar. He prayed that they were not too late, but Sirion's depiction of the situation didn't give him much hope. When they reached the hall that Sirion described, Dinim had to steel himself before looking in on the scene.

The hall was enormous. Huge pillars were situated about the dimly lit chamber, a structural support bastion for the large vaulted ceiling. At the center there was a small congregation of about fifty dark robed priests. They surrounded a circle of what appeared to be five large mirrors. Each one stood at least ten foot-lengths in height, and all faced inward towards one another. Within the circle of mirrors sat a human boy. He was almost a man, having seen about fifteen summers. He was bound with his hands behind his back and he struggled, perspiration wetting his pale blond hair.

Near the periphery of the circle of mirrors stood a dark robed figure wielding a staff that identified him as Gaknar. Beside the sorcerer was another robed figure. His clothing was colored a deep crimson, a sharp contrast to the black ones worn by the other clerics and priests. *This man is not one of the fold. Why is he here?* The man began the incantation to his spell and Dinim felt a shock race through him. *Damnation! This man is a Dimensionalist! Those aren't just mirrors, but conduits that will aid the caster in the completion of his spell. They will be the portals through which the daemon emerges!*

Dread filled Dinim's chest as the Dimensionalist became surrounded by an array of floating runes that pulsated with a reddish glow. The man raised his arms high overhead and he felt another shift in energy. This was a powerful spell.

"No..." Dinim made to step forward only to be brought back by the restraining hand of Sirion at his sash. Then, from out of the darkness, came a wind. At first it was gentle, but it quickly turned into a gale that whipped the hair from around their faces, seeking to take their breaths away with its onslaught. It careened about them furiously, and with it was the voice of Gaknar raised into a cackling laugh of glee. Dinim shut his eyes, not wanting to believe they were too late. *Hellfire! Only a Dimensionalist can open a portal! That was why Gaknar wanted me. But Aasarak had foiled his attempts, and Gaknar was forced to find another. The Mehta had either bribed or threatened this other Dimensionalist in order to get the man to do his bidding.*

Brief moments later, the stone beneath their feet began to quake. A rumbling filled the air, accompanied by the aura of impending doom. The interior of each of the mirror-portals began to glow eerily yellow. The voice of the crimson spellcaster rose over the sound of the quake. When a second voice joined that of the first, Dinim opened his eyes and saw Gaknar reading from a large tome sitting on a pedestal within the circle.

The glow from within the mirror-portals became brighter and the air was rent by a shrill keening. Everyone put their hands over their ears, the wail so piercing it was painful. Then, from out of the portals emerged a pale mist. Slowly it crept outward, whirling and eddying about until it reached the center of the circle. The group was transfixed. Everyone realized they had come too late and that they were in terrible danger, but they couldn't leave, the awesome power culminating into something the world had never seen before.

The boy at the center of the circle stared with wide eyes at the mist whirling before him. For a moment he was still, but then he struggled at his bonds again, a desperation to his movements that hadn't been there before. Dinim felt someone bump into him from behind, and saw Sirion restraining Laura. The young cleric responded to the boy's fear and she wanted to go to him. She almost managed to call out, but Sirion put his hand over her mouth just in time.

The crimson-robed Dimensionalist stood aside, his work complete. By the expression on his face, all the man wished to do was to leave this place, escape from this evil daemon cult and its crazy master. The whirling mist became dense, veins of blue and gray permeating the mass. The boy knelt before it, wildly struggling against his bonds. The intensity of the gale increased, and Gaknar's voice rose high over the noise. He heard a name, and Dinim knew the daemon for whom Gaknar called– Tharizduun of Malchur, one of the most powerful daemons in the Nine Hells.

Suddenly, there was a thunderous *clap*, all the energy in the chamber coalescing at the center of the circle. The mist slammed into the boy, rocking him back onto his heels. His head was thrown back on his neck, and his mouth opened. He screamed in agony as he looked up into the darkness of the vaulted ceiling. His body took on a strange glow, as though a light shone from the inside. Then he seemed to grow, his body taking on mass that hadn't been there before. His legs and arms thickened with muscle, and his height increased. As he continued to scream, the voice began to deepen. The ropes binding his wrists broke, and his arms rose from his sides and extended upwards. Dinim stared in awe. Tharizduun had been released upon the world.

Fear coursed through him, followed by hopelessness and despair. What was done could not be undone. Unless... Dinim focused on the large, ancient tome sitting on its pedestal. If the spell that allowed Tharizduun to enter his host could be reversed...

Dinim shook his head. *No, it will be too risky. But then, what more have we to lose? With a greater daemon such as this one loosed upon the land, the world will be thrust into chaos. Hundreds and thousands of people will become slaves of Tharizduun and his worshippers.*

Dinim looked up and found Sirion regarding him intently. It seemed the usually impassive ranger was hoping he had some plan, no matter how flimsy, to make right what had just happened. Dinim knew that Sirion didn't really care for him all that much, that Sirion felt he was a charlatan, someone who just wanted to look good. But when Dinim turned to face the other man, his plan at the fore of his mind, it must have shown through his eyes. Sirion's countenance changed, an expression of determination altering his face. The ranger inclined his head to Dinim, almost as though to say, *I am at your service,* and a slight grin shaped his mouth.

"I need that book," Dinim whispered into the space between them. He focused on the tome in the distance and Sirion followed his gaze. The ranger then nodded almost imperceptibly. "I also need time, time enough to reopen those portals."

Sirion's eyes widened, almost as though to say, *You can do that?* But the expression was only momentary and he was nodding again. The two men turned back to the rest of the group. The Wildrunners stood there wearing expressions of defeat. Sirion made his way over to Sorn and the rogue nodded when he heard what Sirion had to say. Immediately Sorn slipped into the hall and crouched within the shadows cast by the huge columns.

"We need a distraction and..." Before Sirion could finish his sentence, Arn was at the ready. Then, without warning, the big man was whipping out his sword and running towards the congregated priests. "Arn! Arn, stop!"

"Damn fool!" Naemmious cursed and followed his friend into the hall.

With wide eyes, Anya, Laura, and Breesa just watched as the men raced towards certain demise. Dinim could see that Sirion was angry but he swiftly quelled the rising tide. Now was not the time; they needed all of their wits if they had any chance of succeeding. The surprised priests, their attention diverted from the ceremony, were preparing to face Arn and Naemmious. Sirion nodded to Dramati and the corubis bounded away in pursuit of Naemmious and Arn. Anya entered the hall and positioned herself behind one of the massive pillars. She readied her longbow, and within moments shot her first volley of arrows into the crowd of priests. Meanwhile, Laura remained positioned near the entrance, ready to help any of her comrades if they became injured in the fight. Breesa stayed nearby, waiting for a good opportunity to use her illusionary skills, and Triath did the same.

Taking advantage of the diversion, Dinim started to run towards the circle of portals. He would call upon the skills he'd learned under the guidance of his master and reopen them. It would take a lot of power, more than he had at his beck if he were to try it alone. This endeavor was a long shot, but he hadn't wanted to tell Sirion that. Besides, Dinim felt that Sirion already knew their chances of succeeding were low. Stating that fact out loud wouldn't have helped their cause any.

Dinim continued toward the scene. Tharizduun, within his new host body, still knelt on the floor, his arms wide in supplication. The portals were closed, but continued to exude a faint glow. It was testimony of the power present in order to open them and call forth into this world a being that, always before, had been unable to exist there. Now that such a daemon had been called and successfully placed into a host body, Shandahar was in dire peril.

Dinim had almost made it to the circle when a crimson shape collided into him. The two men fell in a tumble of arms, legs, and robes, each one cursing beneath his breath. But when Dinim realized who the man was, he was flooded with purpose. *Aha! Just the man I was hoping to meet!* Before the man could get to his feet, Dinim grabbed his arm. The man recoiled, the hood falling back from his face to reveal a Cimmerean. His purple eyes were wide with fear, and seeing Dinim, he cringed away. "Please, I didn't want to do it, I swear to you."

"Wait! I am a friend," said Dinim. "You and I, we can undo what has been done here!"

The man shook his head. "No, it is too late, much too late!"

"Please, help me rectify this horrible wrong. I swear it can be done!" Driven by desperation, Dinim told the lie with ease. He wasn't entirely certain it could be done, only *imagined* it could. Regardless, only together would he and this other Dimensionalist be able to reopen the portals. Then, with the tome Gaknar had used to facilitate Tharizduun's seizure of the host body, he would endeavor to evict the daemon from his newfound residence.

From all around came the sounds of the unfolding conflict: the battle calls of Arn and Naemmious, the angry declarations of the priests, the sickening sound of arrows penetrating flesh, and the cries of the wounded. But he ignored all of that, focusing instead on the man before him. The other mage regarded him in turn, probably wondering how he came to be there, at that moment, to thwart his escape.

"Please, we don't have much time."

Something in Dinim's voice must have turned the man to his favor because the Cimmerean nodded and helped him to his feet. Together, the men stepped behind the pillar closest to the circle of portals and momentarily discussed their plan. They readied their spell components and began their first incantation...

Pulling Stalker free from its harness, Sirion slipped deeper into the hall. He had no strategy, only that he would also try and maintain the diversion. He was especially concerned for Sorn, who needed to get precariously close to the enemy to retrieve the book. He locked his gaze onto Gaknar, hoping the sorcerer's attention would remain on the boy-daemon still located at the center of the faintly glowing circle. However, he quickly realized the sorcerer's eyes weren't on Tharizduun at all, but the comrades Sirion had just left behind.

Gaknar finished an incantation, his eyes riveted on Triath, Laura, and Breesa. A glowing red bean flew past and Sirion's heart skipped a beat. *Ah Hells...*

The blast of searing heat swept over him from behind, knocking him, face down, onto the hard, stone floor. It was hot, so terribly hot. He fought to breathe, but his companions suffered much, much worse. He'd been in their place before, other battles that often seemed like lifetimes ago because he'd seen so many.

The heat finally dissipated, and with his back smoldering from the *Flamesphere* spell, Sirion slowly stood and inspected his weapon. Protected beneath his body when he fell, Stalker was unscathed. He chanced a look behind him and saw his friends also rising. Everyone seemed to be functioning. Thrusting away his pain, he resolutely turned back to the enemy and moved towards Gaknar again. If needed, Laura would help the others. It was her calling, and she was good at it. If anyone could help them it was she.

Sirion approached the ceremonial area. The daemon-spawn within the circle had risen to his feet and was slowly taking in the scene. Sirion knelt into a crouch, Stalker gripped tightly in his palms. He looked about, swearing that he remembered seeing the Mehta of the Daemundai across the way just moments before. He felt a prickling along his scalp just before he sensed movement from behind. He swiveled on his heel to find himself face to face with the hideous visage of Gaknar.

Before Sirion could react, the sorcerer had him by the throat. The man was unnaturally strong, with physical power no ordinary mortal could possibly possess. Gaknar lifted him up from the floor and Sirion gasped for air. He groped ineffectually at the clawed hand and kicked out, hoping to connect with a leg. Gaknar just gave an evil leer before Sirion felt a prickling on his neck.

Oh gods, no...

Sirion's head suddenly began to spin and he felt a strange rush. Following it was pain, the type of agonizing pain he had felt only once before many years ago when his uncle had shredded his body and left him for dead. Hatred for Sydonnia swelled, lending him strength in spite of the agony. He swung his staff and Gaknar's smile turned into an expression of surprise followed by fury as Stalker struck. The sorcerer instantly released his throat and stumbled back, landing on the ground half a farlo away. The old book flew from Gaknar's arms and he screeched in rage. Gaknar flopped over onto his belly to go after it, but Sorn was already there. The rogue scooped the book up from the floor, and as quickly as he had come, was gone.

A terrifying scream echoed throughout the chamber and Sirion's attention was momentarily drawn to the circle. The red-robed mage grappled there with the boy-daemon. Tharizduun was strong, extremely strong, and the man didn't have a chance. Yet, the mage continued his efforts to divert the daemon's attention, buying time for Dinim to work his magic.

Sirion's gaze was drawn back to Gaknar as he rose from the ground. The Mehta focused on him with slitted, blood-red eyes. Sirion tried to back away, but his movements were sluggish, pain from the poison gripping his joints. The dark sorcerer lunged forward and struck him, razor-sharp claws burrowing into the flesh of his cheek. Sirion fell back and Gaknar was instantly upon him.

Once again, that clawed hand was around his throat, squeezing, slowly squeezing, until he could scarcely breathe. Sirion grasped Gaknar's arm, tried desperately to exert enough pressure so the sorcerer would release him. He heard his heart pounding, and his vision began to darken at the periphery, but not before he saw someone step up beside the Mehta.

Magical steel hissed through the air and it sliced through flesh and bone. The arm in his hands was suddenly heavy and the fingers around his throat spasmed. Sirion jerked it away and the arm dropped beside him. He instinctively put his own hands around his neck as he gulped for air, looking up to find Anya standing there, sword in hand, chest heaving.

A sudden piercing shriek made them slap their hands over their ears. Gaknar's mouth was open unnaturally wide, and he clutched the stump of his arm in his hand while the severed half of his forearm and hand writhed on the ground. The sound was frightening, something he could never have imagined.

He grabbed at Anya's leg and she tried to help him stand while continuing to hold the sword brandished at Gaknar. The cry abruptly ended as sorcerer's gaze returned to focus on him. In that instant, Sirion knew he was doomed.

His instincts shouted at him to run, but his body refused to obey. Gaknar slowly levitated from the ground, voluminous black robes fluttering in the rising winds. The Mehta began to chant and Sirion had the sickening feeling it was the words of a spell. Something gripped his boot at the ankle and he looked down to find it was the severed hand slowly crawling its way up his leg. With growing alarm, he tried to pull it off, but it dug its claws into the leather of his pants and continued towards his torso.

Dinim heard a scuffle behind him and tore his eyes off of the struggle between the red-robed mage and his adversary. He turned to find Sorn standing there, the pale flesh of his face beaded in sweat. Cradled in his arms was the tome he needed, a huge book with thick leather binding and red runic designs. Dinim clasped Sorn's shoulder as he took the volume, then knelt and riveted his attention onto the book.

I have to forget what's going on around me and concentrate. If this book can set Tharizduun free, it can imprison him again.

Dinim cast a *Detect Magic* spell, hoping there were no locks or traps on the book. He thought not, since Sorn had retrieved it so shortly after Gaknar had used it. Gaknar hadn't the chance to re-trap it, but it was possible the book had a spell that relocked it after every use. Much to his dismay, the book was both locked and trapped.

This is just great. Nothing ever comes easily. Dinim looked up, wracking his brain on how to proceed. *I could use Dispel Magic, but I hate to use the energy.* "Damnation..."

There was a tap on his shoulder and Dinim turned to find Sorn still standing there beside him. The half-Cimmerean nodded to the book. "Allow me to try." Sorn hunkered beside him and Dinim silently handed the volume back over to the other man. Sorn swept his hands over the leather binding and then the lock, examining the area closely. He then untied the drawstrings on the pouch at his waist and withdrew the tools of his trade. These were smaller than the usual, the mechanism on the book much smaller than those on the doors and chests that Sorn was most accustomed to dismantling. Quickly and efficiently, Sorn worked at the clip, carefully manipulating it so as not to set off the trap.

Meanwhile, time seemed to slow down. Dinim chanced a look around the hall, and horrified at the events unfolding before his eyes, he just watched in disbelief...

...the fall of the Wildrunners.

From across the chamber, Triath released the power of his mind, a force made from the air itself. Dinim watched it strike Gaknar where he hovered over Sirion and Anya, slamming the sorcerer to the ground. Arn and Naemmious, no longer backed-up by the lady archer, were struggling in their fight with the remaining priests. Dramati seemed to be holding his own for now, but Dinim wondered how long that would last. Laura and Breesa, who had strayed too close to the skirmish, found themselves also fighting the against the priests for their lives.

Dinim turned back to Sorn. The faelin continued his work, sweat beading his pale brow. Inwardly, Dinim urged the other man to make haste, feeling the time slipping away from them. His Dimensionalist companion continued to divert the attention of Tharizduun, but the fight was coming to a close. He was severely beaten and burned. His blood streaked the stone floor and had splattered the front of his robe, almost indistinguishable against the crimson backdrop. One arm was broken and hung limply at his side. Once more, Tharizduun's fist connected with the mage's face. Blood sprayed from his nose and splattered onto the naked boy-daemon. Tharizduun licked what landed on his lips, the corners of his mouth turning up into a malicious grin.

Despite the sounds of melee, Dinim heard the soft *clink* of metal. He looked back to find that Sorn had finally rid the tome of its trap and lock. Hurriedly, he opened the book, flipping to the table of contents. Not finding one, he turned to the prologue and began to speed read. That was one of the many fine skills he had learned from his master. Picking out the information he needed, Dinim flipped through the pages, quickly finding those he sought. He then settled himself for a more thorough perusal.

Unfortunately, time was of the essence. The Cimmerean mage wouldn't last much longer, and then there would be nothing to keep Tharizduun within the circle.

Gaknar was gone, suddenly and irrefutably gone, and the disembodied hand destroyed by Anya. The winds in the hall picked up once again, and despite his ignorance of most things arcane, Sirion was aware of the magically charged atmosphere. He saw Triath run across the hall to join Dinim and Sorn, who were situated not too far away from Anya and himself. Sirion felt a wave of relief. Sorn had been able to get the book to Dinim, and Triath was heading over to offer what protection he could.

Sirion nodded to his sister and the two quickly made their way to the others. When the two reached their comrades, Triath was in a state of intense concentration. Dinim was also focused on his work, pouring over the large tome in his lap. Sorn stood over his friends, at the ready in case of any trouble. Sirion frowned when he noticed that Laura and Breesa were not with them, and neither were Arn and Naemmious. Sirion was about to look for them when a disturbing sight walked towards them from within the circle of portals.

The boy-daemon's pale body was covered in blood. Sirion focused his gaze beyond and saw the form of a man crumpled on the ground; the crimson-robed mage had finally fallen.

Without thinking of the consequences, Sirion stepped forward to meet Tharizduun. Looking into the blue eyes, Sirion could see the daemon within, the unwavering gaze murderous. As Tharizduun was about to step beyond the bounds of the circle, Sirion stepped within, holding Stalker before him. With all his might, Sirion then swung the staff.

Without flinching, the boy-daemon deflected the weapon. Sirion watched the staff spin out of his grip to land several farlo away. The power behind that parry was enormous, yet he knew that he couldn't allow Tharizduun to leave the circle. Sirion lunged and they grappled. His hands slid over blood slicked skin that was so warm, some would call it hot. The struggle was only momentary. Before he realized what was happening, Sirion was lifted from his feet. He flew through the air and collided into someone.

They fell together, the hardness of the floor knocking the breath from his chest and bruising his backside. He struggled to right himself and found Anya doing the same. Sirion looked for Tharizduun and his heart sank. The daemon was already walking beyond the circle. Tharizduun's strength was like nothing Sirion had felt before, and getting him back inside of it would be a feat.

Unimpeded, Tharizduun strode towards Dinim and Sorn. Time seemed to slow and both men just stared through wide eyes. *By the gods, if Tharizduun reaches Dinim, this is over and we have lost.* The daemon took another step, and another. Then he stopped. Tharizduun frowned and splayed his hands over an invisible surface. Sirion let out a breath. Until then hadn't realized he'd been holding it.

Triath pitched his voice to reach everyone's ears. "This area is protected. I don't know how long I can hold the shell, but for now we are safe." His face showed traces of continued concentration, but other than that, he seemed unaffected by what it was costing him to hold the protective wall.

Worried about Arn, Naemmious, Laura and Breesa, Sirion took a moment to glance towards the area where the rest of the group had been fighting the priests. He saw Dramati sniffing over the fallen bodies, and close by was Laura crouching over the prone form of Arn, Naemmious standing over them protectively, Breesa at his side. Alarm swept through him. "Triath, the others look like they are in trouble."

Triath looked where Sirion indicated and shook his head. "There's nothing I can do to help them. No one may enter the shell if they were not already within the area of effect when I erected it. All my energy and concentration has to remain on this or it will dissipate." His expression became pained. "I'm sorry."

Sirion shook his head. "Don't be. You are doing great just as you are. I'll take care of it."

Triath frowned. "What are you going to do? If you leave, you can't get back in!"

Sirion spied Stalker lying a few farlo away. He then glanced over to where Dinim and Sorn sat pouring over the book. *For now, they will be protected by Triath's power...*

"Sirion, stop!"

Ignoring Triath, Sirion stepped beyond the boundaries of the shell. He ran over to Stalker, swept the weapon into his hands, and rushed over to the rest of the Wildrunners. "Sirion!" Anya's voice sounded behind him and grinned to himself. He should have known she would follow.

Sirion approached and heard the agitated protestations of Arn. "Let me up already! I'm going to be fine!" The big man swatted at Laura's hands as he struggled to sit up.

Laura's eyes flashed. "No, you're not! That potion has only restored a fraction of your vitality. You're allowing it to give you a false sense of security!"

"What do you want me to do? Keep lying here like a dead fish?"

"No, I want you to be careful this time. We are easy targets out here and we need to get back to the others."

Before Sirion could speak, Dramati had bounded over to greet him. Through their link, he felt his companion's relief and he ran his hands through the thick fur around the corubis' neck. "Anya and I are here to help."

Naemmious grinned. "It's good to see a friendly face."

"I bet. How are you holding up?" By the look on the half-oroc's face, Sirion had his answer, but Naemmious wasn't about to let on to Laura about his true condition, not with Arn so injured. "Better than Arn."

Arn frowned and rose to his feet. "Shut your gob, Naemmious."

"Both of you be quiet!" hissed Anya. "This isn't the time or place. Let's just get back to the others."

Suddenly an ominous sound emanated from where he and Anya had come. Sirion turned in place and was just in time to see a sheet of flame shroud Triath's protective shell. For a few moments the fire burned before it began to dic without anything to feed it. *Ah Hells! I hope Dinim is ready.*

Dinim's heart pounded a wild staccato rhythm against his ribs. Instinct urged him to flee with the tome and hide somewhere removed from his companions. It meant leaving the sanctuary of Triath's shell, but it would ultimately fall to the daemon one way or another, and he didn't want to be there to experience it. The agony in Triath's scream when the last spell hit indicated the man could withstand the onslaught only so much longer before he buckled.

Dinim leaned into Sorn and hurriedly whispered his intent. *Tharizduun is concentrating on another spell, and now could be my last chance!* Clutching the book tightly beneath one arm, he fled into the darkness beyond the shell, stopping only when he reached the farthest mirror portal. He crouched behind it and caught his breath, then sat, cross-legged, on the ground. He placed the tome before him, opening it once more to the appropriate page. He reached into his components pouch and pulled out a smaller bag. He opened it and poured the contents into his hand.

Dinim muttered the words from the book as he poured the crystal sand from his palm onto the ground, creating a circle around himself. The sand glowed eerily green and the grains melted together into a liquid flowing mass. Dinim held his fore and middle fingers into the molten crystal and then inscribed runic symbols into the air. Concentrating deeply, he sought to remember the words he'd read from the tome. He cringed to think what could happen if he misspoke even a single word.

Sirion saw Tharizduun prepare for another assault. He hoped that Triath could sustain it for a while longer, for it was the diversion Dinim needed to continue his work. Tharizduun seemed to be unaware of the mage's departure, too busy concentrating on destroying the barrier.

Sirion felt the hairs on the back of his neck rise in warning. Abruptly remembering that he and Anya had never found the body of Gaknar after their last encounter, he turned in place, battle-ready with Stalker poised before him. A few farlo away he saw the sorcerer, one clawed hand held before him as he cast a spell, his few remaining priests arrayed behind him.

Sirion pitched his voice for everyone to hear, "'Ware!"

The group was ready. Naemmious and Arn spun around, swords drawn, and Anya shot her first volley of arrows. The projectiles fell away as they touched the sorcerer's robes and Anya cursed eloquently in Hinterlic. Sirion joined Naemmious and Arn in their rush towards the priests, but barely a moment later, the spell was loosed and the energies coalesced into several small bolts of lightning that arced outward from Gaknar's fingertips. Sirion attempted to dodge the incoming missiles, but the bolts passed through his body. His muscles contracted spasmodically before blackness overwhelmed him.

Sirion groaned and opened his eyes to find himself lying on the ground. A concussive blast shook the area and he groggily lifted his head to see a shower of fiery meteors striking the protective surface of the shell. Triath's agonizing screams could be heard from within as he struggled to hold it. Sirion scrambled to his feet, wincing in pain. Beside him, Anya also rose, as well as Naemmious and Laura. Neither Arn nor Breesa moved from their prone positions.

Laura rushed over to Breesa, turning the girl over onto her back. She leaned over her and placed an ear to the girl's mouth before putting her fingers to Breesa's neck. A strangled cry emerged from Laura's throat and she covered her face with her hands.

"He's dead."

Sirion turned to the sound of Naemmious' voice. The half oroc knelt at Arn's side, eyes wide with disbelief. Sirion's head spun. *No, this can't be happening. My friends are dying, and there's nothing I can do about it!* An ache spread through his chest and moved up to his throat. He quelled the urge to release his grief, to scream his anger at the injustice of it.

Suddenly there was a strange sound. It was almost inaudible, but Dramati perceived it with no trouble, his head turning in the direction of Triath, Sorn, and Dinim. Sirion followed suit and the sight that met his eyes almost stilled his heart in his chest. The shell was down and Triath knelt on the ground, his head in his hands.

Laura gave a cry from behind the hand covering her face as Gaknar strode, unimpeded, towards Triath. Meanwhile, Tharizduun, realizing the tome wasn't there, made his way in the direction Dinim had gone.

Dinim inscribed the fourth rune in the air before him, the eerie glow turning from green to golden. It shed a greater light and he narrowed his eyes to filter it out as he inscribed the rest. Finally, he was finished and his voice faded away. Nine golden runes glowed in the space before him, shimmering and wavering with mystical energy. He took a deep breath, knowing what he needed to do next. Dinim needed to undo what Gaknar had done. He would have to start from the end and make his way to the beginning– every word, every gesture, every nuance.

Dinim closed his eyes and raised his arms upward as though beseeching the heavens. Other casters had suffered dire consequences doing what he now attempted– to cast a spell backwards. He hoped that Sorn would come through to tell Triath the role he would have to play. And he hoped they would get to him before Tharizdune did.

I'm too late... too late! Sirion ran towards Triath, hoping, praying he could stop the inevitable. Gaknar stood over his friend, a fiendishly long dagger in his grip. *Gods, no...*

Sorn suddenly emerged from the shadows cast by the nearest portal. He threw himself at Gaknar and landed on his back, stabbing downward with his own dagger. The cult-master screamed, arching backward to dislodge Sorn.

Triath scrambled out of the way, making it to his feet and running in the direction Tharizduun had taken to find Dinim. Sorn pulled his dagger from Gaknar's back and stabbed again. The sorcerer screamed once more and fell. Sorn leaped away before he could be pinned by the body, and landed in a crouch.

Leaving Sorn to deal with Gaknar, and hoping the rest of the group had followed to help, Sirion rushed after Tharizduun. It wasn't long before he saw Dinim, the Cimmerean encircled within a ring of molten gold. His rich voice was raised in an incantation. Strange words passed from between Dinim's lips, the words of ancient magic. The air felt unusually charged, the presence of magic so strong that even someone like him, who wasn't a Talent, could feel it.

Then, from out of the darkness, the form of the boy-daemon appeared.

"No!" Sirion reached out as though to stop what was about to happen, his legs carrying him just outside of the glowing circle of portals. Behind him, he heard the muttered voices of Anya, Naemmious, Sorn, and Laura. Everything seemed to happen all at once, and everyone acted on desperate impulse– a last attempt at survival.

Dinim finished his final incantation. Winds swept through the chamber-the winds of powerful magic. It was only then he realized Triath was there at his side, the man's eyes glazed with concentration. Tharizduun was there as well, approaching ever closer...

Suddenly the daemon was thrown back, back, back, until he was once more within the circle of the portals. In shock, the daemon looked up from his place on the floor. Then, realizing what had happened and where he was, Tharizduun quickly jumped to his feet...

But it was too late. The runes swept forward and circled the daemon with sparkling light. Faster and faster they spun until, from the host body, began to emerge the same mist the group had seen when they had first entered the hall. Tharizduun shrieked in rage. He struggled to retain custody of his host, clinging to it with all of his strength. Then, realizing the futility, he began to cast his own spell. Dinim realized the imminent danger, but he was in no position to do anything about it. So much raw energy cavorted about the place already, certain to cause a misfire. He hoped it wouldn't have an effect greater than the original spell.

Transfixed, Dinim watched as the thick mist was pulled within the portals leading back to the Hell from which it had come. Just before the boy slumped to the ground, Tharizduun's spell was discharged. Dinim felt it right away, the miscast spell interacting with the charged energies already eddying haphazardly about within the circle. He then felt something else– the atmosphere abruptly activating again. He looked in the direction of the new disturbance to find Gaknar at the periphery of the circle. He was casting a spell at one of the portals, most likely hoping to destroy it and forestall Tharizduun's departure. Alarm swept through Dinim and he screamed into the resulting maelstrom, *"You stupid fool!"*

A small vortex appeared within the center of the circle and the light emanating from the portals went out. The mist was gone, Tharizduun having been pulled back into the Hells. However, the wild magic spiraling out of control created a light of its own, making it just as easy to see. It was almost as though the sun's rays had found a way to this place under the ground.

Sirion watched in horrified fascination as Gaknar's spell hit the eddying mass of energy. The spells spun and collided, creating an electrical cloud. It swiftly enveloped Gaknar and his gnarled body disintegrated upon contact. The unharnessed magical energy moved towards the vortex, somehow attracted to it, and the vortex increased in size and intensity. Instinctively, everyone lowered themselves near the ground, seeking protection.

A piercing shriek encompassed the scene and the spiraling cloud of magical energy reacted with the vortex. An arm-like projection emerged from the twisting mass, reaching randomly. Before he could react, the beam caught Sirion full-force, enveloping him within its intense energy. The magic washed over him and he screamed. The pain was excruciating, and every muscle in his body contracted at once. The magic coursed through him, touched those deepest parts of him he kept locked away. It touched the essence of him... that untamed, wild part of him he had developed over the past several decades. It touched his animal nature and let it come forth. He felt himself changing, his physical form altering. The pain ripped through him and his mind could no longer comprehend, could no longer endure, the torment.

THE SHAKE

It was before dawn. Adrianna lay there, silently wondering what had awakened her at such an early hour. She looked all around without rising and saw the rest of the group still sleeping with the exception of Armond, who was taking the final watch. She regarded him where he stood at the edge of the encampment. He seemed to have a tense expectancy about him, almost as though he sensed something. She frowned and crawled out from beneath her bedfurs, thinking to approach him...

Then the world began to shake.

Adrianna screamed and cowered close to the ground. The trees shimmied and a few leaves showered down. Rocks shifted in their places and the mountains groaned. *Oh gods, what's happening? Is the world ending?* She heard Tianna call out in a fear-filled voice and Armond had dropped to a crouch. Dartanyen stumbled over to join him and both men looked up into the dark sky. Just as she followed their gaze, the shaking abruptly ceased.

By the wan light cast by Shandahar's third moon, Adrianna saw something swirling within the darkness of the heavens. She squinted her eyes and could barely see what had, at first, been imperceptible. It was color. Waves of rippling, glowing color of every hue eddied and flowed within the darkness above.

Adrianna clutched at the ground again as the tremors began anew. She heard Bussi and Amethyst curse from their bedrolls on the other side of the firepit behind her, and Zorg had approached to stand with Armond and Dartanyen. The shaking continued, and unlike the last time, the tremors didn't cease. Instead, they became more intense with each passing moment. The trees shook and bracnches and leaves showered down. All about them the rocks and boulders tumbled from their moorings and fell around them.

Louder and louder the quaking became, and the mountains crashed all around them in a deafening symphony. Adrianna just huddled there on the furs, feeling the movement of the ground beneath her and thinking it would be torn asunder. She felt the presence of magic, and within the depths of her mind, there were whispers of momentous events that could change the future of the world forever. She heard someone screaming and belatedly realized it was her own voice before blackness claimed her.

Adrianna awoke to find Tianna kneeling over her, the priestess' cool hands on her face and forehead. In the light of a new dawn Armond and Dartanyen spoke in excited tones and Amethyst and Zorg stood close by in the near distance. She looked up into the sky and saw nothing out of the ordinary. "What happened to–"

"I was worried for you." Tianna's voice interrupted her. "I heard you screaming one moment, and then suddenly you stopped. I ran over here to find you unconscious. Are you all right?"

She frowned. "I think so. Before blacking out, I remember feeling a pressure right here." Adrianna rubbed her temples and vaguely recalled sensing the flow of great magic accompanied by something sinister... "The world was shaking."

Tianna nodded.

"Is everyone accounted for?"

"Yes, we were lucky that only a few boulders were dislodged." Tianna pointed to the large rocks near the encampment.

Adrianna looked where she indicated and tried to rise, but quickly lay back down and moaned. "Ahh! My head aches."

Tianna placed her fingers over her skull, and after feeling around for a moment, whispered the words to a brief prayer. Adrianna closed her eyes and allowed the healing magic to rush through her. "Thank you."

Tianna smiled and nodded, stepping away to help the rest of the group prepare for travel. Adrianna took a while to rest, but it wasn't long before she was loading Sethanon. Dartanyen had already told them that the next couple of days would be the most difficult, for they would be traveling through a stretch of the pass that was known to be the rockiest. It wasn't uncommon for a lloryk or larian to lose footing and twist an ankle or wrench a knee. They would need to take care and travel slowly so as to save their animals, and quite possibly themselves.

Finally, they were on the move. Dartanyen took the lead with Tianna following close behind, then Zorg and Armond. Adrianna noticed Zorg still moved about with some stiffness after his encounter with Sabian's spell. She cast a glance in the mage's direction and narrowed her eyes. *His spell was strange; I've never seen anything quite like it before. It was powerful, too powerful for that situation. Indeed, there had been an abundance of trolags, but not so many we couldn't have persevered with brawn alone if need be. Sabian may have been trying to help, but instead he had put everyone at greater risk. He's much older, and a senior journeyman. He should know better.*

By midday the trail had changed. Over the past days the trees had been gradually thinning, but now they were almost entirely gone. Before them was a narrow defile upon which only two animals could travel abreast. Along each side of the trail were walls comprised of huge rocks, some of them sheer and others craggy. Along the path there were smaller rocks that shifted under their feet as they walked and the lloryk and larian picked their way carefully along.

Armond pitched his voice for all to hear. "The force of the shake must have caused the steep slopes to crumble. It's why the path is so hazardous."

Dartanyen furrowed his brows. "If these rocks can fall, so can others."

Armond nodded. "Maybe, but I believe that as long as the ground is quiet, the mountains won't fall."

The band traveled a while longer before Dartanyen's fear came to pass. It wasn't nearly as powerful as the quake from that morning, but it was enough. The world shook and the mountains responded. Loose rock and debris tumbled down the steep slopes as people, lloryk, and larian scattered. Adrianna released Sethanon's ropes and ran towards the left slope, squeezing herself within a narrow crevasse before the larger boulders fell.

The avalanche was over a few moments after the shaking stopped. When the dust cleared, Adrianna stepped out of her haven to find the path altered. She stumbled about in the debris until she came across the rest of the group. They were all a bit worse for wear, bruised from falling rock and cut from falling over the precarious terrain. Bussimot was missing for a while but finally found pinned beneath a pile of rock. Sabian and Dartanyen worked to free him while Tianna mended wounds on Armond and Amethyst.

The group slowly set up camp. Dartanyen and Adrianna gathered the lloryk and larian they found nearby while Tianna worked her healing magic on Bussimot. Three of the burden beasts were missing, but no one wanted to go in search of them for fear they would experience another shake without the rest of the group nearby. They ate from the food rations they had brought, and when darkness approached, Tianna was the first to fall onto her bedroll, asleep before anyone could bring her a portion of the meal.

All through the night the ground grumbled and trembled. It was the same the following day and night. Fortunately, only small pebbles and dust responded to the movement. Everyone got very little rest, but they trudged laboriously onward. They were fortunate to find two of their missing animals alive. The third was found crushed beneath a boulder. They were able to move it and salvaged what they could from the travel pack it had been carrying. They also took the opportunity to partake of the meat. Rations would soon get low, especially at the rate they were traveling. Dartanyen built a fire and Armond cut into the larian. They ate well that night and the next morning before they were forced to move on.

Adrianna sneezed and it misted into the early morning air. Her head throbbed and her throat was sore. She growled under her breath at the inconvenience. Maybe it was the change in climate and altitude when they climbed the mountain, or perhaps a result of physical duress and lack of sleep. Maybe it was all of those things, but at some point, she'd managed to fall ill.

The day progressed and she was forced to sit astride when fever made her too tired to walk. Sethanon's task was ten times greater, but she saw no other way and gave the lloryk loose rein to move of his own accord with the rest of the group. Tianna gave her some herbal tea to drink, but it was all the healer could do to help; her goddess-given healing powers only encompassed illness or injury that was of the unnatural variety.

In spite of her illness, Adrianna was the first to hear the tremor emanating from deep within the ground. She looked up, listening and hoping it wouldn't get worse. After a moment she saw Dartanyen and Armond also responding to the quake, one that she instinctively realized wouldn't dwindle away like the others. "Another shake!" Dartanyen shouted. "'Ware and take cover!"

Once again, the group scattered as the mountains trembled all around them. This time Adrianna saw no refuge. She remained astride Sethanon and did her best to dodge the rocky debris tumbling down the slopes, hoping his animal instincts would save them. She closed her eyes and clutched his thick mane, pressing her cheek to his sweaty neck. Legs wrapped tightly about his barrel, she felt his muscles contract and relax as he maneuvered them between missiles of flying rock. The lloryk grunted as they struck him, and she cringed when they hit her unprotected back. Fear kept her from opening her eyes to see how the others fared, and she prayed a litany in her mind.

Finally, the shaking stopped. The rock ceased falling, and in the near silence, Sethanon's heavy breathing filled her ears. She coughed on the dusty air and covered her nose and mouth with the end of her cloak. She remained slumped over Sethanon's back for several moments until she saw Dartanyen and his larian picking their way among the piles of rock. She urged her lloryk over to see him standing over the still form of a larian half buried in debris. Her eyes widened in dread when she recognized it as the pale beast Tianna rode.

Dartanyen scanned the area and called out for the others. A faint reply came from their left and it wasn't long before Amethyst and Armond made their way over. Zorg and Bussimot approached from the other side a while later, but their worries increased when Tianna never appeared from the rubble, and neither did Sabian.

The group branched out and began to search, calling out for Tianna and Sabian as they walked among the rocks. They received no reply from either one, but they found the body of Zorg's lloryk not far from Tianna's larian. The other animals had managed to keep themselves unharmed with the exception of Armond's bronze larian. It had injured its leg, but they hoped some healing could be offered to the poor beast.

Finally, they found Tianna, the sound of her weak voice giving away her location. Zorg gently picked her up and carried her to a place clear of rubble. Adrianna stayed with her as the men and Amethyst went in search of

Sabian. Tianna had a few bruised ribs, and her ankle was twisted. In broken sentences, she instructed Adrianna to bind the ankle. It hurt her to breathe, much less speak, and with each movement, she gave a pathetic moan. Adrianna was afraid the ribs might be more than just bruised, but the healer remained adamant that Adrianna bind her ankle.

Adrianna had just finished when Zorg carried over the limp form of Sabian. The mage's face was paler than usual, and his breathing shallow. He had blood crusted over his right temple, and the area all around it was discolored. "I found 'im buried beneath a few layers of rock," said Zorg as he lay Sabian gently on the ground near Tianna.

The healer rose to tend him, but Adrianna pushed her back down. "No, you haven't the strength!"

"But I must! He needs me!"

Adrianna looked up at Dartanyen indecisively. After a moment of thought, he nodded. Adrianna released Tianna and the woman crawled over to Sabian. She slowly rose to her knees and placed her hands on his head. He looked at her out of heavy-lidded eyes full of pain and weariness. Tianna closed her eyes and remained in that position for a long time. Finally, with a deep sigh, the priestess dropped her hands to her sides and slumped her shoulders. Adrianna knelt down beside her. "What is it?"

"I can't do it. I just can't do it."

Adrianna wrapped her arms around her friend and held her close, her tone soothing. "It's all right. You're just weak. You need rest to get strong again."

Tianna continued talking as though she hadn't heard, "What kind of healer am I if I can't help those who need me?"

Adrianna looked at Sabian. He seemed a little better than before, albeit pasty pale. She tugged at Tianna's elbow. "Come, let me give you some tea to help warm you." She supported a limping Tianna to the small, nearby fire that Dartanyen had built with bits of sticks and twigs he'd found lying about. Once Tianna was settled, she returned to Sabian. His eyes were closed in sleep. With Dartanyen's help, she brought the mage to his bedroll. She covered him with a thick blanket, wrapping it all around and under him to keep out the cold.

The group rested there for the remainder of the day and through the night. In the morning they decided to move on, knowing they needed to get themselves out of the perilous corridor of rock as soon as possible. Zorg distributed the loads from Sethanon and the blue lloryk mare equally onto the other larian. Tianna would ride Sethanon while Sabian was loosely strapped to the blue. Despite her illness, Adrianna walked. She refused to ride Sethanon with Tianna, afraid her added weight would cause him to misstep on the treacherous ground.

They moved slowly and carefully, hoping to be out of the pass without any more mishap. Finally, the path began to slope downwards, signaling they had reached the final stretch of their journey. The remaining lloryk and larian walked with lowered heads. Their once shiny coats were covered with layers of dust and the insides of their nostrils were red with irritation. Their tri-cloven hooves were beginning to crack with the constant stress of walking on such hard debris-laden surfaces, and it would take several moon cycles for them to heal.

Adrianna only vaguely glanced around as she walked. It was difficult for her to remain alert when she was so tired. She was certain it was the same with everyone else. She noticed a cave along the path to their left. It appeared like it might have been hidden before the quakes came. Her nose picked up a strange, unfamiliar odor as they passed, and the hairs at the back of her neck began to prickle. "Dart..."

Bearing clubs, battle-axes, and fierce battle cries, the oorgs rushed towards them from the mouth of the cave. They were tall and muscular, all standing at least a foot-length taller than Zorg. They wore animal hides and pieces of metal that served as armor and their hair was thick and black, hanging in ropes to their shoulders and down their backs. Greenish brown flesh sported wart-like bumps, and the lower jaw protruded to give them a menacing appearance. The largest of the four oorgs pulled his green lips back to display gruesome yellowed canines.

The burden beasts pulled at their ropes and reared. Sabian slid from the blue lloryk's back and Adrianna struggled to retain a hold on Sethanon to keep Tianna astride. Dartanyen, Armond, Zorg, and Bussi leaped into action. Zorg drew his massive blade just as the largest of the four oorgs was upon him. Dartanyen had nocked an arrow and was shooting it quicker than Adrianna thought possible. Cursing her lack of strength and her inability to soothe Sethanon, she unceremoniously pulled Tianna down to the ground and let the lloryk go. He galloped after the other animals down the path.

Adrianna quickly scanned the area, fighting the fear that arose. These creatures could be powerful adversaries, especially since the group had been battered so badly by the shakes. Amethyst threw a dagger at the oorg Dartanyen shot with his arrow, and Bussimot ducked beneath another one, savagely slicing between its legs. Armond faced off with a third oorg, swinging his blades in an awesome display of skill. Adrianna closed her eyes, seeking to rid her mind of the surrounding distraction– the shouts of her comrades, the impact of metal against metal, and the snarling of the savages. She brought the magic to her, caressed the strands of energy, manipulated it, and bent it to her will. It answered her call, flowing to her without hesitation, and then waited for her to use it, to guide it.

A stream of fire erupted from her fingertips, striking the oorg leader where he stood hunched over the prone form of Zorg. The monster wailed and clutched his chest, swinging around crazily and brandishing his rusty blade. Dartanyen put an arrow into him, followed closely by another. The thing fell to the ground and writhed there for a few moments before he died.

Shaking, Adrianna stood there, watching as Time seemed to slow. She saw Bussimot hit the ground after being thrown by his adversary, and Amethyst was struck down by her own shortsword as the enemy turned it against her after pulling it from her hand. Armond was the only one having any luck. She noticed his lips moving, and for a moment it sounded like he was singing. The tall faelin rushed at his opponent, his swords glowing pale red. The oorg gave an agonized scream as the blades cut into him and the stink of scorched flesh assaulted her senses.

Adrianna blinked, her mind making its conclusion much slower than it should. Armond was no ordinary swordsman. He was a Talent.

Adrianna took a deep breath and suddenly things were back to normal. She put a hand to her forehead, feeling vaguely out-of-sorts, and she swayed on her feet. A blood-covered oorg stepped up behind Armond. She screamed a warning as the club struck, sending him to the ground. She struggled to concentrate again, her incantation urging the magic to do her bidding. Moments later, more fire was sprouting from her fingertips, striking the monster standing over Armond. Adrianna's vision dimmed before she saw the oorg fall. She wavered and her knees buckled just as a pair of arms caught her.

Dartanyen's voice was alarmed. "Damnation Adria! You're burning up!"

He lay her down behind a large rock and gave her some water. She rested while he and a bloodied Armond set about finding their comrades. She was concerned, but the swordsman seemed well enough as she watched him go about his tasks. Amethyst slowly made her way over to Adrianna unassisted, blood from her injury seeping through her blouse and between the fingers clenched over it. Adrianna helped the girl down beside her, too weak to do anything more than that.

The men brought Tianna and Sabian over to their spot. Tianna had managed to pull the mage out of harm's way after being so roughly deposited onto the ground when the animals decided to flee, but since then, Sabian had been vomiting. He was unable to move much, and he was ghostly pale.

Tianna shook her head. "It's the head wound. It's making him sick. If we don't find help soon, he might die from it."

Once again, the group made an early camp. Dartanyen and Armond searched the oorg cave to be sure no others lurked there. Tianna was still unable to call upon her goddess for magical healing, but at least she could use her skills as an herbalist. She tended the wounds of Amethyst, Zorg, and Bussimot, using her array of medicinal ointments and salves. She also prepared a medicinal tea that would help ease their pain and another for Adrianna to reduce her fever. She attempted to help Sabian again, and cried when she wasn't able.

The next morning Adrianna awoke to the sound of hooves on loose rock. She groggily opened her eyes to see Sethanon standing above her. He put his head down and blew gently onto her forehead. Slowly she sat up, looking around the camp and noting the late hour. Half the group was still sleeping, and the others simply too tired to wake them.

"I got up this morning and decided to have a look down the trail. I found them not far from here."

Adrianna turned towards the sound of Dartanyen's voice. Dark smudges rested beneath his eyes and her heart went out to the man. Much of the responsibility of setting up camp and keeping watch throughout the night had fallen to him.

The person lying on the sleeping roll beside hers stirred. "Ah Hells," said Armond. "We overslept. We had best get moving. I don't want to spend any more time than necessary in these mountains."

"I agree," said Dartanyen. "But I'm not sure the others are able."

They took a moment to glance around at everyone sleeping under their blankets. Adrianna took in the pale faces, the blood on the cloths Tianna had used the evening before, and the pot of cold tea resting over a pile of ash from the fire.

"Well, we should at least make the effort. It doesn't behoove us to stay here," Armond sighed.

Dartanyen gave a nod. "I know. Let's load the animals ourselves and then wake them. We should let them rest as long as possible."

Armond agreed and the two of them set to work. Adrianna packed away Tianna's pot and medicines while the men redistributed the loads on the lloryk and larian. Amethyst awoke with the activity. Grimacing every once in a while with the pain in her side, she slowly packed her sleeping roll away and then went about rousing the rest of the group. Strangely, no one protested despite their hurts. Perhaps they hadn't the strength. Or maybe they saw no point in grumbling, since they, too, wanted to be out of the pass. With rope from the packs, Armond and Dartanyen worked to tie Sabian onto the back of the blue lloryk mare, and Zorg on Sethanon. That done, the weary group set off along their wretched path. It wasn't long before Adrianna was drained. Her head pounded mercilessly, and she was chilled despite the thick fabric of her cloak. She walked beside Sethanon, her hand clutching his dark mane. She leaned against the solidarity of the animal, and he looked back at her with concerned eyes, somehow understanding she needed his strength.

The day passed uneventfully. Armond rode at the center of the group, trying to keep everyone from falling behind. Moving was slow, but Dartanyen pushed the group knowing the end of their journey within the pass was near. Armond could see that he worried about Adrianna, who didn't seem to hear him anymore, Sabian, who wouldn't awaken from his comatose sleep, and Zorg, who had sustained a massive injury across his chest by the oorg leader. Bussi, Tianna, and Amethyst also suffered in silence. *By the gods, we can't stop to rest because Dartanyen and I may never get them moving again. Not only that, but Sabian and Zorg need a priest as soon as possible, and without attention, Adrianna and the others will also get worse.*

Dusk approached. Dartanyen continued to keep the group moving, but Armond wasn't sure they could keep it up much longer. The lloryk and larian were getting more jittery by the moment and people were just too tired to keep going. Then, like a beast waking from its slumber, the ground began to shake. Armond leaped into motion and tried to quiet the fractious burden animals. From the front of the procession, Dartanyen and Bussimot stopped and turned to look back. Armond met their gazes and, for a split a moment, the three men just stood there. This time, there would be no escape; the group was just too incapacitated.

Dartanyen hurriedly mounted his larian and shouted down at the halfen. "Bussi, give me your hand!"

The man shook his head wildly in protest, his expression panicked.

"Damnation! Just give me your hand, you stubborn fool!" Dartanyen leaned down from the back of his larian and gripped the halfen's arm, roughly pulling the short man up to sit behind him. The animal then reared and bolted down the trail, Dartanyen and Bussi both holding on for dear life.

Armond acted quickly, gripping Adrianna about the waist and swinging her onto the back of Sethanon in front of the slumped form of Zorg. She lay low and gave the beast his head so he would have a chance to get them through the quake as he had the times before. Meanwhile, with help from Amethyst, Tianna mounted the lloryk mare in front of Sabian. Once she was astride, the mare started to run, following the larian carrying Dartanyen and Bussi.

The quake intensified and the mountains responded. Armond rushed over to Amethyst, struggling to keep his larian from bolting after the two that had already left. He pulled the girl forward, urging her to mount. Much to his relief she obeyed, her fear of the coming avalanche outweighing that of never having ridden astride before. Armond mounted behind her, and the beast began to run, Sethanon alongside. Adrianna gripped the lloryk's dark mane and pressed her face against his neck. Amethyst did the same and Armond pressed his chest against her back.

The ground gave a violent heave and the mountains answered and began to fall. Armond saw Adrianna close her eyes and put all her faith in Sethanon. He hoped Zorg wouldn't topple, wondered if the bonds that held him were tight enough. He prayed that the weight of both himself and Amethyst wouldn't mean the death of them, that his larian would manage to persevere despite the extra burden.

The roar of the mountains filled his mind. When all was through, Armond hoped to see all his comrades on the other side.

8 Decaren CY593

It was warm, almost *too* warm. Adrianna awoke in a bed with the fur pulled up to her chin. She pulled it away to reveal a thick, down-filled blanket that was probably the culprit. Sitting up, she surveyed the room. Three rows of beds dominated, and a fireplace took up much of the far wall. The place was empty except for herself, but she could tell that others had been resting in the beds nearest hers. She vaguely recalled the room from other times she'd awakened, but she had no recollection of how long she'd been there.

Adrianna rose and found herself garbed in a soft, white gown. The fabric was thin and she crossed her arms over her chest with the instant chill she felt in the air. She walked around the room looking for her clothes and frowned when she stumbled a few times. She wondered about the weakness, but didn't let it stop her from finding a robe. She donned it and made her way towards the door, all the while wishing she had something for her bare feet. They'd been so toasty warm in the bed. She left the room, hoping to find her missing comrades, her host, some answers, maybe even some boots.

Adrianna walked through the corridors, realizing almost immediately the place was a temple. Symbols of devotion and worship to Tencyndor, god of travelers, lined many of the walls, along with paintings and tapestries. Within all of the portraits, Tencyndor was portrayed with curly, chin-length, chestnut hair and had a smudge of it on his chin. His eyes were friendly, and his mouth often bore an upward curve. She stopped before one such tapestry noting one of the figures out of the corner of her eye. She already knew which one was Tencyndor, having seen him in several other depictions already, but it was not he who had garnered her attention.

The tapestry was elaborate, portraying three people standing alongside a magnificent throne upon which was seated a man dressed in intricately embroidered robes. His hair was platinum silver and swept down his shoulder in a series of braids plaited together into one. He exuded an aura of power and Adrianna applauded the tapestry creator for their ability to capture it. The throne was carved into the visage of a dragon and given a dark varnish. The eyes were made of emeralds and the opalescent horns shimmered with a rainbow of color.

To the right of the throne, Tencyndor was flanked by two companions. One was another man. He had long black hair, bound into a rope with bands made of gold. He was tall for a faelin, and slender, and his features were handsome to behold. However, it was more the woman who captured Adrianna's attention. She was a vision of beauty, her hair the color of moonspun gold. She wore a sleeveless, shimmering bronze gown cut up the length to display shapely, pale legs. But there was something else about the woman, something familiar about her. It was an object about the woman's arm, a golden serpent. She put a hand to her own arm and felt the adornment still there beneath the fabric of the robe. *How strange. I've never seen an object such as this before, yet now I'm seeing it curved about the arm of a woman within a tapestry depicting gods!*

Reluctantly, Adrianna turned away. Deep in thought, she continued down the corridor. *The last thing I remember is running down the mountain path astride Sethanon. Zorg was with me, and Armond and Amethyst riding alongside...* She turned a corner and nearly collided into a man. She stumbled back, a hand to her chest, her heart beating rapidly beneath her palm.

The priest gave a relieved smile. "By the gods, you sure gave me a fright, young lady." His smile was warm, and it reached his blue eyes, making them sparkle.

Adrianna returned the smile, liking the priest already. He was middle-aged, wearing beige robes and a symbol of Tencyndor about his neck. His hair was brown and cropped short. "My name is Hans. You must be Adrianna. Your companions have been wondering when you would awaken. Come, follow me and I will take you to them." His gaze shifted to solemnity. "Although I must warn you, two of them are still not well and we are doing all that we can for them. They may not be ready for travel for quite some time."

Adrianna looked the man, her heart in her throat. "Which ones are they?"

The priests' eyes were apologetic. "Zorgandar and Sabian."

She nodded, unsurprised. She swallowed her fear for them and then grimaced, her thoughts taken away from her comrades and onto something much more mundane. "My feet are cold."

The man chuckled. "I will get you some slippers."

She followed him through the corridors and into a great hall. It reminded her of the one in which she'd found herself whilst in the Temple of Hermod when she'd recovered from her injuries sustained in the necropolis beneath Sangrilak. Dartanyen, Armond, Tianna, Bussi, and Amethyst were there, and young novices served big platters of food they set in the middle of a large oval table. There was curried tobey and spicy rice with nuts, stewed burbana with white, yellow, and orange tubers, freshly baked bread with savory crust, aged cheeses, boiled ptarmigan eggs, and fresh fruits of all kinds.

Armond rose to offer the first embrace. He held her hard against him, his action speaking words he didn't wish to say aloud. Dartanyen and the others followed. Her eyes were full of tears by the end, and she had to blink them away to keep her composure. Hans pulled her a chair next to Armond and once she was seated, he took the place on her other side. Other priests also entered and joined them for the meal. While the tyros poured watered wine, the platters were passed around until everyone had their plates heaping with food. Hans asked one of the novices to bring a pair of slippers and within moments her feet were warming up inside them.

The eldest of the priests regarded them through smiling eyes surrounded by years of wrinkles. "You were lucky to escape the Ratik Pass. Not everyone does, you know."

Dartanyen took a bite and nodded. "Our luck was amplified when you found us, Father Simeon. For that we are eternally grateful."

"It was early; dawn had barely touched the horizon. When we first approached, most of you had fallen from the backs of your lloryk and larian. Interestingly, they had chosen to stay with you instead of running away," said one of the priests.

Dartanyen nodded. "I remember, Brother Joric. They stood a vigil over us. I wanted to move, but my body wouldn't let me." He gave a chuckle.

Father Simeon smiled. "You must treat them well."

Dartanyen shrugged. "We do our best."

Hans turned to Adrianna. "Your companions were wondering when you would finally awaken. You have been sleeping the last five days since being here. You were very sick with a serious illness that causes weakness in the limbs and high fever that often causes a person to become delirious. It's called Tanager Fever because we think that it's caused by the bite of the Tanager Fly that makes its home in the Ratik Mountains."

"You said strange things in your sleep, Adria, things that made absolutely no sense," piped Tianna.

Adrianna frowned and wondered silently to herself what those things were.

"Bussimot was pretty bad off as well. If not for his strong constitution, he would have fallen long before the last quake," said Armond.

"Yes, he was bedridden almost as long as you, Adria," said Amethyst with a mouth full of rice.

Adrianna asked the question that was in her mind since first seeing everyone around the table. "How are Zorg and Sabian? Brother Hans says they are still in recovery?"

The table became quiet and her heart sank. Father Simeon spoke in a sad voice. "They both required many medicinal potions, and even more prayers, to bring them back from the brink of death. Sabian still may not make it with his mind intact, but we have done all we can for him."

Adrianna just nodded, her appetite diminished. *Damnation, if not for me, they wouldn't be here and we would never have journeyed through the pass. If not for me, we wouldn't be worried about my father. If not for me...*

Suddenly there was a light hand at her shoulder. "Adria, this isn't your fault. We all made our own decision to come. You didn't make us journey with you." Armond's voice was gentle.

"I know, but I can't help feeling responsible."

"You can't think that way. You will beat yourself into the dust, and before long, there won't be any of you left. Please, you must remain strong."

She nodded. "I'll try."

Bussimot groused from across the table, "Good, now eat up. Yer too thin, girl."

Two days later, Zorg awoke from his healing rest. He was pale and lackluster, but he lived. Sabian continued to sleep and was monitored all hours of the day and night by priests and priestesses of Tencyndor. The next day he finally awoke. At first he didn't know who they were. All they could do was stand there beside his bed, looking at one another, pity for him shining in every set of eyes. But, as the next few days went by, pieces of his memory began to return. Sabian's recovery was rather swift after that, and once he was up and walking about, everyone began to prepare for the ride to the city of Celuna, which was only a day's journey from the temple.

It was on the last evening of their stay Adrianna chose to speak with Armond. His expertise with his blades was phenomenal, and his Talent only increased his skill. Adrianna wanted to know about him, to hear the story of how his Talent developed. Armond seemed to be a secretive type of person, one who didn't share information about himself to just anyone, so it was with a tentative step she approached.

Armond sat alone in the general hospice, the place where Adrianna had found herself when she first awakened. The group continued to sleep there during the night, for the priests had not a larger space available for them elsewhere in the temple. He sat at the big table at the far end of the room, where many of them continued to keep their travel packs, weapons, and other personal effects. He examined one of his blades, bringing it close and rubbing a thumb over the edge. She walked over and sat down at the table across from him and watched until he looked up from his task.

"Adrianna," he said, nodding in greeting.

She nodded in return. "Armond, I have something to ask."

He placed the sword down on the table before him and gave her his undivided attention. "What is it?"

Adrianna paused before answering. "During our skirmish with the oorgs, I noticed something."

He nodded. "I knew that someone would, sooner or later."

"Why have you never spoken of it?"

He shrugged nonchalantly. "No one asked."

Adrianna frowned. "But none of us knew to ask."

"Now you do, and you have. I don't understand why you are so concerned."

"Because you have a rare gift. You can do so much more than–"

Armond interrupted her with an upraised hand. "I know that I have some Talent. But I'm not like you. My Talent is different. I can only use it to enhance my proficiency with my weapons."

Adrianna regarded him skeptically. However, she couldn't entirely disbelieve him. She supposed it would only be natural for there to be varying degrees of Talent, just as there were varying degrees of other abilities, such as singing or swimming. "All right," she acceded. "Will you tell me a little about it?"

Armond leaned back in his seat and regarded her contemplatively for a moment before he began. "I discovered it when I was but a boy, probably at about the same time that you began to notice something different about yourself when you were young. I perceived an energy in the world, an energy that exists all around us. Not long after, I realized I could affect it. My grandfather noticed me changing, responding to that energy. He took me aside and began to train me to be what I am today– a Bladesinger.

"I don't cast spells the way you do. Instead, I sing to the energy, coax it to me, and channel it into my weapon. For me, it is my swords. For others, it may be a hammer, an axe, or a pair of daggers. My grandfather taught me many things, but training me in my Talent was the greatest. Without him, I wouldn't be anything like what I am today."

Adrianna stared fixedly at Armond. His eyes had become piercing and his expression intensely serious. This was all new to her, for she had never learned about the intricacies inherent in her gift. *What is that he calls himself? A Bladesinger. It has a nice sound to it.*

Armond continued. "The song you heard during the battle is called *Flame-blade*. There are others I can use, such as *Chill-blade*, *Light-blade*, and *Quick-blade*. Just like you, I have to practice to learn something new. It takes a lot of skill and patience to get the song just right."

Adrianna nodded and then was quiet. She wanted to ask something of him, but didn't quite know how to go about it.

Armond continued to watch her, probably wondering what she was thinking. "What? I can tell you want to say something."

She hesitated. "Well, I was wondering if you would ever let me hear you sing one day. I just want to hear it without the added background noise of a raging battle all around me."

Armond's expression registered surprise for a moment before the corner of his mouth pulled up into a grin. "It would be my pleasure, my Lady."

Adrianna returned the smile. *Hells, he probably thinks I'm a bit strange. But that's all right, I can handle that. Most everyone is strange in some way or another.*

Sabian made a full recovery, and after leaving the sanctuary of the temple, the group journeyed to the city of Celuna. Once there, they asked around for Adrianna's sister, and when their search bore no fruit, they discussed their next plan of action. Everyone decided on the more easterly route to Dresdyn as opposed to the more northerly one to Kamden. The hope was that they would spend less time in the forest, which might slow them down. They bought a covered wagon, and within it they stored all of their belongings except for the weapons they kept at their sides at all times. It also allowed for some people to sleep during the day so they could be more awake during their shift at the nightly watch.

The group traveled at the southern outskirts of the Vanderess Forest. A mixed population of people lived there. Many of them were Hinterlean faelin, but there were also mixed race fae, some humans, half-breeds, and others. Dartanyen was in good spirits, entertaining everyone with animated stories that portrayed his younger years spent in the Vanderess. Laughter dominated the day, but unfortunately it was a hot one, unseasonably warm for this time of year. The lloryk pulling the wagon got tired faster than usual and they realized they were going to need to start alternating the animals to take on the burden of this task. The scattered trees of the forest edge offered some respite from the sun's rays, but didn't take away much of the heat.

Finally, the sun began to set. A chill swept over Adrianna, but it had nothing to do with the cooler air. She dreaded the night. Since her illness, the terrible dreams from her past had returned tenfold. After leaving Andahaye to return to Sangrilak, she'd had them a few times, but it was nothing like they were before her apprenticeship with Tallek. She reminded herself that everyone had nightmares every once in a while, but the illness had caused something to break loose, and a floodgate had been opened. Sometimes she spoke in her sleep; twice already she had been shaken awake by Tianna, who was usually the person sleeping closest to her.

The group found a suitable place to make an encampment. Adrianna helped take care of the animals before settling down inside the back of the wagon with the others to eat the meal Tianna and Bussi had prepared. She was startled when she heard Zorg's shout. His food suddenly forgotten, Dartanyen jumped to his feet and was out the rear of the wagon before anyone else could react, swiftly followed by Bussimot. Adrianna heard the ring of steel rending the early evening air as she, Tianna, Amethyst, and Sabian also slid out of the wagon. Using it as a barrier, they kept it at their backs until they reached the front. Adrianna then glanced around the corner to view the scene.

There were ten of them, mostly spellcasters and dark priests. Three were warriors, the metal of their armor shining through the black fabric covering it. They each also wore a large sword that hung from a belt about their waists. The priests and mages kept a distance from the group, but remained close enough so their spells and prayers would be effective.

However, one of them stood further back than the others. His face remained hidden within the dark recesses of his black hood. His arms were crossed at his chest, and his robes were so long that they pooled at his feet. When Adrianna saw him, an icy chill raced up her spine. *Who the Hells are these people? Have they been following us? Are they Thane's spies?*

She had no more time to speculate as the first spell was thrown, the missiles knocking Zorg back. He recovered quickly and was standing again an instant later, his blade at the ready. Bussi stood alongside, his battle-axe resting in a two-handed grip, and Armond with a blade in each hand. Another wizard cast his spell. He pointed his finger and uttered the last of his incantation, releasing a black bolt of crackling energy at Amethyst, who had broken away from them and was creeping deeper into the forest, hoping to sneak up on the enemy from behind. Luckily, she'd been carefully watching, and she effortlessly dropped to her knees and rolled, coming to her feet a few moments later.

Dartanyen remained close to the side of the wagon, keeping enough distance between him and the foe so he had enough space to use his bow. He loosed an arrow, striking one of the priests in the shoulder and interrupting his spell. Meanwhile, Adrianna quickly cast her own spell, a protective one that would remain with her until discharged. Taking a rapid glance about, she saw that Zorg, Bussi, and Armond each had engaged a dark warrior in combat and that Dartanyen had loosed another arrow, one that found home in the chest of another adversary.

Amid the sounds of battle, Adrianna suddenly heard a gasping sound from behind. She turned to find Sabian lurching towards her, clutching at his neck. She reached out to catch him and saw a ghostly, eerily glowing hand around his throat. She hurriedly scanned the battle scene as she held onto him, hoping to find the mage casting the creepy spell. Then, without any warning, Adrianna felt a *whoosh* beside her. She whirled around to find one of the dark priests falling at her feet, the tip of a scimitar protruding from his side. At the other end of it was Tianna.

"Help me with Sabian! He has a spell choking him!"

Tianna nodded and pulled her blade free, moving to Sabian's other side. Adrianna began to move away from the fallen priest when she suddenly felt something grab a hold of both her legs. Still holding onto Sabian, Adrianna stumbled and pitched forward. They both fell to their knees and the dying priest clawed at her, his bloody hands reaching for her throat. Without thinking, she placed her palm against his head and discharged her latent spell. The priest jerked spasmodically and released her. He cried out in agony and his eyes rolled back in his skull.

She kicked the body away and swiftly turned back to Sabian. He continued to struggle with the ghost hand, his strength waning. He was pale and lay slumped beside her on the ground. Tianna knelt beside them and shook her head, obviously not quite sure what to do. A shout to their right brought their attention to Armond, who was struggling against another priest. Scimitar in hand, Tianna rose and sprinted away to aid him, leaving Adrianna alone to help Sabian.

Oh gods...

Once more she turned back to the battle scene. Right away she saw that another *Spectral Hand* spell had been cast. That hand had found a target in Zorg, who clutched at his neck while still trying to fight off the enemy. Adrianna stood from her place next to Sabian and moved away, hoping to shift her point of view so that she might find the casters responsible for the spells that afflicted Sabian and Zorg. She had backed herself up to the tree-line before she saw them. The mages were standing at the edge of the battle to her right.

Adrianna gave a smug smile and incanted the words to her spell, closing out the surrounding disturbance. Once cast, and the reddish-orange orb flew towards one of the wizards and struck him solidly in the chest. The man fell into his comrade and they both landed on the ground, ending their concentration. She glanced over at Sabian to see the hand was gone. Relieved, she looked for Zorg, and it was replaced by alarm.

The big warrior had fallen before his opponent. The enemy stood over him, brandishing a gigantic black sword. Nearby was Armond, who had also fallen. He held his left arm close to his chest, and the front of his tunic was covered with blood. One after the other, two bolts struck the warrior standing over Zorg, and Adrianna was pleased to know that Dartaneyn was still up and fighting.

Adrianna suddenly felt an odd tingling sensation at the nape of her neck, a feeling she tended to get when she was being watched. She turned to see one of the spellcasters standing a few farlo away. It was the one she had noticed at the beginning, the one who had stood back from the melee. He pulled the hood back from his face, fixing her with a malicious stare, a slight smile playing about his thin, bloodless lips. A chill crawled up her spine. It was strange the way he watched her, so intently like he was...

She felt something– an odd *tap tap tap* inside her mind, a feathery tickle.

Adrianna heard a battle-cry nearby. It was Bussi. At the periphery of her vision she saw the halfen crazily swinging his battle-axe and vaguely remembered another time she had seen him so blood-thirsty.

Riveted in place, Adrianna continued to watch the spellcaster. Her throat was dry and her palms sweaty. He didn't move, just watched her with his evil stare. Someone slipped from out of the lengthening shadows cast by the trees behind the wizard. For a moment Adrianna thought it was one of the warriors that had been fighting the rest of the group, but she quickly realized he looked different. He didn't wear black fabric over his armor, and his helm was not of the same design as the dark warriors her companions fought. Stepping past the mage, he walked towards her. When the man reached up and pulled off his helm, her heart stuttered.

Time seemed to stop, the sounds of fighting in the background melting away. She'd hoped she would never see that face again, a face that had haunted her since that terrible night more than nine years ago. He was human, with hair that was dark, almost black, and skin colored a pale bronze. His eyes were black, bottomless pits without a soul. *By the gods, he somehow followed me. Now, after all these years, he will repeat what he did with his comrades alongside the road to Andahye.*

Adrianna bunched her muscles to run...

...but her legs refused to move. She wanted to open her mouth to scream, but it was a though she was paralyzed. Adrianna heard someone laughing and her eyes darted in the direction of the spellcaster. He held her gaze for a moment, an evil smirk on his face, but then she turned her eyes back to watch the warrior as he approached. He stopped in front of her, his body uncomfortably close. Tears wet her face and her heart felt as though it would burst from her chest. She wanted to escape, to run recklessly into the forest. But even if she could, she knew he would catch her.

There was no escape.

The warrior looked down at her, a smug smile curving his lips. He placed a hand on her right breast and took a deep inward breath, slowly massaging the nipple. "Mmmm," he groaned, "I remember the feel of you, the way your flesh yielded to me as I took you." He leaned closer and sniffed the air around her face. "I remember the smell of your fear." He smiled malevolently. "Do not worry, my sweet. I have returned and I shall have you again. This time I won't let you go." His dark eyes gleamed as he slowly removed his hand. He then turned and walked away, slipping back into the shadows from which he had come.

Then it was as though he had never been. He had disappeared, the wizard along with him.

Released from the *Paralysis*, Adrianna's legs buckled and she fell. She took several deep breaths before glancing wildly about. While she was preoccupied, the enemy had been dispatched. Those who were unable to flee lay dead on the ground. Shakily, she stood and made her way towards the rest of the group. Dartanyen and Armond stood over Tianna, who knelt beside Bussimot. No one commented as she approached, and no one asked her about the strange warrior. Everyone's attention was riveted onto the halfen. *It's as though they never saw him.* Adrianna bowed her head, suddenly overcome with fear and desperation. *They may never help me, and there is no escape.*

Tianna continued to pray over Bussi but finally looked up, her eyes shadowed. She shook her head and gestured for Dartanyen to take her place beside the halfen. Adrianna took a deep breath, her mind finally realizing the magnitude of what was happening. A small trickle of blood flowed from the corner of Bussi's mouth and his breathing was labored. His leather vest had been cut in several places, some from the enemy's blades, and others from Tianna's as she'd struggled to remove it.

Dartanyen knelt beside his friend, placing a hand on Bussi's shoulder. The halfen looked up at Dartanyen out of eyes glazed by pain. "Did I git 'em all?"

Dartanyen smiled a sad smile. "Sure, you did! Once again you saved our backsides. They are all lying in a bloody heap over there." Dartanyen gestured towards the battlefield.

"Is everyone all right?"

Dartanyen paused for a moment. "A little bit bruised, but otherwise good."

"Dart–" Bussimot suddenly started to cough. Dartanyen sat him upright and held him until the fit ended. When he pulled away and lay Bussi back down, blood spotted his leathers, tunic, and trousers.

"Hush, no need to talk anymore. Right now. Rest."

"N... no. I need ta tell ya, I don' think I'm gonna be able to travel with y'all anymore." His voice was low and slightly slurred.

Dartanyen leaned closer to his friend. "Hist! Don't be silly, Bussi. You will be fine in no time." The tears streamed, unchecked, down Dartanyen's face. "We'll just have to keep you tied up the next time– make sure you don't get into trouble like this anymore."

Bussi spoke as though he hadn't heard. "We've 'ad some good times, 'aven't we old friend?"

Dartanyen could only nod, unable to speak. He held tight onto Bussimot's hand, as though trying to keep him in the world of the living. Desolation was written on his face, and his lids blinked away the tears that threatened. A few heartbeats later, the brave halfen was gone. Adrianna swallowed past the lump in her throat, felt her own tears running down the sides of her face. When she glanced over at Tianna, she saw that the other woman was no better.

Early the following morning found the group working in silence. Tianna built a new fire and continued to tend Armond and Zorg. Amethyst collected a bunch of dead branches at the tree line while Adrianna helped Dartanyen gather the bodies of the dark priests, mages, and warriors into a pile. They collected coin and other usable equipment from the bodies, but discarded any weapons; Adrianna *Detected* a dark taint about them.

They cleared a circle around the pile, being sure it was free of tall grasses and shrubs. Dartanyen, Adrianna, and Amethyst each took a long branch and thrust them into the heart of Tianna's fire. Immediately the branches caught flame. They went to the pile and stabbed at it with the fiery ends until it began to burn. Once the flames were strong and steady, the group left the vicinity of the burning bodies and moved downwind. It was midday when they set up a new camp and finally tended to their fallen companion.

While Tianna and Amethyst cleaned Bussimot's body, Dartanyen and Adrianna built a makeshift pyre. When it was ready, they placed the halfen's body on it. Alongside him, they placed all of his possessions, including his favored weapon.

By the time they were finished, the shadows of another evening approached. When the sun began its descent, the group solemnly stood around the funeral pyre, each member bearing a torch. Tianna looked up to the sky and spoke in a strong voice.

"Dear Goddess Beory, I pray to you.
Please help me accomplish my task.
Please help me guide this man.
Please give me strength.
Please give me power.
Dear Goddess Beory, I pray to you."

In a manner of great ceremony, she then led everyone into a recitation of their fondest memory with Bussimot. Finally, once all words had been uttered, they thrust their torches to the pyre.

Well into the night the pyre blazed. No one slept, everyone keeping a mourning vigil. It was a private time, a time to ruminate over their memories of the deceased and to say farewells. The next morning, all that remained was the blackened skeleton of Bussimot on a bed of charred debris. Beside the bones lay the flame-scorched, steel blade of his battle-axe.

First Battle

T he group rode towards the city of Dresdyn. Dartanyen's mood settled over him like a dark cloak, shadowing him from the rest of the group. Adrianna had also fallen into melancholy. Not only did her thoughts constantly turn to the warrior in the woods, but she thought about the man who had died while in service to her. That was without mentioning the pile of blackened skeletal necromancers and priests lying a couple days away, a group of individuals possibly connected to her father.

It was beginning to get dark when the weary group of travelers entered Dresdyn. Right away they began to search for an inn, looking forward to the luxury of a hot bath and something to eat other than jerked ptarmigan, potatoes, carrots, wild onions, and berries. They found one rather easily, one that looked reputable enough: The Pewter Pot. Dartanyen stopped the wagon in front of the establishment and gestured for Adrianna to accompany him.

The inn was crowded when they entered, the air filled with pipe smoke that emanated from a large group of halfen sitting at a table in the middle of the common room. Dartanyen led the way among the busy serving girls and stopped at the bar. A burly, dark-haired human man approached. "How ken I 'elp ya?"

"We are looking for room and board for at least two nights. You have the space?"

"I have only three rooms left. They're yours if ya have the coin."

Dartanyen looked at Adrianna and she gave the nod of approval. He counted out some gold and slid it across the countertop.

The innkeep handed Dartanyen four keys. "The fourth one belongs to the bath house."

Dartanyen nodded. "Many thanks."

"It's free of charge." The man crinkled his nose. "Ya need it, my friend."

Dartanyen made no response, but Adrianna hid her smile as they made their way back outside. He raised the keys for everyone to see and Armond was already prepared. Still hitched to the wagon, he led the blue lloryk mare around the side of the building. Adrianna and Amethyst followed with the rest of the animals, which followed them without urging. Two stable-hands ran out to greet them, first unhitching the blue and taking her and Sethanon into the stable. Moments later they returned for the larian.

Once the animals were settled, everyone followed Dartanyen into the tavern and up the stairs. At the first landing, he stopped to hand one of the keys to Adrianna. She gave him a nod, but before turning away, she saw the forlorn expression on his face. Always before he had shared a chamber with Bussi, but now it would be with Sabian. It was going to be a rough night for him. She wished there was something she could do to help, but nothing of this world would ease the pain of his loss.

That night Adrianna dreamed. It was the same dreams she had suffered for so long after her arrival into Andahye, before being taken under Master Tallek's wing as his apprentice. It was the ones that left her weak and panting for breath. They were almost always the same, with very little variation, something her mind devised to torment her. But sometimes they were more, something about them that made her wake screaming in the night, the reality too much for her to bear.

The mists parted and he was there waiting for her, the same smile playing upon his lips, the same evil glint in his eyes. She cringed before him, remembering the cruelty of his touch and all she had suffered at his hand. She fled through the trees, the sound of his laugh following behind, dogging her every footstep...

Adrianna jerked awake, sweat pouring down her neck and back. She expelled her breath in ragged gasps, struggling to breathe. Amethyst stirred in the other bed and Adrianna shrank away from the sound. *He* was there, watching her from within the shadows cast by the moons, waiting to take her back to insanity. She began to cry pitifully to herself, knowing it was happening all over again.

And she would surely die this time since she had not the last.

Adrianna silently followed Tianna and Amethyst downstairs to the common room. There were few others awake at such an early hour, but Adrianna took note of the small groups of Hinterlean faelin seated at some of the other tables. They hailed from the Vanderess Forest, Dartanyen's homeland to the nearby north, and maybe a few from the realm of Elvandahar and the Sheldomar Forest near Andahye. The entire realm of Monaf, and possibly this city more than most, was the most diverse area this side of the Drujasu Sea. Its population was not only rich in faelin and humans, but halfen that resided in the Hesbron Hills and Ratik Mountains.

Adrianna spied Dartanyen, Zorg, Armond, and Sabian sitting at a table against the far wall of the common room. She and the two other women seated themselves as a serving wench approached. The men asked the girl to bring bread, cheese, and eggs to break their fast and soon they were eating the food she brought. Adrianna picked at her eggs, tired from travel and nightmares that kept her from sleep. A part of her just wanted to go back to bed, but her drive to ask around about Sheridana kept that thought at bay.

The front door of the inn opened to admit three men, two humans and a Hinterlean. They went to the bar, ordered some food and ale, and then went over to a large table at which there were seated five other men. The three began to talk in excited whispers, their comrades' eyes widening with what they heard.

The group took their time over their meal, and Adrianna realized she wasn't the only one who was still tired. Armond ordered some mead to wash down breakfast and they just sat around and took stock of supplies. As the morning wore on, the heard excited mutterings all around, the tale from the three men having spread like wildfire through the small tavern. Armond especially was intrigued.

"Hey, there's something going on around here. Maybe we should find out what it is." His eyes were alight with curiosity.

Dartanyen only shrugged, Zorg continued his eating, and Sabian looked back down at his book.

Armond looked at the women, and when he realized they didn't really seem to care either, he shook his head and stood abruptly from the table. He went to the bar and started speaking to a man seated there. Moments later, two more men came to join them. Soon, Armond was in conversation with at least six men, each one excitedly adding his own piece of information to the story that was circulating the inn.

When Armond finally returned to the table, the group's interest was finally piqued. At first, he said nothing, but when everyone continued to silently stare, he rolled his eyes and divulged the information.

"Rumor speaks of a beast lurking about at the outskirts of the Vanderess Forest. It has been hunting the livestock that roam that area." Armond paused, looking from one person to another. "No one has seen a beast quite like this one. They say it is at least twice the size of any wemic, and that it wears a thick ruff about his neck like a kyrrean. The Vanderess rangers have been following it for a couple of days now, trying to determine exactly what it is and where it came from. The druids consider the beast an enigma and don't know what to think of it."

Armond regarded everyone as they pondered his words.

Dartanyen shrugged. "Perhaps we should go hunting for this creature ourselves."

Adrianna glanced at Armond. He wore a mask of indifference, but she knew he was secretly gratified that someone was seeing things his way.

Zorg was also indifferent, but in his case, it was the real thing. He truly didn't care one way or the other if they went looking for the beast. Neither did Sabian. However, both Amethyst and Tianna seemed curious about it, especially Tianna, who was intrigued by anything from the forest.

Adrianna held in her irritation. She was curious, but not enough to go looking. It was a distraction, one she didn't need. It was silly to waste their time on the ranting and ravings of a few farmers and livestock breeders when they had other things that needed to be done. However, with the majority of the group swaying towards a search for the unknown creature in the woods, they prepared for their foray into the Vanderess. They took the equipment they thought they would need and then left the city in the direction of the forest. Adrianna couldn't help grumbling to herself along the way, and she thought she heard something similar from Zorg a time or two.

It wasn't long before they reached the outskirts of the forest. Within moments of entering the tall trees, the canopy was thick overhead. They walked only a short time before Vanderess rangers melted out of the surrounding trees. The men had thick brown or red hair, many with shades in between, and skin tanned a golden bronze from days spent in the sun. They wore sleeveless tunics with leather trousers of simple make, and their boots reached to about mid-calf. Most carried longbows over their shoulders, each man's weapon slightly different than his comrades.

One of the men stepped forward. "Greetings wanderers. What brings you to our forest?"

Dartanyen stepped forward in response. "Greetings Tirvorn. I thought that you of all people would have remembered me."

The other man's eyes widened with surprised recognition. "Dartanyen Hildranis! It's been a long time." He stepped forward and the two men grasped one another's forearms. "What brings you here after so many years?"

The other rangers relaxed their stance. Looking around, Adrianna could see that many of the men knew to whom Tirvorn was speaking. A few slipped back into the trees from which they had come, but several others stayed. "We have heard rumor that a strange beast has taken up residence near here. We were thinking about tracking it down and having a look at it."

Tirvorn nodded. "Yes. It definitely is a most unusual animal. I have never seen anything quite like him. We have been keeping track of him for a couple of days now, but he is a most elusive creature. He has a way of slipping away from us."

Adrianna sighed, her attention wandering away from the men to the surrounding environment. The forest was beautiful. The leaves on the trees were colored the vibrant green of approaching summer. The vines were beginning to make their climbing ways up many of the trunks. There were

238

so many kinds of flora, all creating a harmony of color that painted the forest in every shade imaginable.

Adrianna slowly meandered away from the rest of the group, going first to one flower, and then to another. She saw one vine that had dark green leaves that were outlined by a paler greenish-yellow. One bush sported leaves that were not green at all, but some strange shade of purple. Before she knew it, she was far enough away that she could no longer hear the conversation without straining. *I don't understand what all of the talk is about anyway. They just need to get on with it. If they would get going, they would see the animal for themselves soon enough. Mayhap this is all just a bunch of protocol. Dartanyen obviously knows these people and it is probably out of respect that he's stopping to make conversation before traipsing around in their lands.*

Adrianna continued to walk deeper into the forest. It was a peaceful place, one in which she found she could stay, if given the opportunity. Her thoughts turned inwards and she wondered how her life might be in three or four years. Would she continue to practice magic? Or would she find other things in life with which to occupy her time? Would she have a choice? And the man she saw in the battle– how real was he? Would he continue to haunt her? She began to feel a strange sensation. The hairs on the back of her neck rose and she knew she was being watched. No, not just watched. Stalked. Then she sensed something else. Unbidden feelings and emotions flooded her senses– curiosity, caution, and the thrill of the hunt.

Confused, Adrianna stopped and looked into the dense foliage before her. She saw nothing, but she knew something was there. Intriguing scents wafted into the range of her strangely heightened sense of smell. She felt nervous and edgy, the need to stay concealed consuming her. Then, as suddenly as they'd come to her, the emotions were gone. For the briefest moment she felt bereft as the sensation left her– almost lonely.

Adrianna frowned and started to walk again. She was moving for only a short while when she stepped into an open area. In its center was a small lake. The clear blue water lapped lazily at the shore and she was awed by the beauty of the place. She looked out across the lake and saw an island of rock rising from the center. Sitting atop the massive rock was a large animal.

It was beautiful, with the grace of a feline and conformation of a canine. Its copper colored fur was thick and dappled with darker patches. Around its neck was a luxurious mane. It turned to look at her and, once again, Adrianna experienced the sensation of a mind on hers. She knew without doubt that it was the creature, and that it was male. She could tell he was curious about her and, for an animal who was supposedly wild, he didn't seem menacing.

Alarm rippled through her consciousness just as she heard movement behind her. The creature jumped from the rock and into the water, quickly swimming to the opposite shore. Tianna stepped up beside her just as the animal leaped onto land and disappeared into the forest.

Silently, Zorg motioned to follow the creature. Dartanyen nodded and the two men began to walk around to the other side of the lake, Amethyst and Armond following closely behind.

"This is so exciting!" Tianna whispered. "He was so close. You must have gotten a really good look at him."

Adrianna nodded with a twinge of sadness She was sorry the animal had been frightened away. He had seemed so content sitting there watching her.

Tianna grabbed her arm. "Come on. I want to get another glimpse of him."

Adrianna shook her head. "I'm just going to stay here for a while longer. I feel tired, and it would be nice to bathe my feet."

Tianna nodded. "I suppose it will be safe enough. The Vanderess rangers are close, and if anything should happen, they are only a shout away. I will tell the rest of the group to swing in this direction when we come back through."

Adrianna nodded and sank to her knees while Tianna ran off to join the rest of the group. She removed her soft hide boots, climbed onto a rock, and lay down, dangling her feet into the cool water. For quite some time she remained there, pondering what she had experienced in the presence of the strange animal. She deliberately left thoughts of her nightmares behind, reveling in the tranquility of the forest, the beautiful scenery, and the feel of the water lapping at her ankles. Goosebumps rose on her arms when heard something from the trees behind her, but then remembered it was probably the rangers keeping their watch. Just as she managed to relax again, she felt the strange sensation of a mind touching hers once more, followed by a prickling at the back of her neck.

Oh gods...

Adrianna rose on one elbow and whirled around to find herself face to face with the large creature. She went still, holding her breath to keep from disturbing him. He was so close she could feel the warmth of his breath on her cheek. She held her ground, his gaze mesmerizing pools of molten amber. She sensed a brimming of intelligence, and as she looked deeper, a momentary feeling of...

There is something familiar about him, I just can't place what it might be! We must look a sight– a huge beast poised above the small, supine body of a faelin girl. He's so close, all I have to do is just reach out...

Slowly she raised her hand. Slowly, slowly... She inhaled sharply when he met her halfway and put his jaw into her hand. She caressed his face, sliding her fingers slowly along until she got to the mane around his neck. It was softer than she imagined it would be, much like the fur of an ermine, only longer. Adrianna smiled and chuckled to herself. *I can't believe this. He's letting me touch him like he knows me!* She felt an answering response from his mind, one of contentedness, and she felt a surge of affection. *I can scarcely believe I have already formed an attachment to this animal, and he has some kind of telepathic link to me. I can feel his emotions, just as he can feel mine!*

She whispered the words, "Who are you? Where are you from?" He rotated his ears to listen. Interestingly, she felt as though no one had ever before listened to her so closely.

Feeling a sudden shift in his demeanor, Adrianna tensed. He could smell the others, the members of her "pack", and he felt defensive and wary. They were close, and he knew they were hunting him. A low growl emanated from his throat. She put a hand on his face, soothing him with her mental voice. It seemed to work and he sat on his haunches beside her, gazing into the forest several farlo away.

Dartanyen, Armond, and the rest of the group slowly emerged from the trees, making their way over to Adrianna and the strange creature at her side. At that moment, she looked like a dryad or a nymph, one of those mythical creatures told about in children's stories. She looked so surreal with a beast such as this one sitting so tamely beside her.

The group stopped a few paces away. No one said anything, and Adrianna appeared to be gauging her new friend wondering how he was going to respond to them. The animal remained motionless, as though he was guarding her, and Dartanyen sensed apprehension emanating from the rest of the group.

"Don't worry. He won't hurt anyone," said Adrianna.

Amethyst raised a skeptical brow. "How do you know?"

The rest of the group regarded Adrianna with the same question in their eyes.

She paused. "I can sense it." Then, realizing how strange that statement sounded, Adrianna continued, "He told me. I can understand what he's feeling. Somehow we are connected. His mind is open to me, and mine is open to him. He can understand my thoughts just like I can understand his. I know this sounds crazy, but it's the truth." She stopped and took in the expressions of incredulity and disbelief on everyone's faces.

Dartanyen cleared his throat. "So, you know he won't harm us because he speaks to you with his mind?"

Adrianna nodded, stopped, and then shook her head. "Yes. I mean, no. It isn't like that. He doesn't communicate with speech. It is his emotions I sense. And right now, I sense no aggression."

Dartanyen nodded. "I see."

Adrianna slid her boots onto her feet and stood up. "So, are we ready to go?"

241

Dartanyen nodded again. "If you are. Although, I have a feeling the Vanderess rangers are going to find this situation a bit, ah, interesting." He gestured towards the animal.

Adrianna abruptly tensed and Dartanyen saw the beast was on alert, his gaze focused on the other side of the lake. Within moments, Tirvorn and his men emerged from the forest. Just like the group had done not long before, they slowly approached Adrianna and the creature. Once the rangers reached the area, they stopped. Adrianna remained silent as they all regarded her.

Tirvorn was incredulous. "You know, we have been trying to get close to this animal for days now. It seems he has chosen you."

Adrianna frowned, confused. "What do you mean, 'chosen'?" The animal's ears pricked forward.

"When a corubis cub is old enough, he is introduced to several pre-pubescent boys and girls who will endeavor to learn the skills of a ranger," explained Tirvorn. "Out of them he will choose his companion, that person with whom he will share his life's experiences. This very moment, my own corubis companion roams this forest, hunting for her next meal."

Adrianna nodded and pursed her lips. "That is very interesting. However, you are forgetting two very important things. This animal is not a corubis, and I am not a young girl with hopes of becoming a ranger."

Dartanyen was surprised by her petulant response, and she seemed to be wondering about it as well because she turned to look at the animal sitting quietly beside her. If, indeed, she felt emotions from the creature, she might be taking them on as her own and acting on them.

Tirvorn grinned. "Fiery are we not? I suppose I deserved that. I sometimes forget that outsiders are not accustomed to our ways." He gave a thoughtful pause. "But I would really like to know– what is it that you have done then? How did you bring him to you? Is it some type of spell? I have never encountered one like it before."

Adrianna narrowed her eyes. She looked towards Dartanyen and he gave a discreet shrug and shook his head. She thought he must have said something to Tirvorn about her Talent, but he hadn't said anything about her to anyone. Tirvorn was merely making a stab in the dark, not really knowing what she was about, but determined to find out. Nevertheless, it was quite an accusation for him to make, spellcasters being far and few, and they were not a very popular group either.

Adrianna regarded Tirvorn intently, assessing him. "I assure you, I haven't any knowledge of such things. He simply approached me whilst I was bathing my feet in the lake. I've realized I can understand what he is thinking. It's like we share some type of mental link."

Dartanyen watched Tirvorn out of the corner of his eye while the other rangers whispered animatedly among one another. He couldn't help feeling the same excitement. Tirvorn was right. For some reason, this animal had chosen Adrianna, linking himself to her the way a corubis pup will when first impressing upon a young faelin ranger. He smiled to himself. The young woman would no longer be in need of protection. This animal would do the job nicely all by himself. Somehow, Dartanyen knew the beast would wish to stay with Adrianna. The creature had bound himself to her, had shared himself with her. And inadvertently, Adrianna had opened herself to him as well.

"I think it's about time that we took our leave. We only have a few hours of the daylight left in which to replenish our supplies before we are back on the road again tomorrow morning," said Armond.

"Yes," agreed Adrianna, "we have spent enough time." She turned back to the Vanderess rangers. "Thank you for allowing us to spend the morning in your forest. It is quite beautiful here." She glanced back at the creature wistfully as she left his side.

Tirvorn nodded. "You are welcome back anytime. It was good to see you again, Dartanyen."

Dartanyen inclined his head. "And you as well, Tirvorn." He turned away, with the rest of the group and brought up the rear. He watched the animal out of the periphery of his vision as they left. The creature had stood from his place, but stayed where he was, unmoving, until Dartanyen could no longer see him through the foliage. *Hmm, I was so certain he would want to stay with her...*

The group walked until they were out of the forest. There was a tug of nostalgia and a surge of emptiness swept over him. Being back in the Vanderess had help soothe Bussimot's passing. He refocused his thoughts on the rest of the day. If they walked fast, the group would be back in the city within the hour and they could get something to eat before asking around about Adrianna's sister and restocking their supplies. Dartanyen suddenly heard a yelp from behind him and turned to see Amethyst had stopped, her eyes wide as she stared at the large animal jogging up alongside them.

I knew I was right! I knew it!

The sound had also captured Adrianna's attention. Her eyes met and locked with those of the animal. By the faraway expression it was obvious to see that they were communicating. Her expression shifted to one of amazement and she turned to Dartanyen. "He wants to come with us!"

He couldn't keep the grin from turning up the corners of his mouth. *He wants to come with YOU.* Yet he said nothing, merely giving her a nod before turning back to the path before them.

The group traveled east from Dresdyn. From the back of her new companion, Adrianna watched as the zacrol passed beneath them. She called him Cortath, a name she had chosen a couple of days into their journey. He seemed to like it, and responded to the name as though he had always borne it. The lloryk and larian grudgingly allowed the beast within their ranks, but continued to be wary of such a large predator.

Dartanyen decided they should sell the wagon, claiming they needed the gold. Tianna rode astride Sethanon; both human and lloryk seemed to take to one another rather well. Amethyst was learning to ride on the gentlest of their larian so she didn't need to sit in it anymore, and Sabian rode the new larian purchased with some of the coin from the sale. However, everyone knew the most compelling reason why Dartanyen sold it. They no longer traveled in the presence of a halfen who refused to ride, claiming he needed to keep his feet on the ground.

The days passed very quickly for Adrianna. The world had become a brighter place in spite of the darkness that prompted their journey. That first day, when she had mounted Sethanon, Cortath had given her a strange look. He then sent an inquiry to her through their link. She was surprised by his perplexity. Mystified, she sent a query back, and he responded by crouching on the ground. Her interest piqued, she dismounted the lloryk and approached her new friend. She placed her hand alongside his face, and stroked the soft fur of his silky mane. With his head, Cortath nudged her to his side, and with his mind he urged her to his back. Adrianna hadn't considered such a thing, riding astride the back of this magnificent beast. But when she seated herself so comfortably behind his withers, it seemed so right, and Cortath was pleased to have her there.

The ride was nothing like she had ever felt before. He was fast... so fast that the air took her breath away, tugged at her clothing, and whipped her hair about behind her as they ran. That night, when everyone had settled down to rest, Cortath came to her, settling down beside her with his head on his paws. Hesitantly, Adrianna had leaned back against his warm side and he'd simply sighed, feelings of contentment filtering to her through their link. She'd remained that way all night, and every night since.

Cortath had come to mean so much to her within the short time she'd known him. Somehow, he had given her a piece of herself, a piece she never realized was missing, one that could be wild and free. With Cortath she felt safe, safer than she had ever felt before in her life. It wasn't just that she felt protected during the day; during the night as she slept, dreams from the past came to haunt her. But now, instead of succumbing to them, she needn't face them at all.

Because her friend was there to chase them away.

2 FINOREN CY593

The gap had slowly narrowed over the past weeks as the Azmathous followed the group. It had taken some time, but finally Thane was able to track them down after their departure from Sangrilak. For a while, it seemed that his daughter and her rag-tag band of friends had dropped off the face of the world. However, he had the good fortune of picking up her trail in the city of Celuna. By then it was a bit old, but he and his minions had ridden hard, and here they were, so close he could almost smell her.

Thane grinned to himself. Soon he would finally set eyes upon Adrianna after so many years. He had enjoyed the torment he'd made her suffer thus far, inflicting wounds on her dear cenloryan friend and then burning Mairi and Hafgan to a crisp within the very house in which Adrianna had been raised. He knew she was afraid, for she'd fled Sangrilak before he could get there after being informed of her location. He had considered going back in the city to kill the cenloryan and burn down his wretched inn, but he hadn't wanted to take the time. Now he wished he'd done it, for it would have brought him so much gratification during the nights he'd spent seething from the loss of his daughter.

But then he'd found her again, and the pleasure of the hunt that came after was exquisite.

Thane looked to the sky; dawn wasn't far away. With the approach of daylight, his powers would diminish. However, he was unconcerned. He and his men would have the group destroyed for quite some time before the first rays of the sun lit the landscape. Thane dismounted his dark steed and motioned for his men to do the same. They crept closer to the encampment and the shadow lloryk followed behind.

A small fire flickered weakly in the center of the camp. Beside it was the slumped form of a young woman. Thane felt his mouth turn up in to a smile. They were fools to leave a mere wisp of a girl in charge of the nighttime watch. However, that fact would now be to his advantage. Thane motioned for his men to circle the camp, and once they were ready, they began to close upon the sleeping band.

Adrianna turned over on her bedroll, pulling the blanket up to her chin. She felt a chill and briefly considered retrieving another one from her pack. Even though she was asleep, she realized that it was summer and she shouldn't need to use another cover. Not only that, but the warmth of Cortath's body should be keeping away any chill. Drowsily, she opened her eyes, and at that moment, she heard something at the periphery of the camp. Tianna stirred on the bedroll beside hers, and her mind lurched into wakefulness. Adrianna sat up and looked in the direction she'd heard the noise.

The sight that met her eyes numbed her mind to anything else. In the center of the camp, outlined by the pale light of the dying fire, was the tall form of a man. His shoulders were wide– she could tell despite his armor, which was all black. He wore a horned helmet, and the only thing not concealed by it were the man's eyes. They stared at her where she lay, piercing as they reached into the very depths of her soul. Without having seen him for almost a decade, she knew his identity, knew beyond any shadow of doubt.

"Oh gods," Adrianna choked out the words and her heart skipped a beat.

Tianna responded, half asleep. "What is it? Go back to–"

She abruptly stopped. So attuned to the natural world, Tianna immediately sensed that something was terribly amiss. She sat up suddenly, and when her eyes focused on the man standing within the circle of their camp, she cried out, "'Ware! Intruder in the camp!"

There was a momentary flurry of activity, the men grabbing at their nearest weapons. Several dark figures emerged from the darkness around the encampment and the group quickly realized they were surrounded. There was a lull, almost like the calm before a storm. The man standing in the center of the camp raised his hands to his helmet and pulled it off. The face behind the helm was ghastly, only a grotesque shadow of the man Thane used to be. The skin was shrunken around the bones of his face and his thin, brown hair hung in lank tangles down to his shoulders. The only part of him that remained unchanged were his eyes, and they continued to watch Adrianna with an uncanny intensity.

Adrianna stared back at her father. She rose from her bedroll, never taking her eyes away from his emaciated face. Terror coursed through her, clutching her heart in a vice-like grip. It was all so much more real now that she could see the abomination he had become. Thane reached out a hand and stepped towards her. Adrianna felt herself become still, just the way a burbana does when it is being hunted by a fox.

His voice was deep and grating. "Gemma! My dear, beloved Gemma! How long I have waited to set my eyes upon you once more."

Adrianna felt her heart thump against her ribs. *By the gods, he is mistaking me for my dead mother. Do we really look so much alike?*

He stepped a few paces closer. "I have missed you so–"

Suddenly he stopped. His eyes narrowed into slits, and the expression of benevolence was wiped away and replaced by loathing. He bared his teeth in a grimace of disgust.

"Ah, it is you. Adrianna, for a moment you had me fooled. It is wrong, so wrong that you should look so much like her. It is your eyes; they are different. Yes, my Gemma had eyes the color of a crystal blue lake in winter." Thane paused for a moment, drawing his sword from its scabbard with a fluid hiss. "You know why I am here, do you not? For a long time now, I have awaited this moment. I should have killed you when you were but an infant, having just emerged from your dying mother's belly. But I was too soft then– too *human*. Now I am not so encumbered. Come, why not accept the inevitable? Give yourself to me easily, and I will make your death a painless one."

Finding herself mobile once more, Adrianna shook her head. She stumbled back from her father, widening the distance between them.

Thane sighed. "Ah, such a pity. I don't understand why you refuse to make this easy for me. Always you have been nothing but a burden." He raised his arm, glancing at his minions where they stood around the encampment. Meanwhile, the group was silent, watching the scene unfold before them. A brief moment or two passed before Thane lowered his arm. "Kill them."

The ring of steel rent the air, and Adrianna found her attention momentarily diverted. Fear for her companions was thrust to the foremost in her mind and Thane took the opportunity to lunge. His blade *whooshed* past her face, and at the last moment, she managed to leap out of his way. She began to run, but remembering the camp was surrounded by the undead, she came to an abrupt stop.

Thane still stood near the fire, the flames highlighting the paleness of his skeletal face. His lipless mouth grinned, and she saw the pleasure he took in causing her fear. All around, her companions fought for their lives against an enemy that was much too powerful. *Can this really be the end? We are all going to die out here in the middle of nowhere?* It would have been nice to see Sheridana, even if it was just one last time.

Thane began walking towards her and she ran again. She darted about the melee, saw Zorg fall from a well-aimed kick from his opponent, and Sabian being hit from a deflected spell. Eyes gleaming, Thane played her game, following her weaving path. She was startled to see Amethyst take a ruthless punch to the gut from one of the undead. The girl gave an agonized scream, and when the fist was withdrawn, there was a claw dripping with blood.

Adrianna's eyes strayed too long, and when she looked back, Thane was nowhere in sight. Panic washed over her and she turned in place, praying to see him somewhere in the melee. She saw Tianna run to Amethyst's side, blocking an attack on the fallen girl. Dartanyen loosed a volley of arrows into the chest of another warrior, and Sabian incanted the words to another spell. Terror swelled within her. *Cortath, where are you? Why did you chase all the other dreams away but leave me alone with this one?*

Then suddenly Thane was before her, a looming presence that came from out of nowhere. She moved to run, but it was too late. He easily caught her around the waist and flung her to the ground, the impact causing the breath to abandon her chest. He flipped her over to face him, and Adrianna cringed at the hatred she saw in his eyes as he stood over her. The ring of steel filled her ears as he drew his massive blade once more. She wanted to close her eyes, but for some reason they refused to obey. *Dear gods, please tell me this is just a bad dream. Please don't let this be the end!*

A savage snarl infiltrated her thoughts and a smudgy blur rushed at Thane. Cortath's large form slammed into the knight and her father fell back. Cortath swiftly leapt away and manuevered himself between Adrianan and Thane. She mangaed to scramble away as Thane slowly rose, the full weight of his menacing glare on her companion. Cortath just glared back, unruffled by the unspoken challenge. The knight shifted his sword into his other hand and rushed forward. Cortath crouched and rolled at the last moment as the broadsword swept overhead in a downward arc. He sank his teeth into Thane's leg, and when the knight fell once more, he maneuvered himself on top of his adversary, pinning him to the ground. However, Thane had found the opportunity to grab his dagger. The knight reached up, took a fistful of Cortath's mane, and plunged the jagged blade into the canine's chest.

Cortath's cry pierced the air and Adrianna's guts spasmed. The beast went limp and Thane kicked the animal away before rising to retrieve his fallen sword. Her friend struggled to his feet. Blood stained his mane and dripped to the ground but he refused to back down. Cortath looked like he would die before he let the abomination touch her again.

All of a sudden, a shrill whistle pierced the air and Thane looked up at the sky. The first rays of dawn were about to emerge and he nodded in solemn acknowledgment. Picking up his fallen helm, he turned to Adrianna.

"This isn't over, dear daughter. Already I am looking forward to our next meeting. The feel of your heart stuttering beneath my hands will bring me to the brink of ecstasy."

As though he understood what Thane said, Cortath growled. With the last of his strength, the beast lunged. Thane easily shrugged him off and went to mount the black lloryk that appeared out of the shadowy darkness. He raised his arm as he cantered away, his minions following behind.

With the eminent threat suddenly gone, Adrianna fell back and cried great, heaving sobs that left her breathless. Cortath approached any lay beside her. Reflected within his amber eyes was the conviction that he would never leave her side again.

REUNION

The group rode under the cover of the night. Despite their weariness they kept moving, keeping as much distance between themselves and the enemy as possible. Since their ill-fated meeting with Thane, they kept in near constant motion. They'd fled the scene as soon as they could after the undead left, riding hard until they reached the Dresnjik River. With the coin scavenged from the priests and necromancers they'd met en route to Dresdyn, they bought their way across. Once on the ferry, they tried to rest, knowing they might not have the chance later, but peace of mind was hard to find and sleep a hard-won commodity.

Adrianna was withdrawn. She ate little and spoke to no one. Cortath was her shadow, silently staying by her side as she fought her daemons. Tianna took advantage of the down-time and dressed wounds the group had acquired during the skirmish. She'd seen to Amethyst and Adrianna right after the battle, but Sabian, Zorg, and Dartanyen hadn't the chance to be tended. Out of the three, Sabian seemed to be in the worst condition. However, with adequate sleep, Tianna felt he would quickly regain his strength.

Amethyst's wounds were the most profound. The claw-like weapon the enemy had used was wickedly curved, ripping through her vulnerable belly and causing severe blood loss. Much of her insides had been damaged and the girl was lucky to be alive. Tianna had managed to slow the bleeding whilst on the battle field, but still spent most of her time with Amethyst during the ferry ride, praying arduously to her goddess for the power to heal her. It was well past midday by the time Tianna stopped her ministrations. Then, lying beside her patient, she fell asleep.

Chest heaving from her mad dash, Tianna remained hidden in the foliage with fear rampant in her mind. By the gods, that man is Thane Darnesse! And these people are all dead! *Opposite her, on the other side of the encampment, stood six shadowed animals. They appeared to be one with the darkness, and if they hadn't been wearing barding, she might never have taken notice of them. They were the size of lloryk and the color of the night. Outlined only by a layer of fog, it swirled about them when they moved. It seemed to rise from the ground upon which their hooves trod, and with each stamp of a foot more mist arose.*

Nearby, Amethyst and a dark shrouded figure faced off, each wielding a shortsword. Amethyst reared away from a sweep from her opponent, the bone blade just narrowly missing her face. She swung in retaliation, just to find her blade pulled from her grip by the vein-like whip he suddenly produced from within the folds of his cloak. Stunned, Amethyst fell back. The weapon cracked through the air again and it wrapped around one of her legs. She squealed as the shrouded figure pulled her to the ground. Thinking quickly, Amethyst pulled a dagger from her boot and plunged it into the strange fleshy whip, pinning it to the ground. The shrouded figure hissed angrily and reached within the folds of his cloak again as he lunged at the girl. He punched her in the stomach and an agonized scream rent the air. When the enemy pulled back, he held a bloody claw in his hand.

Quashing her fear, Tianna rushed into the fray and ran past Sabian. The spell he cast was deflected, the magical bolts bouncing off the enemy to rocket back and hit him mercilessly in the chest. She drew her scimitar and stopped when she reached Amethyst. She just barely managed to block the next attack on the fallen girl and the enemy fell back, giving a hiss from within the folds of his hood. He turned his focus onto the healer and rose from the ground. He arched back and was about to crack his whip, when five bolts of magical energy struck his chest.

Angrily, the enemy turned to his new attacker and Tianna followed his gaze. It was Sabian. With the spell he had used to save them, the young mage had left himself open to attack from his own rival. The dark foe lay gnarled hands on Sabian's shoulder and he stiffened and cried out before collapsing.

As swiftly as she could, Tianna pulled Amethyst away from their adversary while his attention remained focused elsewhere. Once far enough away, she knelt over the young girl. Amethyst writhed in agony, holding her hands over her belly, dark blood seeping between her fingers. Tianna moved the girl's hands away and gasped, swiftly replacing them with her own atop the horrible wound.

Struggling to keep calm, Tianna began to pray, her voice weaving among the noises of battle. Within a few moments, she felt the healing magic from her goddess...

Dartanyen watched Tianna. She moaned in her sleep and he wondered what horrors her dreams held. Every so often, he would swing his gaze in Amethyst's direction, a frown on his face. The only thing that kept him away from her was the gravity of her wounds. Because she had fallen asleep at the watch, Thane had almost killed Adrianna. Without Cortath's intervention, he surely would have. Not to mention, the rest of the group had also been in great danger. Dartanyen's disappointment was profound, for this wasn't the first time she had been derelict in her duty and he knew that he would never be able to trust her again. This worried and saddened him both at the same time. It was difficult to travel with someone who couldn't even be depended on for the nightly watch.

It took the ferry all day to cross the river, and everyone was happy to be on dry land as the sun began to set on the horizon. Dartanyen immediately set a good pace, one the animals had the physical capacity to handle after resting for most of the day whilst on the ferry. Throughout the night the group continued to ride. Finally, in the early hours of the morning, they arrived at the outskirts of the city of Torrich. Dartanyen considered passing the city, but when he saw Sabian, Tianna, and Amethyst all slumped over the backs of their larian, he chose to stop.

Once through the city gates, they approached the first inn they found, The Tarnished Tankard Tavern. It looked a bit more upscale than what they were accustomed, but Dartanyen felt they deserved a bit of luxury after what they had recently endured. He nodded to Armond and Zorg and the two men dismounted. The activity awakened the stable hands, and the lloryk and larian were taken right away. Dartanyen was glad they didn't have Cortath there with them; Adrianna had asked him to remain outside the city gates. The animal would have brought them too much unwanted attention.

Armond, Zorg, and Adrianna roused the remainder of the group while Dartanyen proceeded to ring the bell at the entrance to the inn. After a few moments the weary owner appeared at the door. Dartanyen informed the man that he needed lodging for himself and six others. The innkeeper assured him there was room for everyone.

Once everyone was inside, Dartanyen gave the required amount of gold and the innkeep handed them keys to their rooms. They all bade one another a good rest as they headed for their respective quarters. Dartanyen supported a weak Sabian down the hall and once within the room, he settled the mage onto one of the beds. Then, after removing his boots and shucking his outer vest, Dartanyen fell onto his own bed. Before long he was asleep.

Not wanting to awaken Tianna or Amethyst, Adrianna tip-toed across the dimly lit room. Once at the little vanity table, she grabbed a towel, a bar of soap, and a flask filled with some pale, amber liquid, putting them all in her bag with some fresh clothing. It was the beginning of the day, the perfect time to bathe her grungy body. It had been days since anyone in the group had the opportunity to have a proper dunking, and she wanted to be the first one to it.

She left the room and walked about the establishment for a while, searching until she found the women's communal bathing chamber. She walked inside, pausing at the entrance to collect another towel, and went to the large pool in the center of the room. She shucked her clothing and sighed as she stepped into the steaming water. It was still early, and since she was the only one there, she used the entirety of the pool for herself. She smelled of the contents of the flask, and drank when she discovered it was a fruity wine.

Adrianna took her time washing. It wasn't every day one had the luxury of bathing in a thermal pool. Thoughts eddied about in her mind, and they ultimately settled onto Cortath. The wounds he'd attained from their run-in with the Azmathous had healed so swiftly she could hardly believe it. She mentioned it to Tianna, and after several moments of thought the other woman said she imagined that mayhap it was an innate ability. Adrianna couldn't help wishing she had the same gift.

When she was satisfied that she was finally clean, she got out of the water and dried off. She stepped into fresh tunic and trousers and combed out her tangled hair. After wadding up her dirty clothes and stuffing them into her bag, she left the bathing chamber, making sure to take the half-emptied wine flask with her.

Feeling a bit hungry, Adrianna made her way to the dining area. No one had bothered to partake of a meal the evening before because it was late and they'd been so tired. Upon entering the common room, she looked about and noted only a few patrons present, none of them her comrades. One man sat alone at a large table, some parchments strewn about in front of him. Adrianna went to the bar and asked the burly man there to bring her a fresh breakfast of fruit, bread, and nuts. She then walked across the room to the corner table, passing the man sitting alone with his parchments. He looked up as she walked by and smiled. "Good morn to you my Lady. Would you care to join me?"

Startled, Adrianna's step faltered, but she smiled back. The handsome faelin swept his hand towards the empty chair beside him. His hair was blond, and his complexion pale. His eyes were the color of palest purple. There was something about him, something familiar...

"Yes, that would be nice. Thank you." Despite the fact that he was a strange man in an unfamiliar city, she didn't hesitate as she sat down next to him, placing her bag on the chair beside her and the half-emptied flask on the table. She brought her gaze to his. "Would you care to share the rest of this with me?"

The young man gave a winning smile. "It is such a pleasure to be graced by the presence of one so lovely as you." He held her gaze with his own, plucked her hand from the table, and kissed the top of it. A warm tingle traveled down her spine and into her belly. "Of course, I would be willing to share."

Adrianna flushed and smiled. He was more intoxicating than the wine from her flask. She snagged his mug and poured some of the wine, then took another quaff. She belatedly wondered how much of her reaction to this man was a result of the drink.

"Who are you?" Adrianna folded her arms onto the table and leaned forward.

He took a drink from his mug and moved in close. His voice was husky. "My name is Dimitri."

"Dimitri." She whispered his name, rolling it over her tongue. She sucked at her lower lip as she gazed into his eyes, her hand still caught within his. "So, what brings you here?" She indicated the parchments lying haphazardly about on the table.

He smiled. "Only the most important work. Perhaps you can help me with it."

She grinned. She'd never flirted before, but it came easily with the help of the wine. "Maybe. What's in it for me?"

His eyes sparkled. "Well..."

"Good morning, Adrianna." The sound of a familiar voice shattered the moment. Startled, both she and Dimitri snapped out of their shared reverie, and they turned towards her companion.

Adrianna hesitated only briefly as her thoughts regrouped. "Hello, Armond. How was your rest?"

Armond regarded Adrianna with an odd frown. "Good. Thank you." He turned to her table companion. "Who is your friend?"

Dimitri swept his hand towards the other chairs situated around the table. "The lady just settled down to break her fast. Please, join us. My name is Dimitri."

Armond regarded the other man intently. Adrianna turned from him to look at Dimitri again. *He is so familiar. Why is he so familiar?* Then it struck her. *Dinim.* Her eyes widened involuntarily and her heart skipped a beat. Without turning his head from Armond, Dinim caught her surprised, but delighted, expression. One corner of his mouth turned up in the crooked grin typical of the man she knew.

Meanwhile, Armond looked from Dinim to Adrianna, scowling minutely. It didn't take him long to figure it out. She watched as the truth dawned on him. Ever so slowly, Armond began to smile. Then he was sitting down at the table with them. "How in the world did you know we were here?"

"Oh, I asked around here and there." With that statement, Dinim idly looked about the room as though making certain no one was listening in to the conversation. Adrianna and Armond also looked about and saw the remainder of the group had risen from their beds. Tianna, Amethyst, Zorg, Dartanyen, and Sabian were all slowly making their way down the stairs.

Adrianna looked at Dinim once more. She was glad to see him and that he was well. She caught him glancing in her direction and his smile widened. *Drat the man! He tricked me, and so well, too. What was that between us? If Armond hadn't come, what would have happened?*

Dinim glanced sidelong at Adrianna. She had a half-smile on her lips. Her cheeks were flushed, and her eyes sparkled. *Did I do that? Or is it just a result of an excess of wine? I was so close; I could smell it on her breath.* Hells, she was seductive without intending to be, and that innocence made her all that much more enticing. He remembered the way she sucked at her lip and the whispered voice she used as she spoke his name...

Dinim shook himself out of the memory. Now wasn't the time. He had much to say, and unfortunately most of it was bad news.

One by one the rest of the group joined them at the table. It took a few moments, but soon everyone knew that the faelin calling himself Dimitri was Dinim in disguise. Sabian clapped him on the back in greeting, and Dartanyen shook his hand. Everyone was curious, wanting to know about the Wildrunners.

Tianna leaned forward in her seat, her tone quiet. "So, what news do you have? How is Sirion?"

Dinim paused to regard Tianna. It wasn't fair that he had to be the one to tell her what had happened. He supposed it had to be someone, but why him? He hardly even knew this woman. When he didn't answer right away, her face paled and she sat back in her seat, almost as though she wanted to get as far away from him as possible.

"Gaknar, the leader of the Daemundai, was successful in bringing Tharizduun into our world. It was difficult, but I was able to reverse the spell and send him back. However, the battle devastated the Wildrunners' ranks. We started out as nine, but in the end, all that remained were five. For a few days we stayed together for protection while we recovered from the wounds we received in the battle, but finally everyone went their separate ways."

Tianna's hands gripped the edge of the table and she nodded. "You say only five remain. Who was lost?"

Silence reigned. Tianna's eyes filled with tears and her lips trembled.

Dinim swallowed heavily. "There was nothing we could do. At the end of the battle, Sirion was caught in a magical crossfire. The energies of several spells being cast at the same time caused the creation of some kind of vortex. He was sucked into it and never made it out."

Tears streamed down her face. "You never found him?" she asked brokenly.

"No."

Her mournful expression shifted to denial. "Then I don't believe you," she whispered.

Dinim felt tears gathering at his own eyes. "Tianna, I'm so sorry."

She shook her head and rose from her seat. "No, it's not true!" Her voice rose.

Dinim stood as well, holding out his hands to her, palms up in supplication. "I know this is difficult for you to accept, but nothing remained after the vortex scoured the ground. He's gone."

Tianna screamed, "No! I don't believe you!" She spun on her heels and ran from the table. She raced up the stairs, and the sound of a door slamming could vaguely be heard a moment later.

Dinim looked around the table. Everyone stared at him with varying levels of shock. Adrianna's was the worst. The expression on her face almost stilled his heart, for it was the one that most mirrored the desolation on the face of the young woman who had just run from the table.

Finally, she rose and Dinim watched as she slowly turned away to follow Tianna. He just stood there, shoulders slumped. The rest of the group was silent for a few moments, absorbing what had just transpired, but then began to offer their condolences. Food was brought, and they ate their meal in silence. Afterward, Amethyst went for a walk around the city and talk slowly resumed.

Armond leaned forward. "So, really, how did you know where to find us?" His voice was low as he spoke, remembering Dinim's reaction when he had asked the question before.

Dinim was glad for the conversation. Their earlier silence had probably been a gesture of respect, but it had bothered him. He immediately began to relax as he replied. "Actually, it was more difficult than I had let on."

The other men leaned forward in their seats, all bearing expressions of curiosity. "After the battle, we left the Ubekwe Valley, a place outside of Grondor," Dinim continued. "We made our way back to the city, and after a couple days of rest, we said our farewells and went our own ways.

"Grondor is a large city. A person can find anything his heart desires, if only he knows how to look. I had promised Adrianna I would find her when I was able. Hence, I needed to find some way to locate her. I knew she was probably somewhere within the central portion of the continent, but that narrowed my search only marginally. I needed help, something beyond my realm of expertise.

"I decided I needed a scrying device. It would be the perfect way to find Adrianna. I went to several shops, but none of them carried such a thing. The shop owners told me that such items were difficult to obtain, not to mention extremely expensive. I began to lose hope, but then I noticed the gypsies. I thought perhaps one of them would be willing to help me. I'd heard stories about gypsy magic, and that many of the women have certain, rare abilities. So, I went up to one of the men and asked if he knew someone who could help me. At first, he chuckled and called some of his friends over. For a while, they all laughed at my expense. Then I decided I needed to take a chance. I needed to show these men what I really was so they wouldn't think me a mere charlatan."

Dinim paused. Dartanyen, Zorg, Armond, and Sabian were engrossed in his tale. They watched him from wide eyes, taking in every word of his story. "So, what did ya do?" asked Zorg.

Dinim smiled. "I cast a spell."

"An' then what happened?"

Dinim's smile widened. "They stopped laughing at me."

The men grinned, imagining the shock value of that act, an act that had become commonplace to them, an act that was a rarity for most others. Dinim continued. "I showed the gypsy men that I had coin, and that I would pay for any help they could offer. They looked at one another, and then back at me. They then led me along a line of wagons that comprised a sizable caravan. At one of the largest ones they stopped. One of the men entered the rear of the wagon for a few moments and then returned. He told me that I was permitted to go inside. That is when I met the old woman."

Dinim stopped once more and regarded the men around the table. "Go on, tell us what happened next," urged Zorg.

"In return for my services, she scried for Adrianna."

"What type of services?" asked Dartanyen.

"I traveled here with the caravan as a guardsman. My job was to use my Talent to offer aid if needed."

Dartanyen nodded. "Well, I must say, I'm glad you have rejoined us. We have quite a bit to discuss."

Dinim nodded, noticing the pensive tone of Dartanyen's voice. "I figured as much. Let's go up to one of our bedchambers. I don't want to take the chance that anyone may overhear."

Dartanyen agreed and the group rose from the table. They made their way up the stairs and into the room Dartanyen shared with Sabian. The men settled about the room. Dinim twisted a ring off of his middle finger and his facial features shifted back into their customary place, his hair changing back to its natural color. For a moment there was silence.

"Why the subterfuge?" asked Armond.

"When I am travelling alone, I often feel safer in disguise. I've made quite a few enemies over the years," explained Dinim.

The men simply nodded. Dartanyen then started to recount their tale, telling Dinim about their perilous journey from Sangrilak through the Ratik Pass. He spoke of the strange animal, Cortath, and finally about their first meeting with Lord Thane. Dinim took it all in quietly without interrupting.

After Dartanyen was finished, it was quiet again. Dinim stood from his place on the floor and went to the door. "Let me think about this for a while. I will plan on seeing you for the evening meal."

Dartanyen and the other men nodded. Dinim left the room, only to return to his own. He sat at the small table, pensively considering the actions they should take next. The group was in terrible danger. Thane wasn't far away, and probably knew exactly where they had gone. Somehow, they had to find a way to take Thane off of their trail. Tonight, they would be especially vulnerable.

Dinim stood and went over to the window. He looked out over the city street, watched the passerby as they went about their business. Somehow, Thane had managed to track the group this far. Dinim knew he had spies, but they weren't the only means with which he'd followed the group. Thane and his minions had the ability to travel with super-natural speed, and Thane's powers of 'persuasion' were great. If nothing else, he'd hired some scavenging sods to find out where the group had been by checking registry logs at inns and by asking the locals about any groups of wanderers that had passed through recently, especially any that had a young woman in their ranks that fit Adrianna's unusual description.

Dinim swept a hand through his hair as his mind raced through tens of possibilities. *We have to find a way to escape and remain undetectable, at least until we find a way to deal with the threat. And we have to find it fast.*

Adrianna sat on the steps of the Tarnished Tankard Tavern. She gazed sightlessly past the people that walked by, her heart heavy. *He's gone. I can't believe Sirion is gone.* She blinked away tears and sniffed away the ones that gathered in her nose. *There was something about him, something that called out to me. I'll never know what it was. The way Tianna describes him, he was something outside the realm of ordinary. I only caught a glimpse of that. I wish...*

Adrianna shook her head and wiped at the tears that slipped past her weary defenses. She'd managed to keep it all at bay while she offered comfort to Tianna, but now that she was alone, it all came out in a jumbled heap of mixed emotions dominated by grief. *I hardly knew Sirion. Why is this affecting me so deeply? Oh, gods, if I'm feeling this way, I can only imagine what Tianna is going through.*

Thoughts of her friend caused a small deluge. Tianna had clung desperately to her as she sobbed. She'd spoken in broken sentences, professing her love for Sirion, and her wish to see him just one last time. As Tianna's heart broke into a thousand pieces, Adrianna had felt her throat close. It was hard to breathe, and even harder to swallow. She had never loved anyone like that except for her sister..

Sheri, will I ever see you again? Will I live long enough to finally find you?

Through their link, Adrianna felt Cortath probe gently at her mind. He was worried and wanted to come to her. Adrianna refused him, reminding him of the mayhem his presence would cause in the city. Adrianna insisted he remain where he was, hidden in the tall grasses at the outskirts. She could feel Cortath's hunger, for he had forgone hunting while in the vicinity of the city, and she promised to bring him meat when she was able.

It was then Adrianna heard a commotion down the street. At first, she ignored it, but then, as it seemed to be getting closer, she looked in the direction from where the noise came. She saw Amethyst running towards the inn.

The girl saw Adrianna sitting there and called out. "Adria, quick! Get Tianna!"

She jumped up and went back into the inn, running up the stairs to the room she shared with Tianna and Amethyst. "Tianna, wake up! Something is going on outside. Amethyst told me to come and get you."

Tianna hurriedly left the bed and grabbed her medicine pouches on her way out of the room. The women ran down the stairs, and by the time they reached the veranda, the disturbance had reached the inn. Dinim had already arrived on the scene and was helping a blood-drenched man down from a lathered larian. The poor beast looked like it might fall at any moment. Adrianna scanned the gathering crowd and noticed one of the stable hands.

"Oi, stable boy!" Adrianna called over the noise. "Get this animal to the stable. Give him some water, walk him out, and rub him down."

The boy nodded, took the animal's ropes, and lead him away. Meanwhile, Tianna helped Dinim bring the man up the veranda stairs. He had been badly beaten, and could hardly support his own weight. The innkeeper held the door open as they brought him inside, then he took Tianna's place to help Dinim get him up the stairs. They deposited the man onto the bed of the first room they came to. Tianna entered behind with all of her bags and medicines and Adrianna told the innkeeper to get some hot water and clean cloths. Amethyst stood out of the way, near the far wall, silently watching Tianna use her skills on the dying man. Once Adrianna had the water and cloths, she attempted to clean his many wounds. He groaned when she touched his broken body, and she wondered how he had been able to ride.

The women worked for several hours, Tianna making prayers to her goddess, and Adrianna applying herbal salves and giving healing draughts. Finally, the man achieved some level of comfort and Tianna took a step back. Tiredly, she looked at Adrianna. "Thank you for your help."

"You're welcome." Adrianna looked at her friend speculatively. "You should get something to eat. You haven't had anything all day."

Tianna was about to shake her head, but when she noticed the expression on Adrianna's face, she altered her response. She gave a grudging nod and the two women left the room and went downstairs. The rest of the group was in the common room taking their evening meal. Space was made for them at the table and food placed onto the extra plates awaiting them.

Dartanyen was the first to inquire. "How is the poor man? Will he live?"

Tianna nodded. "I think so. His wounds are extensive, but I think I was able to tend most of them before I burned out. I really need to rest after this."

Adrianna noticed Dartanyen and Dinim share a glance and knew what they were thinking. The group could ill afford to stay in the city much longer. Dusk was approaching, and Thane would soon be on his path again. She felt her appetite diminish and she pushed back her plate. Zorg noticed and frowned. "Eat up now, little lady. Ya needs ta eat more 'cause yer too thin."

Adrianna just stared at him for a moment, his words reminding her of Bussimot, who used to say the same thing. The rest of the group must have remembered too, for the table was suddenly silent. Zorg was a quiet man, not much into words, but he'd noticed her and cared enough to say something. Adrianna grinned and Zorg smiled back. The rest of the table seemed to let out a collective exhale as she pulled the plate back and picked up her fork. She forced herself to eat a small portion more, just to satisfy Zorg, who nodded when he saw her eating again.

After the meal, Tianna and Adrianna went back to see their patient. To their surprise he had awakened. He slowly turned his head when they entered the room. Tianna sat down beside him. "How do you feel?"

The man spoke slowly. "I've been... better." His speech was broken and it was apparent his mouth was dry. Adrianna took a cup and filled it with water. She brought it to Tianna and the healer placed it to the man's lips. Slowly he drank, some of the water leaking out of the corners of his mouth to trickle down his chin and onto his neck. When he was finished, he lay his head back onto the pillow.

Tianna patted his shoulder. "Do you think you have the strength to tell me what happened to you?"

The man nodded. "I was traveling... with a merchant caravan... towards the city. We were attacked..." The man paused, fear in his eyes. "They were hideous to behold... creatures made from the stuff of nightmares. They were dead... dead..." The man's voice trailed off and Tianna and Adrianna looked at one another from across the bed. They knew who it was. Thane was coming for them.

"Can you tell us anything more?" Adrianna asked the question, afraid of what she would hear, but needing to know.

The man turned towards her. "They began to slaughter everyone, even the children." The man's eyes filled with tears. "Despite the pleas of the women and the cries of the children, they wouldn't stop until every last person was dead." The man lowered his gaze. "Except for me. I was hidden. It was after they began to burn the wagons that others came."

Adrianna frowned. "Others? What others?"

His voice gained in strength. "They were men, at least twenty of them, all wearing black robes. They looked like vile warlocks and dread priests. I don't even want to contemplate to whom they answered. They surrounded the undead abominations that destroyed the caravan. There were two of them that began to speak, one representative from each side. I don't understand what they said; the language was unfamiliar. Then fighting broke out. I huddled in the grass, far enough away to keep from getting killed in the crossfire, but close enough to know how the fight ended."

The man stopped and shuddered.

Tianna's voice was low. "And how was that?"

"When all was done, the dark priests and warlocks had fallen. All that remained were the living dead."

Adrianna's mind whirled. *My father and his minions decimated a band of priests and sorcerers more than three times their size.* The icy grip of fear closed around her heart. They had to leave Torrich as quickly as possible. Tianna put a hand on the man's forehead, smoothing back his damp hair. "You should rest now."

But the man continued, determined to finish imparting what information he knew. "But they were weak. They'd suffered in the fight. They mounted their dark steeds and cantered away from the city."

Adrianna took the man's hand in her own. "Are you sure?"

The man nodded. "I was able to drag myself to my larian and get onto his back. I rode in the opposite direction."

Adrianna let out an explosive breath, relief washing over her. She squeezed the man's hand, grateful for the information he had imparted in spite of the discomfort it must have caused. "Rest now. You will be safe here." She rose from the bedside and looked up at Tianna. "I will inform the others."

Tianna nodded as she turned and left. Adrianna immediately went to Dartanyen's room. She knocked on the door and, within moments, he opened it and ushered her within. She saw that Sabian and Dinim were there as well. Their travel packs were already sitting on the bed, ready to go. Adrianna sat down beside the packs and watched Dartanyen as he began to don his studded leather. "You won't be needing that tonight."

Dartanyen looked up and gave her a look of disbelief. "Are you crazy? You know Thane is hot on our trail. I don't care how tired Tianna is. We have to leave Torrich tonight."

He went back to his vest. Adrianna raised an eyebrow and shook her head. "No, I don't think we do. Thane won't be coming for us tonight. He is currently..." she struggled to find the right word, "...indisposed."

Dartanyen sighed and dropped his hands from the buckles. "What do you know the rest of us do not?"

Adrianna managed to keep a straight face. "Thane has been detained by physical limitations and will not be traveling anywhere this evening."

"And how do you happen to know this?"

"The man Tianna and I have been healing today was awake for a few minutes. He told us a few things."

"Well, tell us what you know!" urged Sabian.

When Adrianna was finished talking, the men were regarding her with wide eyes. The magnitude of the destruction Thane wrought with nothing other than the six men in his company was astounding, and she could see those thoughts mirrored in their eyes.

"It looks like someone bought us some much-needed time," said Dartanyen.

"Another night of sleep will do us good," Sabian said quietly, taking his pack off the bed.

Dinim nodded. "This gives us an opportunity to rest and put some extra distance between us. He could be incapacitated for another night after this one, but we can't be certain. We still need a strategy to keep ahead of him."

"I agree," said Dartanyen. "Let's get some rest and talk about it tomorrow morning. I'm going to tell Armond, Zorg, and Amethyst the change of plan."

Adrianna turned to leave, but Dinim's voice forestalled her. "I think I already have an idea." She turned back to see him smiling at her and she wondered what she'd said or done to deserve it.

"Let's hear it," said Dartanyen.

"The gypsy caravan that brought me here left today for the city of Risset. If we ride hard tomorrow morning, we should be able to catch up with it a little past midday. I think it would be a good idea for us to travel with them, for there is safety in numbers. Not only that, but the old gypsy matriarch might know some way to keep Thane off of our trail."

Dartanyen turned to Sabian. "What do you think?"

The mage nodded. "I think we should do it."

"Adrianna?"

The men looked at her expectantly. More than she thought it would, she was pleased they respected her opinion. She liked Dinim's proposal; the idea of someone being able to help keep them from her father's clutches for a while longer was enticing. "I agree. If Dinim thinks the old woman can help us, we should do it."

Dartanyen smiled. "All right, then. I'll go tell the others."

THE GYPSIES

The sun had barely crested the horizon when the group left Torrich. Once outside the city, Cortath rushed over to greet them, expressing his happiness by running around the group, rubbing his large head on Adrianna's back and torso, and making rumbling sounds deep in his throat that reminded them of a large cat. They had brought him a haunch of leschera meat and the group waited patiently while he ate. When he was finished, they began to move in earnest. At first Cortath was sluggish and Adrianna wouldn't allow him to carry her. After the first hour his pace picked up, and with his friend finally on his back, he caught up with Dartanyen and was happy to share the lead as they traveled.

At Dinim's urging, the group rode fast all morning. By midday they could tell the caravan wasn't far ahead, and a couple of hours later they saw the wagon train in the distance. When the group finally got close enough, several mounted guards broke away from the train. They stopped several farlo away and the group followed their cue. Despite the distance, there was immediate tension in the air. Most of the men stared at the large animal Dinim had come to know as a loyal, fierce protector. However, he could understand how the guards might be afraid, for the beast was bigger than most other predators and appeared quite intimidating. He noticed that one of the men was familiar and realized it was the same guard who had taken him to meet the old matriarch a few days ago.

Dinim gestured to Dartanyen to fall back and he rode forward to meet the gypsies. "Greetings. I apologize if we have caused you any unnecessary alarm. We have ridden hard to catch up with you, hoping you would be willing to have us in your midst. We have a skilled archer and two swordsmen to help out with guard duties and the nightly watches. What do you say?"

The familiar man recognized Dinim and he visibly relaxed. The other guards looked at one another and then back to Dinim and the rest of the group. "What about yon animal?" asked one of the men in accented Common, pointing at Cortath.

"He won't hurt anyone. This beast is a friend. The woman who rides him is his companion and she will take care of him. He won't be a burden."

Most of the men remembered Dinim from when he traveled with them before and they nodded. The man who Dinim knew more personally spoke. "You all are welcome to travel with us. It is always good to have some extra warriors to take the watch. However, I have forgotten your name."

"I am Dinim, and this is Dartanyen, Adrianna, Tianna, Amethyst, Sabian, Armond, and Zorgandar." Dinim gestured towards each of the group members.

The man nodded. His gaze rested a moment longer on Amethyst, Zorg, and Tianna as the three members of the group who were human. It didn't surprise Dinim, for the gypsies were human themselves. "I am Thalen Firasat. Come. Let us catch up to the caravan. We must let Ami Rayhana know of your return. She likes you and would be upset if I didn't tell her you were riding with us again."

Thalen smiled as he turned his lloryk. The other guards followed suit and soon all of them were galloping into the vicinity of the caravan. The populace stared at them as they rode through, the women and children watching them from the wagons, and the men from astride their lloryk. Finally, they arrived at the large covered wagon at the head of the procession. In an unfamiliar tongue, Thalen spoke to the driver, telling him they had been joined by some wanderers. They conversed for a few moments longer and then Thalen returned to them.

"Maroch has given his permission. I will inform Ami of your presence. Make yourselves at home among us. An hour before dusk we will stop for the night. We will talk more then."

Dartanyen nodded. "Thank you so much for your benevolence. It is good of you to take us on. We look forward to speaking with you again tonight."

Thalen nodded and waved as he rode away. Adrianna looked around, taking in the new environment. The people were Denedrian, an itinerant people that originated from the western side of Ansalar, with features much like Amethyst's. Their skin tone was bronzed, appearing as though they spent all of their time in the sun. Their hair was dark, ranging from medium brown to jet black, and their eyes also were dark, all varying shades of rich brown.

The gypsy women, especially, were creatures of beauty. Their dark, almond shaped eyes and full lips gave them an exotic appearance. They tended to be full-figured, having all the right curves in all the right places. More than once she caught Zorg and Armond glancing at one woman or another with expressions of appreciation. However, it was more than just the color of their eyes and the shapes of their bodies. It was the way they dressed and the aura that surrounded them. These women seemed to have no modesty as they stared at the male newcomers, casting them seductive glances and positioning their bodies just so... the low necklines of their blouses displaying ample cleavage.

The gypsies were a proud people, and this quality manifested itself in the way they lived. They led a nomadic existence, traveling from one side of Ansalar to the other. They traded their wares for those things which they couldn't grow or make make themselves, and they performed entertaining escapades that left their audiences clamoring for more.

The gypsies were also a colorful people. The women wore long skirts made of layers of multihued, diaphanous material and billowy-sleeved blouses embroidered with intricate patterns. They wore their hair long, often contained within shimmering nets. About their waists they wore belts made of silver or gold bedecked with multitudes of chimes that tinkled as they moved. Around their arms they wore decorative bracelets, and at their earlobes they wore long dangling earrings. The men wore billowy trousers with brightly colored sashes, often with cloth bands about their foreheads of yet another color. They too, had ear piercings, and wore thick, decorative armbands made of bronze, silver, and gold.

After a few more hours of traveling, the caravan slowly came to a halt. The order to stop started from the front wagon, and by word of mouth, the command trickled down the line of wagons until it finally reached the end. Some of the riders helped, calling out as they galloped down the line, "Stopping for the night! Everyone halt your wagons; we are stopping for the night!" The wagons at the end drove until they reached the front of the line, and within the hour the wagons had all formed a circle. Meanwhile, the women-folk bustled to life, starting the campfires and beginning their work on the evening meals. The women worked together, partitioning themselves into groups with each group performing a different task. Before long, the tantalizing aroma of cooking meat was wafting through the air.

The group found a place of their own within the protective circle of wagons. They lit a fire and began to prepare a meal. Cortath left the area to hunt, and after only a short while he returned with a fat ptarmigan. He presented the fowl to Tianna, who took the offering and thanked him. Amethyst took the bird and began to pluck the feathers while Tianna continued to cook the barley. Adrianna set out her bed-roll along with those of Tianna and Amethyst. The men laid out their own rolls and settled down to tend their weapons and armor.

Before long, Thalen approached the group. With him were two women, each of whom carried a large platter full of roasted meat and vegetables. Dartanyen stood and greeted the men as the women went over to their fire and set the platters down beside it. "We have brought you some food," said Thalen. "While you are with us you need not prepare your own. We will be more than happy to share what we have."

Dartanyen nodded. "Thank you, this is very generous. The food looks delicious." The women beamed when they heard Dartanyen's remark. "But next time we will bring some meat for the stew-pot. We have a very good hunter in our midst." Dartanyen indicated Cortath.

Thalen nodded. "We would appreciate any offerings you care to give us."

Dartanyen gestured towards the fire and the food. "Would you care to join us? It appears there is plenty of food, and Tianna makes wonderful tea."

Thalen nodded. "That would be good. We can discuss the night watch and the daily guard duties."

Everyone sat about the fire and passed the platters all around. The food tasted wonderful, seasoned with an array of spices that had become familiar only very recently since their journey this side of the Dresenjik River. The men talked about which shifts they would take while they traveled with the caravan. Dinim was the first to rise after finishing his meal. "Thalen, could you direct me to Ami's wagon? If it is not too much of a bother, I would like to speak with her for a few moments."

"It should be no problem at all. Hers is the red covered wagon across the way," he replied, pointing across the central campfire.

Dinim nodded. "Thank you, my friend."

Adrianna watched him walk across the camp and noticed that he garnered the attention of many of the gypsy women. Unlike most other people, human and faelin alike, the gypsies didn't seem to care about his race. She wondered about that for a moment as she watched many of the young men and women gathering at a large fire they had built in the middle of the circle of wagons. Their talk was animated, and some had begun to play music. They saw something in Dinim other than the color of his skin and eyes, and even if they weren't looking any deeper, they found his features to be attractive, much the way she did.

"Would you like to join us at the bonfire? I am sure you would enjoy the stories and the camaraderie. Not only that, but we would like to hear some of your stories as well," said Thalen.

Dartanyen, Armond, Zorg, Tianna, and Amethyst all agreed to attend the bonfire while Sabian chose to settle down on his bedroll with a book. Adrianna remained behind as well. She was in no mood to join in any festivities. Sirion's death and the recent experience with her father prevailed in her mind. She still sported a big, dark bruise beneath her ribs, testament of his intense hatred. Without Tianna, she wouldn't be faring this well, for she was certain Thane had broken something inside her with his well-aimed kick. Actually, without Cortath, she probably wouldn't be alive to ruminate over it like she was now, and the group would probably be dealing with the threat of Thane without her.

Adrianna put her hand into her friend's thick mane. She didn't know what she would ever do without him, didn't even want to contemplate such an existence. Already, it seemed like she'd known him all of her life and that he'd always been by her side.

Divining her thoughts, Cortath put his big head in her lap, telling her that he loved her too. Her heart melted. *Love.* Yes, Adrianna loved this creature.

She loved him more than she had loved anyone in a long time. She stroked his face and Cortath closed his amber eyes. Somehow, he filled a rift in her life she never knew existed until now. He made her complete, and she did the same for him. It was like they were meant to be... that Fate had brought them together that day in the Vanderess Forest.

Adrianna lay down and Cortath readjusted himself until they were both comfortable. As they lay there, Cortath curled protectively around her, and Adrianna looked out on the bonfire. She spied her comrades and saw that Dinim had joined them. She couldn't help noticing the gracefulness of his movements, the way he tilted his head when he smiled, and the way he carried himself with confidence. He was an incredibly handsome man; the gypsy women's covetous gazes were testament of that. Adrianna rolled her eyes. They had accosted Armond and Zorg as well, sitting next to them at the fire, leaning into them as they spoke, batting their lashes and smiling seductively. One woman sitting beside Zorg was leaning so close her rotund breasts touched his arm. He didn't seem to mind, his deep, throaty laugh sounding throughout the circle.

However, it wasn't just the gypsy women who were having a good time. Adrianna noticed that Amethyst seemed to fit in perfectly with these people, smiling and talking animatedly with several of the other younger men and women. Tianna also sat near the fire, and beside her was a handsome man. Her melodious voice floated through the air, followed by her laughter. Adrianna sighed, her eyes beginning to close. She supposed Tianna needed something... someone to take her mind off of Sirion's loss. Adrianna didn't necessarily agree with the methods Tianna used, but she supposed it was more favorable than some others she could employ.

Adrianna yawned and watched as Dinim suavely rid himself of the women clinging to him. As he walked towards the group's fire, she thought of rousing herself. Perhaps now would be a good time to talk about a few things on her mind, but she couldn't find the energy to do anything but reach a hand in his direction. She was so tired, and so comfortable lying there beside Cortath. Her eyes drifted shut, and she dreamed no dreams.

It was still dark when everyone awoke, Meriliam still hanging in the predawn sky. Since it took more time to get so many people started in the mornings, the caravan broke camp before dawn so as to make maximum use of the daylight hours. It was loud, everyone talking as they quickly took down the tents and loaded the wagons. The umberhulks rumbled and trumpted their displeasure, and children ran amok, weaving in and out of the wagons.

Tianna was in good spirits as they packed away their bedrolls and Amethyst grumbled about the early hour. Adrianna caught Dinim looking at her a couple of times. She looked down at her tunic and then at her trousers, seeing if there was something amiss. She asked Tianna if there was anything about her that needed fixing. Her friend just gave her an odd look and shook her head.

Finally, everything was packed up and the wagon circle began to unravel. It started with the lead wagon, the red one Dinim had visited the evening before, and the others followed behind in some predetermined order. They journeyed north, keeping the Dresnjik River to the west, moving at a set pace. Travel was a bit slower than what the group was accustomed, but the company was good. Dartanyen, Zorg, and Armond took part in guard duty along with the other warriors, and they shifted positions at regular intervals throughout the day.

Adrianna estimated close to one hundred and twenty people in the caravan. Many of the gypsies rode within the wagons, but some did not, choosing instead to travel on the backs of their lloryk, riding around and making conversation among themselves and the group. Adrianna rode astride Cortath. He was ever her good friend and companion, staying with her even though he really wanted to jog at the front of the caravan, scouting ahead to see what lay before them. Once they realized he was no threat, most of the populace accepted him without any reservations. The children especially liked him. From the back of their wagons, they stared at Cortath and his rider through dark eyes. They were engaging and asked Adrianna multitudes of questions. She just smiled and answered them all.

Late in the morning Dinim sidled up beside her. For a while he just rode there, saying nothing, but finally he broke the silence. "Dartanyen told me about your meeting with Thane."

Adrianna nodded. She knew this topic would arise, just not when. And now that he was there beside her, she didn't quite know what to say even though she'd wished for his presence since leaving Sangrilak.

Dinim hesitated and then continued. "He told me you were wounded."

Strangely, she felt defensive and she pressed her lips into a thin line. "Tianna was able to heal my injuries."

Dinim's eyes flashed. "Your physical wounds maybe, but not the ones in your mind."

Adrianna frowned. Now that the terrible subject had been broached, she couldn't stop the surge of anger and helplessness that swept through her. She regretted the words as soon as they left her mouth. "What the Hells would *you* know about it?"

Dinim's eyes darkened and his lips tightened. "More than you know."

Chagrined, she shook her head. "Oh gods, I'm sorry. All of this has just been very difficult for me. You had a duty to the Wildrunners, but all I've wanted was your presence at my side. I must profess, I am quite a selfish creature. Please tell me you won't be going anywhere soon."

Dinim's demeanor relaxed. "You have my word, but will you forgive me for leaving?"

Adrianna regarded him intently. He wore a despondent expression on his face, but his eyes were bright. He was funning her and she couldn't help playing along. She struggled to keep the smile off her face. "I suppose I could consider it."

"Please do, my Lady, for I don't think I could live another day without the warmth of your lovely smile upon me."

She rolled her eyes. "Oh, hush. You are such a scoundrel!"

Dinim grinned wider and Adrianna broke out into a smile of her own. She fell into a fit of giggles and then composed herself. "So, have you any information that might help us?"

"I'm not sure. However, I was able to find some background information. Tonight, let's sit and talk about it. I have a couple of books I can show you."

Adrianna raised an eyebrow. "Where did you get them?"

He used an innocent tone. "The library in Grondor."

"They let you borrow the books?" she asked in surprise.

He was quiet for a brief moment. "No."

Adrianna glared. "You *stole* them?"

Dinim leaned over and placed a forefinger at her lips. "Shhh. Lower your voice, my dear. I don't want the whole caravan knowing I'm not just a scoundrel, but a thief too." His eyes twinkled.

"You are incorrigible."

"Yes, but you like me," he said, waggling an eyebrow.

Adrianna turned away in mock dislike. "I'm not too sure about that now. I had no idea you were a thief."

"But you liked me when you knew I was a scoundrel?"

Adrianna narrowed her eyes and turned back. "You are also an impossible rake."

Dinim only chuckled.

It was near the end of the day when the trackers discovered grang spoor. The caravan was instantly alert of any possible threat, however, nothing approached. Even the groups of dumb grang were not so foolish as to attack a retinue so large. A few zacrol later, the signal was given and the caravan began the process of stopping for the day. The wagons curled into a circle again, and before long the evening fires were made and meals prepared. Adrianna watched the young gypsy women. They were temptresses, wearing

269

their low-cut blouses and long skirts with slits up the sides to reveal golden flesh browned by the sun. They captivated Zorg and Armond with their dark beauty, but somehow, Sabian and Dartanyen seemed unaffected. Sabian stayed preoccupied with reading his books, and Dartanyen was busy either observing those about him or conversing with the other men in the caravan.

After the evening meal had been eaten, and everyone was settling down to some camaraderie before turning in for the night, Thalen approached. "Ami Rayhana wishes to see you all. She wanted to meet you sooner, but she has been very busy with other things. She offers her apologies."

Dartanyen nodded and everyone stood and followed Thalen. They walked across the center of the camp, passing several wagons before approaching the largest one. Once there, the brightly colored flap was pulled aside and a woman gestured for them to enter. Disconcertingly, Adrianna saw the woman smile at Armond as he passed by.

Once inside, the group was ushered toward the front of the wagon, and there, sitting at a round table, was an old woman. Her face was deeply wrinkled, but Adrianna could tell she had once been very beautiful. Silver hair was pulled back to reveal delicate features and her eyes were a rich chestnut brown. She regarded them intently for a moment before speaking. "Welcome. Everyone calls me Ami Rayhana. You may call me Ami as well. Please have a seat." She gestured towards the other eight chairs around the table. The woman who bade them enter stood at Ami's left side, watching the group. Everyone silently seated themselves as Cortath settled himself on the floor nearby. Adrianna found herself sitting with Dinim on her left and Armond on her right.

Ami placed her hands on the table and regarded the group intently from dark eyes. She looked at each person in turn. "You are all in danger," she stated ominously.

Adrianna startled and then narrowed her eyes imperceptibly. *What does this woman know that would cause her to believe we are in danger?*

"I have seen what follows you. He is a powerful adversary, but nothing compared to what will come after. You must all come together to overcome your enemies. You must realize one others' strengths and weaknesses, accept them, and work together to fulfill the destiny set before you."

The old woman looked again around the table. Adrianna shook her head and found she was angry. This wasn't what she wanted to hear. She had always known there was more to this than just Thane, but she'd been keeping the hope that once her father was dealt with, it would be over and she and her friends could return to their lives.

She spoke without thinking, the words tumbling from her lips like the rocks in the Ratik Pass when the world quaked and shook the mountains. "What are you talking about? How do you know this?"

Ami replied in a quiet voice. "I see many things. That is my Gift."

Adrianna raised a skeptical brow. She'd heard about gypsy seers. They were charlatans that liked to take people's gold, telling them what they most wanted to hear.

Ami closed her eyes and her brows furrowed. "My eyes show me you have been down this path before." Her hands began to shake and she reached out to take the hand of the woman beside her. "The dead will begin to walk and it will herald the end. Four times the Death Master has won, and he will do so again unless the prophecy comes to fruition."

Adrianna felt Armond shift uncomfortably beside her and she felt much the same. She didn't understand a single thing this woman had just said, but part of her deep inside sensed the importance and it was frightening.

Ami opened her eyes and turned to look at her. The emotion reflected there was easy to decipher, a sadness so intense she could almost feel it. "Your path has been preordained, a destiny given to you before birth."

Adrianna trembled. *This woman is scaring me. Why am I letting her do that? I have enough fear in my life without some crazy old lady added to the mix.* Anger welled up and she welcomed it, recognizing it as the fuel she needed.

"You're wrong! There is no destiny!" Adrianna rose from her seat. "If Thane is stopped, we will all go back to our normal lives. If he isn't, well, maybe we will all die. But this torment ends with him!" Adrianna stopped. The group stared at her, as well as Ami and her daughter. Her tone shifted to one of derision. "I say there won't be an adversary for us to face after Thane, because we won't be there to deal with it. So much for your dung-eaten *Gift*!"

Ami's tone was soothing. "You have so much hurt and anger within you. Your family can help if you let them—"

"You know nothing about me! I have no family except a father who wants to kill me, a brother I haven't seen in over two decades, and a sister who' been gone for just over half that time. You talk as though you know what I'm feeling but—"

The old woman's voice rose over Adrianna's. "The undead lord will not cease until your heart stops beating! For now, his vision is clouded, but he will find you again. You can't run from him forever. And after him there is another, one so dark and so foul that he will raise an army like no other that has been seen on the face of this world. If he succeeds, another Cycle of the curse will end, and the future will never come to pass."

"What you are talking about is craziness!" Adrianna turned to her comrades. "I want out of here. I'm ready to go."

Dinim stood up beside her and gently took her arm. "Adrianna, let's just listen to her for a moment."

She pursed her lips and looked into his eyes. "Dinim, you can't be serious. This is a farce, and I want to leave."

"Adrianna, please just sit down," implored Dartanyen.

She suddenly stopped. With wide eyes she looked around at her comrades. Holding her breath, she regarded everyone through the tears that clouded her vision. *These people have a future. Am I really so ready to possibly take that away from them?* She spoke around the lump in her throat. "What have I done? I have dragged you all here, into this Hell my life has become. Already, one of us has died. And for what, just to face even more adversity? After Thane there will be more of this nightmare?" Adrianna gave a swallow so heavy she almost choked on it. "I am so sorry... so sorry for everything."

She abruptly turned from the table. Dinim tried grabbing the sleeve of her tunic, but it slipped out of his hand as she darted away back through the wagon. She jumped from the back and into the night, Cortath swiftly following behind.

Adrianna ran back to the group's campfire, her thoughts too jumbled to be coherent. Hot tears stung her eyes and ran down her face, the air cooling them on her cheeks. After a few moments she slowed and noticed her surroundings. All around her there was laughter and music. Off to one side there was a group of entertainers, their music lively and upbeat. Near them were some dancers, their hips gyrating with the beat. It was the music of gypsies, different than any she had heard before. The dancing seemed to have been made for just this type of music; they went together so well. She saw some of the men handing out mugs of some kind of drink, and before she knew it, she was walking over to get one for herself. The man smiled affably as he handed her the mug of warm liquid.

Adrianna took a long swallow of the brew and walked around the extensive encampment for a while. She watched the festivities as she drank, and before long the mug was empty. She finally made it over to the group's fire. No one was there. They must have gone to enjoy the festivities– even Sabian, who spent most of his time with a book in front of his face. Adrianna looked towards the central bonfire where most people were gathering. None of her comrades were to be seen. Cortath took himself over to her bedroll and lay down beside it, placing his head on his paws. He seemed more tired than usual.

Adrianna looked down into her mug. Sadly, the spiced ale was gone. Without thinking twice, she went to get another drink.

Adrianna imbibed two more and walked slowly around the encampment again. Unashamedly she watched the enthralling movements of the gypsy women. The dancing, and the music that went with it, was seductive. It caught the attention of the men, including Armond and Zorg, whom she finally saw surrounded by three or more women. Sadness crept up to her like a predator does its unsuspecting prey and her chest ached. *How many more nights like this will we have, nights when the sky is clear and almost every star in the heavens can be seen? How many more good times will we have before our enemies strike us down? I thought once I found my sister everything would somehow be all right. But that's impossible. Thane will still be hunting me, Sheri, and everyone with us.*

Adrianna shook away the thoughts, allowing the music and the effects of the brew carry her along. Memories swirled sluggishly around in her mind as she continued to drink the intoxicating beverage. As she walked around the circle of wagons, she began to dance to the sound of the music. She loved dancing; Master Tallek had introduced it to her while she was his apprentice and she always looked forward to the days he would send her across the city of Andahye to learn.

Even though they were rather provocative, she mimicked the movements the gypsy women made. Before long she found herself ensconced within the shadows cast by some of the larger covered wagons. She continued to dance for a while, but paused when she heard some sounds coming from a nearby wagon. Intrigued, she slowly crept towards it. As she got closer, the sounds became more distinctive. Someone was moaning, and there was labored breathing. She continued to creep alongside the wagon, and when she reached the juncture between it and the next one, she peered around the corner. The scene that she discovered was unanticipated.

It was a man and a woman. They strained against one another in a tumble of bare arms and legs. The man lay partially on top of the woman, her paler complexion a sharp contrast to his darker one. Suspicion glimmered in her mind, but when she saw the chestnut hair fanned out on the ground and heard the timbre of the moans, she knew who it was. Adrianna backed away from the scene, taken aback by what she'd seen, yet strangely stirred. She didn't notice she wasn't alone until she bumped into someone standing behind her.

Startled, Adrianna spun around and came face to face with a man. She struggled to collect herself as he offered her a smile. In spite of the shadows, she noticed he was very attractive. Black hair swept back from his forehead and was braided along the sides, and light brown eyes regarded her appraisingly. His gaze briefly settled beyond the wagons to Tianna and her lover. "Captivating are they not? Your friend is lovely, and I'm not surprised Hansel got to her first."

Adrianna stepped back. "I... I don't know."

The man looked back to her and widened his smile. "Come now. I've been watching you watching them." He spoke softly, almost seductively. "I saw you dancing. You are beauty in motion– an enchantress."

She felt her cheeks burn and hoped he couldn't see. So easily he disarmed her. "I... I'm sorry. It wasn't my intention to enchant anyone."

The man suddenly bridged the gap between them. He captured her hand, pulled her close, and put his other hand at her waist. "Why should you be sorry? I'm not. I loved every moment of watching you." He led her into a dance, moving them to the sound of the music in the distance. "By the way, my name is Errow."

"I am..."

"Adrianna. I know who you are."

His husky voice tickled her ear and a trill of fire raced down to the tips of her toes. Her mind whirled as her body followed his in the dance. *He's been watching me for who knows how long and caught me spying on two people in the act of making love. He even knows my name. Gods, he's so close...*

Too caught up in her thoughts, Adrianna faltered. Errow tightened his grip and pressed her tightly against him. Her senses suddenly flared to life. She brought her face close to Errow's chest, inhaling the scent of him. It was almost as intoxicating as the spiced ale. An ache began in the lowest portion of her belly and she took a handful of his sleeveless tunic. The world spun and she allowed herself to move to the music in the arms of a handsome stranger.

This man wanted her, could feel it in the way he held her and the response of his body to her nearness. He had sought her out, wanting her before he even met her. And somehow, a part of her wanted him too. Perhaps it was the brew, or maybe the scene she had witnessed between Tianna and her lover. It confused her, frightened her, and excited her all at the same time.

Finally, the music ended and they swayed for a few moments longer. Adrianna looked up and Errow's gaze was smoldering as he looked down at her, his eyes sweeping over her face. His hands did the same over her back, and then down to her backside. He was close, ever so close, and she felt his breath on her eyes, her nose, and her lips. Her hands swept over the fabric of his tunic, feeling the contours of his muscular chest. Errow's hands slid from her backside to her waist, and then up her sides to her breasts...

Euphoria suddenly shifted to despair.

Fear washed over her in a wave of dark memories. The past rose to the surface of her mind– another man, his dirty hands, his rank mouth, his dagger on her naked flesh.

Adrianna pushed against Errow's chest and he stumbled back. "Stop!" She took a couple of deep breaths and backed away, her heart threatening to beat out of her chest. She looked into his face, saw his expression of surprise, and then reluctant acceptance.

"I... I'm sorry. I didn't mean to lead you on. I'm sorry..."

He shook his head. "No apologies are needed, Mi'lady." Errow's eyes searched her face, and she saw the concern reflected there.

She swallowed past the sudden lump in the back of her throat. "I need to go. Good night." Adrianna turned from him and ran. Her head swam with the effects of the brew, but she at least had enough wits about her to make it back to her own fire without needing to ask someone for directions. As she neared, she saw that Dartanyen, Sabian, and Amethyst were already there. Cortath was sitting up next to her bedroll, looking out in the direction from which she was coming. She felt a questing at her mind, but she blocked him out. This was something she couldn't share, even with him. She slowed her pace to a jog, and then to a walk. Nonchalantly she approached, and with a show of being overly tired, she sank onto her blankets.

Cortath curled beside her bedroll. Through the link she felt his hurt, the sting of her rejection echoing in his mind. She felt sorry for the hurt she caused, but she refused to let him have any idea about those dark aspects of her past. No one could ever know about those things, horrible things she was afraid to allow her mind to linger upon for too long.

But Adrianna couldn't help but remember. Tears crept down her temples as she unlaced her tunic. She slipped a hand into the front and traced the scar than ran between her breasts. No decent man would ever want her, not after he knew what had happened to her. But that was fine, because then no one would see her for what she really was, *and for all of the many things she was not.*

The following morning the camp was sluggish to awaken, everyone's physical state reflecting what had been enjoyed the night before. As the encampment got ready for travel, Zorg and Armond emerged from a nearby campfire, their clothes a bit wrinkled, and their hair a bit tousled. It had definitely been a good night, one Armond wouldn't mind replicating in the near future.

As the caravan moved off, Armond grabbed a skewer of quartered burbana meat left over from the evening before and mounted his lloryk. He rode leisurely as he ate, not expected to participate in the guard duty until just past midday. Before long he saw Adrianna riding astride Cortath up ahead. He noticed her solemn demeanor and, glancing around, he spied some the gypsy women from their wagons. Their expressions of contempt were difficult to miss, and Armond wondered what she could have possibly done to warrant such animosity. He nodded in greeting when he approached and fell in beside her. "How are you faring this morning?"

She gave a lopsided grin. "I'm all right, I guess. I think I may have drunk a little too much of that spiced ale last night."

He felt his hear melt and smiled back. "I think we all drank a little too much last night." He then regarded her ponderously. The warm winds blew errant strands of pale hair across her face, and she impatiently brushed them aside. She was a very lovely woman, possibly more beautiful than any he had ever met before. Her beauty was entrancing and had captured the attention of many of the men in the caravan. She was oblivious of this, and it made her all the more fascinating. Thinking on it now, it was the same thing that probably made the women so hostile.

Last night as they sat around the bonfire, he and Zorg had heard some of the men talking about Adrianna. Many of them expressed simple attraction. Others expressed more, and a few were downright lewd. He'd found himself feeling protective, knowing she was undeserving of the treatment about which the men fantasized. And now, as he looked upon her face, he knew he would never tell her what he'd heard even though she needed know in order to stay alert and wary. I *will just have to be vigilant, protect her myself if need be. And mayhap I will tell Dartanyen and Dinim so they can watch over her too.*

Adrianna watched him with a quizzical expression, trying to figure out what he was thinking. Knowing he had a rather stoic countenance at times, he offered another smile to diffuse any worrisome thoughts she might have. She seemed to relax, and it was at that moment Tianna rode over. Armond was well aware of her activities the previous night, and by the slight shift in Adrianna's demeanor, she knew about them too. Of course, being human, Tianna recognized none of this and immediately struck up some light-hearted banter.

Armond slowed his larian and eventually he was far enough away that he wasn't bombarded by Tianna's incessant chatter. It wasn't long before Dinim was riding up beside him. He nodded to the Cimmerean in greeting and the other man did the same.

Armond had come a long way since that day in the Temple of Hermod when he'd fought with the doppelganger he'd thought was Dinim. He'd been raised with a strong prejudice against Cimmereans, for they had brought much hardship throughout his family's history. But now, since knowing Dinim, Armond had begun to realize that prejudices could be evil things, and that not everyone fit the representation they were forced to bear. It was very obvious that Dinim was a good man, and somewhere in the world there were probably other good Cimmereans. Likewise, he was certain there were bad Hinterleans, Savanleans, and Terraleans to balance it all out.

After a few moments Dinim was riding ahead. Most likely, he was in search of Adrianna's company. Armond hadn't missed the glances the mage threw her way every once in a while, not to mention the scene he'd interrupted between she and Dinim at the inn in Torrich. It had become rather evident that the Cimmerean harbored some feeling for the young woman. Armond couldn't really blame the man. Although, Armond strongly felt that personal and business relationships should be kept strictly separate. During a fight, it could be difficult to keep a cool head, even without the added strain of having a loved one present. It simply wasn't an option for Armond– never was and never would be.

Adrianna looked on as her friend waved and rode ahead towards the rest of the group. Last night's tryst had done Tianna quite a bit of good, for her eyes were bright, her smile dazzling, and her laughter cheery. It heartened Adrianna to see her so vibrant after the tragedy of Sirion's death, and it made her feel more upbeat about her own situation and about what had happened the evening before. She heard someone approaching from behind and turned to find Dinim riding up. She smiled as he positioned his larian beside Cortath and he returned the gesture. "Good morn to you, Mi'lady."

Adrianna inclined her head. "And to you, Mi'lord."

"It is good to see you rested."

"Indeed, it is. I find myself in much better spirits today."

"I was thinking perhaps we could take a look at some of my parchments. There is a wagon not too far away where we can sit and look over the books I 'borrowed'."

Adrianna's smile widened and she nodded. Dinim led her to the wagon Thalen had said they could use for the day. He handed her his larian's ropes, and with his pack slung over one shoulder, he jumped from the back of his mount and into the rear of the wagon. He then tied the larian to the anchor afixed to the side and helped her leap from Cortath's back into the wagon beside him. Once situated, they sat down and began to take the books and parchments out of his pack.

Adrianna pulled one of the books onto her lap and opened it. She flipped through the pages until she came to one that had the hideous picture of a half-eaten corpse. With a look of disgust, she turned to Dinim only to find him watching her. He grinned when he saw her expression and then passed her another book. "Here, this is what you're looking for."

Adrianna took the book and regarded the open pages. Scrawled across the top, in large letters, was the word *Azmathion* and below it ***The Box of Death***. Adrianna grinned. "You found it!"

Dinim nodded. "It took me a while, but I was somehow able to hunt it down."

Adrianna paused for a moment and frowned. "How did you know that my father was Azmathous in the first place?"

"Well, when I was captured by Gaknar's priests, I was brought to the temple beneath Sangrilak. Only a single day later, the temple was overrun by priests of Aasarak. I was subsequently confiscated, and my identity given to the doppelganger Ixitchitl so that it could act as a spy for Aasarak. I escaped the guards, but not my prison. I was forced to live in the temple for many weeks, waiting for the one they called 'Lord Thane' to come for me. It was during that time I learned of the Azmathous, that Aasarak had begun to master the power of the Azmathion, and that he was beginning to amass an army of his minions."

Adrianna shook her head, Ami's words running through her mind. *The undead lord will not stop until he feels your heart stop beating! For now, his vision is clouded, but he will find you again. You can't run from him forever. And after him there is another, one so dark and so foul that he will raise an army like no other that has been seen on the face of this world. If he succeeds, another Cycle will end, and this future will never come to pass.*

She shook herself out of the memory when Dinim continued. "Thane is a follower of Aasarak, and it seems he is one of the first of the Azmathous that Aasarak has created. Others have been created since then, at least six by your account. This book describes the Azmathous made by the creator of the Azmathion a long time ago, including their desire for revenge against those whom they perceive to have done them wrong. At first the Death Master can create only warriors, but as he gains in strength, he can make sorcerers as well. Aasarak has become very powerful very quickly if he has managed to harness a sorcerer already."

Adrianna fought to steady herself. She couldn't even think about Aasarak right now. She needed to focus on her more immediate problem– Thane. Even now he was coming for them. "So, what exactly do you know about Thane? Does this book tell us what powers he and his followers may possess?"

Dinim shook his head. "No. Each of the Azmathous is different. The abilities of each will depend upon the skills he or she possessed in life. If the warrior was a swordsman, then he will be a master with that weapon in death. In addition, they all have some powers in common, such as the ability to cause uncontrollable fear, supernatural strength, and immunity to non-magical weaponry."

"Well, at least that's a start," she said.

"Indeed."

Adrianna frowned. "I'm afraid, Dinim. Even now we're being hunted. He will find us traveling with this caravan, and he will kill everyone–"

Dinim interrupted her. "No, he won't."

She shook her head. "How can you say that? You know what my father is capable of doing!"

Dinim put an arm around her shoulders and pulled her close. "He won't find us. As it turns out, the caravan is protected. I spoke to Ami, and she told me the Firasat clan carries an arcane device that will make it impossible for Thane to see us. When he tries to scry for you, he will find only cloudiness. The power of the device will keep him from seeing us for as long as we are with them. When we part company, we will no longer be within the area of effect. Only then will Thane be able to track us again."

Adrianna gave a relieved grin. "So, you were the one who told Ami that we were in danger?"

"No. I told her nothing about Thane. I just told her that a debt collector was following us, and that he owned a seeing orb. That was when she told me about the anti-scrying device."

She frowned. "You're funning me."

Dinim raised an eyebrow. "You want to bet?"

Adrianna pouted her lower lip. "No."

"Then hush. You should know better than to think I would let anyone know about our business."

Adrianna nodded and said nothing more. But one thought reigned: *How in Shandahar does Ami known about Thane?*

The Firasat clan caravan continued to travel north alongside the Dresnjik River, across the kingdom of Durnst toward the city of Risset. The days turned into a week. The gypsy women continued to watch Adrianna with expressions of disdain. They never made outward displays of hostility, but she could feel it lurking behind their frigid stares. She saw the man, Errow, only once. He smiled as he passed by her on his larian, but that was all. Tianna continued her lustful affair, taking nightly jaunts across the encampment to meet her lover. Her spirit seemed to be recovering from Sirion's loss, and it was good to hear her tinkling laughter.

However, Adrianna found it difficult to capture happiness for herself. She experienced solace and some measure of joy in her companionship with Cortath, but that didn't take away pervading feelings of guilt. She was constantly looking over her shoulder, afraid of who she might find standing there. She felt sorry about the way she'd treated the gypsy matriarch. The old woman hadn't deserved her wrath, and Adrianna knew she needed to offer her apologies. The woman had shown she and her friends nothing but kindness, and Adrianna had repaid her with disrespect.

Adrianna was pensive as Cortath carried her over to Ami Rayhana's wagon. The cover over the rear entrance was closed. She was wondering how she should alert the occupants of her presence when the cover was pulled aside. One of Ami's daughters stood inside the wagon, smiling kindly. She gestured Adrianna within. Cortath moved close to the wagon, and when she made it off of his back and into the back, he jogged away to walk where he chose. He would come back when she needed him. All she had to do was call to him with her mind.

"Ami has been waiting for you."

Adrianna nodded and followed the woman into the recesses of the wagon. The cover closed behind them and the area dimmed considerably. "Ami has been resting. That is why it is so dark, but when she wishes it, we will pull back the cover and let the light in."

Adrianna only nodded again. Looking ahead she saw a soft glow of light. It got larger, and then she saw the withered countenance of Ami Rayhana cast by the light of the nearby glow-sphere. The old woman smiled. "Sit my dear child." Ami gestured toward the pile of pillows situated opposite her. "Would you care for a refreshment? Some tea perhaps?"

Adrianna smiled. "That would be nice, Ami."

Ami's daughter turned to a small pot, poured the tea into a cup, and handed it to Adrianna.

Adrianna inclined her head as she accepted it. "Thank you."

There were a few moments of silence while the two women drank their tea. Adrianna found that it was quite good, almost as good as the tea Tianna made for the group in the mornings. "You have come to ask me about what I have seen," stated Ami bluntly.

Adrianna looked up at the old woman and regarded her intently. "I have come to apologize to you for my wretched behavior a few nights ago."

Ami chuckled. "An excuse for everything, have you?"

Adrianna contained the sigh that threatened to emerge. The old woman was perceptive. Indeed, there was a part of her that wanted to hear what Ami had seen in her visions, but there was an even larger part of her that did not. Yet here she was, sitting in front of the strange seer, sharing a cup of tea. She supposed there could be more to her visit than a simple apology. "Is there something more that you would like to tell me?"

"To share with you, yes." Ami paused. "There is more to you than meets the eye, my dear. I have seen your dreams. Through the years I have learned that dreams can be changed, altered to fit the needs of the world, altered through space and time to be a mold for one place... one warrior."

Adrianna frowned. "You speak in riddles, Ami. Please be plain with me."

The old woman pursed her lips. "The world will need a hero, and prophecy has foretold the coming of one who will open the path to a new era. She may even save the world from becoming lost forever."

Adrianna shook her head. "I'm sorry, I don't know what any of this means for me. Perhaps I shouldn't have come."

Ami Rayhana got a distant look in her eyes, and her voice began to rise. "There will be born a child, and she will be a beacon of light within this world of approaching darkness. With her a new era will begin, and the dragons will call her Sister. The tipping Balance will cause the ascendancy of an old power. When the time comes, the angels will fall. The daughter will open a new way, and when all seems lost, a new people will answer the call."

Adrianna stared at the seer. She had never heard words of prophecy spoken before, yet she knew she had just heard them uttered from this woman's mouth. The old woman closed her eyes, and her body slumped. Ami's daughter came over and situated her more comfortably upon the pillows. Adrianna stood up. She was more than a little rattled, and felt the need to escape.

Ami's daughter turned to her and nodded. "It is always disturbing when Ami has a vision."

Adrianna nodded in return, calling Cortath as she walked to the rear of the wagon. He was already waiting when she pulled back the cover, and she easily slipped onto his back. She urged him away from the wagon and moved as far away as they could go. She mulled over Ami's words, and her hands wouldn't stop shaking. The words of the prophecy bore no meaning to her, yet she felt the power of them. All she could do was wait, for she was sure the prophecy would come to pass.

And she would understand, whether she wanted to or not.

Sheridana positioned her larian beside the wagon and prepared to dismount. She secured the beast's ropes about one of the bars on the lattice afixed to the side of the wagon and patted the sweaty neck affectionately. She then gripped the lattice and pulled herself out of the saddle, stepped a couple of feet and then angled herself into the opening.

Carli looked up with a smile at her arrival and held out a plate. "I just finished preparing lunch. Here, sit next to me."

Sheridana obliged, took the proffered plate, and sat beside her friend. For a moment the two women ate in silence. Fitanni was taking her midday nap and the other occupants of the wagon were either on guard duty or taking their meal elsewhere.

Five days ago, the caravan had left the small city of Kranton behind, and it was about time. Sheridana had tired of the city after being stuck staying there with her small family for longer than she cared. When she happened to discover that the visiting gypsies were planning on leaving soon, she went to them and asked where they were traveling next. When they told her they were going southwest along the river, she asked if she could join them. Clan Mustafa readily welcomed her into their ranks.

Traveling with a caravan this large, it was easy for Sheridana to keep herself occupied. She made herself useful by helping with daily guard duties and contributing her share to the evening stewpot. The gypsies were a vociferous people, and there was never a dull moment. She and Carli captured the attention of many of the young men right away. Sheridana spurned their advances with ease, not interested in the purely physical relationships they offered.

However, she noticed Carli was entranced.

When the silence stretched, Sheridana turned to her young charge. Carli stared into the distance outside the wagon, a half smile curving her lips. "You still thinking of that boy?"

Carli blinked and turned, her smile widening. "Maybe."

Sheridana gave a small sigh but the girl forestalled anything she might say. "I know! I know you don't like him."

"It's not that I don't like him. I actually think he's a nice person."

"Then what is it? Why shouldn't I think about him?"

"It's because of our situation; in less than a handful of days we will leave this caravan behind. But even more, because of *his* situation, and what he is. Gypsies are a very transient people, and that reflects in their relationships. Only a fraction of the children you see running about here know who their fathers are."

Carli gave a belly laugh. "Sheri! Aren't you moving a bit fast? I've hardly thought past holding his hand!"

Sheridana shook her head and gave a toothy grin. "You don't know how tempting men can be."

Carli rolled her eyes. "Stop worrying so much. I know we are leaving, and he's not so magical that he can lure me into his furs that easily."

Sheridana gave her a skeptical look. She would continue to watch over her young charge as best she could, no matter what assurances Carli gave.

Seeing this look on her face, the girl rolled her eyes again and shook her head before shifting her expression into one of solemnity. Her voice was low, "I heard some talk today."

"What about?"

"Some of the guards were talking about a merchant caravan camped at the eastern banks of the river near the city of Torrich. It was attacked. The entire caravan was brutally killed, women and children too. Only one man survived. He spoke about the ambushers like they were something from out of the worst of nightmares."

Sheridana listened as Carli continued to talk. The path they were taking would bring them closer to where this rumored ambush took place, but she was determined to stick to their route. Taking another would only cost her more time, time she wasn't willing to spare anymore.

In another three days they would be reaching the city of Risset. Once there, she and her family would rest for a couple of days and then leave the city early in the morning. They would ride south along the river until they reached a place where they could cross; she knew of one just south of the Shelarea fork. They would hire the ferry to take them across the river. The journey would take most of the day, and at the end of the ride, they would be in the Kingdom of Monaf. They would then ride to the closest village and stay there until they found a means in which to travel to the city of Kamden safely.

Sheridana sighed. She was getting closer. The air was becoming warmer with each passing day, not just because of the season, but because they were moving southward. Once they reached Kamden, they would stock up on their supplies and then journey to Celuna. From there they would traverse the Ratik Mountain Pass that would deposit them near the city of Driscol. She couldn't wait to be in the Realm of Torimir after so long, and she would be able to start her search for her sister…

And she would be whole again.

SISTER

Adrianna sat alone near the evening fire. She made a valiant attempt to read the open book before her, to no avail. She was simply too jittery to concentrate. They had been with the caravan for just over a week and there was only one more day of travel before they reached Risset. Once at the outskirts of the city, the caravan would camp for the night. The next morning, the gypsy men would enter the city and see if there were any business ventures for them there. If they found some, the Firasat clan would stay. If not, the men would stock up on supplies and the caravan would move on towards the next city. Meanwhile, Adrianna would have begun asking around about Sheridana. Hopefully she would meet someone who had heard of her, or possibly the group with whom Sheri had been traveling called Thritean's Pride. If not, she would consult with her comrades and they would decide if they should move on with the caravan or part ways.

Cortath bounded up with a fresh kill in his jaws. He dropped the furred, six-legged animal at her side and sat down beside her. Adrianna smiled when she picked up his offering. "Thank you, my friend!"

A few moments later on his way by with a brace of ptarmigan, Dartanyen nodded cordially and collected Cortath's burbana. He took the meat to Tianna, who would prepare it for the evening meal. Adrianna sighed and rose to her feet. She might as well help, for she was getting nothing done by just sitting there. Not to mention, she was certain Tianna would appreciate it.

Late in the afternoon the next day, the caravan reached the outskirts of Risset. In the distance, another line of wagons could be seen situated closer to the city. Some of the men rode out to meet the other caravan. After an hour they returned and cheers went up among the wagons when the identity of the other train was revealed. There was a close friendship with Clan Mustafa and it was the perfect excuse for a celebration. It was rare they received the opportunity to spend time with a familiar family.

The caravans moved closer together, and once they met, the wagons were situated in a huge circle. It would be a particularly safe encampment with the city so close and the presence of so many of their own. Soon, the camp transformed into a place much like the one from several evenings before– with musicians, dancers, games, and an excess of good drink and food. A few people had relatives from the other clan, and families were reunited for the evening. Some familiar, well-known travelers passing by on their way through towards the city stopped and mingled with the crowd for a while, making the scene even larger.

Adrianna stayed near the group's wagon, watching the goings on, tending the fire, and stirring the contents of the pot positioned over it. Suddenly Tianna was sweeping into the camp. She was quite a vision, wearing a blue and yellow skirt and a green blouse. Adrianna was hauled away from the fire and dragged behind one of the wagons.

Tianna's eyes twinkled. "Take off your clothes."

She looked at her friend with an expression she was sure bordered on shock and some cloth was pressed into her hands.

"Put these on instead."

She looked down to see a red and yellow, gold-embroidered skirt with a gold colored sash in her arms, as well as an orange blouse with similar décor. She just stood there for a moment, staring at the cloth.

"You will look beautiful in this," Tianna reassured her excitedly. "Now take off your tunic and trousers and put it on."

Adrianna obeyed, donning the blouse Tianna had brought. Tianna helped her step into the skirt, and then fastened the loosely woven, shimmery gold sash about her waist. Adrianna looked at her friend, waiting for her to mention the long scar, but Tianna didn't pay it any heed. While the healer examined her ears, Adrianna struggled with the blouse, which seemed too small. When Tianna noticed her attempts to pull the blouse down over her belly, she slapped away her hands and repositioned the blouse beneath her breasts.

"It is meant to be worn as such– like mine." Tianna displayed herself.

Adrianna frowned and shook her head, glancing down at her exposed belly. She realized that it wasn't just too small, but also too low-cut, something she would never wear had she the choice. The evening air hit her flesh and she felt naked.

"No way. I look like a harlot." She plucked at the cloth, trying to adjust it to cover her cleavage, but her hands were slapped away again.

Tianna chuckled. "You look very fine, Adrianna Darnesse. And you don't look like a... a harlot. Anyway, you deserve to have a good time. I bought the clothes so you could have a new experience– you know, let yourself go for a change."

Adrianna looked down at the ground. She hadn't told her friend about the night she'd drank so much brew that she was nearly swept away by a dark, handsome stranger. She let Tianna take her by the shoulders to lead her back to the fire. She was bade to sit while the healer took something out of her belt pouch. Tianna then placed the small object in the flame, turning it this way and that for a few moments before turning back to Adrianna. "Now, don't move. This will only hurt for a moment."

"Tianna, what are you– **Ouch!**" Adrianna screamed the last and put a hand up to her ear. Tianna quickly took the hand away from the area, removed the needle from her lobe, wiped the wound with something that smelled medicinal, and then placed a decoration there. Tianna repeated the procedure with the other ear. At the finish, she had pierced ears.

Adrianna frowned. "You could have told me first," she said petulantly.

"If I had, you would never have let me do it."

She stuck out her lower lip. "You are probably right," she agreed.

Tianna smiled. "Come on. Let's get something to drink." Then she stopped. 'Wait, these are for you too." Tianna took a pair of gold-colored slippers from her bag and handed them to her.

Adrianna placed the shoes on her feet. *Gods, what will the rest of the group say? I can't let them see me like this.* But it was too late. When she was finished lacing the slippers, she looked up to see Dinim striding into the camp.

Adrianna's mind whirled and her face flushed. She thought about hiding behind one of the wagons, and was about to dart away, when Dinim noticed her. Adrianna saw his eyes widen, and he slowed his pace as he approached. Finally, he stood before her, his lavender gaze drinking her in from head to foot. "Wow," he exclaimed. "You look so..."

"Different," she supplied in a monotone voice, not really wanting to know what he was going to say.

"Yes, definitely that," he replied almost breathlessly. Tianna stepped up to them. "We were just about to get something to drink. Do you want to come with us?"

In the distance Adrianna heard the music begin. She walked toward it with Dinim on one side and Tianna on the other. When they reached the bonfire, someone offered them each a drink. They graciously accepted the mugs and Adrianna took a few swallows. The drink seemed stronger than she remembered, the liquid racing like a warm river down her throat. Beside her, she heard Dinim clearing his throat and her suspicions were verified.

Before she knew it, they had joined many others near the entertainers. Excitedly Tianna tapped her shoulder and then pranced away, going over to the musicians and joining them. Tianna began to sing, lifting her beautiful voice in accompaniment to the others. For a while Dinim and Adrianna watched the performers, the instruments being played, the people singing, and the women dancing. Adrianna continued to drink from her mug and, after a while, realized it was almost empty. The music began to infiltrate into her thoughts, and she swayed slightly with the music. Someone refilled her mug and she continued to drink.

Dinim and Adrianna walked around the bonfire a few times, laughing at some the antics of the children, as well as the adults. They walked slowly, side-by-side, enjoying one another's company, their sides bumping every now and again. Adrianna noticed the way many of the people looked at her, especially the women, who didn't even try hiding their contempt anymore.

"Dinim, what is going on here? Why do that hate me so much?"

He turned to look at her. "They don't hate you, Adria. They're just jealous."

"But why? What have I done? What could they possibly be jealous about?"

Dinim stopped and she followed suit. "There is something about you, an aura to which people are drawn. On top of that, you are an exceptionally beautiful woman. Hasn't anyone ever told you that?"

"No, not really." Then she chuckled. "I know you are just saying it to be kind."

He shook his head. "No, no I'm not. Really, let me explain..."

In the distance Adrianna heard another round of music struck up by the musicians. "Come on! We should go back over near the entertainers. I want to hear Tianna sing. She has such a wonderful voice, don't you think?"

Adrianna took Dinim's hand and he swallowed what he was going to say to allow her to lead him towards the music. It was a great diversion from a conversation that had shifted into uncomfortable territory. She didn't know if what he said was true or not, and at this point, it didn't matter. Parting company with the gypsies was a great possibility depending on the information she attained on the morrow, and the hateful glares would be a thing of the past.

They stopped before the entertainers and stood there for a few moments, listening to the music. After a while Tianna stumbled over and thrust a full mug of ale into Adrianna's hand. Now that she wasn't singing, Tianna's voice was a bit slurred. "So, what did you think?"

Adrianna wrapped her arms around her friend's neck. "I think you're wonderful!"

Tianna laughed and returned the embrace. "You don't mind if I stay here a while longer?"

She waved Tianna away. "Go! Go be happy and sing. I'll be here listening."

Tianna gave a little squeal before going back over to the entertainers. One of the men gave her a hug and kissed her soundly on the lips. Adrianna chuckled and felt a nudge at her side. She turned and Dinim handed the mug back to her. She raised a brow when she noticed half of the ale was gone and he gave her an innocent shrug.

Adrianna listened to the music, content to just stand there and sway. It was nice to have Dinim there with her, and given the massive bonfire, they discussed the properties of various fire-based spells. Once again, she'd imbibed too much ale, and the familiar sensation of euphoria enveloped her. She felt warm and was glad for the light fabric of the clothes she wore. She would have to thank Tianna for them later.

"Dance with me, Adrianna."

She turned to see Dinim holding out his hand, a half smile turning up one corner of his mouth. He looked so debonair standing there, one black eyebrow just a little higher than the other and the white streak in his hair more noticeable since it had grown out. "Don't mind if I do, kind sir."

Adrianna took his hand and Dinim pulled her towards him. Suddenly she remembered the last time they'd stood so close– it was when she'd discovered that Mairi had been killed. He'd held her while she cried bitter tears of loss, his arms wrapped protectively around her. However, the memory slipped away as he placed his hands at her hips and began moving with her to the cadence of the music.

Her world spun. Desire surged through her, and it couched with the excitement of being alive at this time, in this place, with this man. The combination was more intoxicating than any ale. As they danced, her body melted into his and she never knew she could be so close to someone. Adrianna became a part of the music, the rhythm moving all about and within her, and she let it carry her away.

Suddenly she was no longer in Dinim's arms but in front of him. She raised her arms and let her body move to the seductive cadence, circled Dinim as she danced, her hips bumping him lightly as she moved. She felt the feather-soft touch of his fingertips on the bare flesh of her arms and waist. His movements accompanied hers, and then his hands were on her waist, at the small of her back, drawing her back into him. Her body moved against his and they began to move together in synchrony to the music, each moment that passed causing her yearning to intensify. Her senses spiraled out of control, and all that existed was Dinim...

Finally, the music paused. From her place within the circle of Dinim's arms, she looked up into eyes dark with passion. His breath was warm on her cheek, and where her palm rested on his chest, she could feel the beating of his heart.

"That was wonderful," Dinim whispered. His voice was deep and his breath tickled her ear. Adrianna pulled back to see the desire written over his face. She deeply inhaled a shuddering breath and fire curled low in her belly. Dinim leaned towards her and she went to meet him...

"Adrianna, that was great!" Suddenly there was a hand on her arm, and it wasn't Dinim's. She turned to see Armond standing next to them, smiling appreciatively. "Where did you learn to dance like that?"

Heat suffused her face and she pulled away from Dinim, suddenly feeling self-conscious. Dinim seemed to be feeling the same way and was running a hand through his hair.

"I learned while I was studying in Andahye. Master Tallek felt that it would be a good outlet for me, so he hired someone to teach me how to dance." Feeling strangely disturbed, Adrianna wrapped her arms about her middle and backed away. "I'll be back soon. I need to take a moment to cool off."

Adrianna fled the scene, looking about as she walked away. She didn't see the rest of the group. It was just as well they hadn't seen her wanton display of affection. She wouldn't have known how to explain it, and mere drunkenness wouldn't have been believed. She shook her head. This was the second time Armond had interrupted, inadvertently stopping something from happening between she and Dinim. She wondered about that as she recovered from the thrill of being so close to him. *What would have happened between us? How far could it have gone?*

Perhaps I will never know.

15 FINOREN CY593

The next morning the group rose early. They assembled the lloryk and larian, loading the animals with their travel packs. They then said their good-byes to the Firasat clan. It was a sad parting, for friendships had been made during the many days of travel together. But it was tempered with gladness for they had high hopes Adrianna would find some information about her sister in the city.

It took them only a couple of hours to reach the outskirts of Risset. Just like last time, Adrianna was sad to leave Cortath behind. Through their link she promised that she would come to him sometime the next day. She watched as he sank into the tall grasses, his demeanor much less lively than usual. She frowned with concern, wondering if something was amiss, but then realized that it might just be the separation that had him so lackluster.

Once through the city gates, the group made their way to the first reputable inn, The Wayward Wyvern. They paid for the accommodations and immediately went to their rooms. Adrianna immediately felt the urge to take a look around the city. She wanted to get a feel for the place before she started questioning the residents. The best way to do that would be to just keep her ears open and her mouth closed. However, the need for a bath screamed at her, and the first thing she did when she reached the room was order one. One at a time, she, Tianna, and Amethyst shared the hot bath. It was good to feel clean again, and it put everyone in better spirits. The women then piled their dirty clothing into the lukewarm water and left them to soak.

When the three women finally made it back down to the common room, the rest of the group was already partaking of an early evening meal. Adrianna seated herself next to Dinim and looked around the table. It seemed that everyone had maximized on the luxury of bathing, for there wasn't a dry head among them. Helping herself to the leftover food at the table, she ate heartily and then accepted a mug of mead. Finding herself more tired than she thought she would be, Adrianna leaned back in her chair. She supposed it wouldn't hurt to start her search until the morrow. It was such a different attitude than what she had felt upon first entering the city, but now that she'd reached her destination, she felt a little more relaxed.

Late afternoon melted into early evening and the crowd in the tavern grew. Ale and mead continued to flow, loosening everyones tongues. The group spoke animatedly amongst themselves, simply enjoying one another's company. Every now and then Adrianna looked around the room, taking in all the people entering the establishment. It was a more diverse populace than she would have imagined, although nothing like Sangrilak. Most of the people were human, with most of those being of Recondian descent. The few faelin she saw were either Terralean or Savanlean. A few people took a look or two in their direction, but no one seemed to care much after that.

Laughter drifted from the direction of the bar and Adrianna focused her attention to it for a moment before she lost interest and returned to the story Dartanyen was telling. It was a tale he'd told them once before, one from his younger years about a girl who had gone missing from her village. He got to the part where he'd come face to face with a terrifying wild boar when she heard the laughter again. Her interest piqued once more, she turned towards the bar. A woman was seated there and she was talking animatedly with the man beside her. Her back was turned to the rest of the room, so Adrianna couldn't see her face, but she had dark hair that was plaited into a long rope that hung down her back. She focused on the woman's voice, and when a reply was made to something the man said, familiarity rushed through her.

Adrianna stared, her heart cavorting about in her chest, and Dinim nudged her in the side with his elbow. Once again, the young woman laughed at something the man said, and Adrianna knew why the voice affected her so much.

By the gods, can it really be? Saying nothing to the rest of the group, Adrianna rose from the table and slowly made her way over to the woman seated at the bar. She was jostled about a bit by busy serving girls and thirsty patrons, but finally she stood behind the woman. Hesitantly she reached out and touched her arm. "Excuse me..."

The woman turned around on the stool, deep blue eyes regarding her questioningly. The woman's expression then altered into one of disbelief. "Adrianna?"

A wave of relief passed through her and she almost choked on her words. "Sheridana, is that really you?"

"By the gods, Adrianna, what are you doing here?"

Sheridana slid from the barstool and pulled her into a hearty embrace. Adrianna squeezed her eyes shut and returned the hug. She took a deep breath; her sister still smelled the same. She spoke past the lump in her throat. "I came here looking for you."

Sheridana's broken voice was muffled by the curtain of thick, curling hair over her shoulder. "I have missed you so much."

Adrianna blinked away the tears in her eyes as the best friend she'd ever known continued to hold her. The power of the moment was extraordinary and threatened to steal her breath away. A piece of her had been lost for a long time, and now that she'd found it, she didn't quite know what to do except hold it close. A decade of years separated she and Sheridana, but the bond they shared was still there, unbroken.

Sheridana could hardly believe the good fortune the gods had smiled upon her. Adrianna was the epitome of beauty, not even remotely like the awkward girl she'd left behind when she chose to accompany their father and Ian all those years ago. *Why did I ever leave? My life was fraught with one trial after another. But then, if I hadn't gone, I wouldn't have conceived Fitanni. I suppose some things are meant to be, even if we can't find the explanations for them anymore.*

Adrianna took her hand. "Come with me. There are people I want you to meet." Adrianna led her across the common room to a table seating two women and five men. "Sheridana, these are my companions, the group I have been traveling with for the past few moon cycles." Adrianna gestured around the table, introducing her to people whose names she'd never remember the following day. The only one who stuck out was a Cimmerean man called Dinim. It wasn't every day she saw one of his kind walking around, and the look he gave her wasn't friendly like the others. To all outward appearances it looked that way, but she knew better.

Sheridana pulled up another chair and seated herself beside Adrianna. Dartanyen beckoned to a serving girl, and when she approached, he asked her for a loaf of bread and another few tankards of ale.

The human woman with long hair gave a wide smile. "It is so good to meet you! Adria has told us a lot about you."

Sheridana just smiled in return. She doubted Adrianna had said much and imagined the woman was trying to be friendly and start conversation. It was strange to hear other people call her sister by her short name. She'd have to get used to it. Sheridana glanced around the table, uncomfortable sitting with a bunch of people she'd never met before, alongside a sister she hadn't seen for several years. However, she forced the feeling aside. Everyone seemed willing to incorporate her into their conversation.

The men made small talk while they ate and drank, and Dartanyen asked her a few questions about how far she'd traveled, from where, and with whom. When she mentioned she'd arrived with the Mustafa clan, the big man, Zorg, told a story about his recent experience with the gypsy men and Tianna followed with her rendition of the evening before when she'd been a part of the entertainment. She mentioned Adrianna and the two women bickered back and forth about the amount of spiced ale they drank. Sheridana just stared at them both for a moment. It was then she noticed it— a small, folded bit of parchment near her right elbow. She picked it up, unfolded it, and read what had been written in fine, precise handwriting, *"Congratulations on the birth of your daughter."*

Sheridana took a deep breath and stiffened. She read the note again and crumpled the parchment in her fist. She looked up and around the table until her gaze rested on the Cimmerean man. His cold gaze met hers and she knew the message was from him. For a moment she considered saying nothing, merely allowing it to slide by. But she couldn't do that. She had to know how he knew about Fitanni. He had suddenly become a threat, and the need to protect her family was strong.

Sheridana rose from her seat and held the crumpled parchment before her. "What is the meaning of this?" she demanded, her voice harsh even to her own ears. "How do you know about me? Who the Hells are you?" She trembled with fear and anger. She knew that she was causing a stir, but she refused to sit passively by and allow this man to bully her.

Dinim remained seated as he looked up at Sheridana, unconcerned. "My name is Dinim Dimitri Coabra. All it means it what it says."

Sheridana waved the fist with the parchment. "How do you know so much about my life?" Her voice rose in pitch. "Are you some kind of spy?"

With a single, fluid motion, Dinim stood from his chair and smirked at her. "It means nothing more than what it says. Why can I not congratulate you on such a momentous event? Were I mocking you, I may have announced it to the entire room." With that statement, Dinim raised his arms into the air.

Sheridana only gaped at him, her eyes full of the horror of what he was about to do.

"Attention everyone." Dinim waited until just about every person in the room was looking toward the group. "I just want to congratulate this young lady upon the birth of her daughter. Such a joyous thing should not go unheeded, don't you think?" Dinim looked at Sheridana as he spoke his last words and everyone began to applaud. The faelin man called Sabian who was seated on Dinim's other side began to chuckle as though he had just heard a joke, jabbing the Cimmerean in the ribs gleefully with his elbow.

Sheridana swallowed convulsively and felt sick to her stomach. Once more Dinim smiled at her, the smile a serpent might give its prey as it tightened its coils. The group regarded her intently and Adrianna's body had stiffened beside her. With wavering eyes Sheridana looked into his smiling face, and realized that she had made a mistake. Too soon she'd hoped to find some kind of camaraderie with these people.

"I can't believe you just—"

"Well, you'd better believe it," Sabian interrupted. We know a lot about you, my dear."

Sheridana stared at the men through wide eyes. *Who the Hells are these people? What else do that they know and how do they know it? Why do they care to know it?* Dinim turned to regard his companion with a strange expression, but Sabian just kept staring at her with an odd intensity.

Escape. I have to escape. With only that thought in mind, Sheridana spun on her heel and rushed from the table.

Shock coursed through Adrianna and at first all she could do was stare. *How could Dinim do this? Why would he do this? Sheridana had done nothing to him, yet he has humiliated her in front of an entire tavern full of evening customers, not to mention the rest of the group!*

Her voice was higher pitched than she thought it would be, mirroring the shock she was sure characterized her face "Dinim, what have you done? I can hardly believe you would be so malicious as to hurt someone like this, especially someone so important to me!" She swallowed heavily and almost choked. "Mere words can't begin to describe how disappointed you have made me."

Blinking away tears, Adrianna turned from the table and walked away. No one stopped her as she made her way towards the front of the inn, and deciding she needed some fresh air, she walked out onto the small veranda. It was a nice night and the wind blew gently through her hair. It was the coolest weather she had felt in days. The tears that threatened to fall when she confronted Dinim would no longer be held back and she leaned her back against the wall and began to cry. *By the gods, what is happening? The Dinim I know would never have done such a heinous thing. I just want to wake up from this terrible dream.*

Adrianna wiped away her tears and finally looked up at the clear night sky, the bright orb of Steralion dominating. No, this was no dream, and Dinim really was a pile of lloryk dung. Her sister was upstairs, within this very inn, probably wishing that she had never seen her this night. A part of her wanted to go to Sheridana, but the other part wouldn't allow it. *What if Sheri doesn't want me? We haven't seen one another for almost a decade. Whatever connection we once shared is frayed. Sheri probably wants to be alone—*

But no, wait. That's not possible. She has a child.

The tears ran anew. Sheridana had a baby and Dinim somehow knew about it. He knew her sister had a child and he had chosen not to share that with her. Instead, he'd told that lloryk's ass, Sabian. She'd trusted Dinim, put all of her faith in him. But for what? Just to have her heart crushed beneath his boot-heel. She suddenly remembered the evening before, how she'd behaved so wantonly. He must have loved watching her act like a little idiot.

Fortunately, Armond had been there to stop her from possibly making a mistake she'd later regret.

Maybe I would never have behaved that way if I hadn't imbibed so much of that gypsy brew. What the Hells is in that stuff? Damn it all...

Adrianna pulled herself away from the wall. She wanted to leave, walk off the excess energy that burned through her. She knew it was just her anger, but she absolutely didn't want to go back inside the inn, possibly to face Dinim, and then lay awake all night thinking about what she had done, or not done. Adrianna leapt from the veranda and onto the street. She knew where she wanted to go.

Into the shadows of dusk she ran away from Dinim, away from her sister, away from the hurt she knew would follow her anyway. Once she was out of the city, darkness fell, but Adrianna continued through crop fields that reminded her of the ones back home in Sangrilak. It wasn't until fatigue made her slow down that she recognized the folly of what she'd done.

She stopped in the middle of a field. It was quiet but for the song of hespartus. It was dangerous for a lone woman to be out at night; there could be anything hiding in the tall barley. Adrianna opened her mind, hoping Cortath was somewhere near. He was closer than she'd thought he would be, and within moments he materialized in front of her, his shape appearing larger than usual in the light cast by Steralion and the newly emerging Hestim.

Her fears assuaged, Adrianna rushed up to her friend, wrapping her arms about his neck. He brought his head down over her shoulder and the warmth of his breath washed over her back. She simply held him for a while, then climbed onto his back and bade him take her where he'd been keeping himself. For a short while they walked, Adrianna lying over his back. They left the field behind and when he finally stopped, she slid down and saw that he'd found a small copse of trees. Beneath the largest one, she saw the indentation in the grasses where he'd been resting. Cortath took himself over to that spot and lay down.

Adrianna followed. She was tired, and more than willing to join her friend in his nest. She settled down beside him and Cortath placed his head on his paws and closed his eyes. For a few moments Adrianna sat there and stared at him. His communication with her through their link was barely minimal. She was accustomed to feeling and experiencing so much more. She didn't receive any negative emotions from him, so she knew he wasn't upset about something. She ran her hand over his soft fur and probed their link. Something else was there, something she couldn't pinpoint, and it gave her a bad feeling.

Adrianna lay her head against Cortath's warm side. He didn't curl around her as he usually did, nor did he adjust himself to make her more comfortable.

He merely lay there, his eyes closed. He breathed deeply and slowly, as though he'd already fallen into slumber. Adrianna gently caressed his face and ran her fingers through his silky soft mane. Cortath didn't stir. Finally, she curled up into a ball next to him, pressing her back into his side. Before long, exhaustion took over and she was fast asleep.

Dinim slowly walked down the stairs, his head aching from drinking too much ale the night before. He didn't recall making it up to his room, and awoke in the same clothes he'd been wearing the day before. His sleep had been restless, his mind replaying the whole horrible scene over and over again.

Dinim cringed when he heard the voices at the bottom of the stairs. "Are you sure she never came back?" asked Dartanyen.

Tianna's reply was petulant. "What do you mean, '*are you sure*'? We share a room. For the love of Beory, of course I'm sure!"

"What's going on here?" Dinim came into view and descended to join Tianna, Dartanyen, and Armond.

Armond turned to glare at him. "Adrianna never returned to the inn. Tianna has been up waiting half the night." Armond's tone was accusatory, and his glare bordering on menacing.

Dinim felt a chill sweep through him. Because of his idiocy, she had left the tavern. Because of him, she had wandered, alone, into the night. Something had probably happened, and it was all his fault.

Tianna must have seen the myriad of expressions passing over his face. "All right, let's not jump to any conclusions. Just because she didn't come back to the inn last night doesn't mean something has happened to her."

After that statement, there was silence. No one knew what to say, all realizing that, most likely, something had happened to Adrianna. Why else would she not have returned? "Gather the rest of the group, Tianna. We need to start looking for her," said Dartanyen quietly.

Tianna nodded and went up the stairs to do Dartanyen's bidding. Armond followed her, casting one last nasty glance at Dinim as he left. Silently Dinim stood before Dartanyen. Finally, the other man spoke. "I don't know why you did what you did last night, nor do I want to know. All I want to say is that it was wrong of you, but I think you know that already. Adrianna has shown you more kindness and given you more friendship than anyone else in this group, yet you betrayed her trust in the worst way." Dartanyen paused and shook his head.

"I don't know why I did it. I have wished, a million times over, that I had told her about the child."

Dartanyen put a hand on Dinim's shoulder. "We all make mistakes. It is the way we rectify them that makes us good men."

"I don't think Adrianna will ever forgive me."

"You don't give her enough credit."

Dinim lowered his head. "Perhaps."

After a moment they both looked towards the stairs. Zorg and Sabian were making their way down, wiping the sleep from their eyes and dressed in nothing but their trousers. Amethyst followed behind, the epitome of alertness. Dartanyen raised his voice for all to hear. "Let's split up into pairs. I want to have the whole city scoured by the midday hour."

Adrianna walked slowly down the street back to the inn, worry dogging her every step. There was something definitely wrong with Cortath. She could tell he was ill, but couldn't get anything definitive in regards to what it could be. Through the link, all she could feel was his lethargy and the sensation of cold, which she had come to believe was a fever. *Oh gods, what am I going to do? I've neither seen, nor heard, of any other creature quite like him. All I can do is tell Tianna and hope she can help.*

She put a hand to her forehead. She'd awakened early, hoping to make it back to the inn before anyone became alarmed. She hoped the others hadn't begun to worry about her, and if they had, she hoped they realized she would have found solace with Cortath.

Adrianna walked up the stairs to the inn. She was still tired and wished for the opportunity to go to bed. However, she needed to find a meal for her friend. It was apparent he hadn't bothered to feed himself because his stomach rumbled to her all throughout the night. Despite his belly's indications, Cortath didn't bother rousing himself to obtain a meal. She was about to open the door, when someone from within did it for her. Startled, Adrianna jumped back, her hand to her chest. From the entryway Dartanyen stood there staring at her, and behind him was the rest of the group.

Ahh Hells...

Tianna rushed out of the inn and grabbed her by the arms. "Adrianna, where have you been? We've been worried sick about you!"

Adrianna's eyes widened with the passion she heard in Tianna's voice. "I went to spend the night with Cortath. I didn't think you would worry about me. I'm sorry–"

"Don't ever do that again!" Tianna said angrily. "You are no different than anyone else in this group and should let us know when you are going somewhere. How dare you–"

Dartanyen placed a staying hand on Tianna's shoulder. "I think she gets the point."

Adrianna regarded her companions standing at the doorway. They were about to go out looking for her. She must have been wearing an expression of chagrin on her face, because Dartanyen gave her an 'it's all right' look. Adrianna noticed Dinim standing with all of the rest. Why he even bothered she couldn't begin to fathom because he obviously didn't care about her. Perhaps he did it because Dartanyen asked him for the favor.

All of a sudden Tianna rushed at her. Adrianna steeled herself, but quickly realized her friend was merely embracing her. "I was so worried about you, Adria. I'm sorry. I didn't mean to yell at you. It's just that I love you so much."

Adrianna blinked, touched by the words, and patted her friend's back. She hadn't known how much she'd come to mean to Tianna. She felt the same and Tianna had become like a sister to her. *Sister... where is Sheridana? I hope she hasn't left. I have so much to say, and haven't been given the chance. Perhaps I should have followed Sheri last night after all, but then I never would have realized Cortath's illness...*

Adrianna whispered into her ear, "Tianna, I think Cortath is sick. Please, you have to come and help me find out what is wrong."

Tianna pulled away, a frown furrowing her brow. "All right, I'll go and get my bags." She turned and went back into the inn, followed by Zorg and Amethyst.

Armond stepped over and put a hand on her shoulder. "I'm glad to see you are all right. I'm sure Tianna will figure out what's wrong with Cortath." He offered her a smile before turning and following the other two back into the building.

Dartanyen was last to approach. "I will accompany you and Tianna to Cortath." Adrianna nodded as Tianna came back out, bags in tow. "Let me go and get a couple of the larian." Adrianna only nodded again, her mind already questing for Cortath. She only hoped Armond was right and that Tianna was able to help him.

Thane stared into the sultry night sky. If he were alive, he would smell the dampness of the surrounding grass and the perfume of the nearby simoas. He would feel the heaviness of the air against his skin, and with his superior faelin sense, easily recognize if it would soon rain. He probably would have striven to find some type of shelter, unwilling to spend his night in a raging downpour. Now it simply didn't matter, for such mortal things had ceased to affect him.

The evening after their last meeting, Thane had begun his endeavor to track Adrianna and her group towards the Realm of Durnst across the Dresnjik

River. At first, he and the other Azmathous were slow, for they had been weakened in the fight she and her comrades had given them. The days passed, and just as they were regaining their full strength, Thane and his minions encountered a caravan. Out of simple need for destruction they easily decimated it, however they were so focused on the caravan they hadn't noticed the approach of Grimwell and several more of Lord Aasarak's priests and sorcerers. Before Thane realized it, he and his Azmathous found themselves surrounded.

Over the past several moon cycles, Thane had become somewhat of a rogue. He had begun to break away from Aasarak's influence, allowing his strong desire for vengeance to finally overlay allegiance to his creator. Meanwhile, the other Azmathous had followed his lead, somehow bound to him through the power of the artifact Aasarak had used to create them. Thane knew he was taking a chance, but he simply wasn't able to ignore his desire any longer. Adrianna needed to die, and he would be the one to bring about her death.

Aasarak was undoubtedly upset. He had communicated Thane's lack of obeisance to Grimwell, and the priest had been compelled to bring Thane to task. At the scene of the destroyed caravan, words were exchanged and a battle ensued. Thane and his minions had managed to defeat the priests, but not without cost. Weakened, and unable to continue tracking Adrianna, they had backtracked to an easily defensible, relatively hidden location. It had taken them at least two nights to begin recovering their strength, and by then Adrianna was long gone. When Thane was ready and attempted to scry for her, the translucent gem had remained clouded.

In spite of being unable to determine her location, Thane had continued. When he didn't find Adrianna in the closest city, Torrich, he began to scour the countryside. It wasn't until almost a fortnight later that Thane was able to detect her again, and he immediately began to track her further north.

Now he was heading towards the city of Risset. Adrianna's death had become a fiery obsession, even to the exclusion of communicating to his master. The runic pendant resting against his chest had gone untouched for several fortnights in spite of the compulsion for him to use it. Not only that, since the battle with Grimwell, he had the price of some of Lord Aasarak's most favored priests on his head.

Thane clenched his hand over the hilt of his broadsword. Hells, if only he hadn't decided to leave the night of their last meeting, if only he had persevered to destroy Adrianna despite the arrival of the dawn. But the large canine was an element he hadn't considered, and his band had been weakened. He'd chosen to let her go to fight another day, and unfortunately it had been too long in coming.

But now he was getting close again. This time he would show no mercy. As each day passed, he and his minions grew in power, when next Thane met his daughter, he would crush her as he should have done that night over a fortnight before.

Adrianna sat in the common room, picking at the remnants of a meal she'd ordered well over an hour or two ago after returning to the inn with Tianna and Dartanyen. The healer hadn't discovered what was wrong with Cortath. She'd noted the mild fever and his lethargy, but didn't find any seeping or open wounds that might be the cause of an infection. Even though she hadn't the skill to heal animals, Tianna had even tried praying to her goddess. When she placed her hands on Cortath, she felt nothing festering inside his body that would cause his illness.

"Adria, maybe Cortath is just worn out and needs a rest."

"But that doesn't seem right. The time we spent traveling with the gypsy caravan was relaxing. Nothing was expected of him, and he rested as often as he wished."

Tianna shrugged. "I don't feel anything wrong with him. I've done all I can."

The fork clattered when she dropped it onto her half-eaten plate. *No, it isn't lack of rest that's wrong with Cortath. Perhaps he has a simple, common ailment and needs extra care for a few days. Everyone gets sick, even animals. He ate the meat we brought when we went to see him and seemed to enjoy our company. Mayhap I should stop fretting so much and accept Tianna's expertise.*

Adrianna pushed aside any niggling feelings about Cortath, slumped back in the chair, and thought about the other thing that was bothering her. *I know what I need to do. I need to go to Sheridana and explain away the damage Dinim wrought last evening. Then I have to somehow tell her that our dead father is hunting me down so he can kill me...*

Adrianna leaned forward into the table and put her head in her hands. *Indeed, Thane will continue to come after me until I'm dead. I can't run from him forever. One of these days, I have to face him. He can dispose of me easily, and with me dead, maybe the rest of the group will be saved from his wrath. But what of Sheridana and her child? Will he leave them alone too?*

Adrianna felt a hand settle onto her shoulder. She jumped and brought her head up to see Sheridana standing there beside her. Her sister quickly retracted her hand. "I'm sorry. I didn't mean to startle you."

Adrianna shook her head. "No. It's okay. Please sit." She gestured to the chair beside her.

Sheridana took the proffered seat. For a few moments there was silence. "Your friend Tianna– she came to my room."

Adrianna raised an eyebrow. "Really? When was this?" She was surprised for Tianna hadn't said anything to her about it.

"Later this morning."

Adrianna nodded. "So, what did she have to say?"

For a moment Sheridana just stared at the hands he had clasped on the table before her. Adrianna regarded her intently, and when her sister finally looked up, her eyes shone with unshed tears. "She said you have been moping about all day."

Adrianna nodded again, feeling her own tears begin to threaten. "I suppose I have."

Silence reigned once more. Adrianna struggled with what she should say. Maybe it should be, *Dinim usually isn't such a bastard. He didn't mean to hurt your feelings.* Or perhaps, *Dinim is such an oaf. He doesn't realize what he is saying sometimes.* But Adrianna didn't want to say either of those things. She didn't want to defend him that way. Mayhap she should say, *That man, he is such a lloryk's ass. I don't really know him very well.* Damn, she didn't really want to lie either. But she had to say something...

"Sheri, I am so sorry about last night. I..."

Sheridana put a hand on top of Adrianna's. "Don't be. It's fine."

Adrianna caught her sister's gaze. She saw hurt reflected there, but even more she saw love. She rose from her seat and Sheridana followed. She grabbed her sister's arm and pulled her close, clutching her as close as she could.

Sheridana whispered in her ear, "No matter what, I feel good to be with you. Nothing will separate us again."

Adrianna finally pulled away. "I feel the same. Come. Let's take a walk. It's a nice evening."

"All right, just let me run upstairs for a moment. I need to let Carli know I will be away from the inn for a while."

Sheridana turned and began to make her way up the stairs. Sad, and more than a little hurt, Adrianna called out, "Aren't you going to let me see your baby?"

Sheridana stopped and turned around. Even though Adrianna tried to hide it, her sister must have divined something of her emotions. A flash of guilt passed over Sheridana's face and she gestured her forward.

"Yes, of course! I'd love for you to meet Fitanni. Please, come upstairs with me. You can meet Carli too."

Filled with excitement, Adrianna joined Sheridana on the stairs. *Fitanni, I've never heard that name before, but it sounds like a girl's name. I have a neiya!*

Sheridana led the way up the stairs and Adrianna followed her to the third room on the right, not far from the one she shared with Tianna and Amethyst down the hall. She opened the door and they stepped inside. The room was just like hers. There were two beds, and sitting on one was a young woman with dark brown hair reading a book. On the other bed lay a bundled form. The child was asleep, a fisted hand held up to her tiny mouth. Golden curls were damp with sweat, and tears rested on plump cheeks just below closed eyes.

The young woman smiled. "She has been crying for you, Sheri. I believe she thought you would rock her to sleep."

Sheridana gently seated herself beside the baby. She swept a finger down one rosy cheek and then stroked the hair from the child's forehead. She smiled tenderly and waved Adrianna close. "This is Fitanni. She is everything to me."

Adrianna sat on the bed and leaned over the sleeping baby. Most of the child's features appeared to be human. Her ears were rounded instead of arched and pointed and her face was not so angular. "She is beautiful."

Sheridana whispered, "She is the greatest thing I have ever done." Adrianna looked up to find her sister regarding her solemnly. "Someday you will understand. When you look at your children, you will see a miracle, a gift from the gods, and you will treasure them with every breath you take."

Adrianna was taken aback by Sheridan's passion. She'd never thought about having children, didn't know with whom she could possibly consider having any. But now that she thought about it, she assumed she would feel about her children the way Sheridana felt about hers. Maybe, if the future allowed it, she would know what it felt like to bear a child and to love it one day. Just as the thought entered, Ami Rayhana's words echoed through her mind, and sadness followed. For her, the future had become bleak. It was unlikely she would have the opportunity to experience such happiness.

Sheridana placed a hand on her arm. "Come, I want you to meet my good friend Carli. She has been such a blessing to me these past moon cycles."

Adrianna just nodded and allowed Sheridana to lead her over to the young woman who had kept herself inconspicuous. She nodded and smiled as she was introduced, maintaining the facade that all was well. She had some time; she needn't share the horrible truth with her sister just yet.

Adrianna walked through the hallway to her chamber. It had been a long day as the group prepared for travel and she hoped to have a brief rest before the evening meal. Everyone had met early that morning to discuss the route they would take once leaving the city, and they agreed to travel south along the Dresnjik River just long enough to find a good crossing. They would then go to the city of Kamden. It was a different route than the one they had taken to Risset, but they didn't want to retrace their steps in the happenstance that Thane was following. Other than that, they had no other plan in mind except that they saw no reason to continue north through unfamiliar territory.

The group had also discussed Sheridana and everyone agreed they would be increasing their number by three instead of just one. The men were leery about the idea of traveling with a small child, but Adrianna and Tianna convinced them that it was for the best. They really had no other option because Sheridana would never leave the baby…

And Adrianna would never leave Sheri.

When she finally got the chance to take Dartanyen aside, Adrianna told him she hadn't yet spoken to her sister about Thane, but that she would do it sometime over the next few days while they traveled. All he'd done was shake his head in silent disagreement. She knew Sheridana was wondering what their rush to leave the city was all about. Adrianna hated that she hadn't told her about their father last night, but she couldn't bring herself to broach the terrible subject when she was enjoying spending time with her sister after so long of being apart.

So enveloped in her thoughts, Adrianna startled when someone stepped into the hallway ahead. She relaxed when she saw it was just Dinim. She moved to step around him, but he blocked her way with his body and a well-placed hand onto the opposite wall of the corridor.

With a heavy sigh, Adrianna glanced up at him balefully. "Dinim, please get out of my way."

He shook his head. "I've wanted to talk with you all day but you keep avoiding me. Listen to what I have to say; when I'm finished you can order me to leave if you still wish it."

Not seeing any way to escape, Adrianna crossed her arms beneath her breasts. "Fine. I'm waiting."

"First, I want to apologize for my behavior a couple nights ago. Honestly, I don't know what came over me. Whatever sickness it was is gone now, and it will never return. I have already offered an apology to your sister and she accepted it more gracefully than I could have expected. Second, I want to tell you that I have wished a hundred times over I'd told you about your sister's baby before I left to rejoin the Wildrunners. A part of me thought that Volstagg would tell you, but when everything spun out of control a couple nights ago, I belatedly realized that he had not. I'm so sorry you found out like this. You have to believe me when I say that I would never intentionally do anything to harm you. Ever."

Adrianna regarded him intently. "So, it was Volstagg who told you about the child?"

Dinim nodded.

"How did he find out?"

"Thane told him."

Adrianna's thoughts swirled. *If Thane knows about the baby and spoke about her to Volstagg, that means he has an interest in her. Knowing our father, it isn't a healthy interest.* "What else did Thane tell him?"

Dinim shook his head. "I don't know."

She narrowed her eyes. "I don't know if I believe you."

He raised his arms away from his body. "I swear I don't have anything to hide." Dinim's gaze was beseeching. "Adrianna, I won't betray your trust again. Please give me another chance."

With bated breath Dinim watched Adrianna's resolve crack. It was hard to tell her he had nothing to hide when he knew Thane's desire to murder Sheridana's baby was almost as strong as his lust for his youngest daughter. But quite truthfully, she didn't need to know that. It would only add another element to her fear, and right now, all he wanted was to get back into her good graces. He sorely missed her companionship, and the last two days he realized how much he depended on it. It was she who kept the boredom and monotony out of his days, and she whom he dreamed about at night. Images of her dancing before him: the bare flesh of her waist, mesmerizing dark eyes, hair the color of moonlight, and captivating movements aroused him like no woman ever had before. Even before she'd danced for him, he'd lay awake many nights unable to sleep.

Dinim reached out and put his hands on her shoulders. "Adrianna, I will never keep anything from you again. I consider you my equal, and no matter what, I always have you and the rest of this group in my thoughts. Please..."

She gave an audible sigh. "All right."

Dinim frowned. "All right, what?" Inwardly he smiled. He'd finally managed to break through to her.

"All right, I forgive you already. Now, will you please get out of my way? I'm tired, and I want to get some sleep before the evening meal."

Dinim stepped aside, sweeping his arm down the corridor. "As you wish, Mi'lady."

Adrianna shook her head and moved past him. She couldn't help the small grin that surfaced and chuckled inwardly at his antics. She felt as though a weight had been lifted from her shoulders, and it was with a lighter heart she entered the bedchamber. The room had become a disaster as they made final preparations to leave the next morning. She assumed Sheridana's chamber looked the same, possibly even worse as she made preparations with a baby in mind.

Adrianna's grin broadened. In spite of the threat looming over her, she found she was happy. Even if it was for just that moment, her heart was lifted. In spite of the odds, she had found her sister. She had also found good friends in Tianna, Dartanyen, Armond, Zorg, Amethyst, Dinim and even the unpredictable Sabian. She had Cortath as her boon companion and protector. Her dreams had almost entirely gone away since he'd joined her, and he somehow filled all those dark places in her soul where there had once been only fear.

For that moment, Adrianna felt everything just might be all right. Maybe, just maybe, they would find a way to persevere over Thane, and then they could begin their journey back home.

EPILOGUE

The Deathmaster, Lord Aasarak, stood upon the desolate battlefield. The sky was darker than usual, the clouds covering the moons so the pale light barely filtered through. Cold, too, the northern winds swept down from the Sartingels to blow across the bleak plain. This tortured place was the site of the epic struggle fought between faelin and humans during a time in which the two races held very little tolerance for one another. It was one of the largest battles to ever be fought on this side of Ansalar, and neither side claimed ultimate victory. In the end, both armies had been forced to retreat and a century-long cold war ensued.

The long, embittered, and bloody Battle of Shinshinasa had been a defining moment in the history of Shandahar. Aasarak looked forward to taking advantage of what had been left behind so long ago.

From the voluminous folds of his dark robe, the dark Lord pulled out the Azmathion. Created by a mathematical genius, the artifact was difficult to interpret. One could manipulate the bones into all manner of fascinating geometric designs, utter any one of hundreds of spells, and dust it with even more types of elements–and still get nothing.

Aasarak had spent lifetimes unlocking the secrets that lay within the intricate puzzle. Not just one lifetime, or two. The Curse of Odion had been through *four* repetitions, four Cycles of the same people living and dying for centuries, then everything coming to a grinding halt and starting all over again. A very long time ago, an old wise man had told him about this curse, and to corroborate his crazy claim, Aasarak left clues and messages behind for his young self to find in the upcoming Cycle so that he might come into contact with the Azmathion and learn its secrets earlier in his life.

It worked. Shandahar was now nearing the end of the fifth Cycle. He had more power than he ever could have dreamed, and it was all because of the Azmathion.

The first power he learned was how to raise the newly dead. At the beginning he could raise only one corpse at a time, but the more he grew in power, the more corpses he was capable of raising at once. For the longest time, it was the only secret he had been able to unlock, and for so long he'd struggled to raise his armies, piece by little piece.

However, at the beginning of the last Cycle, the Azmathion led him to the discovery of a necromantic grimoire, the Azmatharcana. The text gave Aasarak the knowledge necessary for him to create something much more powerful than the mindless automatons he raised from graveyards. Called

Azmathous, these beings were required to pledge their allegiance to him upon their death. A man by the name of Icarus Barsados had been his first endeavor. He was a warrior, a good man beaten down by the trials of life, but tempted to live on despite the price. He was followed by several more. That was in the fourth Cycle...

This Cycle he made the decision to go in search of something stronger. Thane Darnesse, a man already caught up in darkness, one who warred with his very soul.

It didn't take Aasarak very long to realize he'd made a mistake by choosing Thane. The man was twisted by his hate and need for vengeance. The strong emotions he carried in life had made Thane that much stronger in death. Aasarak was unable to harness such strength for long, and when Thane and the other Azmathous finally left Aasarak's side, he was left with nothing but the misfortune of having to begin anew with another man, Hodorin Krasser.

However, it hadn't been much longer after Thane's creation that he unlocked the power to raise the ancient dead. Once losing control of Thane and the other Azmathous, Aasarak chose to focus his energies upon this endeavor instead, visiting one city after another, skulking around in the darkness of the night from cemetery to cemetery. By now, he had amassed quite a legion, the beginning of the army he would use to bring about the downfall of civilized Ansalar.

But his forces still weren't growing fast enough. Aasarak gave a hideous grin. The Azmathion hummed within his palm, almost as though in anticipation of what was to come. He spoke the words of the required incantation, then shifted the bones into the necessary configuration. The strange runes inscribed upon the new surfaces glowed briefly before a sickly green mist began to emerge. It slowly drifted to the ground and crept about to circle his robe-covered feet. This was going to be one of the best nights he had ever lived...

Because he had finally discovered how to raise hordes.

Like a disease, the mist spread across the old battlefield. From behind, Aasarak heard the nervous snort of Hodorin's shadow lloryk. Aasarak raised his arms upward, reveling in the power surrounding him. The ground quivered and his attention was brought to the dead lying beneath his feet. The sands of time had covered the remains of the fallen humans and faelin who had fought in that ill-fated battle, but if one looked closely enough, a leg bone here and a skull fragment there could still be seen.

Aasarak concentrated all of his energy onto the task. First one, and then another disturbance could be seen beneath the thin layer of dirt. The corpses slowly rose from the places where they had died, their comrades never having removed their bodies from the field after the battle was through. The armies had been so decimated, they could scarcely think about the living, much less the dead. So, they had lain there, forgotten, over the decades.

The way Aasarak considered it, they had merely been waiting for him to come for them.

The dead rose from all around. Aasarak cackled with glee, and the shadow lloryk voiced his agitation. Aasarak turned to his newest Azmathous, gestured for Hodorin to begin leading the way north from the plain towards the mountains. With weapons in hand, the newly-risen skeletal corpses fell into place and followed.

Aasarak continued his arcane litany, watching the plain come to undead life. When he was through, there would be hundreds at his disposal. It was a race against time, but he was getting closer and closer to success.

GLOSSARY OF TERMS

Aertna (airt-na) – that place faelin-kind believe to exist within every man somewhere between his mind and his soul

Alcrostat (al-kro-stat) – the largest city within the realm of Elvandahar – residence of the Sherkari Fortress, home to the King

Alothere (al-o-thayr) – large porcines that are cousins to the wild boar – they live in the forests and steppes of the temperate regions of Shandahar

Andahye (an-duh-high) – mystical city located at the northern edge of the Sheldomar Forest – it is the place where many mages receive their arcane training

Ansalar (an-sal-ar) – one of the three continents of Shandahar – it is the most inhabited

Azmatharcana (az-math-ar-kana) – a mystical tome that delivers many necromantic secrets, including those contained within the Azmathion

Azmathion (az-math-ee-on) – the arcane artifact that gives Aasarak much of his power – it is a geometrical work of art, and one must work the puzzles contained within it in order to divine its secrets

Azmathous (az-math-us) – the most powerful of Aasarak's undead creations – with the power of the Azmathion, they are reborn and are able to retain the skills and abilities they possessed in life

Behiraz (be-heer-az) – a worm of gargantuan proportions, it lives beneath the ground finding it's prey by the vibrations they make upon the surface. Swift and deadly, very few survive an encounter with one

Buffelshmut (buffel-shmut) – a slang term for buttocks

Burbana (bur-ban-uh) – a small ermine-like animal with exquisitely soft fur

Calotebas (kal-o-tee-bas) – a large foul-tempered herbivore that lives near swamps – the taste of their flesh is equally as repugnant as their personality

Cenloryan (sen-lor-yan) – a creature made of the twisted magic of the Kronshue, it has the lower body of a lloryk and the upper torso, arms, and head of a human

Chag (chag) – a drink made from the large seeds of the chagatha plant, which grows in the more southern regions of Ansalar

Chamdaroc (sham-dar-ok) – a shrub that grows within Elvandahar and other forested regions of northwestern Ansalar – it has small white flowers that are said to have intoxicating qualities

Cimmerean (sim-ur-ee-an) – one of the faelin sub-races – also known as 'dark' faelin, they live in vast labyrinths below the surface of the world

Common (com-mun) – the universal language across most of the main continent of Ansalar

Cortubro (cor-too-bro) – a realm situated north of Elvandahar

Corubis (kor-oo-bis) – large canines that have tawny fur with dark dappling – they live in packs headed by an alpha male, but many of them find companionship with faelin, especially hinterlean rangers

Croxis (krok-sis) – a plant that has hallucinogenic properties, often making the person feel a false sense of well-being – the extract is called croxian

Daemundai (day-mun-die) – an organization of those who strive to give daemon-kind influence and power in Shandahar

Daladin (dal-a-din) – a hinterlean house in the trees

Denedrian (den-ed-ree-an) – one of the human sub-races – they are largely nomadic, originating from the western plains and deserts

Dimensionalist (dim-en-shen-al-ist) – a sorcerer who specializes in otherworldly knowledge and travel

Doppleganger (dop-pel-gang-er) – a bipedal being once thought to be made of magic, it is a daemon that has the ability to shift its shape into any humanoid between four and eight feet tall – it is a master of trickery and disguise that works for the most powerful of sorcerers

Elvandahar (el-van-da-har) – large forested region in the vee of the Terrestra and Denegal Rivers – it is ruled by hinterlean faelin, and bears the largest population of these people

Esfexanar (es-fex-an-ar) – a deadly poison often used to subdue someone – it causes the person to fall unconscious and to have after-effects such as slurred speech and tiredness

Eukana (yoo-kana) – a mixture of assorted nuts and dried berries that Hinterlean rangers carry on long trips

Farlo (far-low) – the equivalent of several feet

Filopar (fil-o-par) – one of the five domains of Elvandahar

Fistantillus bush (fist-an-til-lus) – a plant bearing poisonous thorns that can make a person violently ill for several days

Grang (grang) – slightly shorter than halfen, these small, bony humanoids live primarily on the steppes – they are primitive and voracious, but not very smart, their greed often getting in the way of thieving strategies

Griffon (grif-fon) – large animals that have both feline and avian features – they are friendly and intelligent, and can often be found in the company of druids

Hamzin/Hamza (ham-zin/ham-zuh) – the title given by the King to the one who rules within one of the five domains in Elvandahar

Helzethryn (hel-zeth-rin) – one of the dragon sub-races – at maturity their color ranges from pale gold, to deep bronze, to fiery red – they have the highest propensity towards *bonding* with other species

Hestim (hes-tim) – one of the three moons of Shandahar

Himrony (him-ron-ee) – a type of grass that grows abundantly throughout the central Ansalar – the preferred vegetation of larian

Hinterlean (hin-ter-lee-an) – one of the faelin subraces – they live in treetop villages within temperate forests

Hralen (her-ay-len) – the name used for the household staff within the Sherkari Fortress

Humanoid (hue-man-oyd) – any creature that walks upright on two legs (bipedal)

Hybanthis (hie-ban-this) – a vine that has poisonous blue thorns – poison has brain-based affects that heighten a person's emotional state, making emotions difficult to handle

Isterian (iz-ter-ee-un) – the name used for the guards that keep patrol throughout the Sherkari Fortress

Karlisle (kar-lyle) – the human realm neighboring Elvandahar on the other side of the Denegal River

Kleyshes (klie-shays) – one of the five domains of Elvandahar

Krathil-lon (kruh-thil-lon) – a forested glen located within the southern reaches of the Sartingel Mountains

Kronshue, Brotherhood of the (kron-shoo) – a 'technological' society that dominates eastern Ansalar

Kyrrean (kie-reen) – large blond felines with dark brown dappling and oversized paws – they make their existence on the warm temperate plains and borderlands

Larian (layr-ee-an) – with only minor differences, these are smaller cousins to the lloryk – they are able to carry faelin and most humans

Leschera (le-sher-uh) – very gentle, larian-sized, deer-like creatures that grace the temperate woodlands

Lloryk (loor-ik) – large muscular equine-like creatures that are able to carry humans and small orocs – they are omnivorous and beneath the top coat of silky fur, have modified hair shafts that appear similar to scales one would see on a reptile

Lycanthrope (lie-kan-throap) – one afflicted with the disease of lycanthropy – they are humans, faelin, or hafen that can transform into animals (beginning with prefix *shir* – wemic, althothere, or kyrrean) – the disease is spread through the bite

Lytham powder (lye-tham) – a component used in a spell that creates a noxious vapor

Mehta (may-tuh) – the title given to the leader of the Daemundai

Meriliam (mer-il-lee-am) – one of the three moons of Shandahar

Merzillith (mir-zil-lith) – otherwise known as a mind flayer, this inter-mediate daemon is from one of the Nine Hells – it has psionic power, the ability to use the energy of the world in a way that is different from the Talent possessed by mages

Mirpur (mir-poor) – one of the five domains of Elvandahar

Monaf (mon-af) – the human realm neighboring Torimir on the other side of the Ratik Mountains

Morden (mor-den) – one of the halfen sub-races – they live in deep caverns within the mountains

Murg (murg) – an alcoholic beverage distilled from fermented cane sugar

Necromancer (nek-ro-man-ser) – a sorcerer who focuses on the darker aspects of spellcasting

Nefreyo/Neiya (nef-ray-oh/nay-yah) – the familiar terms used for nephew and niece

Oorg (oorg) – one of the humanoid races of Shandahar, they are even larger than orocs and are often called giants – they often fight with brute strength alone, but aren't good with any type of real strategy

Oroc (or-ok) – one of the native races of Shandahar – they are muscular and broad, standing at least six to seven feet tall – faelin are their greatest enemies, and the two races find any excuse to maim and kill one another

Pact of Bakharas (bak-hair-us) – an agreement between daemon and dragon kind that does not allow one or the other too much influence over Shandahar

Papas fruit (pay-pas) – a small pink orb about the size of a nectarine – it grows on the papas tree, which is prevalent throughout the temperate borderlands of Ansalar

Ptarmigan (tar-mig-an) – a squat, grouse-like bird that is often hunted for its flavorful meat

Rathis (rath-is) – the leaves of this plant are known for their pain-relieving capabilities

Recondian (re-con-dee-an) – one of the human sub-races – they mostly live in the central regions of Ansalar

Reshik-na (resh-ik-na) – an order of druids that lives within the Elvandaharian domain of Filopar

Rezwithrys (rez-with-ris) – the largest of the dragon sub-races – at maturity their color ranges from silver to steel blue to metallic violet – they have a propensity for magic

Samshin/Samshae (sam-shin/sam-shay) – the son/daughter of the hamzin or hamza

Sangrilak (sang-ri-lak) – a very diverse city located in the northwestern quadrant of the realm of Torimir

Savanlean (sav-an-lee-an) – one of the faelin sub-races – they live in majestic cities built into mountainsides located in the more northern regions of the Ansalar

Shagendra (shuh-gen-dra) – the root from this plant can be used to make a person's mind vulnerable to suggestions – also causes general lethargy, dulls the senses, and slows reflexes

Shockwave (shok-wave) – a game that is popular throughout the continent – involves cards, bones, and no small amount of strategy and luck

Steralion (stir-a-lee-an) – one of the three moons of Shandahar

Tabanakh drink (ta-ban-ak) – a drink prepared by the druid elders as a right of initiation for their tyros – it has properties that exaggerate the visions of those who are so *gifted*

Talent (tal-ent) – (adj) the ability that some people possess to harness the energy of the world and use it – (n) someone who uses magic

Talsam (tal-sam) – the root from this plant is ground into a powder from which a pain-relieving tea is made

Tankard (tank-erd) – a vessel for holding liquid – it is the equivalent of approximately two mugs and is usually used in taverns

Terralean (ter-a-lee-an) – one of the faelin sub-races – they inhabit many of the borderlands between the forests and steppes and are the most widespread

Thalden (thal-den) – one of the halfen sub-races – they live within the temperate hills

Thritean (thrye-teen) – very large silver felines with black striping and six legs – they live in cold northern forests

Tobey (toe-bee) – a small, goat-like creature – many nomadic peoples breed them for the creamy textured milk they produce

Torimir (tor-eh-meer) – the realm neighboring Elvandahar on the other side of the Terrestra River

Tremidian (tre-mid-ee-an) – one of the human sub-races – they live on the eastern side of the continent

Trolag (trol-ag) – one of the humanoid races of Shandahar, they are tall and stooped, their long, gangly bodies covered with dark brown wiry hair – they have the ability to heal quickly

Umberhulk (um-ber-hulk) – large, stout burden beasts with thick umber colored skin virtually devoid of hair – used to pull carts in cities, towns, and many times even in caravan trains

Varanghelie Vault (vair-an-gay-lee) – a highly protected storage facility located within Andahye – it is where many people keep their most valuable possessions

Wemic (weh-mik) – in some places better known as wolves, these animals appear to be distant cousins to some worgs – they run in temperate to sub-arctic forests and have never been tamed

Worg (woorg) – medium sized canines that tend to make their residence in urban areas – they come is all sizes and shapes, all depending on which city they are from

Wraith (rayth) – a corpse that has been re-animated – they are mindless, following the commands of their necromantic masters – their bodies are ravaged by the effects of decay and they wield only the simplest of weapons

Wyvern (why-vern) – a large snake-like creature with four stubby legs and a poisonous barbed tip on its long sinuous tail – it lives in shallow caverns in temperate climes

Zacrol (zak-rol) – the equivalent of about a mile

ABOUT THE AUTHORS

Tracy R. Chowdhury (aka Ross) was born in the small town of Tunkhannock Pennsylvania in 1975 and moved to Cincinnati Ohio when she was twelve years old. Growing up, she was an avid reader, especially of fantasy and science fiction, and she loved to write. She attended college at Miami University in Oxford, Ohio and studied her other passion, Biology. She graduated in 2002 and worked in cancer research for several years. During that time, she picked up her love for writing again, and in 2005, her first book, *Shadow Over Shandahar– Child of Prophecy*, was put into print. With the help of her co-author, Ted Crim, the sequel was published two years later.

Tracy currently lives in Montgomery, Ohio. She is married with eight children, a big dog, and four cats. She does home renovation work, and in her 'spare' time she continues to write and promote her books. In 2011 the novels were picked up by a small press and her original duology was re-mastered and separated into smaller volumes to make a series. More books have followed, as well as several short stories. And now, she and her husband own their own publication company! More information about the books can be found on her website at www.worldofshandahar.com, and she can be found on Facebook and Twitter.

Ted M. Crim was born and raised in Cincinnati Ohio. He spent most of his early youth in Over-the-Rhine, but moved to upper Price Hill when he was about eight years old. He was always interested in fantasy role-play, and enjoyed playing Dungeons & Dragons with his friends. When he was a junior in high school, he went into a vocational program called Animal Conservation and Care located at the Cincinnati Zoo & Botanical Garden. He received his certificate in 1989 and worked in animal care for several years.

It was during that time Ted met his good friend, Tracy, and they shared an interest in Dungeons & Dragons. She was a writer, and it was upon the first campaign they played together that her first book, *Shadow Over Shandahar–Child of Prophecy*, was based. Together, they brought the world and the characters to life into a novelized format. He attends many of the conventions and festivals at which the books are sold, and goes by the moniker, Pirate Ted!

Ted is currently working on his new fantasy series and gaming system. More information about the books can be found on his website at www.worldofshandahar.com, and he can also be found on Facebook.

OTHER BOOKS TO ENJOY:

DARK MISTS OF ANSALAR

BLOOD OF DRAGONS

T.R.Chowdhury & T.M.Crim

Authors of *Shadow Over Shandahar*

The legendary Pact of Bakharas has been broken and daemon and dragon-kind are free to make the world of Shandahar a battle-ground in an epic struggle that has lasted centuies.

Young sorceress Aeris Timberlyn is burdened with the task of persuading a new Talent to return to the academy to persue training in the arcane arts. Accompanied by her brother and their companions, she travels through dangerous lands in search of him.

Picture a hero.

I bet he's tall, muscular, and chiseled... forthright and chaste with bright shiny armor... takes on all challengers face-to-face... lots and lots of honor?

Yeah. I am not that guy. I am the antithesis of all of those things.

In this world, with so much gold at stake, with the most powerful people in the kingdom taking notice...

That shiny hero? Yeah, he dies.

I am the guy that can get the job done.

I am Fox Crow.

ELVISH JEWEL

The Chronicles of Rithalion
Volume One

TRACY RENÉE
JAMES DANIEL **ROSS**

Imagine living over one hundred years without a home, without a family, without responsibility. Imagine being alone in the wilderness with nothing but memories of the long ago past. Imagine dreaming of the day you might find something worth living for... worth dying for.

Elvish Jewel.

Doomed by his forbidden love, discarded by the crown, forgotten by the people, a disgraced hero rises from the ashes to combat the rising darkness. Accompanied by a novice priestess of the God of Death, this armored savior will crash headlong into the ranks of the undead. As the legions of the unliving surround and entrap him, he faces the dark truths of his own failures and discovers the limits of his warrior will.

In a world beset by nightmares, another is coming. Two of the mightiest nations in the world are clashing in a war that will shake the Great Veddan River Valley to its core. The fae elves and the bronze dwarves look upon one another as foreign and alien, their conflict fueled by dark powers and bigotry. Pride and misunderstandings foil peace at every turn, and two star-crossed lovers shall suffer as their people descend into bloodshed.

AND FORTHCOMING:

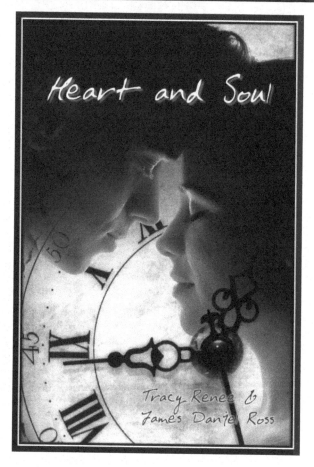

Heart and Soul

Tracy Renee & James Daniel Ross

Seth and Kaila: writing partners, friends, lovers. Their relationship is a rocky one, and an arguement sends Kai out into the night in tears.

A terrible accident leaves Seth suddenly facing the worst days of his life. Deep within the embrace of a coma, Kai struggles for her life, her mind trapped within the world she and Seth have created. And as the days pass, she continues to weaken.

The only thing keeping Seth from insanity is their book manuscript, and as the love of his life slips closer to death, he is desperate to finish what they started together. As their darkest hour approaches, Seth finally realizes what might save Kaila's life, and it is a race against the clock before she is lost forever.

VISIT THE WEBSITE AT
WWW⬚WINTERWOLFPUBLICATIONS⬚COM
FOR

BREAKING NEWS
FORTHCOMING RELEASES
LINKS TO AUTHOR SITES
WINTERWOLF EVENTS

Made in USA - Kendallville, IN
42733_9781945039034
07.12.2022 1353